# HUNTING ODESSA

Cover image: Auschwitz concentration camp Poland.
Courtesy Shutterstock.

*This book is a work of fiction. Any resemblance to actual events or persons, living or dead, is entirely coincidental.*

"Hunting Odessa," by Douglas Clark. ISBN 978-1-951985-21-9 (softcover); 978-1-951985-22-6 (hardcover); 978-1-951985-23-3 (ebook).

Published 2020 by Virtualbookworm.com Publishing Inc., P.O. Box 9949, College Station, TX 77842, US. 

**By Douglas Clark**

Belfast

Take Five

Shell Game

Evermore

Critical Mass

Fault Lines

Provoke the Devil

The Irish Spy

Endgame

Hunting Odessa

*To Josie for her invaluable editing contributions and the forbearance in sharing a writer's life.*

# HUNTING ODESSA

A NOVEL

DOUGLAS CLARK

*ODESSA* was the American codename for the German *Organisation der ehemaligen SS-Angehörigen,* translated as the Organization of Former SS Members.

Distinct from the regular military elements of the Third Reich, the *Schutzstaffel* became the instrument of Nazi genocide and mass murder. The breadth of SS power ranged from the secret police, the *Gestapo,* the intelligence service the *Sicherheitsdienst des Reichsführers-SS,* or SD, combat troops of the *Waffen-SS,* mobile death squads of the *Einsatzgruppen,* and the *SS-Totenkopfverbände* Death's Head detachments operating the concentration and extermination camps.

# CHAPTER 1

LAUSANNE, SWITZERLAND | DECEMBER 1943

---

The hotel room in Grenoble, France was drafty with a chilling wind coming off the Alps. However, it did possess the luxury of a private bathroom with a bathtub. A temporary refuge for perhaps no more than a day. Arriving by train the prior afternoon from Lyon, Marc Fraser and his wife Fiona Marchand knew the *Gestapo* would soon discover their identities. Their clandestine activities in the French Resistance exposed after participating in the murder of an SS officer and the failed attempt to kill the Lyon head of the *Gestapo*, Klaus Barbie. *Gestapo* agents and the Nazi-collaborating French *Malice* across occupied France undoubtedly alerted by now. Heighten security possibly armed with their photographs made escape to neutral Switzerland difficult.

How to get across the border? Must be a better way than attempting to cross at some remote wooded area. Probably guarded by roving German patrols. It was also cold in November at these higher elevations. They were not dressed for a trek in rugged terrain making nighttime out of the question.

Consulting his map of France, what about Lake Geneva? What drew his attention was the line in the middle of the lake defining the French-Swiss border. Looked to be less than twenty kilometers across the lake. Maybe a boat for hire? Steal one if necessary? Should be easier than his desperate ocean escape made from Bilbao, Spain to France during the civil war in 1936.

The map indicated a small French town on the southern shore off the lake, Thonon-les-Bains. No way to know if it was assessable by rail. If not, difficult to get to without raising suspicions.

Turning to Fiona, he said, "Here," putting his finger on the map. "If we can cross the lake into Switzerland we will be safe. I know someone in Switzerland who will help us."

After the chance assistance by the train conductor to escape this far, their fortunes continued to improve. Returning to the train station in the morning there was only one French gendarme in sight. Fraser looked at the train schedules. There it was. Thonon-les-Bains. The route went north from Grenoble via a town called Bellgarde-sur-Valserine then skirted the Swiss border east to Thonon-les-Bains on the south shore of Lake Geneva. A four-hour trip with a departure at noon. Enough time to buy some clothes and warmer overcoats before setting out.

With fresh clothes, a shave for Fraser and a touch of make-up for Fiona, they felt human again. Fiona was almost cheerful. Fraser cautioned her they were not yet out of danger. Must not let their guard down until they crossed into Switzerland. Well-dressed with first-class tickets they looked the part of their cover story. The ticket seller commented that Thonon-les-Bains was nothing more than a remote spot on the map. He commented, *in winter an unusual destination for people like you.*

The movie business ploy again became a convenient cover that explained everything.

"Need an ocean background scene from a boat on the water. Wintertime. Not allowed to film on the Atlantic coast or the Channel with the German military defenses. Therefore, Lake Geneva is a stand-in. A large enough expanse of water for what I need."

Arriving in Thonon-les-Bains in the late afternoon allowed some time to reconnoiter. Not much of a town in winter. Few people were about on this blustery November afternoon. A cold breeze out of the northwest blew across the lake. No German soldiers in sight. No French gendarmes patrolling the small marina. An unguarded border? Not likely. Probably just keeping warm somewhere.

Using their cover story, they arranged for a charter immediately after setting eyes on the perfect boat. A handsome mahogany motor launch. Big enough, fast enough. A good charter boat for the summer crowd in season. The captain was an older man with a gray beard. Weathered complexion. Looked like a sailor. Wool pea coat over a turtleneck sweater, smoking a pipe.

They told the man they needed to scout the view using the remaining daylight then into the twilight hours. After sunset, they needed some night shots looking back on the lights of the town from out in the lake. Perhaps they could use him as an extra in the movie? They would pay well for the four hours work but they had to push off right away. Fraser handed over enough money to counter any objections.

Once well out into the lake, Fraser asked, "Do the Germans run patrol boats out here?"

"Oh yes. Two fast patrol boats. They moor at a dock a short ways from here. That a problem?"

"Could be. Here is the situation. That was all lies about making a movie. You are going to take us over to the Swiss side of the lake. Is that a problem, old timer?"

The man remained silent, no expression readable. After sizing up Fraser and Marchand the man said, "It is if I get caught coming back. Germans are a little sensitive about people sneaking into their territory. The patrol boats are armed. Not worth the risk no matter what you are willing to pay."

"Not sure you understand, Monsieur. First, you have no choice." Fraser pulled out the Webley revolver from his overcoat pocket. "Second, I'm going to pay you double. Or if you prefer, you can decide to escape occupied France with us and stay in Switzerland. I will even help you. You do not have to return."

Puffing on his pipe, "Since I have little choice, I will take the offer of the money. Not much of that this time of year. Times are difficult. I cannot leave my wife alone. Poor woman is not doing well with her arthritis. The winter cold gets harder each year. Harder yet with so little food.

"No need for that big gun, Monsieur. Do not see myself jumping a young fellow like you holding a gun. If you are running from the Germans that is not my affair."

Fraser smiled. "Then head to Switzerland. Can you get us all the way to Lausanne? Don't care to walk too far in the middle of a cold night."

"Guess so. Be close to three hours though. I must keep the speed down to make less noise. No need to announce our presence out here at night. I do not know if the Germans patrol at night, but I suspect they must. Big lake though. Keep as quiet as possible. Only the engine noise. If there are any patrols boats out they should not hear us above the noise of their own engine. No talking. No lights. No smoking."

Within ninety minutes darkness descended under a moonless dense overcast. Looking toward Fiona the old man said, "Looks like you're a bit chilled out here, Madame. There is a bottle of cognac down below. Some shot glasses. Perhaps we should all take the chill off this damp night."

The shallow draft fast boat had a shallow hold in the bow section. Marchand ducked her head and stepped down inside.

Just as she disappeared below there came the sound of a large engine coughing to life in the distance. A patrol boat? Were the bastards sitting idle just listening? The engine noise grew louder.

Seconds later a strong search light beam traversed in an arc while approaching fast in their general direction. Only a couple of hundred meters away. Close enough to hear commands yelled in German.

"*Merde!* I am cutting our engine," the old man said in a loud whisper. "It is our only chance. Stay absolutely quiet and hope they do not spot us with their search light. No talking."

A much larger craft by the sound of the engine. Could they out run it? No way to know. If they ran for it and guessed wrong, surely fired on by machine gun. The old man was right not to try making a run. Avoiding the search beam their only hope. If luck held, they could then resume at low speed. As long as they continued to hear the patrol boat engine then the Germans would not be able to hear the speedboat's engine.

The tactic to sit silent and hope the German patrol boat passed without sighting them proved only partially right. The Germans did not see them. The search light never picked them out in the blackness. However, the German boat's speed lifted its bow causing the search light to play over the low-sitting speedboat as it closed the distance to only a hundred feet.

Fraser looked on in horror as the patrol boat approached at high speed. Its position and proximity obvious by the search light. *Heading directly toward them!* He instinctively tried to get to Fiona in the hold but he was too late.

The heavy patrol craft with its bow raised out of the water under speed came over the top of the bow of their motor launch. The impact smashed the wooden hull of the smaller boat then slammed down with its greater weight forcing it under water. A terrible noise of splintering wood as the smaller boat's bow section broke away.

The German boat pushed through the wreckage of the smaller craft under power to a short distance away before stopping.

The halves of the severed wooden boat sank immediately. The old man was gone, presumably thrown overboard. Frantic shouts in German came from the patrol boat. The water immediately closed around Fraser in the sinking rear section of the motor launch as he desperately reached down hoping to grab hold of Marchand. However, the severed bow section sank quickly into the black water underneath him.

His water-laden overcoat and suit dragged him down. Sinking two meters below the surface with no further breath, he thrust his way to the surface. Even then, it was all he could do to tread water to keep afloat. Everything was black. Biting cold. No stars, no moon.

Something struck him in the head. Then a shout in German, "Take hold of the pole."

A German soldier hauled him on board the patrol boat using a Shepard's crook rescue pole. With difficulty, the soldier hoisted Fraser out of the water dropping him face down on the deck.

The intense cold of the water already began to inhibit the use of Fraser's freezing fingers. His only thought, *Fiona was gone.* Drowned in this cold black water.

From the other side of the patrol boat two other soldiers were seemingly searching for someone in the water. Calling out for 'Fritz', one soldier worked the search light now pointing toward the rear of the patrol boat. A comrade obviously thrown overboard in the collision.

The soldier rescuing Fraser turned him over. Even while shaking with cold, Fraser reached into his waistband and withdrew the Webley revolver. Would it still fire after soaked in the water?

The young soldier pulled back in surprise raising his hands. Fraser then yelled at the other two in German, "Halt what you are doing. Make no move for your weapons or I will shoot."

The other soldiers turned in Fraser's direction. Immediately, the one holding the search light swung it around into Fraser's eyes. Turning away from the glare, Fraser saw the other soldier reaching down for a submachine gun on the deck. Fraser fired twice hitting the soldier and spinning him over the railing into the water. The younger soldier that hauled him out of the water scurried away out of sight.

The search light beam now fell downward toward the deck. The soldier working the light let it drop trying to get to the mounted machine gun. A mistake that cost him his life as Fraser scrambled closer as the man reached the machine gun but too late. Two shots from the reliable Webley killed him.

The remaining soldier had time to find a weapon. A rifle. At least not a submachine gun thought Fraser. Nonetheless, the soldier was now pointing the weapon at him. Fraser pointed his revolver at the soldier while stepping closer to him. The barrel of the rifle now only a meter away. A standoff.

"No closer! I will shoot!" the soldier said. "Drop your gun!"

This close, Fraser judged the soldier probably no older than seventeen. The heavy Mauser rifle shaking slightly. Fear, cold, or the weight holding the weapon?

Continuing to point his own weapon, Fraser said, "Just us now. Your comrades are dead. You and I too if that is the way it must be. You shoot and I will still get off a shot. Right into your face. I will not lower my weapon so you must kill me. Can you do that?"

Fraser had no idea how this would go. Did not matter anymore. Seconds passed. Fraser's hand was also shaking as the effects of hypothermia became more acute.

"Help!" A faint cry from the other side of the boat. From the water? "Help me!"

Fiona?

For a split second, the soldier diverted his eyes toward the direction of the voice. It was long enough for Fraser to grab the barrel of the rifle while ramming the Webley into his throat.

The soldier released his grip on the rifle.

Fraser flung the rifle overboard then pushed the soldier toward the side of the boat. Fraser reached down picking up the submachine gun and throwing it into the water.

"Find her you sonofabitch!" Fraser yelled in German. "The search light!" he said pushing the soldier toward the still illuminated search light.

Within seconds, the light beam found her. Ten meters from the boat. Too far to grab her with the rescue pole.

Marchand struggled frantically to keep her head above water. Fraser grabbed the soldier by the front of his tunic and pointed the Webley in his face. "Help her!"

As the soldier looked at Marchand bewildered about what to do, Fraser pushed him into the water.

As the soldier's head bobbed up spitting water Fraser pointed the gun, "Save her or you also die."

The soldier was his best choice. Fraser was in no shape to rescue Fiona. He was dangerously cold, having difficulty now even focusing his thoughts. A death sentence if captured by the Germans.

The soldier shed his water-soaked overcoat, but saving someone from drowning was a different skill. With her wet clothing weighing her down, Fiona Marchand could do little to help as hypothermia rendered her limbs unable to function. Once the soldier got to her, it was all he could do to stay afloat. Slow progress back to the boat. His head going under repeatedly as he struggled to keep her head up. Yet he was young, fit, and motivated to save his own life.

After several agonizing minutes, he got her to the boat. All Fraser could do was keep her afloat with the rescue pole hooked onto her overcoat while the soldier hoisted himself to the deck. The soldier reached down and grabbed her coat while Fraser pulled her up with the pole. Eventually Fraser tucked the Webley into his waistband to use both hands.

Once on deck she was barely conscious. Fraser by now was also struggling physically. His fingers barely able to grip the revolver as he pulled it out of his waistband.

Shivering, the soldier said, "In the pilothouse. There is heat below from the engine. Blankets too."

They dragged Marchand into the shelter of the patrol boat's pilothouse. Lifting an access door in the floor, revealed a storage hold below.

Fraser said, "Get the blankets."

The soldier started to disappear below when Fraser said, "Bring a weapon from down there and I will kill you."

Fraser began stripped off all of Fiona's wet clothing. Difficult using only one hand. He still had to hold the gun on the German and his fingers were not working well.

The soldier brought out several blankets from below. Fraser ordered him to help finish undressing Fiona. Under different circumstance, her naked body would delight the young soldier. Right now he was freezing. Nothing else mattered than getting warm. He knew he had to help the woman before allowed to tend his own needs.

They wrapped Fiona tightly in several blankets.

"We should move her below," the soldier said. "The engine's heat exchanger is rigged to provide some heat into the pilothouse. Comes up from the engine compartment. Much warmer down there. Running the engine faster might produce more heat."

Fraser and the soldier moved Fiona below into the cramped hold, wrapped tightly in the blankets like a mummy. She appeared better but still looked in a bad way. Deathly pale. Her breathing was shallow and seemed at a reduced respiratory rate. Fraser increased the engine rpms. He could feel the blessed warmth coming from a vent in the hold. He hoped enough to save Fiona.

Shaking uncontrollably, Fraser knew he must quickly get warm. The soldier looked no better. They must get out of their water-soaked clothing. All they had were blankets and the clothing of the one dead soldier on the deck.

Fraser left the shelter of the pilothouse. Dragging the dead soldier near, he said to the young soldier, "Strip his clothing off. Hurry!"

After the soldier removed his dead comrade's coat and uniform, Fraser said, "Give me the overcoat. You get the uniform."

The soldier nodded appreciatively. He expected Fraser might take all the clothing and let him freeze to death. Perhaps shot later when no longer needed. Still, he was alive for now.

Fraser removed all his wet clothing including his underwear. Wrapping a blanket tightly around his body under his armpits, he draped the overcoat around his shoulders. The German's jackboots offered some warmth to his feet. Still cold, hypothermia possibly averted.

With dry clothing and a blanket wrapped over his shoulders, the soldier joined Fraser in the pilothouse for the meager warmth coming up from the engine.

Fraser sat holding the Webley in his lap. "Do you know how to get us to Lausanne on the Swiss side?"

"No."

"Do you know how to handle this boat?"

"No."

"Neither do I but we will learn. Get below and see if we are taking on any water from the collision."

The navigation chart next to the wheel suggested a heading of north-northeast to Lausanne. However, he did not know their current position.

The soldier returned from below reporting no unusual amount of water in the bilge.

Fraser checked the fuel gauge. No way to tell if enough to get them to the Swiss side of the lake. He pushed the throttle forward and increased speed. No need to be quiet. It was a German patrol boat.

Once a few lights became visible indicating they were nearing the Swiss shoreline, Fraser turned parallel to the shore. Reducing speed, he was looking for a populated spot suggested by more lights. Once on land, they needed to find help quickly. Fiona needed to get to a warm environment with medical attention. There remained the problem of finding help once on shore. Fiona could not walk. Carry her? Send the German for help? Becoming harder to think clearly.

The problem resolved quickly as a search light beam played across their boat.

From a loud speaker in German came, "Halt! Idle your engine. You are in Swiss waters. Put down your weapons." The Swiss obviously saw the German military markings. "Stand down. Prepare for boarding."

Fraser cut the engine. The Swiss patrol boat slowed as it eased closer.

"Drop your weapons. Show your hands."

Fraser yelled back, "We are French refugees escaping France. Commandeered this German patrol boat. Need medical help. Injured on board."

To the soldier he said, "Stand up. Raise your hands," punctuating the order with the Webley.

Fraser bent down to Fiona, "Hang on, Fiona. We made it. You'll be warm soon."

She managed a weak smile, mouthing silently, "I love you."

As the Swiss boat came along side, the enormous relief Fraser felt gave him a sense of generosity toward the young German soldier. Why not? He looked like a kid. Not every German was part of the *Schutzstaffel.* Nor every SS a sadistic murderer and torturer.

"You're a lucky young man. Germany is losing the war. No need now to die for the Führer. Your war is over. You are young with a life ahead of you. Now you can eat Swiss chocolates, drink beer, and make love to pretty *fräuleins.*"

The Swiss patrol boat made for their base in the small lakeside town of Morges. Huddled below to keep warm, Fraser sat close to Fiona trying to impart his body warmth. A Swiss border guard brought a steaming cup of coffee, which Fraser coaxed her to drink. She was still in a bad way evidenced by her quivering cheeks. Given a set of weather gear to wear, Fraser sufficiently recovered his core temperature.

Thirty minutes later the patrol craft docked. Having radioed ahead, the ever-efficient Swiss had an ambulance waiting. Bundled in layers of blankets, the attendants closed the ambulance doors. Two Swiss border guards restrained Fraser from joining her. In German, one said to him, "She will be well cared for in the hospital in Lausanne. Only thirty minutes from here."

"And me?" Fraser asked.

"You have entered Switzerland illegally. We are taking you into custody."

At the police station, they mercifully provided clothing. Shabby workingman's clothing, but at least laundered, and a pair of badly worn work boots.

"I am an American citizen," Fraser said to the Swiss officer sitting across the desk.

"Really?" the incredulous officer said. "How is it you were in France?"

In English, Fraser replied, "I am a journalist. My name is Marc Fraser. The woman is my wife. Her name is Fiona Marchand. I would appreciate you contacting the United States Embassy as required by protocol."

Twenty minutes later, after being ushered into an office, a sergeant handed him a telephone.

The American consular officer asked him his name followed by a string of questions. Interrupting, Fraser said, "Sir, are you familiar with a fellow American by the name of Allen Dulles?"

The consular officer remained silent for a moment. "Dulles you say?"

"Yes. Allen Dulles. The head of the American Office of Strategic Services in Switzerland. He is there in Bern I believe."

"Are you claiming to be with the OSS?"

"Affiliated you might say. Mr. Dulles knows me."

The OSS, America's WWII spy agency operated in neutral Switzerland under the full knowledge of the Swiss government. So did Britain's MI6 and Nazi Germany's Reich Main Security Office, the *Reichssicherheitshauptamt* or RSHA. While neutral, Switzerland walked a precarious line. Surrounded by the Axis powers of Nazi Germany, Austria, Italy, and German-occupied France, Swiss banking served to finance the Third Reich's war effort.

Neutrality was a balancing act for Switzerland. The threat of German invasion countered by the need for the Third Reich to use Swiss neutrality to convert German Reichsmarks to internationally accepted Swiss francs. This allowed Germany to purchase materials critical to the war effort. It further offered Germany the means to launder gold and other assets plundered from conquered countries into Swiss francs. That included works of art and of course the confiscated wealth of Jewish victims of the Holocaust.

From the Swiss perspective, this arrangement preserved their independence while earning vast wealth for banking billions of Reichsmarks. An arrangement with the devil. Outside the Swiss banking industry, prevailing Swiss popular sympathies were largely anti-Nazi accounting for Allied intelligence presence. Like Lisbon in neutral Portugal, Bern Switzerland was a denizen of Allied and Axis spies.

Although under detention in a dreary locked room at the border guard barracks, Fraser received a hot meal and warm clothing. Concern remained for Fiona's unknown condition. Two hours later his circumstances abruptly changed.

Following the sound of a key in the locked door, in walked Allen Dulles. Well-dressed in a vested tweed suit, ten years older than Fraser, Dulles looked like a lawyer, which he was.

"Been a long time, Marc," Dulles said pumping Fraser's hand and placing his other hand on his shoulder. "Obviously circumstances went badly in France?"

"I will tell you all about it, but first, what about my wife? They took her to a hospital in Lausanne."

"Don't be alarmed. I already checked before I took the train here. She is doing fine. No injuries apparently, just the effects of the cold. We will go to the hospital immediately."

"I'm to be released?"

"Oh yes. You and your wife will soon become legal residents of Switzerland. At least for the duration of the war."

Three days later Fraser and Marchand boarded a train for Bern. Marchand suffering no residual effects from her ordeal.

Discharged the previous day, she took charge of shopping for clothing for both with money provided by Dulles.

"So Mr. Dulles is the American intelligence chief in Switzerland? At the hospital, he sounded as if you were old friends, Marc. How are you acquainted?" Fiona said on the short train ride to Bern.

"I met Allen in 1933. Before he was an intelligence officer. Back then, America did not have an intelligence agency. The Office of Strategic Services came into being only after Pearl Harbor. Before that, it was only the Navy and Army that engaged in intelligence. Mostly signals intelligence. Radio traffic, codes, and the like. The OSS was formed under control of the Joints Chiefs of Staff to wage espionage behind enemy lines. True spying, but also nastier operational stuff like the British SOE we worked with in France."

"Dulles doesn't look like a military officer? More like a professor."

Fraser laughed. "No, Allen isn't military. He is a lawyer. Served in the State Department during the First World War. In the twenties and thirties he was a legal adviser to the League of Nations."

"So how did you come to know him?"

"You recall when I told you William Randolph Hearst himself sent me to Europe as a foreign correspondent for his newspapers in 1931 after I broke a major story in Los Angeles. Based in Paris, the overwhelming news of the time was the growing popularity of the National Socialist German Workers' Party, the NSDAP. Specifically its charismatic leader, Adolf Hitler.

"Just months after Hitler became Chancellor of Germany in 1933, Hearst arranged a personal interview. The old man had real pull. The day after the Hitler interview, I was having a drink at the Adlon Hotel bar. Dulles walks in with Hamilton Armstrong, the editor of the prestigious American journal *Foreign Affairs* who I recognized. In terrible German, Dulles asked if I was at the Reich Chancellery the previous day. Said he was also there as part of disarmament conference.

"Anyway, I impressed Dulles and his friend Armstrong when I explained. Not only did I interview Hitler, but Göring also. I also obtained Göring's authorization to visit the Nazis' first actual concentration camp outside of Oranienburg. Internment of political opponents mostly. Since not specifically prohibited, I took photographs."

Disembarking the train at the Bern station, Fiona said, "That was ten years ago. How is it you know Dulles is in Bern and head of the American OSS?"

"You recall what I told you happened in Spain?"

She looked at him. "Of course. Your adventures as you called them. Eventually connected to events in France that now brings us to Switzerland as refugees."

"What I mean, what happened in Spain started with Allen Dulles. You might say he introduced me to espionage. Somehow, he knew of my reporting assignment to Spain just before the onset of the Spanish Civil War. Persuaded me to see the U.S. assistant military attaché in Paris. I learned to develop my own microdots. Real spy stuff. That is how I transmitted sensitive information from inside Franco's Nationalist Army. Concealed the microdots under postage stamps. Fake letters mailed to *my lawyer* in New York.

"Let me guess. The esteemed international lawyer Allen Dulles."

Fraser smiled and nodded.

"*Mon Dieu.* I fear we have escaped from the frying pan into the fire. What exactly does your Machiavellian Mr. Dulles have in mind for us?"

# CHAPTER 2

BERN, SWITZERLAND | DECEMBER 1943

---

Armed with a map of medieval Bern purchased at the train station, Fraser suggested they walk to Allen Dulles' residence. Only a few days before New Year's and cold, but a clear sunny day. Number 23 Herrengasse was only a kilometer distance from the train station. An easy fifteen-minute walk since they carried only a single suitcase with their few new clothes.

Dulles' address was a fine old mansion. Modernized, the building now consisted of four spacious apartments. Soon after arriving in Bern in the fall of 1942, Dulles secured the ground floor apartment. It served as not only as his residence, but also a working office. Given his espionage portfolio, he could not very well operate out of the U.S. Embassy, or anywhere nearby. The Herrengasse address provided for discreet access, including a back door into a garden. Located close to the heavily trafficked Casinoplatz concert hall sector, Dulles' visitors could easily explain their presence among the shoppers and strollers.

Dulles did look the part of a professor. Graying hair, a neatly trimmed mustache, rimless glasses, and smoking his signature pipe, he answered the door.

"Marc. So good to see you. And the lovely Madame Marchand," greeting them both in atrociously poor French pronunciation. "So glad you recovered from your ordeal on the lake. Please come in."

Fraser smiled reflecting on Dulles' multi-lingual fluency yet apparently with little improvement of pronunciation since their first meeting ten years ago.

Seated in Dulles' study, enjoying coffee, Dulles said, "I am well aware of the services you and Marc rendered working with the French Maquis, Madame Marchand. British intelligence kept the OSS well informed once we entered the war. The code name referenced in dispatches as *Odysseus* I guessed to be Marc. You see, Madame Marchand, Marc used the byline for his pieces secreted out of Spain as *Odiseo*. The Spanish rendering of *Odysseus*."

Marchand said, "Since you refer to my husband as Marc, please call me Fiona."

Dulles the charmer who loved the ladies, especially attractive ones like Marchand, smiled warmly. "Thank you, Fiona. Please call me Allen.

"I now understand the connection of the code name *Penelope,* the wife of *Odysseus* in Homer's great adventure tale. How did you two operate? Extraordinarily difficult to move about freely I imagine. Especially with the *Gestapo* firmly entrenched in Paris and the occupied zone in the north."

"I worked for a film production company. A natural vocation given my early background in Hollywood," Fraser said. "The Germans encouraged the French film industry to continue making movies. Surprising amount of creative freedom tolerated. Allowed me to travel freely with special authorization. Worked with a good friend in the movie business."

Marchand interjected, "That good friend was my brother, Henri."

"The three of us became committed to resisting the occupation," Fraser said. "I traveled by train using the ploy of scouting potential filming locations using my *Comité d'Organisation des Industries du Cinéma* travel authorization. The Vichy government controlling the COIC had wide latitude to produce movies, under censorship of course. Movie going was one of the few entertainment outlets for the French during the occupation. The Germans thought it beneficial for controlling the French populace.

"I developed many sources and harvested intelligence from local Resistance groups. Careful always to obscure my identity. Henri and Fiona managed the clearinghouse functions from Paris. A script set in Marseille served for two trips to Provence where Fiona and I visited her parents in Aix."

Dulles said, "Your network of sources obviously delivered some impressive results. British intelligence credited your detailed information on the massive German dry dock in Saint-Nazaire that led to the spectacular commando raid in early 1942."

"A stroke of luck. Unfortunately, we also shared in a series of personal disasters after that success," Fraser said.

"In July of last year we lost Henri," Fiona said with some emotion. "Caught up in the massive roundup that became known as the Vel' d'Hiv Roundup. The Vélodrome d'Hiver was a bicycle racing stadium used to confine most of the Paris arrestees. Over 13,000 people sealed inside in the summer heat. Little food and water. Only five lavatories. As bad as the physical conditions were at the Vélodrome it was only the beginning of a worse ordeal for those imprisoned."

Fraser added, "We believe Henri was just in the wrong place at the wrong time. It was a Vichy operation conducted by French police to roundup Jews. Probably suspected him as Jewish. We never found out."

Fiona added with a tinge of anger, "We learned they transported the detainees to French-run internment camps outside of Paris. From those camps followed a horrific journey sealed in railway cars for days without food, water, or sanitation as the trains made their way east to concentration camps in Germany."

With grief and anger over the loss of her brother evident in her expression, "Our own countrymen complicit in helping these *Boche* pigs. We have no idea of Henri's fate."

"Things only got worse," Fraser said. "Tasked by De Gaulle to organize the many Resistance groups under the central control of General De Gaulle in London, Jean Moulin returned to France in March of this year. With my mobility and familiarity with the heads of all the Resistance groups, the job fell to me to secretly escort Moulin."

Dulles pulled the pipe from his mouth, "Good lord. Are you saying you knew all the Resistance leaders? A major blow had you been captured by the *Gestapo*"

Fraser just nodded. "Made me a bit nervous working outside my routine and cover legend to shepherd the most wanted man in all of France about the country.

"That became all too evident after the *Gestapo* captured Moulin outside Lyon. Eventually that led to personal ramifications. But let me first backup and explain events that never appeared in intelligence dispatches."

Dulles interjected. "Excellent. Might I suggest we continue over lunch? I have a place in mind. It is early and we should be able to secure a table in the back out of earshot."

While Dulles was charming and gracious, he wanted to hear all the details of Fraser and Marchand's undercover wartime activities. An interview of sorts since he was recruiting. Almost impossible to smuggle in trained agents with Switzerland surrounded by Axis controlled territory. A substantial hurdle in carrying out his charge to infiltrate behind enemy lines to conduct espionage. A shortage of qualified staff limited efforts by Dulles and his few agents in developing productive sources inside Germany. Experienced operatives like Fraser and Marchand represented a singular opportunity.

To look at Allen Dulles' past might not suggest he was the United States' master spy, essentially inside Nazi occupied Europe. Yet prior to Pearl Harbor, there was no history of U.S. organized governmental espionage in the history of the country. The head of the newly formed OSS, William Donovan, had no intelligence background. A lawyer like Dulles, he distinguished himself as a decorated First World War officer, a U.S. District Attorney, and an Assistant Attorney General.

Dulles' background provided an unusually broad understanding of international relations. Because of his extensive work in Europe in the two decades preceding the start of the Second World War, he spoke both German and French.

His early career started with the State Department in 1920. Acquiring a law degree in 1926, he joined the firm of Sullivan & Cromwell in New York where his brother, John Foster Dulles was the managing partner. His legal duties were typically advisory in nature regarding international business dealings. Sullivan & Cromwell was not a typical law firm. The partnership functioned more as a confederation of lawyers engaged in establishing international relationships of power and economic influence that transcended sovereign borders. Sullivan & Cromwell offered investors credible assurances before the age of regulatory financial reporting. They were international brokers and dealmakers.

In 1927, Allen Dulles became director of the private nonprofit think tank Council on Foreign Relations. Serving as legal adviser to the delegations on arms limitation at the League of Nations for many years afforded unique firsthand experience. The opportunity to meet Adolf Hitler, Benito Mussolini, the leaders of Britain and France and other European leaders provided insights into European political instability following WWI. After entry of the U.S. into WWII, Donovan recruited Allen Dulles to become Swiss Director of the OSS. Working out of Bern, his mission was to gather intelligence on German plans and activities by developing a network of German émigrés, resistance figures, and anti-Nazi intelligence officers.

It was a unique high profile posting. Dulles became the highest-ranking Allied intelligence officer in the European theater. Neutral Switzerland, surrounded by Axis controlled territory provided an ideal base of operations. Within the first year, Dulles soon demonstrated his value. British intelligence and the U.S.

Army benefited from the information coming out of OSS Bern for the remainder of the war.

Only a short distance from Dulles' residence, the restaurant offered a grand view of the River Aare on this sunny winter's day. Lunch consisted of trout, boiled potatoes, and fresh vegetables, accompanied by a surprisingly good Swiss chardonnay. For Fraser and Marchand, the fine meal was a particular treat given the years of inadequate food in occupied France. The Swiss clearly did not suffer the same privations as the rest of Europe.

"You left off recounting the capture of Jean Moulin, "Dulles said as he went about the ritual of charging his pipe with tobacco. "Please resume your story, Marc."

"As I said, I need to explain events that started in Spain," Fraser said. "Even though I was using you as the means to secret my photos and copy out of Spain, I never revealed the details that caused me to leave after my second trip there in '37. Fiona knows the entire story but I will give you the short version.

"I was working with a Spanish journalist. A committed Republican and known enemy of the Nationalists. While imbedded with the advancing Nationalists supported by the German Luftwaffe Condor Legion, Loretta Elizalde retreated with the defending Republican troops and the Basque Army. Outgunned, demoralized, with little room for further retreat, defeat appeared imminent.

"The end came in Santander on the northern Spanish coast. Elizalde never made it out. Arrested, she unfortunately possessed photos only I could have taken. Atrocities previously committed in Andalusia and Badajoz. My arrest soon followed.

"Hauled into the same hotel room, the sight of a badly beaten Loretta tied to a chair came as a shock. She revealed nothing although enduring terrible suffering. I tried to talk my way out of this claiming the censor in Seville approved the photos. They did not buy that after discovering my unusual photographic equipment and makeshift developer. Equipment I learned how to use by chap in Paris recommended by your attaché acquaintance, Allen. Allowed me to produce those micro-sized negatives I sent to you concealed under the postage stamps.

"I suffered worse treatment than Loretta. They beat me unconscious. The two officers in charge were Falange Colonel Eduardo Cabrera Fuentes and German SS Sturmbannführer Heinz Konrad Leitner. Their names have significance to later events.

"Finished with the torture, they took us to the wine cellar in the hotel occupied by Nationalist officers. Clearly, we were in for a bad end. I believe they waited only for authorization for my execution since I carried a letter of safe-conduct from Generalissimo Franco himself. Escape seemed impossible. I could not walk. Could not see out of one eye. Suspected broken ribs with debilitating pain when I moved. They dislocated Loretta's fingers on one hand after inflicting terrible bruising on her arms from a rubber truncheon did not make her talk."

Fraser paused for a moment as the intense memory consumed him. Fiona knew the story and placed her hand on his arm.

"Good lord, man, how *did you* escape?" Dulles asked.

"I killed the guards with a knife."

Dulles leaned forward across the table. "A knife? From where?"

"A protection learned the hard way. A corrupt cop stabbed me in Los Angeles when I was a reporter that got too close. The bastard kept it taped to his calf. After that, I kept a six-inch switchblade in an ankle holster.

"The problem then became getting away. I took a bayonet wound from one of the soldiers I killed so I could not make it far. Loretta would not leave me. She knew Santander, coming there to seek refuge with her fiancé a local doctor. She hid us in a small sailboat cabin in the marina only a couple hundred yards from the hotel.

"She stayed with me before venturing out the following night and returning with her fiancé, Dr. Rafael Solano. The good doctor turned out to be an accomplished sailor. After doing what he could for me and administering morphine, we put out to sea. Two days later, we sailed into Biarritz on the French coast.

"I helped them settle in France. Both took up roles helping Spanish refugees fleeing the civil war. Skipping forward several years, as anti-fascists both Elizalde and Solano took up with the French Resistance following German occupation. They wound up in Lyon with Elizalde writing pieces for an underground newspaper and Dr. Solano working at a local surgery. That brought them into contact with Jean Moulin.

"Moulin created the *Bureau d'Information et de Presse* to act as a clearing house for intelligence materials from the various Resistance groups. Elizalde's job was to arrange documents to get to London by various routing methods. One such method was to courier materials to a contact in Paris known by the code name *Odysseus*. After learning *Odysseus* could smuggle out material cleverly reduced photographically to an exceedingly small size, she knew *Odysseus, or Odiseo* in Spanish, must be me.

"Although I did not know it at the time, her contact in Paris was Henri Marchand. He borrowed my code name only to deflect suspicion from me should I ever be arrested.

"In June we received disturbing news. After the arrest of her brother, Fiona took it upon herself to reestablish Henri's network of information gathering from the various Resistance groups for transmission to the Free French in London. She created an ingenious method of receiving sensitive information through the Louvre. You tell the rest of the story, Fiona."

Knowing how disturbing those memories were for Marc, Fiona said, "One of those Resistance groups was *Libération-sud*. Marc knew Loretta Elizalde and Rafael Solano worked for the group in Lyon. Elizalde served as the secretary responsible for transmitting gathered information. I received an unusual coded call from Dr. Solano saying the *Gestapo* arrested Loretta.

"Marc and I traveled to Lyon immediately. Solano told us the *Gestapo* raided his surgery from which he was absent at the time. They arrested Jean Moulin and the principals of *Libération-sud* gathered there on the second floor. The *Gestapo* arrested Elizalde later in a sweep of Lyon. Solano claimed there must be an informer in the group."

"Desperate to rescue his wife, Solano put us in touch with Lucie Aubrac. An extraordinary woman. She recruited the few remaining members of the Resistance group for a daring attempt to free her husband, one of those arrested. Adding to the urgency was the reputation of the Lyon *Gestapo* chief, SS-Hauptsturmführer Klaus Barbie. Recently reassigned from Amsterdam, he carried a fierce reputation for brutality. Known for personally inflicting hideous forms of torture.

"Marc joined the rescue attempt engineered by Lucie Aubrac. While transporting fourteen prisoners from Montluc Prison, the Resistance rescued all the detainees in a daring ambush. However, Loretta Elizalde was not among them.

"One of the rescued prisoners related knowing of a Spanish woman held in Montluc. A Spaniard. According to rumor, awaiting return to Spain. Dr. Solano was distraught. Wanted by the *Gestapo,* there was little he could do alone.

"Marc conceived a dangerous rescue plan. I objected because it sounded almost suicidal. Marc however was determined. He owed Elizalde and Solano a debt of gratitude for saving his life under equally desperate odds.

"Marc reasoned the only possibility of rescuing Elizalde was during her transport back to Spain. If true, that would undoubtedly be by train. With my help, Marc intended to overpower the escorting guards on the train. Solano was to make his way by automobile to Avignon where we would disembark. Marc's cover as scouting a location for a movie would provide the pretext for conducting surveillance at Lyon's photogenic Gare Perrache."

Fraser interjected, "The rumor proved correct. The *Gestapo* was returning Loretta to Spain. To face certain execution for continued agitation against the Franco regime from France in underground Spanish language newspapers.

"When brought to the railway station, she was physically in a bad way. Obviously sustaining injuries under torture by Klaus

Barbie. A Spanish officer supported her by one arm, her other arm by a man in a black leather overcoat and fedora. At least she was alive. I then recognized the others behind her. Falange Colonel Eduardo Cabrera Fuentes and German SS Sturmbannführer Heinz Konrad Leitner. Leitner addressed the shorter SS officer as Hauptsturmführer Barbie."

Fraser let out a long breath before continuing. "We successfully rescued Loretta, Allen, but she died soon after from injuries inflicted by Barbie."

"You rescued her? Care you be more specific?" Dulles said.

Fraser nodded, "Sure. I killed Cabrera in the water closet on the train."

"How?"

"Strangled him with his own necktie. A fitting death. Cabrera was a sadistic criminal no different from Barbie.

"And the two guards?"

"Fiona had a revolver and I got the drop on them. They helped Loretta off the train in Avignon. I then shot them both."

Dulles nodded. "A remarkable adventure. Too bad you could not save your friend."

Fraser said, "That was not the last chapter, Allen. You see Rafael Solano felt no purpose for living without Loretta. He intended retribution by killing Klaus Barbie. Easy enough to do if willing to sacrifice his life.

"Even knowing this was likely a suicide mission for Solano, we agreed to help. We could identify Barbie for Solano. Circumstances took an unexpected turn. Leitner was still in Lyon. Staying at the same hotel as Fiona and I probably because of its proximity to Gare Perrache."

Looking over at Fiona, Fraser continued, "But I got greedy. Had the idea of using Leitner to lure Barbie to a restaurant where Solano could just walk up and shoot him while Barbie sat alone waiting for Leitner.

"After forcing Leitner to call Barbie, Solano and I killed Leitner. A lethal injection of air into his bloodstream. Regrettably, the assassination attempt on Barbie failed. Solano tried to shoot

Barbie as he exited his car instead of waiting until he entered the restaurant according to our plan. Barbie's driver shot Solano before he even got off a shot.

"With Leitner, a ranking SS dead in our hotel, too great a risk for Fiona and I remaining in France. With Cabrera relating Loretta's background, my name undoubtedly came up connecting me now with the French Resistance. Registered in the same hotel after finding the dead Leitner would quickly add Fiona and I to a *Gestapo* wanted list. Fleeing to Switzerland our only chance.

"We hired a boat to cross Lake Geneva at night. A German patrol vessel ran over our smaller boat in the moonless dark. Fiona almost drowned. Got lucky with a Swiss patrol boat coming to the rescue."

Dulles smiled and relit his pipe. "Left out a few details I should think? What happened to the Germans on the patrol craft? Only one soldier survived?"

"I shot the others. Couldn't afford capture and return to Lyon."

Dulles shook his head in an expression of amazement. "The same Marc Fraser I knew from ten years ago. What do you and Fiona intend doing for the duration of the war?"

Fraser looked over at Fiona before answering. "The war is not over for us, Allen. Personally, I want to kill as many of the Nazi *Schutzstaffel* as possible. They are not soldiers, just murderers. I want to be nearby when the Nazis surrender. Help stamp out whatever remains of the SS."

"And you share those sentiments, Fiona?"

"I am not as blood thirsty as Marc, but I share his convictions. I lost a brother to them. They destroyed my country. Some time ago, I committed to resisting the Nazis. Now more than ever."

"Excellent. Interested in jobs with the OSS?"

"What specifically do you have in mind, Allen?" Fraser said.

"You two are a rare find. Committed. Experienced in espionage. Possessing useful linguistic talents. Interesting professional backgrounds that may prove useful as covers. I will need to give it some thought and discuss with a couple of others. Want to make the most of both your talents."

Fraser and Fiona looked at each other both signaling with slight nods.

Fraser stood extending his hand. "You have a provisional deal, Allen. Depends on what you have in mind."

# CHAPTER 3

BERN, SWITZERLAND | JANUARY 1944

---

Fraser and Marchand spent the next three days settling into Bern. Their new home for the duration of the war. Arriving in Switzerland penniless, their first order of business was establishing adequate economic means. Pay in the employ of the American OSS probably provided little more than subsistence. Marchand came from a modest economic background of a family of intellectuals. While by no means wealthy, Fraser was economically very comfortable. With well-paid jobs, he also enjoyed an inheritance from his mother, a granddaughter of James Mayer de Rothschild the founder of the French branch of the venerable Rothschild banking family. Even after coming to Europe ten years ago, his New York bank account remained untouched gaining interest.

In the first week of the German invasion into the Low Countries, Fraser sensed France was in trouble. Following the First World War, France constructed an impenetrable line of massive concrete fortifications on the border with Germany stretching from Basel, Switzerland to Luxemburg. With the Ardennes Forest region deemed a natural barrier to mechanized warfare, the strategy should force any German invasion to come through Belgium, the same as during the First World War. Here the

French would defend from outside French territory with their best divisions.

The Germans did exactly that in May 1940. However, the French defensive strategy fell apart from the beginning. The use of fully mechanized divisions of tanks and mobile infantry by the German *Wehrmacht* proved overwhelming to the lesser equipped French army. Even with a sizable supporting force of the British Army in France, Allied forces appeared outmatched. News reports followed daily progress of the German *blitzkrieg* penetrating deeper into France.

Fearing a French military disaster, Fraser moved funds in his Paris bank account to his New York account. A fortunate move since France fell in only six weeks. The Germans confiscated all French bank and treasury assets. Now in the banking capital of Europe, he could access his New York funds by establishing a Swiss bank account.

With these financial resources, they found a comfortable furnished apartment on Rathaugasse in the same ancient Altstadt district as Dulles' residence. Bern was not Paris, but it did have its own charm. None of the hated *Boche*. After three years under German occupation and the collaborating French Vichy government, experiencing the freedom of a neutral country was something to relish. Fraser could write to his father and sister in the United States. Once part of the OSS, Marchand might find a way to inform her parents in Provence that she was safe and well.

They made the most of those three days. A special event each day dining out with food not experienced for years. Although winter, they walked about medieval old town Bern, returning to their cozy apartment to make love.

After outfitting new wardrobes, they felt better prepared for whatever lay ahead. Although by now obvious the Germans would eventually suffer defeat, when and in what form remained unclear.

They knew their brief leisure period ended when summoned to Dulles' residence. Time to reenter the war.

Seated in Dulles' study was another man in his mid-thirties, well dressed, handsome with receding hair.

Dulles said, "Gerry, let me introduce Marc Fraser and Fiona Marchand. Gerald Mayer, like you, is a civilian employee of the OSS. Not only my right-hand here in Bern, but also the chief of the Office of War Information. The OSS spies on the Nazis while the OWI spreads nasty misinformation targeting the German home front."

Gerald Mayer was the same age as Fraser. Born to an American family, he spent his early years in Berlin. His father was Scotch-Irish, his mother Jewish. Under Nazi anti-Semitic racial laws, that qualified him as Jewish the same as Fraser. While not identifying himself as Jewish, he nonetheless was particularly sensitive to Nazi persecutions.

Educated at the University of California Berkeley, he was fluent English, German, and French. When the United States entered the war, Mayer accepted a job at the National Broadcasting Company. One of his functions was translating Hitler's speeches in real time. Soon afterwards, he joined the Office of War Information, the American clandestine propaganda agency, and then posted to Bern.

Gerald Mayer approached with a warm smile, extending his hand.

"Everyone please sit down. Coffee?" Dulles said.

After settling in with coffee and a plate of Swiss chocolates, Dulles resumed. "I related your backgrounds to Gerry. We have been discussing how best to use your talents. Gerry, I will let you explain our thoughts."

Mayer said, "Considerable talents I must add. Experienced operatives given your exploits in the French Resistance. Your professional backgrounds coupled with your language skills offer unique options."

Switching to French, Mayer addressed Fraser, "Sufficiently fluent in French to claim to be French?"

Fraser replied in French, "I should think so. My mother was French. Spent my summers in France and completed most of my university education at the Ecole Superieur de Journalism de Paris before transferring to Columbia in New York."

Mayer nodded, and said in excellent German, "How about German?"

"Fluent, however nowhere near as good as you. Could not pass as a native German."

"And you Madame Marchand," Mayer said, "How did you acquire proficiency in Italian?"

"A professional necessity in my field of art and art history. Conducting research into original documents requires not only reading Italian proficiently, but also understanding the differences of Renaissance-era language style. Like Marc, my accent prevents passing myself off as Italian. However, I have worked extensively in the great museums of Roma, Firenze, and Milano."

"If I may Interrupt Gerry," Dulles said. "Your background, Fiona, has our immediate attention. With the toppling of Mussolini and surrender of Italy, now an ally, we have need of someone like you. Your art world background will provide the perfect cover once the Allies advance north up the Italian peninsula. Would you consider an assignment in Italy?"

Marchand did not expect this. Thinking more of a safe posting in Switzerland, she realized her naivety. Of course, what Dulles suggested made sense. But leaving Marc?

She looked at Marc. His expression revealed his discomfort of her going alone into the field without him. Yet he could not constrain her. This was war. Her war no less than his. They could not sit idly in comfort in Switzerland while others fought the Nazis.

Fraser said, "Since Germany invaded France, Fiona and I have fought side by side. As much as I hate her to go it alone, I cannot be selfish. She is fully capable of acting as an OSS agent. It is your choice, Fiona."

Marchand reached out and touched Fraser's hand. Turning to Mayer and Dulles, "Yes, I will be willing to go to Italy. Obviously, I can be of greater use there than doing administrative work here. What am I to do in Italy?"

Mayer said, "First, contact with Vatican intelligence, *Santa Alleanza,* using your natural cover as working in the Vatican Museum. From that platform you will act as OSS liaison to various Italian partisan groups working in the north."

"What about Marc?"

Mayer looked over at Dulles, not sure how much he should reveal to Marchand.

Dulles did not hesitate. After all, they were husband and wife, as well as experienced undercover operatives. "Setting your mind at ease, Fiona, Marc will not be venturing into occupied France. That is for other OSS and the British SOE run out of England.

"Too dangerous to return to France given your high-profile exposure there. Marc is too valuable now that he is here in Switzerland. Since Marc knows the leaders of the various French Resistance groups, he will remain involved in that effort of course. London coordinates with the French Resistance. Marc will monitor reports and add any insights from his years of experience in France.

"Things may soon change in France. It is no secret that a third front will eventually open in France. When and where remains the question. Once that happens, the Resistance will play an important role and Marc's knowledge will become valuable. That is much the situation now in Italy since the Italian armistice months ago. OSS-Bern coordinates Italian partisan efforts to harass German forces.

"I see Marc playing a different role than interacting with the French Resistance. Using his cover as a journalist, I want Marc to find Germans here in Switzerland and in Germany to act as informants against the Nazis. Marc's background shows he has a talent for manipulating people to suit his purpose. He can put those skills to great use here. As a neutral country, we are in the belly of the beast. The perfect place to interact directly with the enemy. An enemy that knows it is going down to defeat. Lots of rats trying to leave the sinking Third Reich ship."

"Will he be venturing undercover into Germany?" Marchand asked.

Mayer answered, "No. His German is not good enough to pass as native German."

"Plenty of work here in Switzerland," Dulles said. "As the German military situation deteriorates further, all manner of potential sources and those looking to improve their postwar prospects become available. A matter of vetting those people and making overtures they cannot refuse.

"Now to the matter of your cover names. In transmissions, everyone has an identification number for economy. No particular significance. I am 110. General Donovan is 109. A type of shorthand. You are 531, Marc, and Fiona you are 587. Everyone and everything, friend or foe also has a code name. OSS personnel, foreign sources, organizations, actual spies, well-known people, and those of the enemy. Anyone best not mentioned even by code name in encrypted signals traffic. In your case you will retain your prior code names of *Odysseus* and *Penelope* from working with the French Resistance."

For the next month, Fraser and Marchand underwent intensive training. Each becoming familiar with their respective spheres of involvement and OSS procedures.

For Marchand, she immersed herself in understanding the rapidly changing political dynamics of Italy from Axis partner with Germany to overthrowing Mussolini then switching to the Allied side. Since the invasion of Sicily six months earlier, the Allies now fought German forces after the Italian Army disbanded. A crash course in the Allied military campaign and the cast of players.

For Fraser, it meant understanding what the OSS knew of various dissident elements aligning against Hitler. Peace feelers were even floated from certain high-ranking Nazis and *Wehrmacht* general officers. Conditional armistice feelers to preserve German sovereignty by collaborating with the Western Allies to defeat the Soviet onslaught from the East. With Switzerland both neutral and locked in a symbiotic relationship with Germany, Bern was a hot bed of spies from both sides. Switzerland an ideal working environment.

They both studied the codes used by the OSS. This included the protocols for encrypted transmissions by the ECM Mark II cipher machine. A bulky machine typically managed by a cipher technician from a secure location such as a U.S. embassy or consulate. For Marchand working in the field, this meant training with the portable M-209-B cipher machine used by the U.S. Army. Both cipher systems used the same basic concept of mechanical rotors to encrypt messages incapable of deciphering without possessing the same device used in reverse of the transmission.

While a busy month training in their new roles, it proved a quiet respite. Settled in their apartment, Fraser and Marchand began an active social life. Although intended to support their respective covers, their backgrounds and the circumstances bringing them to Switzerland were fully reasonable with only minor fictions.

They did not explain their true circumstances compelling the desperate escape from France. Simply escaping life under German occupation. Fraser relating the inability to produce films in France without adhering to the uncultured and propagandized Nazi censorship. He would fall back on his long career in journalism now reporting from a neutral country. To establish his credentials, he telegraphed his old benefactor, William Randolph Hearst, to offer his services. Hearst responded within days. Delighted to hear again from his former foreign correspondent and to have a veteran reporting from neutral Switzerland, he offered Fraser a position at a respectable salary with expense account.

Marchand was not only an art expert with an advanced degree in art history, but also a respected restorer of oil paintings. Her niche being sixteenth-century Italian works. A talented painter herself, classes at the Sorbonne provided a strong technical background. Personal curiosity prompted her to study the materials and techniques of the Renaissance masters. Her passion enabled securing her first job at the Louvre as an apprentice to a renowned art restorer. Her restoration talents took her on assignments throughout Europe. Living under the heel of the occupying Nazis having little appreciation for art other than its economic value, became unbearable.

To the question why they did not escape to America, the answer was simply no easy way to escape Europe. Switzerland was the obvious choice. Fraser's bad experience reporting against the Fascist Nationalists in the Spanish Civil War eliminated Spain as an option with Franco in power. Their means of escape explained by *forged documents obtained for the right amount of money. The offer of doing a screenplay for a Swiss filmmaker a further inducement.*

Both understood they were preparing to reenter the war. However, the safety of Switzerland was a welcomed respite to the violence and continual danger of their resistance work in France.

Preparing for dinner with new friends, as Fiona refreshed her makeup at a dressing table, Marc put his hands on her shoulders. "You sure about getting this actively involved. I obviously will worry about you going off to Italy. It is an active war zone."

She touched one of his hands on her shoulder. "We have been over this, Marc. In Italy, I can be of service. I cannot coerce Germans to become intelligence sources as you can. I am not going behind enemy lines. Not like in France having to elude both the *Gestapo* and the *Malice*."

Looking up at him, she teasingly said, "Besides, I have now become skillful with a revolver thanks to an American Marine officer Dulles recruited for my training. Handsome young fellow from Texas. Said my accent sounded like something out of a movie.

Over her shoulder, Marc smiled into the mirror. "I'll bet he enjoyed that assignment. Teaching a sexy French woman how to shoot."

She elbowed him in the ribs gently. "No need to be jealous. I prefer mature men like you."

He chuckled. However, her safety was of paramount concern. Contacting partisans by definition meant venturing into dangerous territory. She would also be a woman surrounded by thousands of soldiers in war-ravaged Italy. All manner of danger. No way to tamp down his concerns but he must manage the worry. They went through this is France. Fiona proved resourceful while handling the constant fear.

"Seriously, I need to provide you with better protection than that cumbersome revolver, no matter how well this handsome young Marine trained you. Now, get your sexy ass moving or Jacob and Ruth will suspicion why we are late."

Among their acquaintances, they quickly became friends with an older couple in their apartment building. Professor Jacob Ausfelder of the University of Bern and his wife Ruth, a concert violinist. Herr Ausfelder was German, and Ruth Austrian. Both Jewish.

Both left German in 1933 when Adolf Hitler rose to Chancellor. Months later, the Reichstag passed the Enabling Act essentially allowing the Chancellor to rule by decree. Dictatorial rule by an anti-Semitic, nonintellectual psychopath. Ausfelder read Mein Kampf. Obvious what this megalomaniacal monster intended for the Jews. Seeing where events were taking Germany with the rise of National Socialism, they realized they must leave Germany. Before the end of 1933, he left his tenured position as professor of history at Heidelberg University in Baden-Württemberg near Stuttgart in the south of Germany near the French and Swiss borders. The University of Bern offered Jacob a position and Ruth soon secured a position with the Bern Symphony Orchestra.

The Ausfelders embraced Fraser and Marchand as fellow expatriates caught up in this terrible war started by Adolf Hitler. They both spoke English and French from their proximity to France. Their only son studying at Cambridge in 1933 thankfully remained in England. Both Jacob's parents were deceased. Emma's two siblings and elderly parents refused to leave Vienna. The last she heard from them was following the *Anschluss* in March 1938 as Germany absorbed Austria into the Third Reich.

Persecution against the Jews of Vienna began immediately. The few letters Ruth Ausfelder received that year portrayed ever-escalating plunder and degradation as the process of Aryanisation began. The last communication arrived just after the brutal *Kristallnacht* pogrom in November of that year. A non-Jewish childhood friend wrote informing her of the deportation of her entire family including two nieces. Rumor identified the destination as Dachau concentration camp.

Marchand shared the loss of her brother to an unknown fate in the Nazi concentrations camps while her parents and other brother remained trapped in occupied France.

Without going into details of events leading to his and Fiona's escape from France, Fraser recounted the deaths of his Spanish refugee friends at the hands of a *Gestapo* torturer in Lyon.

Digressing to less depressing events, Fraser regaled them with his adventurous career as a journalist and his early days in Hollywood. All became good friends with the shared bond of loss of family and friends at the hands of the Nazis.

Over drinks at the Fraser's apartment sitting room before venturing out to dinner at a nearby restaurant, Jacob Ausfelder said to Fraser, "That is good you have found employment with your former publisher in America. Especially after the falling out you related during the Spanish Civil War."

"Well Mr. Hearst is an opportunist. I am in an ideal position just short of being in Berlin."

"What sort of material are you expected to provide here on this island?"

"This island as you call Switzerland, Jacob, is a hotbed of intrigue. Both of the warring sides are here doing secret business. As long as they abide by the rules preserving Swiss neutrality."

Ausfelder replied, "And the Swiss are doing a great deal of business with the Germans. War provides all manner of opportunities for turning a profit. Something the Swiss are good at."

"You sound critical of your adopted country, Jacob."

"As one should be. Critical of those in government. The Swiss are good people. The profiteers are the banking industry with a strong political influence."

Fraser said, "Switzerland walks a narrow line. The Alps cannot serve as a defensive bastion should the Germans choose to invade."

Ausfelder replied, "Yet Swiss banking is the principal reason Germany hesitates to invade."

Dulles briefly alluded to transmissions from both the U.S. Treasury and State Departments accusing Switzerland of essentially funding the Nazi war effort. Choosing not to dwell on the details, Dulles told Fraser his limited OSS staff did not have the resources to dig deeper. He largely avoided the issue given the competing positions of the two U.S. government departments.

"What do you mean?"

"I am no expert but a close academic associate at the university is. Friedrich Bauer is a Professor of Economics. Swiss, not Jewish, but he virulently despises Hitler and the Nazis. He feels Swiss banking collaboration with the Nazis is unconscionable. He maintains a wide range of contacts in Swiss banking, therefore understands its darker side.

"In simplest terms Friedrich says the Third Reich funnels German Reichsmarks through the Swiss banking system. Yet the more outrageous collaboration comes in the form of accepting gold and other assets looted from countries occupied by the Germans. The national treasuries of France, Belgium, and the Netherlands along with stolen Jewish wealth flow into Switzerland.

"The Swiss convert Reichsmarks and looted gold into Swiss francs. A stable neutral currency recognized throughout the world. Not only does this allow Germany to purchase vital war material, but the Swiss also facilitate transactions through shell companies to conceal the commerce. Goods then often flow through Switzerland ending up in Germany. All this earning Swiss banking lucrative income on loans backed with these vast gold deposits with added fees and commissions for these special financial services.

"Germany's access to necessary war goods using stolen wealth becomes severed if Switzerland does not remain a sovereign neutral nation."

Fraser said, "Interesting. I would very much like to talk with your colleague. How much of this is sensitive to publication?"

"Not sure. We are a democracy allowing free speech. However, this is wartime. Please tread cautiously. Please do not attribute my comments or Professor Bauer's in print. Not sure Swiss authorities are magnanimous when it comes to criticism."

"I will remember that, Jacob. Just unnamed sources. Some more wine?"

Carefully crafting watered down material for publication presented no conflict. Fraser's real interest was gathering intelligence and useful sources rather than furthering his journalistic cover. Professor Bauer certainly fit the description of a useful source.

Ausfelder turned his attention to his wife and Marchand, "I apologize ladies for digressing into a rant. Marc tells me you are engaged in a project at the *Kunstmuseum*, Fiona."

The Kunstmuseum, the Museum of Fine Arts Bern, was the oldest art museum in Switzerland with its permanent collection ranging from the middle ages to the early twentieth century.

Marchand said, "Yes. A restoration project on two of the museum's paintings by the late thirteenth century Italian painter Duccio di Buoninsegna. Never had an opportunity to see his work this intimately."

Emma Ausfelder said, "Restoration? I knew you were an art expert, but you physically work on restoring masterpieces?"

Marchand nodded. "Yes I do. Got my first real job that way. Understanding the techniques and the materials greatly enhanced my artistic knowledge of oil painting. I consciously think of the way the great masters painted. It has taken me to the great museums of the world. I never before worked at the Kunstmuseum though. A fine collection I understand."

Like Fraser, Marchand began working her cover as an art expert preparing for eventually going to the Vatican once the Allies liberated Rome.

The following day, Fraser followed through with his agenda to instruct Fiona on how to defend herself in circumstances she might encounter. Not target shooting by a Marine without combat experience serving embassy duty. Worse yet, Gerry Mayer presented her with a bulky .38 caliber Smith & Weston revolver to take into the field. Impractical as a close quarter protective weapon. Good she got the feel of firing a large handgun, but he had in mind something more suitable to augment her defensive capabilities.

After finishing their morning coffee, Fraser was only partially dressed in his trousers and undershirt with Fiona still in her nightgown.

"Stand up. Time for your first instruction into how to defend yourself," he said.

"You cannot be serious. Not now."

"Just do as I say, Fiona. This is serious. You are going into a dangerous environment. As a pretty woman, you are a natural target for assault. Should this happen, you must be prepared to defend yourself. Understand?"

Noting his seriousness, she stood and said, "Very well."

"Now if a man attempts to grab you from the front, your first response is to knee him in the groin. Hard. With all your strength. You are not warding him off, but debilitating him. Of course, that will not be enough. Following immediately, I want you to thrust your hand into his face, hitting his nose with the heel of your palm. As hard as you can."

He demonstrated with his hand.

"I don't know if I could do that."

"Listen. You will if attacked, Fiona. Hit him with all your strength. Crush his nose. Remember I told you about the ex-boxer staging fight scenes at the studio in Hollywood when I was young. Always said go for your opponent's nose."

"And if someone attacks me from behind?"

Fraser turned her around and pulled his right arm around her neck from behind. "Now reach around with your hand. Find an eye. Gouge it violently with a finger."

Fiona mimicked the response and he let go.

"Remember, you are looking to do damage to vulnerable areas. Eyes, nose, throat, groin, and knees. Avoid getting close. Go for the groin only if close enough to use your knee. Never try kicking his groin with your foot or he may grab your ankle and upend you. If he comes aggressively toward you, instead kick hard to his knee with the bottom of your foot."

He made her demonstrate each tactic. Her moves not particularly impressive. Impossible to learn self-defense without practice.

"Now these maneuvers will not resolve the attack. In a street fight, if you put your opponent down you must make sure he does not get up again to hurt you. There are no rules except to escape unharmed. Use anything available as a weapon."

Fraser reached into his pocket and extracted a slim soft chamois holster. Handing it to Fiona, he said, "Take it out."

She knew what it was. Saw it many times on her husband's ankle when they were in France.

Extracting the knife, she pressed the button releasing the spring-loaded six-inch double-edged stiletto blade.

"Wear trousers at all times and wear that at all times. Practice reaching down to extract it. If attacked, never threaten. Stick it into your assailant. This is your life or his."

She said nothing for several moments looking at the knife. Marc never recounted the details, but she knew he used this weapon or one like it to save himself in Spain. The thought sent a shudder through her.

"I don't think I could ever do that, Marc."

"Yes you could if threatened with harm. The best protection is to maintain situational awareness. Always understand your environment even to the extent of anticipating how someone might attack you. It is about being constantly prepared."

Fiona nodded. All his instructions only served to make her more anxious about Italy. "Now let me finish getting ready."

Fraser went to the bureau and opened a drawer. Coming back to the dressing table, he laid down a small pistol and a handful of cartridges. "Take this to Italy as well as that two-pound artillery piece Gerry you. Pick it up. You'll see how much more comfortable this is."

Fiona picked up the small weapon.

"Oh my. Such a little thing. Powerful?

"Enough for use at close range. Fits in your pocket or purse. Get into a bad fix, you empty this into your attacker."

The small pistol was an FN1906 manufactured by the Belgian firm Fabrique Nationale. A ten-ounce automatic pistol with a six-shot magazine firing a .25ACP cartridge.

# CHAPTER 4

BERN, SWITZERLAND | MARCH 1944

---

"Are you and Fiona getting along in your new home? I mean Bern." Dulles asked Fraser. They were sitting alone in Dulles' study, his preferred office. What constituted the small OSS staff based in Bern worked out of the U.S. Embassy. Dulles' separate location kept a courier busy each day delivering classified information between the locations.

The arrangement suited the professional style of Allen Dulles. A consummate networker, the less official surroundings of his private residence allowed meeting individuals preferring to keep their contact secret. As a neutral country, those individuals included enemy nationals and government officials of his host country. Swiss Intelligence officials numbered among his most useful associations.

"Very much. Medieval Bern is easy to like. We have already made friends. As comfortable as Switzerland is, we both appreciate the opportunity to contribute in the war effort, Allen."

"It is America that appreciates your services. Fortuitous for all concerned. Have you been monitoring the dispatches between the French Resistance and London?"

"Yes. By the signals traffic, it seems activity is picking up in the North," Fraser said.

Dulles puffed on his pipe and smiled. "Very observant. Picking up because something big is about to happen. *Operation Overlord.* Even the Germans know that. American and Canadian troops continue to pour into Great Britain. When and where is the most deeply held secret, but certainly the northern coast of France."

"Communicate any insights or recommendations from your experiences with the Resistance to London."

"Of course. The most useful leading up to invasion will be the Ceux de la Libération, the CDLL, and the Organisation Civile et Militaire, the OCM. Unfortunately, arrests last year decimated the leadership of both groups. I do not have immediate familiarity with the current leadership.

"Not sure I can be of much assistance from here in Switzerland. I have however familiarized myself with the various color code-named plans for the Resistance once Overlord starts."

"Very good, but that is just monitoring work because of your familiarity with the Resistance. Your real assignment centers on gathering intelligence from inside the Third Reich. Are you settling into your cover job as a foreign correspondent?"

"I believe so. It provides the perfect basis for approaching people and asking direct questions. In fact, I have a lunch meeting today with a friend and his colleague, an economics professor at the University.

"My friend, an expatriate German Jewish academic, has strong views about what he characterizes as Swiss banking funding the German war effort. Wants me to hear opinions from someone familiar with the Swiss banking industry.

"Interesting?" Dulles replied puffing on his pipe. "A touchy subject with the Swiss. Secretary Morgenthau at Treasury is pushing the Swiss aggressively on what happened to the gold of treasuries looted by the Nazis. Washington is continually pushing us for information. However, Washington does not understand circumstances here. Swiss banking preserves better secrecy than the best intelligence organizations in the world.

"I cannot dilute more pressing priorities to assign OSS resources for what will be difficult and awkward since we are guests in Switzerland. I have a close working relationship with Swiss intelligence. As a neutral power, I can say there is a decided bias toward the Allies. They are a valuable intelligence source. Yet Swiss banking is a sacred cow."

Of course the Swiss are moving closer to the Allies, Fraser thought. Germany is losing the war. Fighting on the East and Italy with a decisive third front in France imminent. German cities bombed day and night.

"Yet if true the Swiss are assisting the Germans in funding war materials, should it not be a priority?"

"Well it is true. The problem remains Switzerland's neutrality. They are in a difficult position. And we have no leverage. Washington must take the long view. Switzerland will be of critical importance to the inevitable reconstruction of Europe. The issues are delicate and complicated."

Fraser was not about to argue with his boss. Dulles obviously lacked enthusiasm for pursuing Swiss financial complicity with The Third Reich. His focus was collecting actionable intelligence on the enemy.

"But you are on the right track," Dulles said. "That is what networking is all about. Hardly need to tell that to you. You have been doing that your entire journalism career. Get what you can from this Professor Bauer. Not likely to divulge anything useful, but report what you learn. Be advised however to tread carefully where Swiss interests are concerned.

"A personal friend of mine, Thomas McKittrick, is the President of the Bank for International Settlements. Based here in Switzerland in Basel. A good source in understanding the movement of money between central banks, including the Swiss National Bank. I assure you, pressuring Switzerland in the form demanded by Secretary of the Treasury Morgenthau and his minions is fraught with myriad complexities. "

"Isn't the B.I.S. the institution setup in the thirties to manage reparations from the Great War?" Fraser said. "That no longer seems to have applicability."

"Nonetheless, the B.I.S remains. A type of independent world bank, now with a wider purpose."

An interesting reaction from Allen Dulles to this seemingly important issue of international finance central to Germany's ability to sustain the current war. Dulles former law firm Sullivan & Cromwell, headed by his brother John Foster Dulles, conducted extensive business dealings in prewar Germany. Yet it was Allen Dulles, at odds with his brother, who demanded closing the firm's Berlin office with Hitler's ascension to power. With decades of experience, Allen Dulles was very much an expert in international business. Odd he lack of interest in the role of Swiss Banking.

"Tell you what. I am attending a social gathering in Zurich on Saturday. The Home of Emil Oprecht. A magnificent home. Emil looks on it as a type of literary solon. He is director of the publishing house of Europe-Verlag. His quests number among the intelligentsia of Central Europe. With you as a published novelist and Fiona an art expert, Emil and his wife will be delighted to include you and Fiona."

Fraser published *Dark Side of Tinseltown* in 1931, a semi-autobiographical novel based on his early exploits exposing corruption in Los Angeles with the movie industry as a backdrop. Retiring from journalism after returning from the Spanish Civil War, he published *Inferno* in 1939, a novel based on the horrors of that war.

"A little over an hour by train. I will get us rooms for the night. I can guarantee a lively evening and a good opportunity to pick up competing sentiments. Certainly will provide you with a network of influential contacts."

Anxious for Fraser to meet his associate, Friedrich Bauer, Jacob Ausfelder invited Fraser to his office the following week.

A corpulent man, balding with thinning gray hair entered Ausfelder's university office. It was late in the morning. Ausfelder and Fraser were chatting over coffee. So ubiquitous to Swiss life, Fraser indulged his passion for coffee so long denied by the years of rationing in occupied France.

"Good morning Jacob. And you must be Herr Fraser. I am Friedrich Bauer."

Bauer rigorously shook Fraser's hand then took the other chair across the desk from Ausfelder.

"Delighted to meet an American journalist. Jacob told me something of your background. Most fortunate you have found a home here in Switzerland. I cannot image life under the thumb of Nazis. It remains only a matter of time before the Allies defeat their criminal regime."

"Thank you, Professor. Jacob raised the subject of Swiss banking financially assisting in the Nazi war effort. Readers in the United States would like to understand why that is possible given Swiss neutrality."

"I would say Swiss banking is more than assisting. They are actively collaborating. Have been since well before the outbreak of this war. How do you think the Third Reich funded its rearmament in the thirties? This of course is well known in official circles of Washington and London."

Fraser said, "I have been isolated from English publications for the last few years as you can imagine."

Bauer nodded. "Of course. However, here in neutral Switzerland we have access to news from both the warring factions. Neutrality is at the heart of the Swiss situation.

"The American press frequently publishes articles, usually buried in the financial sections of the newspapers. Of interest mainly to only those in business and investment banking. Nevertheless, the allegations against the Swiss are becoming more strident. Driven by your Treasury Secretary, Henry Morgenthau."

"And what does Morgenthau accuse the Swiss of?"

"All manner of wrongdoing. Accepting looted treasuries of occupied countries. Also accepting looted private assets, namely assets from Jews disappearing into their concentration camps.

"The Nazis stole the gold reserves of the countries they occupied. Austria, Czechoslovakia, Poland, Denmark, Belgium, the Netherlands, and France. Gold worth hundreds of millions of Swiss francs. The total amount of Nazi looted gold transported to Switzerland amounts close to 400 million Swiss francs. In your currency, something over $400 million U.S. dollars."

Fraser said, "How did you come by these figures, Professor?"

"Professional colleagues. Fellow academics and former central bankers from France, Belgium, and the Netherlands. Those that fled their countries in 1940. Most are working in England, Canada, or America. We communicate regularly."

"The Americans and British are therefore well aware of these details?" Fraser said.

"Certainly. With thousands dying every day, complex financial transactions do not consume public attention in these countries. It does however make the Swiss appear culpable by enabling Adolf Hitler. Which it is. The question remains, culpable by greed or coercion?

"A moral burden for us Swiss. The majority of Swiss citizens are anti-Nazi. How to express that in the face of implicit German threat to Swiss sovereignty? What do we expect our government to do? A dilemma with many variables."

"But you feel the Swiss government should be doing far more to distance themselves from Nazi Germany. According to Jacob, the Swiss fear German invasion. Perhaps there is little choice in tacit cooperation with Germany," Fraser said.

Bauer said, "Absolutely. But at this stage in the war, I do not believe the Nazis can spare the resources to invade Switzerland. Everyone knows the Allies will invade France, opening a third front. More than ever, Germany needs the services of Swiss banking and preserve a conduit to receive essential materials passing through Switzerland.

"You see, these are not just bankers taking in deposits. Their essential service is converting those assets into Swiss francs. The most stable currency in Europe and suitable for payment of goods throughout the world. Swiss bankers hold to the claim they cannot attest to the providence of gold bullion. Therefore, the Swiss claim to have accepted no gold from Germany with mint markings of other countries. Who can say without examination of the gold reserves? Even then, the Germans could easily have reminted the gold ingot removing any trail to its provenance."

Fraser said, "Your position, a blunder for the Germans to invade Switzerland. Of course, that psychopath Hitler repeatedly makes strategic blunders. The reason Germany is losing the war."

"True. However, the Swiss banking industry goes far beyond simply acting as a repository for Nazi gold. In order to purchase goods internationally, converting gold into Swiss francs is not enough. Concealing transactions to disguise Germany as the recipient of war materials becomes essential. Swiss banking therefore actively aids in creating foreign shell companies to act as fronts in sympathetic fascist countries like Spain and Portugal. Then front companies here in Switzerland complete the procurement ruse.

"Some in our government argue this as the necessary reason to allow goods to flow to Germany through Switzerland or avoid German invasion. It certainly allows for extraordinary profit opportunities. Swiss war profiteering is on an unprecedented scale."

"What is Morgenthau expecting of the Swiss?" Fraser asked.

"For one thing, to cease facilitating the movement of war goods to Germany. The Swiss deny complicity and resort to various arguments asserting Swiss neutrality. The other demand is to reveal a full accounting of deposits received from Germany. Again, the neutrality argument by favoring demands of one warring faction against the other.

"However, the real resistance is the demand to breach Swiss banking confidentiality. That approaches an article of almost religious faith. It goes to the very soul of Switzerland's principal industry."

Jacob Ausfelder interjected. "Friedrich speaks of these looted gold reserves from national treasuries. Beyond looted gold, are staggering sums of money and art stolen directly from the occupied populations. Mostly the Jews of course. Following enactment of the Third Reich's Nuremberg Laws in 1935, the flow of Jewish wealth into Switzerland for safekeeping accelerated. As Nazi persecution progressed in its level of barbarism, ransoms for wealthy Jews to escape and widespread confiscation of Jewish property continues to pour into Swiss accounts. And your other statistic about stolen art, Friedrich?"

"Obviously far less precise. Again those displaced French, Belgian, and Dutch academics talk of values in the hundreds of millions of Swiss francs."

"And is Switzerland a repository for this stolen art?" Fraser asked.

Bauer nodded. "Sadly, yes."

"Where is the stolen art kept?" Fraser asked.

"Bank vaults."

"Let me understand what you and Jacob are saying. The entire Swiss banking system is complicit with financing the Nazi war effort, yet the majority of the Swiss population is anti-Nazi?"

Bauer answered, "Essentially that is the situation. Swiss banking cooperation with Germany goes back a long time. It is an ingrained habit."

Fraser shook his head. "In the form of the Nazis, Germany is now different. Do all Swiss banks participate in this ... *cooperation* with the Nazis?"

"Not all. There are many banks standing on moral principles. Unfortunately, the Banque National Swisse, the Swiss central bank is the focal point. At least for the initial receipt of Nazi looted gold deposits. The process is further facilitated by the Bank of International Settlements."

The BIS again. "Tell me, exactly what does the BIS do?" Fraser said.

Bauer said, "Let me provide an example. The Swiss National Bank receives Nazi gold from the German Reichbank. Subsequently it ships gold to the central banks of Portugal and Spain. The gold serves to purchase war material such as wolframite ore for producing tungsten. A vital material for aircraft and tooling manufacturing. The ore ships to Germany moving first through the puppet Vichy French regime then through Switzerland. All purchase transactions and payment take place in Bern. All sanctioned through the BIS. On the surface, these are transactions involving neutral nations. Obscured by the Swiss government is the underlying fact the gold deposit reserves backing the currency transactions are stolen assets. The Swiss are therefore laundering Nazi loot under the auspices of the BIS."

Professor Bauer went on to explain in extensive detail much of which was beyond Fraser's understanding of international banking.

The BIS functioned as a world bank. It was a creation of the world's central banks to deal with reparations of the Great War. Governed by a board of directors from all the signatory countries of its charter in 1930, by 1944 the Nazis virtually controlled the BIS. Located in Basel Switzerland, it was physically assessable to German directors but to none of the Allied or occupied nations.

The sitting board therefore consisted mainly of Germans and Swiss. Among the German directors was the Reichsbank official of the German central bank, the head of the industrial giant I. G. Farben, and the managing director of a Cologne bank as the leading financier of the *Gestapo*. With the chief function of the BIS to facilitate gold reserve transfers among central banks, a perfect set of circumstances existed for Nazi gold to disappear into the secrecy of the Swiss banking system. Adding to the stacked deck, the director of the BIS since 1940 was an ardent American Nazi sympathizer, Thomas McKittrick.

Very interesting. Good material for his cover as an American journalist but little prospects for networking toward seeking out intelligence sources. Dulles was friendly with McKittrick, and his *old boy* network included many leading Swiss bankers. Dulles undoubtedly knew everything Bauer related.

Jacob Ausfelder said, "I know this is not the sort of headline material your publisher is looking for, Marc. Most troubling is the enabling of the Nazis to carry out their genocide of Jews.

"Plundering of Jewish wealth does not serve any German war cause. It simply enriches the Nazi *Schutzstaffel*. They run the concentration camps for profit and provide a flow of renewable slave labor using the *Gestapo*. At the head of this Nazi criminal enterprise is Heinrich Himmler.

"Perhaps a more worthy story lies with exposing the Nazi *Schutzstaffel* wealth concealed in Swiss bank accounts. Himmler and his henchmen likely have their own share."

Fraser looked at both men with an expression of interest, "Do you have something specific where I could start?"

Ausfelder looked over at Bauer.

"There is a German lawyer named Manfred Krüger, here in Bern," Bauer said. "Publicly known to be connected with the Reich Ministry of Economic Affairs. Believed to hold a senior rank in the SS. Runs a company known as Internationale Investitionen, GmbH. Rumored close to both Walter Funk the German Economics Minister as well as Oswald Pohl, head of the *Schutzstaffel* Main Economic and Administrative Office. Krüger is a former banker. Speculation suggests he manages foreign investments for the Nazi SS. The SS is of course a massive economic enterprise."

"As secretive as Swiss banking appears, how did you come by such information?" Fraser asked.

"Not all Swiss bankers agree with assisting the Nazis. Fortunately, we are still free therefore, there is much talk within the banking industry. Herr Krüger's SS affiliation provided by a sympathetic anti-Nazi official in Swiss Intelligence."

"Well, Herr Krüger might prove a starting point for a story," Fraser said.

Ausfelder said, "That is good. As this war draws to conclusion, these criminals will seek refuge. Hoping to make their escape to some fascist-sympathetic country, taking their blood money with them. Compounding the injustice of their astonishing crimes."

Fraser thought, perhaps to reconstitute a Fourth Reich following German defeat.

Bauer said, "However, please avoid any attribution of your source of material to either Jacob or me."

"Of course, gentlemen. I have never revealed my confidential sources."

# CHAPTER 5

BERN, SWITZERLAND | APRIL 1944

---

On the train ride to Zürich, Dulles sat across from Fraser and Marchand. Turning to Marchand he said, "We talked about you going to Rome once the Americans and British liberate the city. Unfortunately, that campaign is proving a daunting task. The Germans are mounting stiff resistance. I want to get a jump on things. Get you to Italy within a couple of weeks?

"Well behind the front lines of course. Naples. Headquarters for both the U.S. Fifth Army and the British Eighth Army. I want you to make contact with Italian partisans in the area. Just like France, there are many resistance groups. Some constituted from former Italian military. Some with political agendas. Part of your task is to sort out which group can be useful. Remember, you are looking for actionable intelligence on the Germans but also information useful in predicting the postwar political composition of Italy."

The daunting prospect was overwhelming. The objectives as part of the French Resistance were clear. Harass the Germans and provide the Allies with information useful for invading and liberating France. Italy was an active theater of war. Her mission objectives vague. She was not like Marc. His professional life involving asking questions. Investigating and sticking his nose into dangerous places. But she reminded herself she was no different from every soldier called on to perform unfamiliar tasks.

Dulles said to her, "You ready for this, Fiona?"

She looked at Marc. Obviously uncomfortable with Fiona venturing off to Italy alone, he simply nodded. She could not remain in comfort in Switzerland while others did their part. Losing her country and younger brother demanded active revenge against the Nazis. A curt nod answered Dulles' question.

The Ausfelders were frequent guests to the Oprechts' home in Zürich, as was Professor Bauer. A stimulating experience in a magnificent setting. They looked forward to the evening as something more than a boring social gathering. They arrived with Allen Dulles by taxi after first checking into their hotel near the train station. The beauty of the Oprecht residence exceeded the description of their friends.

Located just south of the city of Zürich on Lake Zürich, *Zürichsee* in German, the 18th century mansion was the gem among a host of luxurious mansions. It sat on a hill surrounded by gardens with a vast lawn descending to the lake. The neoclassic sixty-room structure stood in brilliant splendor with its white stone façade contrasted by a deep blue slate multi-gabled roof.

Dulles turned to Marchand after exiting the taxi. "Later in the evening I will find an excuse for us to have a private conversation with Archbishop Bernardini, Apostolic Nuncio to Switzerland. The Archbishop is decidedly anti-Fascist. Despises Hitler and Mussolini. His Excellency will facilitate your entry into Italy.

"You, Marc, should have no problem working the guests by regaling them with your many adventures. Best not to recount your many violent encounters. Stay with your journalistic exploits."

The front door opened by a servant in white jacket. Another female servant took their coats. While the exterior was ostentatious the inside immediately reminded Marchand of a museum. Everything from the matching side tables and the decorative chairs in the foyer to the art on the wall represented quality. Her practiced eye appreciated the arrangement of the paintings to show each work in suitable light and complimentary to adjacent works. The paintings crawled up the walls of the double staircase. Sculptures placed to move the eye from piece to piece. More a great hall than merely the foyer to a grand house.

Off to the left, the sound of voices from a large room suggested a lively group of guests.

"Allen, my dear, so good to see you," Said an elegantly dressed and coffered woman in her forties, holding a flute of champagne, as she hurried over to embrace Dulles.

Dulles kissed her on each cheek. This woman clearly a favorite acquaintance as she held his hand. In English he said, "Emmie, these are the two refugees from France I told you about. Frau Fiona Marchand and her husband, Herr Marc Fraser. And this is our beautiful hostess, Frau Emmie Oprecht."

Frau Oprecht replied in very good French, "*Bonjour et bienvenue.*"

In German, Dulles said, "Herr Fraser speaks German, and Frau Marchand, Italian. Both speak English."

Frau Oprecht exclaimed in accented but fluent English, "Oh my. Then we shall converse in English. Outside of dear Allen, I have few opportunities to improve my English skills."

Fraser said, "I should say your English is excellent Frau Oprecht. Thank you for inviting us."

"Thank you both for coming. Allen probably told you Emil and I enjoy surrounding ourselves with artists and intellectuals. We like to think our home is an intellectual oasis in the middle of the horrors of this terrible war. Pulling together artists and thinkers.

"Let me introduce you to Emil. Beware, as an author and journalist he will consume your entire evening if you are not clever enough to escape. Once we have introduced you to the other guests, as an art expert, Frau Marchand, I would like to show you our modest art collection."

"I would love that, Frau Oprecht. Even from a distance in your grand foyer, I recognized several pieces. Far from modest works."

"How observant. I can understand why you are working for the Kunstmuseum."

The guests proved to be an eclectic mix of intellectuals and authors. As briefed by Allen Dulles, the Opechts were decidedly anti-Fascist. Their home became an intellectual salon as well as a haven for escaping refugees from Germany and Italy. The guests this evening included many displaced persons and likeminded Swiss within the Oprechts' wide social sphere.

Emil Oprecht steered Fraser to a group of writers. Emmie Oprecht took the opportunity to give Fiona the grand tour to show off her art.

Like the Oprechts' guests, their art was an eclectic mix of styles.

"Oh my!" Fiona said as they reached a small sitting space at the top of the grand staircase. She walked over to take a closer look. "A Rafael. I have never seen his work outside a museum."

"My prized possession," Emmie said. "I am probably guilty of hording it here upstairs but I so like to gaze on it in the morning and before retiring."

"My current work at the Kunstmuseum is restoring one of their several Rafael's."

"Can you tell if mine is in good condition?"

Marchand put her eye up close to the surface, moving to look at several places. "I would need my strong magnifying instruments, but I would say it appears in remarkably good condition, Frau Oprecht. My specialty is restoration of sixteenth century Italian oil paintings. I worked at the Louvre twenty years."

They descended the staircase and entered the large study. Bookshelves lined two walls to the fourteen-foot high ceiling. The books in various shades of leather bindings. Windows occupied the end wall overlooking the lake. However, it was the long wall opposite the books that captivated Fiona Marchand.

At least twenty modestly sized oil paintings hung with small brass nameplates set beneath each. The style in contrast to older paintings in the ballroom and entrance foyer.

Marchand exclaimed, "How wonderful. Impressionism."

Emmie Oprecht said, "I see you also appreciate style forms different than your Italian Renaissance painters."

Marchand smiled at her host, "Art in all its forms is my passion. While my restoration work specializes on Renaissance works, my personal tastes gravitate to this latter fin de siècle style of Impressionism. Those works are not old enough to require restoration. Few have even made it into museums. The Louvre displays no works later than the middle of the last century. The art world is slow to embrace the new. The work of these artists draws you into the moment. Their use of brush strokes and color to create effects of light invokes an emotional impression."

Looking at the paintings, Marchand said, "I know most of these artists. Most are French or worked in France. Paul Cezanne from my home town of Aix-en-Provence. Claude Monet with his unmistakable brush strokes. These landscapes by Alfred Sisley and Camille Pissarro invite a profound sense of place and season. A magnificent collection. Perfectly presented in this room with its natural light. I could sit in this room for hours and just absorb these paintings, Frau Oprecht."

Emmie Oprecht gushed. "Please. Call me Emmie. You feel like an old friend, Fiona."

Marchand grabbed Oprecht's hand. "Thank you so much, Emmie."

As the two women were about to exit the room, Allen Dulles and a distinguished man walked in. Marchand immediately assumed this must be Archbishop Bernardini. Fashionably dressed in a tailored black suit with clerical collar and pectoral cross, his Excellency looked the picture of a cultured diplomat. On the back of his head, he wore the fuchsia-colored zucchetto, the skullcap with matching sash to signify his bishopric office.

Dulles said, "Fiona, I would like you to meet Archbishop Bernardini. His Excellency is the Apostolic Nuncio to Switzerland. This is Mr. Fraser's wife Fiona Marchand."

As a practicing Catholic, she made a slight bow and reached for the bishop's hand to kiss his ring.

"So pleased to meet you Madame Marchand. I have been speaking with your husband. So few opportunities to talk to an American about this terrible war."

Dulles related a brief background of Bernardini on the train ride from Bern. Excellent English from spending 19 years teaching at the Catholic University in Washington D.C. A seasoned diplomat. From his post in Switzerland, Bernardini took a proactive role in assisting Jews escaping Nazi persecution. He cultivated strong relationships to anti-Fascist Cardinals in the Vatican Curia. He also maintained an active connection to *Santa Alleanza,* the Vatican Intelligence Service.

Allen Dulles shifted his gaze to Emmie Oprecht. By prearrangement, she excused herself to greet other guests claiming she had lost track of time with her newfound friend Fiona.

"Allen has recounted your ordeal in France. Your participation in the French Resistance makes you qualified for Allen's clandestine efforts to defeat Nazi Germany. All Christians should renounce the crimes committed by Adolf Hitler. This persecution of Jews is counter to everything the Church stands for."

Marchand silently thought that was not necessarily the view of the entire leadership of the Roman Catholic Church. Some critics of Bernardini's superior the Holy See called Pope Pius XII *Hitler's Pope* for his lack of denouncing Nazi anti-Semitism. Jewish genocide being the more fitting description.

Bernardini added, "I understand you lost your brother into the depths of these Nazi concentration camps."

"Yes. Mistaken as Jewish but nonetheless, still a victim of anti-Semitism."

Although not Jewish, her brother was a homosexual swept up in a raid of Jewish men. She held little hope of his survival given the horror stories seeping out of the Third Reich.

"Allen has recruited my assistance to introduce you into Italy. Glad to offer the services of my position. My country has suffered much under the Fascist yolk of that megalomaniac Benito Mussolini and his disastrous alliance with Hitler.

"Once the Allies are victorious, Italy must rebuild as part of larger democratic Europe. All of us, including America will soon face a new adversary every bit as ambitious and bloodthirsty as Hitler. I speak of the Soviet Union and that abomination Josef Stalin. I fear Communism every bit a threat to the free world as Fascism.

"Mussolini gained power in the 1920s campaigning against the Communists. No small threat in Italy at the time, nor I fear once this current war ends. Italy shall need the United States to counterbalance this looming threat. With Hitler's failures in the East, Stalin will emerge from this conflict even stronger.

"I tell you this so you have some sense of the many competing political positions you will find in war ravaged Italy. Allen has specifically requested I intercede to *plant,* using his word, you alongside the Vatican's *Santa Alleanza,* or 'Holy Alliance'. In more prosaic terms, the Vatican's clandestine intelligence service. Its motto *cum cruce et gladio,* 'with the cross and sword'. Your cover as that of an art expert and accomplished restorer of Renaissance era oil paintings."

"There are those in the Vatican Museum that know my name, Your Excellency. I did a restoration of a Rafael ten years ago."

Bernardini replied, "Wonderful. With the inability for those with your expertise to travel freely these last years, I suspect there is much work. You can therefore work directly from within the Vatican."

Dulles said, "As I mentioned, Your Excellency, time is critical. It takes time for any operative to develop the necessary relationships in a new place before successfully sourcing useful information. I am sending Madame Marchand to Naples to start as soon as possible. Perhaps you could assist?"

"Of course, Allen," Bernardini said, pausing in thought for a moment. "I know someone at the *Duomo di Napoli, Cattedrale di Santa Maria Assunta,* the Naples Cathedral. The repeated bombings of Naples by the Germans following the Italian surrender caused widespread destruction of the city. Following liberation by the Allies, an old friend, Monsignor Rinaldi wrote to me.

"Several churches in Naples suffered damage. Marcello wrote to me of the many treasures lost. Those that survived now housed in the basement of the cathedral. I am sure he will welcome the help of an expert such as Madame Marchand."

"Is Father Rinaldi connected with Santa Alleanza?" Dulles asked.

"My dear, Allen," Bernardini said with a smile, "Vatican Intelligence does not function in the same manner as your organization. Santa Alleanza exists to protect the Church. More a concept than an organizational identification. All of us that serve in the diplomatic service of the Holy See are indirectly connected with Santa Alleanza. Beyond that, thousands of priests worldwide serve as a vast source of information continually flowing information to Rome.

Marchand felt some sense of comfort that she was venturing into war torn Italy with allies in high places.

"I apologize for imposing on Your Excellency's gracious offer of assistance, but there is one other matter. Do you have *associates* in Naples that might assist in Madame Marchand making contact with Italian partisans?"

Bernardini smiled and said, "I believe that might be arranged, Allen. I shall make inquiries immediately."

Turning to Marchand, Bernardini said, "A genuine pleasure meeting you, Madame Marchand. I admire your sacrifice to continue the fight against the Nazis having just narrowly escaped France with your life. I wish you success in your mission. Safe travels." Bernardini made the sign of the cross saying, "May you carry God's blessing as you do his work."

"Thank you, Your Excellency. Your words and support shall bring me comfort."

Bernardini said, "I believe we should return to the other guests."

❖ ❖ ❖

Two weeks later, accompanied by Fraser, Marchand met with Dulles at his residence. Dulles handed her a letter. "The Archbishop came through. This is from Monsignor Rinaldi in Naples requesting your assistance in helping to recover Church art objects damaged by bombing. He invites you to stay at the rectory as his special guest.

"Now to practical matters. How soon can you leave?"

"Give me a week. Enough time to finish my restoration of the project at the museum and make my good byes. This letter will preserve my cover to the museum director as my reason for leaving. A personal favor to Archbishop Bernardini."

"Excellent. You will travel by Swiss commercial aircraft to Gibraltar. From there by British military transport to Naples. On arrival, report to the American Fifth Army headquarters to a Lieutenant Colonel Masterson with Military Intelligence.

"Here is the signed order from Supreme Command of Allied Expeditionary Forces directing in-theater military personnel to render all assistance to you. It does not mention your affiliation with the OSS."

Dulles handed her the order. "And this envelop contains currency. U.S. dollars and Italian lira. The set exchange rate is 120 lira to the dollar."

"And reporting?" Marchand asked.

"Compose your reports on the M-209-B cipher machine you trained on. Transmit via Army headquarters. File a report at least every other day regardless whether there is substantive information to relay. If for no other reason than to let Marc and I know you are okay."

The last day before her departure was both endearing and wrenchingly difficult. In the morning, Marchand packed. A single military duffle bag. Mostly trousers and sturdy shirts. Only one dress. A pair of modestly dressier shoes compared to the military boots as part of her working attire.

Marchand knew how Marc must feel about her leaving for Italy. She suffered many a sleepless night when he was away on clandestine business with the French Resistance. Although not in direct danger, war-ravaged Italy nonetheless held other dangers for a lone woman. She pointed out to Marc that her mission did not pose the same dangers as faced by those female journalists Martha Gellhorn, Gerda Taro, and Loretta Elizalde he spoke of during his Spanish Civil War experience. Of course, that rational argument did little to alleviate his concern. For that matter, she harbored her own uneasiness.

This was well beyond any of her experiences. Even her work in the Resistance was mostly supportive and in the shadows. Resisting the German occupation like thousands of other French citizens. Here she was out in the open. Her cover only a thinly veiled rationale for a French woman being alone in Italy with war still raging. Savage fighting still raged at the German defensive line midway up the Italian peninsula holding Rome hostage.

A leisurely lunch at the Ausfelders' apartment as a sendoff proved difficult for all. The Ausfelders put up a good front about Fiona's story of going to Naples to help rescue damaged art. Having narrowly escaped Nazi occupied France to go to Italy so soon without your husband, strained believability. The Ausfelders knew of their relationship with the American Allen Dulles. Although not knowing what Dulles actually did, his connection to the United States government in some capacity was common knowledge. Since this was wartime, that likely meant spying.

Everyone shed tears as they left the Ausfelders. Back at their apartment, Fiona said, "That was difficult. I am going to draw a bath and relax for the balance of our last day before leaving."

She came to Marc and grasped his face in both hands kissing him passionately as tears ran down her cheeks. "Want to join me?"

Embracing her tightly, he kissed the tears from her cheek and continued down her neck. The feel of her breasts pressing his chest caused his immediate arousal now amplified by her hand.

He went to the bathroom, turning on the bath water. Returning to the bedroom after adjusting the water temperature, Fiona stood there naked.

Embracing her again, she began unbuttoning his shirt.

Stepping back, she unbuttoned his trousers. With both hands, she pulled down his trousers and underwear exposing his erection.

Stroking his cock, she said, "I was intending to soak a while. Now I want to make love. Right now, Marc. Turn off the bath water and come to the bed. Quickly."

Slipping off his shoes, he did not hesitate.

Returning to the bedroom fully undressed, he settled next to Fiona lying on her back. A glorious sight. He began by kissing her breasts but soon moved downward, his state of arousal intensifying. Kissing her abdomen caused her to moan in anticipation of what he was about to do.

Enjoying providing her pleasure, he prolonged her enjoyment for as long as possible. Eventually giving in she erupted in a sequence of orgasmic spasms.

For the next hour, they made love intent on pleasuring the other, savoring this last intimacy for what might be an indefinite period after Fiona left for Italy.

Later that evening, they relaxed in their robes after bathing together. Opening a bottle of champagne, they enjoyed music on the radio. The mood altered with the nightly broadcast of latest war news. Much of it concerning the fighting in Italy.

Although winter was not truly over, the first week of April was sunny with the hint of spring. After an early morning train from Bern, Fraser and Marchand stood quietly at Zürich Airport. On the tarmac, a Swissair DC-3 was boarding.

As the last passenger, Fiona waited until motioned by a Swissair staffer to board as she kissed Marc. "I love you. Promise you will not venture into either Germany or France. Not sure I trust Allen if he sees an opportunity."

"I promise. Now go. Report your safe arrival. I love you, Fiona."

As the DC-3 took off, Fraser took stock of his circumstances. He understood Fiona's motivation to make the personal sacrifice to go to Italy. She shared the same sense of commitment to fighting the Nazis. Yet confined to Switzerland left him feeling somehow less than actively engaging the enemy. Obviously, the risk was too high for him to conduct missions into France. His language skills inadequate to infiltrate into Germany. Switzerland was at least closer to the front lines than London.

His only answer was to commit himself to making a difference. Find sources to turn on the Nazis. Find means to inflict damage to the Third Reich. Principally, the heart of Adolf Hitler's criminal enterprise the *Schutzstaffel*. The instrument by which Hitler inflicted widespread horror on noncombatants. The secret police, the *Gestapo*. The administration of the concentration camps. The perpetrators of genocide against the Jews. Murders and torturers. Remember Heinz Leitner and Klaus Barbie. Especially Barbie. Undoubtedly still in France. Perhaps someday to see the Butcher of Lyon go to the guillotine.

# CHAPTER 6

BERN, SWITZERLAND | JUNE 1944

---

Manfred Krüger sat in his large fourth floor office in a building occupied by other professionals and businessmen in a fashionable sector of the Bern. One entered from the hallway into a spacious outer office with a secretary and filing cabinets. His wood paneled personal office offered a view of the Aare River from two large windows. Roomy enough to provide a sitting area with expensive leather chairs and a sideboard with assorted liquors in crystal decanters with cut-crystal tumblers. Quality landscape paintings adorned the walls. Krüger enjoyed his creature comforts.

This morning he sat staring out the window on what proved to be a sunny early spring day. It did not improve his mood. A cup of cold coffee sat on his desk. Even the curves of his attractive secretary in a tight knit dress did not improve his disposition.

Returning the previous evening from Berlin left him shaken. The Lufthansa Junkers JU 52 tri-motor held only four passengers. All connected with the government of the Third Reich. The limited nonmilitary air travel usually occurred at night. Daylight in the air could prove dangerous with the long ranging capability of new fighter aircraft protecting American bombers. At night, British bombing made for round the clock bombings of important German cities.

As their plane lifted off from Berlin's Tempelhof Airport, the first explosions of antiaircraft artillery lit the night sky as a British bombing raid started. Having not been in Berlin for months, it was shattering to see the destruction of Berlin in the daytime. Now to experience firsthand the continuous terror of unrelenting bombing left him with dread.

The German Luftwaffe long ago lost the ability to attack Allied bombers at the airfields throughout southern England. Now it no longer even had the capability of inflicting heavy losses on the waves of bombers continually pounding Germany.

There was no reason to believe Germany could survive this war. German forces continued in retreat from the eastern front. A continuous retreat since the Sixth Army surrendered at Stalingrad over a year ago. The Italian front could not hold indefinitely. A new front might open any day with an Allied invasion of occupied France. At best, Germany could only expect an armistice. The same outcome as in 1918. Even more disastrous terms imposed on a defeated Germany this time.

His three days in Berlin proved unnerving. Without any of the higher ranking SS directly stating the obvious dire circumstances, all made it known they were relying on Obersturmbannführer Krüger to secure their secret wealth once the end came.

Krüger's Swiss-based company was nothing more than a cover to export SS assets outside Germany. In the past year, the flow of money accelerated several fold as Germany suffered repeated military setbacks. Even Heinrich Himmler spent an hour intently reviewing Krüger's efforts. The details of moving SS funds out of Germany and securing it in such a manner to prevent discovery took on new urgency.

However, this trip was different. Each of the ranking SS individually consulted Krüger on their personal accounts. In addition to moving official SS funds ostensibly into foreign investment for long-term economic benefit, each of these senior SS officials had personal Swiss bank accounts. Fortunes amassed through diversion from the constant flow of SS profits generated from slave labor and confiscated Jewish assets.

These conversations took on a more detailed review with each of senior official. None dare articulate any direct reference to a possible German defeat, but the nature of their questions reflected concern over future access to their personal wealth. Questions about the business and political climate of South America or neutral locations like Spain revealed their thinking of possible relocation sites when German defeat became imminent.

The *Schutzstaffel* was the most powerful sector of Hitler's Nazis government. By 1944, its head, Reichsführer-SS Heinrich Himmler was the second most powerful Nazi figure. The SS generated vast sums of money. It represented a state-owned conglomerate enterprise. Manufacturing goods using slave labor. Pillaging occupied countries of industrial assets, natural resources, food, art, and wealth of the citizenry. The network of concentration camps provided not only a labor source, but also yielded income from seized personal possessions of the inmates. Money, jewelry, clothing, and following death in the gas chambers, harvesting eyeglasses, hair, and gold dental fillings.

The *SS-Wirtschafts-und Verwaltungshauptamt*, the SS Main Economic and Administrative Office, abbreviated SS-WVHA managed the economic underpinning of the Nazi SS. At its head was Obergruppenführer Oswald Pohl, Krüger's immediate superior. Pohl also was the most senior administrator of the Nazi concentration and extermination camps. Krüger was therefore intimate with the details of the *Final Solution*, the genocide of the Jews. It troubled him only to the extent it made him complicit in unspeakable crimes should Germany lose the war outright. Krüger knew what went on at the concentration and extermination camps.

Himmler talked vaguely of some endgame whereby Germany might conclude an armistice with the United States and Britain realigning their military capabilities with Germany to defeat the Soviet Union in the east. Even some negotiated armistice might include serving up scapegoats for genocidal crimes.

Krüger could never claim being distant from direct involvement. Not only did he report to the head administrative unit of the SS responsible for the concentration camps, there was something else incriminating in his SS background.

After graduation from the university, Krüger joined the Reichbank in 1930. He did not join the Nazi Party until 1933 when Hitler became Chancellor. In 1939, Pohl recruited him to the SS-WVHA. One of his earliest assignments was that of administrator for a newly organized SS unit, the *Devisenschutzkommando,* the Foreign Exchange Commando, or DSK. This was a special looting unit of selected SS soldiers operating in newly occupied Belgium, France, and the Netherlands. Nominally charged with overseeing all bank foreign transactions, their practical function soon devolved into confiscating anything of value, often with brutal consequences for the victims.

Krüger came to Switzerland in 1943. Initially, his portfolio tasked him with concealing SS funds while making foreign investments to provide a sustaining profit stream. In this past year, his mission substantially changed. Deposits now designated to the personal accounts of the senior SS increasingly overshadowed the *corporate* SS accounts. With the largest fortune, Himmler undoubtedly began exercised direct control working closely with Pohl.

These private accounts comprised a very select group. Heinrich Himmler, Oswald Pohl, Ernst Kaltenbrunner, Walter Schellenberg, and Heinrich Müller. Krüger was not senior enough to share in the considerable sums now designated for his superior's personal Swiss accounts. Not about to do all the creative work to conceal the higher-level graft and not benefit, Krüger simply stole from the bigger thieves. He controlled power of attorney to all the accounts under his management. Beyond that, he also engineered the complex array of legal entities to launder and conceal SS funds flowing into Switzerland. Ample opportunities to skim money throughout the process.

Two months later on June 6, while having his morning coffee before heading to the office, the BBC broadcast the news of the Allied landings on the beaches of Normandy, France. For the next hour, he remained transfixed to the radio. A third front. Unless the celebrated General Erwin Rommel could throw the invaders back into the English Channel, this meant the beginning of the end for Germany.

Concerns about his postwar fate turned to genuine anxiety. His comfortable life in Switzerland would undoubtedly change. His legal services business forced to find new non-German clients. What about his wife and two teenage daughters living in Augsburg, Germany? While safe from Allied bombings, how would they survive in postwar Germany without him? Would the Swiss allow him to remain in Switzerland? What about the relationship with his secretary-mistress Helga?

In this frame of mind, he responded to Helga's question when she walked into his office only days following the D-Day invasion, "Manfred, there is a gentleman on the telephone. A newspaper reporter with Hearst Publications. An American named Fraser. Inviting you to lunch."

"Lunch? For what reason?"

"Says you are a prominent German national. A businessman not a politician. Few opportunities for an American reporter to interview Germans here in Switzerland. Would like an interview to get your comments on the latest events in the war."

"Tell him that would not be ..." pausing instead to reconsider. Time to begin exploring postwar options. The Americans and Soviets will dictate the very near future. He should be looking to choose sides. Nothing to lose. Perhaps this American might be useful. "Tell him I accept. Make it Thursday at one o'clock. Where?"

Helga answered, "Maison Charles. Said they have a good wine cellar."

Well at least he could enjoy a good bottle on this reporter's expense account.

Fraser knew Krüger enjoyed wine and French cuisine with information provided by his new source in Swiss Intelligence, Captain Alfred Gisler. Introduced by Allen Dulles, Gisler was anti-Nazi. Understandable being Jewish. Within the bounds of his understood latitude given the general cooperation of Swiss Intelligence of sharing information with the Allies, Gisler pushed that boundary as far as possible.

"Krüger is a Nazi pig," Gisler said to Fraser over a drink. Pushing an envelope over the table to Fraser. "Everything about Obersturmbannführer Manfred Krüger. Even about his secretary Helga doubling as his mistress with his wife and children conveniently out of the way in Germany. Wants to play the role of a worldly international lawyer. No less a murderer than the entire Nazi *Schutzstaffel*."

"You know of course of the Nazi program they call the *Final Solution*?"

Fraser nodded, "Yes. Genocide of the Jews."

Gisler looked at Fraser. "Is that why you still fight the Nazis?"

Dulles undoubtedly related Fraser and Marchand's backgrounds in the French Resistance to Gisler.

"Partly. They also murdered people close to me. Remnants of the Nazi *Schutzstaffel* must not survive following Germany's defeat. I intend to take part in their destruction."

"Krüger is directly part of that. All there in his dossier. His current role is not entirely clear. Beyond managing suspected SS funds moving out of Germany, we suspect he channels some of those funds into foreign investments. We do not possess sufficient details. Swiss banking laws even restrict our efforts."

"Can you not examine Krüger's business files under a legal search warrant?"

Gisler smiled. "Herr Fraser, this is Switzerland. Such an intrusion would eventually lead to investigations into Swiss banking. A sacred cow. Perhaps you are aware of American government efforts pressuring Switzerland to provide an accounting of German transfer of gold deposits from occupied countries to Swiss banks. The Swiss government continues to resist as a violation of our sovereignty. Even Swiss Intelligence must work around the edges.

"We do not believe Krüger is involved with looted national treasury gold. I am told that would come under the control of the Reich Ministry for Economic Affairs rather than the SS."

Fraser said, "However, you say Krüger manages foreign investments, probably using SS funds. Might his expertise not involve concealing purchases of war materials from neutral nations through shell companies?"

Gisler nodded. "Possibly. Maybe probable. However, there is another reason preventing a closer examination of Obersturmbannführer Krüger. Regrettably, he holds a diplomatic passport as an assistant commercial attaché for Germany. Short of engaging in espionage against Switzerland or committing murder, he is untouchable under Switzerland's neutrality stature."

"Speaking as an American journalist, Herr Krüger sounds like an interesting interview subject. Did Dulles ever tell you I interviewed Adolf Hitler and Hermann Göring ten years ago?"

Gisler smiled knowingly, well aware that Fraser was an American OSS operative using a journalism cover. "I trust you will pass along to me anything of interest?"

Shortly after meeting with Gisler, Fraser telephoned Krüger's office. To his surprise, Krüger agreed to an interview over lunch at Bern's best French restaurant.

Krüger accepted the invitation partly primarily because of the disturbing visit to Berlin and the successful Allied invasion of France. Harbingers of certain German doom. Adding to that after back only a few days, he received a call from a fellow SS officer. The soft-spoken officer gave him the creeps.

Krüger interacted often with Adolf Eichmann, the administrative head of the Final Solution. The person chiefly responsible for organizing the concentration and extermination camps. With no particular feelings toward Jews, Eichmann's fanatical anti-Semitism repelled Krüger. A bureaucrat relishing his repugnant mission, embracing Hitler's irrational obsession. Citing the Jews as scapegoats for Germany's failures no longer held any meaning.

Eichmann went to Hungry following the German invasion there in March. His job to deport previously unharmed Hungarian Jews to Auschwitz-Birkenau concentration camp for forced labor or extermination by gassing. A frantic call from Eichmann said he negotiated the release of 1,700 Jews to travel by train to Switzerland. This in exchange for three suitcases full of diamonds, gold, cash, and negotiable securities. Eichmann simply said that Krüger should secure the assets at a Swiss bank.

Eichmann provided no further instructions. Was this for Eichmann's personal use? Krüger never touched such blood money directly. Eichmann was not senior enough to have his own Swiss bank account. An Obersturmbannführer, the same as Krüger. Now a trail leading to another crime connecting him with 1,700 potential witnesses. These combined events of June 1944 sufficiently rattled Krüger to take action to secure his future.

From Krüger's background, the dossier prepared Fraser with a sense of his character.

Born in Augsburg, Bavaria in 1907 to a prosperous middle class family, Krüger received his education at Germany's prestigious Heidelberg University in Baden-Württemberg. Graduating with honors with a law degree, he immediately pursued an advanced degree in economics, gravitating to a career involving international business.

Unlike so many SS members, Krüger came to the Nazi *Schutzstaffel* only in 1939. Since graduation in 1930, he forged a promising career at the Reichbank. With his experience, he joined the SS at the advanced officer rank of Obersturmbannführer, equivalent to a lieutenant colonel in a conventional military. To Fraser, here was a clear-eyed opportunist shifting employers for personal advancement rather than ideological position.

Krüger undoubtedly possessed a Germanic nationalistic stance based on his early years. As an engineer, his father worked at an aircraft manufacturing company producing aircraft for the Great War. The family suffered the difficult years of the Great War and the following decades. While his mother taught school, his father took on various manual jobs in manufacturing before eventually joining Willy Messerschmitt's design team at the reformed Bavarian Aircraft Works in 1927. That background must play on the broadly held German reasons for losing the war. The lack of resolve of the German people. The more extreme excuse of *stabbed in the back* by Jews and Communists. Certainly the injustice of the terms of the 1919 Treaty of Versailles, relegating Germany to a second-class European state for decades. The delusion that the Great War ended in stalemate rather than the reality of German defeat.

Given this new German defeat, Krüger was vulnerable. Not only a senior SS officer involved with concentration camp administration, but also his stint involving the DSK looting unit exposed him to postwar prosecution. Might escape hanging but likely faced imprisonment. Krüger understood his postwar vulnerability.

Fraser's task was to cultivate a relationship while maintaining his cover as a journalist. He must ask the difficult expected questions of an American reporter without alienating him. That was how he built his career in journalism. Manipulating bad characters into making mistakes.

With Allied forces moving south from the Normandy beaches, Germany was now on the defensive on three fronts. Unlikely they could even play to a draw. Krüger was not the type to sacrifice himself for the Reich.

A rainy late spring day but winter was clearly gone as Fraser arrived at the restaurant Maison Charles precisely at one o'clock.

The maître d' said to Fraser in French, "Your guest arrived a short time ago, Monsieur Fraser. I took the liberty of seating him at your table."

Manfred Krüger was average height, trim build, with neatly barbered hair and wire-rimmed glasses. Expensive shoes and a well-tailored gray suit.

"Herr Krüger. Thank you for joining me."

Krüger stood up making a slight bow of his head and extended his hand.

"I trust you enjoy French cuisine," Fraser said German.

"*Mon préféré,*" Krüger replied in respectable French.

The dossier stated Krüger was fluent in French and Spanish, and conversational English. Fraser launched into French. "Excellent. We shall enjoy our lunch with a good bottle of wine?"

Sticking with French, Krüger said, "According to my secretary, you are American with the publisher Hearst? How is it you find yourself in Switzerland?"

Before Fraser could answer, a waiter approached placing menus and thick leather bound wine list on the table.

Fraser said with a smile, "Perhaps you could select good wine. I enjoy Bordeaux or Burgundy equally. Do not concern yourself with prices. A generous expense account you know.

"To your question, I have been in Europe for ten years as a foreign correspondent. Based in Paris. Learned to appreciate the European attention to enjoying the finer pleasures. Grew up in California. Hollywood. My father is in the movie business.

"Working in the French film industry became difficult under German occupation censorship. Even the basics of living became a challenge. Wine scarce even through the black market. Neutral Switzerland became the obvious refuge."

Fraser purposely launched into his background to convey a tone of congeniality to buffer the harder edge of the questions to Krüger that would follow. Set your subject at ease. Establish an initial rapport.

Krüger knew his French wines, selecting a 1934 Château Lafite Rothschild.

They sat in silence while the waiter decanted the wine.

"May I ask why you wish to interview me, Monsieur Fraser?"

"To get a different perspective on unfolding events. You are a lawyer engaged in international trade and business according to your embassy. The German commercial attaché."

"Only an assistant attaché."

"Nonetheless, a prominent figure in the economic future of Germany I suspect. You see, my interest is exploring what lies ahead once this war ends. My questions are more practical than political. You must acknowledge that Germany cannot hope to win this war."

Krüger paused to pour wine in both their glasses. After tasting the wine, he said, "Winning may take different forms. All of Europe must now face a common enemy, the Communists. Not only the Soviet Union, but its ideological reach into the working classes everywhere."

Hitler's recurring bogeyman along with the Jews.

"Where will Germany and for that matter, all of war torn Europe, stand once hostilities end?"

"Do you agree that Germany cannot prevail militarily, Herr Krüger?"

"Prevail. Not in the conventional sense. American resources and the Soviet hordes will eventually prove overpowering. I hope that the United States and Britain can see further into the future. If Germany falls, they must immediately confront the Soviet Red Army. A compromise armistice could thwart further Soviet advances. A unified Europe allied with the West would serve all interests."

My god! Dulles alluded to OSS dispatches out of neutral Sweden about proffered separate peace proposals from Heinrich Himmler. Was Krüger confirming the same absurd scheme?

"And how might that work?" Fraser asked.

"Simply, the western Allies cease military activities in Italy and France. Using their enormous airpower, they join forces with the German *Wehrmacht* to halt Soviet advances westward."

"What about France, Belgium, the Netherlands, and Italy?"

"Well of course Germany would withdraw to previous borders of 1939."

Did this naïve idea originate with Himmler? Did it confirm the Swedish intelligence? Did Krüger suspect him of being a source for U.S. intelligence? Was Krüger merely speculating an unrealistic hypothetical?

"Is Berlin seriously pursuing this with the Western Allies?"

Krüger shook his head. "I do not know. I am not involved with political matters. I am a businessman actually. Just citing an obvious alternative to continuing this war of attrition. All of Europe shall face the destruction of entire ways of life. The economic underpinnings of each state shattered perhaps for decades."

Fraser said, "Interesting concept. However, I seriously doubt there can be any such rapprochement while Hitler remains in power."

Krüger did not take the baited reference to Hitler. "As I said, I see the world through the lens of economics. International trade between countries serves to work against military adventurism. This war is a great mistake for all parties.

"Since the Great War, Britain and France have sought to constrain Germany. First with punitive terms of the 1919 Armistice. Crushing reparations and limitations on German sovereignty. The denial of the rights of ethnic Germans living in Austria, Czechoslovakia, and Poland.

"Adolf Hitler blundered disastrously. This is off the record of course. Invading Poland was an ill-conceived gamble that failed. Invading the real enemy the Soviet Union was premature and poorly executed. Then the greatest blunder of all. For no practical reason, Hitler unnecessarily declares war on the United States only six months after taking on the Soviets."

"I could not agree more. Given clever leadership rather than megalomania, Germany would be in different circumstances today." Fraser took a sip of wine and offered, "Shall we order lunch?"

During lunch, each related their backgrounds tailored to conform to their respective covers. Fraser said nothing of his anti-Fascist activities in Spain and occupied France. Krüger omitted any reference to SS affiliation. He portrays himself the principled German banker and international business lawyer. Refers to Hitler by name rather than Führer.

Creating a natural bond by shared fluency in the same languages, Fraser explained his language skills in French, German, and Spanish accrued from his professional journalistic work in Europe for the last ten years. Krüger claimed his Spanish came from legal work involving Spain and South America where Germany had strong business ties.

With lunch and the bottle of wine finished, Fraser ordered coffees and brandy.

"What exactly do you do in your official role as German assistant commercial attaché?"

Krüger reached into his pocket and withdrew a silver cigarette case. Opening the case, he offered it to Fraser.

"No thank you. I do not smoke. But by all means go ahead."

Lighting the cigarette, Krüger exhaled the first draw of smoke with an expression of satisfaction.

"You might say I act as a broker. You see, countries do not conduct international trade, business enterprises do. I provide the necessary means to navigate the complex rules associated with doing business with foreign companies. A broker of financial services. A business as much of relationships as the legal structuring agreements and contracts."

Fraser read that as hiding prohibited trade in war materials with neutral countries to fuel the Nazi war effort and preserve the pretext of neutrality with the trade nations. Particularly the pro-Fascist states of Spain, Portugal, and those in South America.

"Regardless of the outcome of the war, Europe will require massive reconstruction. That will require private enterprise to provide the resources. Financial resources will become the problem. Other than the United States, only Switzerland can assist in financing on this scale.

"I am only associated with the German Economic Ministry to the extent necessary to perform my duties as a commercial diplomatic official. I see my personal future in remaining in Switzerland, the European center for commerce and financial services once war ends."

A not very subtle pitch. Krüger networking for useful associations following German defeat.

"Very interesting. Bringing hostilities to a close seems the more pressing matter. Little talk about rebuilding the world. I can see a series of articles for my American readers."

They chatted for another hour over a second round of brandies. Both satisfied as having accomplished their objectives.

"A most enjoyable lunch. Less painful then I imagined, you being an American."

"I am a journalist. An observer. I wanted to obtain your opinions not confront you as the enemy."

Krüger smiled. "We should do this more often, Mr. Fraser. Two pragmatic professionals, alone in Switzerland."

Earlier, Krüger confided his family remained in Germany. Fraser simply said he was not married.

Fraser concluded Krüger was a potential intelligence source with a direct connection to Himmler. He could already report Krüger's comments about a separate peace with the western Allies, confirming the Swedish intelligence feeler. Cultivate the relationship further. Circumstances for Germany will only worsen. As defeat becomes imminent, Fraser will put the hook into Krüger by exploiting his fear for survival given his involvement in the SS and the Nazis Final Solution of the Jewish problem.

# CHAPTER 7

Naples, Italy | May 1944

---

The morning after arriving in Gibraltar, Fiona Marchand boarded a British Royal Air Force Douglas C-47 military transport. The same airframe as the Swissair Douglas DC-3 she flew from Switzerland but decidedly different inside. Seating in the military C-47 version consisted of facing rows on each side rather than the commercial forward facing seats. Fitted to carry troops in full battle gear or parachutes, the C-47 was a utilitarian transport designed for maximizing cargo.

Dressed as a photojournalist, the presence of an attractive woman nonetheless created a stir among the British soldiers. Her outfit consisted of cotton twill trousers, a shirt with pockets over the breasts, a leather flight jacket, and lace-up boots. A working outfit whether gaining intelligence or working in her cover in the Vatican Museum.

Seated next to the ranking officer, a captain in his early twenties, she endeavored to be polite to his endless small talk and flirtation. With a camera borrowed from Marc slung around her neck, she played her alternate cover story to account for entering an active war zone. Looking at the faces of these young soldiers soon to face combat made her anxieties seem trivial. The Germans continued to mount stiff resistance holding a line south of Rome. Allied casualties mounted daily.

Several hours flying over the Mediterranean offered time to reflect on what she was doing. An intelligence operative? Coming from the academic and museum world, an alien venture. Yet no less unusual than adapting to occupation life under the despised *Boche*.

Deprived of everything that meant being French while living in constant fear. A fear realized with the arrest of her younger brother only to disappear into some Nazi concentration camp. Her work with Marc in the Resistance restored meaning to life turned upside down by providing an active means to fight the Nazis. It also uncovered skills she never imagined. Times were different and so was she.

She stepped off the airplane at the damaged Naples Airport and walked briskly with confidence toward what appeared to be the former passenger terminal. Every soldier on this fight came from some normal background. Her circumstances no more unlikely than everyone fighting this war.

Inside the building was chaos with a cacophony of shouting voices. Recognizing officers from the enlisted ranks, she entered a line of several officers queued in front of another officer seated behind a table. Taking a place in the line, a young lieutenant ahead of her turned around registering surprise followed by a wide grin.

"Bloody marvelous seeing a pretty woman here. Lieutenant Nathan Carter, Ma'am."

Dressed in full battle dress, Lt. Carter snapped to attention, clicking his heels and giving Marchand a smart British open-palmed salute.

"I am a journalist," Marchand said in her French accented English extending her hand.

The officers were reporting in to receive deployment instructions for their units. The harried officer at the desk with his head down thumbing through paperwork said, "Next?"

Marchand passed her orders to him.

Looking up, the officer said, "Bloody hell! Who are you?"

"Marchand, Fiona. A journalist. I am to report to U.S. Fifth Army headquarters. Perhaps you can direct me where to go?"

"This is a war zone, Miss, not a bloody information service."

Looking at his nametag, Marchand said, "Lieutenant Mallory. If you look at my orders, they are quite specific. Note those orders are from Allied Headquarters. Render all services. I would think information falls within *services*. You will note the signature of a major general.

Somewhat cowed, "Yes, Ma'am. Give me a few minutes and I will see what I can do."

Standing off to the side to wait, she looked around. As the only woman in the area, all the soldiers passing through the processing center looked her over with varying degrees of intensity from curiosity to obvious lust.

A burly American soldier with chevrons on his shoulder denoting him as a senior sergeant approached.

"The limey officer over there tells me I'm to take you to American headquarters. This your only baggage?'

"Yes, Sergeant. Thank you."

The soldier picked up her standard issue American Army duffle bag. "Right this way. I have a jeep outside. Wind might mess up your hair."

"I will manage."

"A photographer, huh? What's a pretty lady doing out here with a bunch of unwashed grunts with bullets flying?"

"Doing my job to get pictures. Been around enough, Sergeant. Seen lots of shooting and a whole lot worse in Spain during the civil war. Used to the hardships."

Playing her cover to the hilt. Building on Marc's recounting of events in Spain, she would play her cover role patterned on the real life photojournalist Gerda Taro.

As the Sergeant drove through Naples, the devastation from Allied bombing was a jarring site viewed close up as the jeep weaved its way avoiding debris. Both the U.S. Fifth Army and the British Eighth Army made their joint headquarters in a municipal building. After passing the undamaged Cattedrale di

Santa Maria Assunta, her cover destination, military headquarters was conveniently close. She suspected her time to split between the two locations depending on how circumstances developed.

The building was another hectic hive of activity. Eventually she located the office of the Executive officer of the Fifth Army Military Intelligence Section.

A repeat of the incredulous reception at the airport.

"My name is Marchand. Here are my orders," she announced to the officer standing behind a desk while handing him her orders.

After quickly reading the orders, he said, "Please be seated, Miss Marchand." Raising an eyebrow in a questioning manner, "A bit unusual the OSS sending a woman here?"

"Probably because of my qualifications, Major."

After a short silence realizing she was not going to elaborate, "Well, we shall do our best to accommodate you. I will need to consult with my boss the colonel. He will return probably by tomorrow."

"Time is short, Major. Are you in contact with any Italian partisans?"

"I am afraid I am not at liberty to discuss sensitive intelligence matters with nonmilitary personnel."

"Read my orders again, Major. They are quite explicit. No mention of first clearing anything with your colonel. Note the rank of the officer signing my orders."

The major stiffened at Marchand's rebuke. "Let me explain our situation. In this campaign, we are sharing intelligence operations with the British. Separating functions, liaison with Italian partisans falls to the Brits. I suggest the quickest way for you to embark on your mission is to start with them. This building houses the joint command headquarters for the American and British Armies."

"Very well. Whom do I see?"

"My counterpart in the British Eighth Army." Shouting through the open door, "Sergeant!"

As a sergeant entered, "Please escort Miss Marchand to Major Rothschild of British Army intelligence."

"One other matter, Major. I will need to periodically transmit encrypted messages to my headquarters."

With an exasperated expression, "Sergeant, also introduce Miss Marchand to Communications."

As she accompanied the sergeant, who carried her duffle bag, he said, "You a reporter, Ma'am?"

"Among other things."

"Sure is a treat to see a pretty woman after all these months. No offense, Ma'am."

Marchand smiled. "Difficult circumstances for all of us involved in this fight."

After visiting the communications center, the sergeant led her to the other wing of the former municipal building keeping up small talk trying his best at flirtation.

"Where are you staying? I'd be glad to escort you to your assigned billet."

"Thank you. However, I will be staying at the cathedral rectory. A guest of the Church. Not far from here I understand."

Marchand's welcome at British Army Intelligence proved more amenable. Major Edmund Leopold de Rothschild was a handsome man a few years younger than she was. Every bit the English gentleman in appearance and demeanor.

His office appeared better ordered and his staff less harried than the Americans.

After introductions and recounting why she turned up in his office, Rothschild offered her tea.

"Interesting assignment. Done this sort thing before, Miss Marchand?"

"Yes. I worked in the French Resistance with my husband for several years. We made our escape to Switzerland when circumstances turned out badly. One step ahead of the *Gestapo*. My husband is American. We naturally joined the OSS working out of Bern. "

"Impressive. I would also add courageous for wanting to continue the fight. You could have remained in comfort in Switzerland. What is your cover?"

"I am an art expert in real life. Employed at the Louvre for many years. Worked on restorations at the Uffizi in Florence, the Vatican Museum, and the Museo di Capodimonte here in Naples. That is how I speak Italian. Vatican Intelligence is expecting me once Rome is liberated. Depending on circumstances, I also pass myself off as a photojournalist imbedded with the army."

"Now to your mission making contact with Italian partisans. My counterpart at American Army Intelligence was correct. We have the principal assignment to liaison with the local partisans for actionable intelligence."

"Well I will not be stepping on your toes. My mission is to gather broader information. Assess the political environment in Italy once Germany is defeated."

Rothschild chuckled. "A tall order. Not sure anyone can gauge what a post-Italy might look like. They have been under Fascist rule for twenty years. Now a return to a constitutional monarchy for the liberated south following the surrender. However, the Communists and Socialists have broad support among the population. My guess is post-Italy will experience continued political turmoil.

"The politics range across the entire spectrum. I can say that because of the character of the many different partisan groups. While the Communists and Socialist represent the largest fighting factions, the resistance movement is by no means cohesive."

She replied, "To be expected. It is the same in France. So how do you characterize the principal Italian groups?"

"Still evolving. Started right here in Naples back in September when Italy surrendered and the Germans invaded in mass. A bloody popular rebellion. Elsewhere, outlawed political groups organized. Initially, most of those willing to take up arms against the Germans were former soldiers of the Italian Army. As other committed anti-Fascists joined the resistance movement, the various groups took on the political affiliations of their members."

"How would you characterize the politics?"

"Oh, decidedly far left. Communist and socialist mostly. The only real centrists are the Christian Democrats. Most of these politically centered groups support a unified central organization the *Comitato di Liberazione Nazionale*, the CLN. Outside that umbrella are groups comprised largely of former soldiers with less political orientation. The most effective is the *1st Gruppo Divisioni Alpine*. Former Italian elite troops operating in the Piedmont region in the north."

"What groups are operating just behind the German defensive line south of Rome?"

"Several. In Rome and the central mountain areas. Moving ahead as our forces move north. Particularly helpful to us British as we pushed north up the east side of the Italian peninsula. We then joined the Americans coming up the west side of the Italian peninsula to concentrate forces directly through the Liri Valley to breakthrough to Rome. The partisans are still important for intelligence and harassing the Germans.

"There is one group particularly helpful operating from Rome. Called the Central GAP Carlo Pisacane. Our contact is their deputy commander. A woman. A rarity among armed partisans. Carla Capponi however, is no stranger to weapons and killing Germans. She periodically slips through German lines to provide valuable tactical intelligence on what is going on in Rome."

"How can I connect with her?"

"For that you will need to consult with my fellow intelligence officer Captain Trakonitz. He largely operates in the field. I expect his return tomorrow afternoon. May I suggest you join us for dinner? I know a functioning trattoria. A few of us go there and donate the food. We get good Italian pasta and local wine while contributing to the economic recovery of Italy."

"Most kind, Major. I would like that. May I ask you a personal question?"

With a puzzled expression, he said, "Certainly."

"Are you related to the Rothschild banking dynasty?"

"Yes I am. In fact, I worked at the family bank in London before the war."

Marchand smiled. "The reason I asked, my husband's mother was a Rothschild. The French branch. Marc said his maternal great grandfather was James Mayer de Rothschild."

"Good lord! What an astonishing coincidence. My paternal great grandfather was Nathan Mayer Rothschild. The English branch of the family. James was his brother. That means we share common great-great-grandparents. That makes us distant cousins. That also makes your husband Jewish under Nazi racial laws. Must have been dangerous in occupied France. And your husband's name?"

"Marc Fraser."

After a very long day, a British soldier escorted Marchand to the rectory of the Cattedrale di Santa Maria Assunta.

Received warmly by Monsignor Rinaldi, she enjoyed dinner and a pleasant evening with the senior rector and two other priests. Tomorrow she promised to examine the many salvaged art objects stored in the Cathedral basement rescued from several churches damaged in the repeated bombings of Naples.

The elderly Rinaldi personally accompanied her the following morning to the subterranean chambers of the cathedral. Stacks of all manner of recovered art objects occupied the hallways of ancient burial vaults. Various alter pieces and statuary stood among broken confessionals and even broken sections of walls displaying frescoes.

She stopped to examine stacks of paintings in frames. A cursory look revealed some important 16th century works mixed in with lesser works of different periods. Everything covered in a dust undoubtedly from pulverized masonry and plaster. Some blacked with soot from fire.

"Monsignor Rinaldi, this is heartbreaking. From how many destroyed churches?"

"I believe what you see came from six churches, my child. But for the grace of God, our magnificent cathedral suffered only minor damage."

"My expertise is restoration of oil paintings. The immediate concern is the environment. From what I see, they need careful cleaning. The dust from plaster and masonry is abrasive and requires careful removal. Soot represents a different sort of problem. There appears little ventilation down here. I fear with the approaching hot humid weather these contaminants will only become more difficult to remove."

"I understand your concerns. What do you suggest?" Rinaldi said.

"A secure place where we can began restoration. What about the Museo di Capodimonte? Was it damaged in the bombings?"

Rinaldi touched his forehead in a gesture of *why did I not think of that*? "I believe it did not suffer serious damage. I shall contact them at once?"

"Perhaps I can help. I worked on a project there years ago. I know the curator, Signore Morra. They have facilities to house and conduct restorations on those art objects at most risk. You can say I will supervise the restoration of the oil paintings. But I will need the services of several people that I can train to assist in the work."

"I shall speak to the mother superior of the Order of Saint Bridget. Her order oversees the care of many paintings at the Hermitage of the Most Holy Saviour on a hill outside Naples. Undamaged in the bombings since it sits outside the city. Perhaps she can offer several of her sisters to assist you."

"Excellent. The sisters should prove ideal for the work. Their discipline will allow for my absences as I conduct my other work." The reference being to work associated with Vatican intelligence to which the Monsignor was aware.

"I welcome your services, Signora Marchand. My good friend Archbishop Bernardini of course informed me of your real mission here in Italy. When the time comes for you to go to the Vatican, I shall make the appropriate arrangements. Until that time, I shall accept God's blessing in His sending you to assist in Italy's recovery by rescuing our artistic treasures."

After a good night's rest, Marchand felt a surge of confidence. Things began falling into place. Stumbling into the British sector and working with the likable Major Rothschild, a distant relative of Marc's, was a stroke of real luck. Might improve her chances of gaining help from Captain Trakonitz to introduce her to this Rome partisan group.

A jeep driven by Major Rothschild called for her at the rectory at seven o'clock.

"Captain Trakonitz will meet us at the trattoria. Let me tell you a little of his background. A most unusual and resourceful fellow. A Palestinian Jew emigrating from Prague, Czechoslovakia in '38 after the German occupation. Lost his family to the Nazis. Speaks Czech, German, English, Hebrew, and Italian. Learned Italian after joining the British Army then fighting Italians and Germans in North Africa.

"Served in the elite commando SAS unit in North Africa. Chaps trained to operate behind enemy lines. Trakonitz proved so talented, he quickly earned promotion to sergeant then to lieutenant for the invasion of Sicily. His mission in the desert was deep penetration reconnaissance. His specialty capturing prisoners on night forays into the desert. Trakonitz usually commanded a small select squad. They typically sought to capture and return with a single soldier for interrogation after silently dispatching others. One can only imagine embarking on successive missions of this type in two years of combat.

"He brought along those skills as we took on the Germans on the Italian peninsula. Trakonitz was a natural to continue reconnaissance efforts behind enemy lines working with Italian partisans."

Marchand understood the unstated use of *dispatched* meant killing the enemy even if surrendering. Silently killing by knife or garrote. Taking more than a single prisoner impaired the unit's mobility to return to their own lines. *Ruthless* more descriptive for Captain Trakonitz than *resourceful*.

"I see why you referred to him as resourceful. That why you use him in the field to liaison with the partisans?"

"Exactly. His service record identifies exceptional skills in unarmed combat. A natural intelligence operative."

"I look forward to meeting Captain Trakonitz. With his blood-soaked past, do you think he will resent working with a woman?"

"Cannot say for sure. Trakonitz keeps his feelings in tight check. A bit intense perhaps. Although in the British Army, he harbors a keen resentment of the British Mandate's restriction of Jewish immigration to Palestine. Not sure how that will play out when the war ends.

"Before joining the British Army he severed with the Haganah, the underground army of the Yishuv, the Jewish community in Palestine. In fact, he was part of the Haganah's elite fighting force the Palmach. This shared in a brief uncharacteristic personal revelation. We have an excellent working relationship but Trakonitz keeps largely to himself."

The small restaurant was on a street suffering comparatively light damage from the months of Allied bombing. "*Buonasera, Guido,*" Rothschild said as he shook hands with the elderly proprietor. Reverting to English, he said, "This is Signora Marchand."

Marchand extended her hand and greeted him in Italian followed by saying she was happy to return to Italy after many years, but saddened by all the destruction.

Guido fairly fell all over himself so delighted to meet this foreign woman fluent in Italian. Carrying on a constant dialogue, he ushered them to a table and brought a bottle of wine and glasses.

"You certainly made a hit with Guido. He is in the back telling his wife about the pretty foreigner that just walked in speaking Italian. His wife does the cooking and Guido manages the customers."

Moments after Rothschild poured wine for each of them, a short British officer of average physical stature approached the table.

"Madame Marchand, let me introduce Captain Pavel Trakonitz."

Offering her hand, her first impression was how short he was. Perhaps 5 feet 8 inches. In her mind, she was expecting a hulking rough sort. Hard to imagine this slight fellow killing enemy soldiers with his bare hands. Yet his hands were exceptionally large for his small frame and his sinewy strong forearms evident with his rolled-up sleeves.

"Major Rothschild said you are Czech. Escaped to Palestine when the Nazis invaded. I know how that feels. I am French, escaped to Switzerland one step ahead of the Nazis."

"What were you doing that put you in danger?" Trakonitz said.

"My husband and I were with the French Resistance. We collected intelligence information not easily transmitted by radio from various Resistance groups then sent it on to London. Maps and photographs. My husband had a cover allowing him to travel throughout France. Useful for obtaining sensitive information on German coastal defenses."

"Now you are with the American OSS?"

"Yes. My war against the Nazis is not over. I lost my brother to the Nazis."

"The Major says your husband is Jewish. Are you also Jewish?"

"No. However, the French police rounded up my brother with a group of Jews and sent him to the camps nonetheless. I do not know if he is alive."

Trakonitz nodded. "I escaped Prague just after graduating from university. My parents and a sister delayed leaving until it was too late. All remaining Jews in Prague, over 40,000 perished. First sent to the Theresienstadt Ghetto but eventually shipped off to the Auschwitz extermination camp in Poland."

Trakonitz recounted his personal tragedy with no expression of anguish. "My story is no different than countless tens of thousands of others."

A wound now held so deeply he refused to let it emotionally surface. Quickly moving away from that subject, he said, "The Major says your orders are to make contact with Italian partisans?"

"Among other things. My mission is to gather intelligence useful in determining the political direction of postwar Italy."

Trakonitz said in excellent Italian, "Do you speak fluent Italian?"

Marchand answered in Italian, "I believe good enough to get along. Do you agree?"

Trakonitz offered a rare smile and nodded.

"Major Rothschild said you often meet with a woman from a Rome partisan group. Any chance that might happen again soon?"

"I received word just today. This Friday. The rendezvous is to be in a small village south of the German Gustav Line. To the east, up in the mountains."

Marchand observed Trakonitz did not reveal the name of the woman or the name of the village.

"Can I join you, Captain?"

Trakonitz looked at Rothschild who nodded affirmatively. "Her orders come from Joint Allied Headquarters. *Render all assistance it says.*"

"Very well. We leave early. Five o'clock. Not sure how long it will take to get there. Probably several hours. The rendezvous is to be at mid-day. A hilltop town recently liberated. The German lines are not far to the north."

"This woman partisan has crossed through German lines before to meet with you?

"Yes. She is resourceful and possesses great courage."

Captain Trakonitz headed his jeep northeast climbing ever-higher hills as they approached the spine of the Italian peninsula. Their destination the hilltop town of Venafro. Slow going with the endless caravans of military vehicles going in the same direction. The spring thaw left the secondary roads rutted. A rough ride that stretched to more than three hours.

Expecting a picturesque Italian town, Marchand looked on a scene of similar devastation to Naples.

"What happen here, Captain?" Marchand said in Italian, intending to settle into the comfort of the language she had not used for years.

"Bitter fighting here for the last six months. In March, Allied bombers mistook it for Monte Cassino just thirty kilometers to the west and hit it hard in a bombing raid."

A significant British Army force now occupied the town.

"Where are we supposed to meet Capponi?"

"At the front entrance to the Castle Pandone. Carla is her first name but she goes by Elena. There is food and water in the back. Hungry?"

"Yes, and thirsty. Already getting hot."

"A cold winter just a few months ago. A tough go for the British forces as we moved north on the right flank of the Allied thrust north."

"Much different conditions than you experienced in North Africa I imagine."

Two hours later a petite woman dressed in hiking attire approached the jeep.

"Elena, good to see you." Trakonitz said as he embracing her. "Any difficulties?"

"Not really. The Germans are preoccupied preparing for retreat."

Capponi turned to Marchand.

"This is Fiona Marchand, Elena. An American intelligence agent. Formerly with the French Resistance so you have that in common."

Marchand got out of the jeep and extended her hand to Capponi. "Quite a trek from Rome. How long?" She said in Italian.

Capponi smiled. "Five days. Partly by mule with the help of locals for food and shelter."

"What information makes this trip so important?" Trakonitz asked.

"As I said. The Germans are preparing to pull back north again soon. I saw all sorts of indications as I came through their lines. The Allies will undoubtedly break through the Gustav Line and then the secondary defensive Caesar C Line. Fortunately, the Germans already declared Rome an open city sparing its destruction. Here is the important information I brought you."

From her backpack, Capponi extracted a leather cylinder and handed it to Trakonitz.

"Inside is a full set of Kesselring's retreat plan once Rome falls. It describes the defensive details of what the Germans are calling the Gothic line. Their main defensive line. It starts north of Pisa and Firenze using the mountains south of Bologna as a natural defense. Extends to the Adriatic just south of Rimini. The Germans are using 15,000 slave laborers to construct bunkers, machine gun emplacements, and even artillery casements.

"The source also provided maps. Photographs of the original documents."

Trakonitz extracted the rolls of full size photographs. Leafing through them brought a look of surprise followed by a broad smile.

"This is astounding, Elena. The source of yours?"

"I prefer not to say. Only my commander and I know his identity. An Italian. Trusted by the German command. Reliable.

What I provided you in the past came from the same source. I know his motivation for spying on the Germans."

Trakonitz handed the photos to Marchand. She understood the map references but did not read German. Yet if legitimate, of extraordinary intelligence importance.

"One other thing. The source tells of an interim plan to stall the Allied advance once the Germans pull back north of Rome. Something called the Trasimene Line. Unfortunately that planning is still evolving so he cannot yet provide any details beyond the operational name."

Trakonitz spent only a brief time examining the photographed documents. It required much closer examination by planning experts to adjust Allied countermeasures. Capponi took the opportunity to eat sandwiches they brought and drink from a bottle of wine. Marchand engaged Capponi by sharing backgrounds.

Anxious to return to Naples with this critical intelligence, Trakonitz spent the next hour pumping Capponi for what information she could provide from observations during her journey.

Making ready to leave, he said, "You returning to Rome immediately, Elena?"

"Tomorrow. I will spend the night with a cousin who lives here then head out tomorrow night, rested and provisioned."

Trakonitz embraced her. "Be careful. I will look you up when we liberate Rome. How can I contact you?"

"Here is my business card. I manage a small food distribution cooperative. Gives me the freedom and cover to move about outside the city to obtain produce to sell to markets and restaurants in Rome."

# CHAPTER 8

## PALESTINE & NORTH AFRICA | 1941-1943

---

On September 29, 1938, Great Britain, France, and Italy signed an agreement with Adolf Hitler in Munich. Under threat of war, the infamous concession to Hitler ceded the ethnic German Czech territory known as the Sudetenland to Germany. To young recent university graduate Pavel Trakonitz of Prague it foretold the end of Czechoslovakia. Just like Austria six months earlier, Germany would soon eventually absorb all of Czechoslovakia into the Third Reich in another bloodless invasion of a neighboring state.

As a Jew that meant the terrible persecution experienced by German Jews would soon descend on the over 100,000 Jews of Bohemia and Moravia regions of Czechoslovakia.

Immediately making plans to escape Prague, Trakonitz hesitated only while attempting to convince his parents and a married sister they must also flee. His entreaties failed. His father, a prosperous businessman with an established construction company, remained in denial. His mother harbored concerns but did not assertively press her husband to leave. For both, leaving everything they worked for, their community of friends and their homeland meant venturing somewhere alien. How would they survive? Perhaps reduced to poverty? What meaning would life hold?

Pavel understood their fears. Eventually he understood that for his parents leaving their life in Prague was its own form of death. They countered his pleadings by suggesting the lurid stories of persecution of German Jews were unfounded rumors. Exaggerated stories resurrecting historical lore of past Jewish pogroms of Eastern Europe and Russia.

In denial of the danger, his older sister and husband proved more exasperating. The brother-in-law was a respected lawyer, she a teacher. Both still young with two small children. Even Pavel's pleadings for the safety of the children did not prevail. Neither his sister nor brother-in-law could conceive of sacrificing their well-ordered life based on unfounded fears.

Trakonitz could better understand his parent's position. The business was his father's life achievement. Specializing in masonry, Pavel worked summers as a laborer for his father rather than the office. A life-lesson his father said. Get an education if you want to prosper. He followed his father into civil engineering at the Czech Technical University. Having just graduated with a degree in civil engineering only months earlier, he did not feel anchored to his place of birth to the same emotional degree as his parents. He also knew the horror stories coming out of Germany were true. Jews constantly harassed. Physically assaulted, robbed, places of business destroyed. No jobs in government or the academic community. Relegated to inferior status under continual persecution. He could not live under such conditions.

Therefore, on March 1939, as the German *Wehrmacht* marched into Prague, Pavel Trakonitz made his tearful goodbyes and fled the following day. He prepared well in advance. His father provided ample money in the form of universally accepted Swiss francs, and his mother several days rations of bread, cheese, and sausage.

Before embracing his parents for the final time, his father secretly slipped a Beretta pistol into his coat pocket whispering. "You have a long journey, my son. In case you encounter trouble."

At that moment, Pavel realized his father understood the dangers he and his wife faced. For him it was not denial but resignation to fate.

His father also understood the perilous journey his son faced. Crossing into German allied Austria to the Adriatic port of Trieste represented a journey of 800 kilometers. His route would take him through major cities, first to Brno, then Vienna and Graz. The plan called for traveling by train. In Trieste, he hoped to find passage on a steamer to Palestine.

He believed he could avoid any unpleasantness as a Jew by simple denial if confronted, while prepared with a cover story. His family Lutheran, his father a Prague businessman. A recent engineering graduate seeking his first job with a British construction firm in Haifa, Palestine. He spoke passable English. University trained, two professors armed him letters of recommendations. He created a false employment offer from a fictitious construction firm.

The four-week journey proved uneventful but emotionally wrenching. Would he ever see his family again? Even though always self-reliant and solitary in his habits, the uncertainty of the fate of his family and realizing he was now entirely alone brought on despair.

Once in Palestine, given his background in construction, he quickly secured a position with a firm doing concrete irrigation construction at a new kibbutz, a Jewish agricultural collective community in Palestine.

From the onset, Trakonitz realized Palestine represented a different set of dangers for Jews. In the last twenty years, great numbers of European Jews, especially Russian, emigrated to the *Promised Land* to escape anti-Semitic pogroms. This upset the prior balance of ethnic demographics with the indigenous Arabs. Caught in the middle was Great Britain. They inherited management of Palestine following the Great War and the fall of the Ottoman Empire under the British Mandate sanctioned by the League of Nations.

Violent attacks to the outlaying kibbutz by Arabs increased in proportion with increased Jewish immigration. In response, Palestinian Jews established a paramilitary organization called the Haganah. In the beginning, lightly armed and operating mostly as small independent defense units, the situation changed following the 1929 Palestine riots. Haganah expanded in size by including not only those in the agricultural settlements but also the cities. It armed itself by transforming from a relatively untrained defensive security to a capable underground army in support of a future sovereign Jewish state.

Pavel Trakonitz discovered he possessed a natural range of military skills. His quick mind and intense concentration brought him to the attention of the Haganah leadership. Eager to build themselves into a real army, the Haganah created an elite strike force, the *Palmach,* in May 1941. Trakonitz proved the ideal recruit.

While undergoing Palmach training, Trakonitz met a fellow Czechoslovakian refugee in 1942. Hungarian Jewish born Emrich Lichtenfeld grew up in Bratislava, Slovakia. As an accomplished boxer, wrestler, and gymnast, Lichtenfeld participated in defending his Jewish neighborhood from anti-Semitic rioters in the late 1930s. His flight to Palestine was more difficult. His ship sank in the Aegean Sea in 1940. He eventually reached Palestine in 1942 after serving in the British Army-commanded Free Czechoslovak Legion in North Africa.

From his martial arts experience, street fighting in Bratislava, and military training, Lichtenfeld developed his own style of hand-to-hand combat. The core principal was to use natural movements for defense combined with immediate and aggressive counterattack methods. Quickly disabling or killing your opponent the objective. Martial arts as combat not sport. Years later, he refined this military style of fighting, known as *Krav Maga,* for the Israeli Defense Forces.

Lichtenfeld was no larger than Trakonitz yet even the largest Palmach recruit with fighting experience could not overpower him. More than that, the brief practice fights usually lasted only seconds ending with Lichtenfeld's opponent on the floor vulnerable to a lethal blow had Lichtenfeld not pulled the punch.

Trakonitz became Lichtenfeld's best student. That caught the eye of a particular Haganah leader, a former Spanish Jew formerly an officer in the Spanish Republican Army. Colonel Felix Martel fled Spain in 1939 following the overthrow of the elected government by Fascist forces commanded by General Francisco Franco. Martel's responsibilities now included helping create the underpinnings of what would eventually become the Army of the State of Israel.

Even David Ben-Gurion, the most vocal political presence advocating the Zionist objective for an Israeli state, understood the need to first defeat the greater threat of Nazism. Palestinian Jews must support Allied military efforts, including the British, in defeating Germany and Italy before forcibly turning on Britain to expel them from Palestine. Therefore, Haganah selected Palestinian Jews to join the British Army fighting in North Africa. Learn military tactics and develop an experienced officer corps.

Lichtenfeld encouraged his prize student Pavel Trakonitz to join. Recognizing his unique close quarter combat skills, Colonel Martel, helped him get into the newly formed elite British Army commando unit called the Special Air Service Regiment, or SAS. Martel understood the SAS not only conducted raids but also deployed on reconnaissance missions to gather intelligence. A vital military skill gained only through experience.

Cut short was Trakonitz's developing career as a civil engineer working to convert the desert into agriculture. His adopted new homeland would not survive without those like him to confront forces bent on their destruction whether Fascist or Arab. Jews would never find a secure place without engaging in war. Hundreds of years of anti-Semitic persecution must end by violent means with Jews standing in their own defense.

During the weeks of intense SAS training in Cairo, Trakonitz's skills in unarmed combat marked him as unusual. Among the recruits and even the instructors, no one could best him in unarmed combat. Promoted to corporal in the 2nd SAS, he shipped out to North Africa, in February 1943.

Arriving in Tripoli with the British Eighth Army and attached to the New Zealand Corps, Trakonitz joined SAS troop 6 of B Squadron. The troop consisted of 16 men further subdivided into four-man patrols typically commanded by a corporal.

In March, Trakonitz saw his first combat in the Battle of the Mareth Line, the last major engagement of the Allied North Africa Campaign. The German and Italian forces by now pushed west out of Libya into Tunisia. The Axis powers faced imminent defeat in North Africa. Hitler recalled his favorite General Erwin Rommel to Germany just a week earlier to avoid his possible surrender.

Arriving at Eighth Army field headquarters in the late afternoon, the B Squadron commander moved his men to a secluded area for briefing. It was dusk with two large bond fires lighting the area as the sixteen men sat in the sand.

"Each patrol leader has a map. Lieutenant Waterfield will be in command. Your mission tonight will be to swing south around the southern end of a string of hills designated on your maps as the Matmata Hills then turn northwest. Your mission is to recon this gap between these lesser hills. The plan of battle is to strike northeast, exploiting a gap in this hilly terrain and attack the right flank of the Italian 1st Army's defensive position. To be successful, it is up to us to infiltrate and accurately assess enemy strength and deployment.

"You shall travel by our jeeps to this point. From there you dismount and move silently by foot. The key is not to engage the enemy. This is a recon mission. If confrontation is unavoidable, use silent means. Take any prisoners if the opportunity presents itself. You leave tonight and return to the forward rendezvous point at 0200 hours tomorrow night. Use the daylight hours tomorrow to observe enemy defenses and movements. That is all. Good luck."

Lieutenant Waterfield called the squadron to attention then said, "Make sure you have ample food and water. We leave in thirty minutes."

Trakonitz led his patrol through the largely featureless arid terrain using a compass and recently learned navigational skills. His patrol were all veterans of the North Africa Campaign but all new to the SAS. Some uneasy rumblings when they learned their Jewish corporal had seen no real combat other than skirmishes with Arabs raiding Palestinian kibbutz.

After observing enemy troop movements from concealed positions the following day, Trakonitz positioned his unit near to what appeared to be a forward observation post on the second night. Well concealed by large boulders on one of the hills, the position offered a good view across the entire gap where the New Zealanders intended to attack. Their position was close enough to identify two enemy soldiers through binoculars by their caps as German. Elements of the German Afrika Korps fighting alongside the Italians.

As darkness fell, the patrol silently ate their rations and took turns napping while waiting to begin the three-hour trek back to their lines. Trakonitz had a different idea.

The observation post was close enough to overhear the enemy talking in low voices. Thirty minutes before pulling out, Trakonitz went to each of his patrol and whispered separately in their ears, "We are going to take these two idiots back as prisoners."

Trakonitz shut down any discussion after their reaction. He selected one soldier to accompany him. The other two would cover them with their rifles.

The soldier named Murphy selected to follow him whispered, "You're bloody mad, Corporal. We're ordered not to engage the enemy."

"Only by firearm." Trakonitz pulled out his knife from its scabbard stuck in his boot a couple of inches to make his point. "The Captain also said to take prisoners if there was opportunity. I say this is an opportunity."

"Fucking shit," Murphy said.

Moving out quickly to forestall further debate, Trakonitz began crawling his way up the gentle slope, the sand making it easy to avoid noise. A reluctant Private Murphy followed him.

Trakonitz's tactic was to come at the Germans from around the large boulder on the right. With hand signals, he motioned to Murphy to move around to the left.

Once close to the German observation nest, Trakonitz found a gap in the rocks allowing him to see the Germans in the moonlight. They were talking in low voices. Speculating about defeat and the possibility of becoming prisoners. Bitching about the Italians. Totally ignoring their sentry duties.

Not waiting for his backup to get into place, Trakonitz sprung down on the unsuspecting Germans.

No way to capture both Germans without a firearm, Trakonitz therefore stuck his knife in one soldier's neck. Quickly turning on the second German trying to bring around his rifle, he fell on him catching the soldier's neck in the crook of his left arm using his own weight to place him in a strangle hold.

The commotion brought Murphy scampering into the scene with his knife drawn. Unseen by either was a third German back in the shadows of a rock overhang. His presence becoming apparent only after uttering "*Was ist los.*"

In a fraction of a second, both Trakonitz and Murphy realized there was another German standing and groping for his rifle on the ground in the dark.

Armed only with a knife, Murphy was too far away to attack before the German got off a shot.

Adapting to the situation, Trakonitz released the neck hold on his German, rose to his knees and threw his knife at the third German. The knife imbedded just below the throat.

Murphy rushed to the stricken German grabbed the rifle then stabbed him in the neck to finish him off.

After seeing his knife strike the German, Trakonitz turned back to the German freed from his hold, now holding a bayonet extracted from his waist. The German had no chance. Trakonitz was in his element, disarming and dropping him in series of moves followed by a debilitating offensive blow.

Whispering, Murphy said to Trakonitz, "Bloody fucking hell, Trakonitz, you almost got us killed."

"Get a boot lace and tie the wrists of this fellow behind his back."

Having secured and gagged the German, Trakonitz said to Murphy, "Get Burke and Dombrowski up here. Find a place to hide the bodies and all their gear. Let their command think they deserted."

Trakonitz's exploits on that first mission brought recognition from SAS command. The German prisoner provided immediate intelligence on enemy positions and strength. The Battle of the Mareth Line still proved a fierce engagement with heavy casualties on both sides. The British and Commonwealth forces subsequently bypassed the Axis defenses at the Mareth Line, and drove deeper into Tunisia. The weight of the Allied offensives eventually resulted in the surrender of 275,000 of the poorly supplied and battered remnants of the German Afrika Korps and Italian forces in May 1943.

Reassigned as instructor for hand-to-hand combat, Trakonitz spent the next two months near the seaport of Suez, Egypt. From here, the British Eighth Army began preparations for invading Sicily. His reputation for unusual manual combat techniques caused SAS command to take notice. Skeptical after meeting the short Trakonitz, a demonstration resolved any doubts.

Trakonitz managed to defeat three successive experienced SAS opponents, all trained in manual combat and larger in stature. Trakonitz disarmed their wooden knife attacks and delivered what in actual practice would be fatal blows. Each mock combat lasted no more than a few seconds.

The commanding colonel simply uttered, "Bloody magnificent, Corporal. Where did you learn to fight like that?"

"From a fellow in Palestine. A martial arts expert who adapted defensive techniques with decisive killing blows. Developed his skills in fighting Nazis in the streets of Slovakia."

"Think you can teach these methods?"

"I will do my best, Sir."

By the end of June, preparations made it clear the British Eighth Army was preparing for another major engagement. Everyone knew that probably meant Italy. Where however, remained a closely held secret.

Newly promoted Sergeant Trakonitz learned of the destination only after 2nd SAS, B Squadron Air Troop boarded a C-47, suited up for a parachute drop on the night of July 9. The obvious destination being Sicily only a little more than an hour flying time to the north.

To any experienced paratrooper, dropping behind enemy lines in the middle of the night carried an emotional impact. Unlike combat, this is a contest with nature. Tonight was worse. Not only moonless therefore falling slowly to earth with no knowledge of your landing terrain, this night they faced a thunderstorm bringing wind and rain.

"Easy, lads," the commanding SAS troop captain said. "Tough weather but the enemy will not be expecting us."

Throughout the troop, murmurs under their breath, *some fucking comfort that is. Break your leg on a rock or land in a tree and break your neck. Land in the middle of the enemy with your pants down. Not a soldier's way to die.*

Even experienced parachute commandos, Trakonitz included, felt exposed during the drop out of the aircraft. Jumping into this wind meant not controlling your drop zone. The troop scattering over a large area.

Trakonitz landed without incident. However, for the next hour, the scattered troop worked to regroup. Using clickers for identification, it sounded like a swarm of crickets. Of the seventeen men, three were missing.

The captain said, "We cannot wait. Must move out. Trakonitz, take the 3rd and 4th patrols. Head toward Rosolini. I will advance with the 1st and 2nd patrols a mile to your west. Rendezvous at Rosolini at 17:00 hours. Regardless the circumstances transmit any intel in code at that time. As we speak, a combined Allied force of 150,000 is making an amphibious landing along the south coast of Sicily. Eighth Army is on the right flank."

The SAS mission was reconnaissance combined with opportunistic search and destroy. Artillery and machinegun bunkers. They carried considerable quantities of explosives.

Already in disarray, Italian forces began withdrawing from Sicily the day following Benito Mussolini's arrest and the fall of his Fascist dictatorship. However, remaining German forces put up heavy resistance.

Trakonitz and his six-man force distinguished themselves. Destroying three artillery batteries and two machine bunkers, they took two German officers two prisoners.

Adding to their mission success was the capture of maps, a codebook, and radio. Fluent in German, Trakonitz then coerced one of the German officers to transmit a disinformation message that a large enemy airborne force of battalion strength was overrunning their position.

The officer was from the elite *Wehrmacht* 1st Parachute Division. A soldier fighting for his country. Not the criminal SS or *Gestapo* Nazi elements. However, this was not about playing fair.

To the younger of the German officers, no more than twenty, Trakonitz said, "I am a Czech Jew. You Nazis killed my entire family. All my friends and their families too."

"I am *Wehrmacht*. A soldier, not a Nazi. I do not kill Jews."

"That does not matter to me. You follow that murderous pig Adolf Hitler. Now you will do as I say or you will die."

"*Nein,*" shaking his head and squaring his back at attention although sitting on the ground.

"Very well. You and your *kamerad* will then both die. I spared you and your captain only because you can be of use. We killed the others Now transmit the message with the proper authentication code."

Trakonitz pulled his knife from his boot. "Unfortunately it will not be as quick as a bullet to the back of the head. Cannot afford the noise. Ever seen someone die with his throat cut?"

In English, he ordered his SAS to hold the arms of the senior officer behind his back.

The SAS looked at each other but did as Trakonitz said. They knew the sergeant was a bloody ruthless sonofabitch, but did not think he would go this far. Then again, looking into his cold pale blue eyes when his blood was up could be chilling.

"I only need one of you. See how you will die drowning in your own blood if you do not cooperate."

The officer got on the radio and delivered the false message.

Trakonitz never explained to his men if he meant to execute his prisoners. They had seen him use that knife to kill in combat so it was not clear if it was a bluff.

The achievement of the mission earned Trakonitz promotion to lieutenant and the Distinguished Service Order citation.

Trakonitz landed in Taranto on the Italian peninsula heel with the British Eighth Army on September 9. With the surrender of Italy on September 3, German forces withdrew from the valuable port to establish a defensive line to the north. Although the landing was unopposed, subsequent fighting proved intense. The Germans better trained and led than the Italians.

A month later, Trakonitz's squadron joined a joint commando raid called *Operation Devon* near the Adriatic port town of

Termoli, anchoring the eastern end of the German Volturno Line. Insertion this time was by water in rubber boats behind German lines north of Termoli in the early morning hours. They caught the German garrisoned in the town by surprise. The commandos gained controlled of all approaches to the port town, then dug in to await reinforcements.

The Germans repeatedly counterattacked with superior strength including tanks for the next three days until elements of the British Eighth Army advancing north relieved the commandos.

For Pavel Trakonitz, his battlefield luck ran out.

Attacking a German machine gun position from the flank by surprise, one of the Germans rose up ready to throw a grenade. Trakonitz was only two steps away and cut the man down with his Sten submachine gun. Unfortunately, Trakonitz's momentum propelled him into the dugout depression as the grenade fell from the German's grasp. Realizing his predicament, Trakonitz rolled against the German he shot hoping the body would shield him from the blast. The grenade explosion killed two Germans manning the machine gun. Trakonitz's exposed left thigh took two nasty shrapnel wounds. Another SAS applied a tourniquet stemming heavy bleeding until a medic arrived.

After convalescing at a field hospital for two weeks, came a transfer to headquarters in Naples and temporary assignment to a desk job with Eighth Army Intelligence.

Major Edmund de Rothschild, executive officer for intelligence, discovered the right soldier to serve for the Italian campaign. Fluent in both German and Italian with interrogation experience. Innovative with an impressive combat record made him perfect for use in the field.

Rothschild sold the idea of pursuing a transfer for Trakonitz to Intelligence to his Colonel. The offer sweetened with promotion to captain.

# CHAPTER 9

BERN, SWITZERLAND | AUGUST 1944

From high-level intelligence sources within the Third Reich, Allen Dulles learned of the latest attempt to assassinate Adolf Hitler within two hours. At 12:42 pm on 20 July, a bomb detonated in a conference room at Hitler's secure field headquarters in East Prussia. After activating the chemical detonator, Colonel Claus von Stauffenberg placed the bomb concealed in his briefcase under a large conference table while standing next to Adolf Hitler.

Stauffenberg left before the detonation, leaving the headquarters by staff car then immediately boarding a plane to Berlin. This was the beginning of *Operation Valkyrie,* the decapitation of the Nazi dictatorship.

Unfortunately, after Stauffenberg left the conference room, another officer moved the briefcase to the other side of one of the supports of the massive tabletop. This saved the life of Adolf Hitler.

Dulles briefed Fraser and the other Bern-based OSS staff the morning following the failed assassination attempt.

"I have been aware of this latest plot to kill Hitler since April. Our sources Gisevius and Waetjen forwarded direct messages from two of the principal conspirators. The conspiracy involved senior *Wehrmacht* and *Abwehr* general staff. They sought a quid pro quo for decapitating the Nazi regime. Unreasonable terms but that is now irrelevant."

Hans Bernd Gisevius and his assistant Edward von Waetjen worked at the German Embassy in Bern. Both were agents of the *Abwehr,* Germany's military intelligence. Both old-line Prussian nationalists and anti-Nazi. They reported to *Abwehr* chief Admiral Wilhelm Canaris and his chief of staff, Colonel Hans Oster, both deeply involved in the assassination conspiracy. Playing their own double game, Gisevius and Waetjen were also reliable sources to Allen Dulles. Possibly with the knowledge of the devious Canaris following the disastrous sequence of German military setbacks over the last eighteen months.

"The situation remains fluid. Certain aspects of what the conspirators call *Operation Valkyrie* are in motion. Fragmented information suggests *Wehrmacht* troops have occupied various Nazi Party offices and arrested Gauleiters and SS officers. However, other reports suggest the coup is foundering following the immediate news that Hitler survived.

"Additional information suggests a purge of the conspirators may have already begun. Several reported already executed at Reserve Army headquarters on Bendlerstraße in central Berlin. Twenty minutes after those executions around midnight last night, a contingent of SS arrived and took control of the situation. Perhaps some of the conspirators turned on their colleagues to save themselves. According to Gisevius, the SS were led by Colonel Otto Skorzeny acting under direct orders from Hitler."

Otto Skorzeny was a favorite SS officer of Adolf Hitler having participated on many daring commando raids. The most famous was the Gran Sasso rescue of deposed Italian dictator Benito Mussolini held at a ski resort hotel in the Apennine Mountains in September 1943.

"This turn of events will immediately affect every source and prospective source. Not for the better I fear. Tell your sources to hunker down and save their skins. The expected purge will eventually run its course."

Fraser commented, "Perhaps the failed attempt will hasten German defeat."

Dulles said, "How's that, Marc?"

"First, Hitler will be obsessed with seeking vengeance, paralyzing the daily running of the war. Second, Hitler will not trust anyone within the *Wehrmacht* general staff. I suspect he will assume even greater direct control over military decisions. Given his consistent record of disastrous military decisions that should benefit the Allies."

After the staff meeting, Dulles asked Fraser to remain.

"As I said, chasing regular army sources as prospective counterintelligence sources against the Soviets will now become measurably more difficult. The *Schutzstaffel* might prove a better opportunity. This failed coup by the *Wehrmacht* will play into the hands of Heinrich Himmler. For some time he has been indirectly pursuing peace feelers to the Western Allies. Looking to split us from the Soviets."

Fraser said, "Might be a ploy by Himmler to ingratiate himself to escape hanging once Germany surrenders. I have seen the reports on the Nazi concentration and extermination camps. That malignant little weasel runs all that."

Dulles said, "Regardless, pursuing vulnerable SS to either turn on Hitler or serve as postwar Soviet counterintelligence assets is the best intelligence opportunity we have. Many must be running scared. Which brings me to this SS lawyer managing Nazi funds using Swiss banking.

"Time to push hard, Marc. Here is some new information on Herr Krüger. Obtained through Gisevius. As a subordinate to Canaris, it appears Gisevius still has access to the dissolved *Abwehr*, perhaps even to Canaris himself."

Heinrich Himmler viewed the *Abwehr* and Canaris as a rival intelligence agency to the expanding reach of the *Schutzstaffel*. Himmler successfully lobbied Adolf Hitler to abolish the *Abwehr* based on suspicions of Canaris' loyalty. Only months before the assassination attempt, Hitler abolished the *Abwehr* and placed Canaris under house arrest. Himmler redistributed the duties to the SS subordinate divisions of the Reich Main Security Office, headed by Walter Schellenberg, and the *Gestapo* headed by Heinrich Müller.

Allied infiltration of the SS therefore took on increased importance.

"Seems Herr Krüger started his service in the SS. The *Devisenschtzkommando*. The Foreign Exchange Protection Commando," Dulles said.

"What is that?"

"The DSK is another branch of the vast SS organization. Created to oversee foreign exchange transactions in Nazi occupied countries, it quickly devolved into organized theft. These handpicked SS steal anything of value among from the occupied citizenry. Currency, gold, silver, precious stones, art. The Jews of course among the primary targets. Bad enough at the start of the war, reports now suggest increased brutality by the DSK."

"And Krüger's role in this DSK?"

"Among other duties, Krüger was the corporate controller so to speak for the DSK at headquarters in Berlin. Oswald Pohl, the head of the SS Main Economic and Administrative Office, *SS-Wirtschafts-und Verwaltungshauptamt*, recruited Krüger from the Reichbank in 1939. He came in with the equivalent rank of a lieutenant colonel and later landed this special job in Switzerland. The SS-WVHA manages all SS finances, supply systems, and business projects. It also administers the concentration and extermination camps. Krüger's hands are very dirty."

The attempt on Hitler provided the perfect excuse to contact the German lawyer Manfred Krüger. Fraser met with him only once since that first interview. That second time was a contrived accidental meeting on the street after following Krüger. The sole purpose was to develop a social rapport before pitching something more.

Telephoning Krüger days after the assassination attempt, the secretary connected him immediately. "Manfred, Herr Fraser is calling."

"Hello, my friend. Things are well with you?"

"Very well. Can you spare time for lunch? My editor is hounding me for more information on what is happening after this attempt on the life of Herr Hitler."

Krüger remained silent for a moment. "I am afraid I can offer very little, but I would enjoy seeing you over lunch. Today will be my treat."

Interesting Fraser thought. Krüger must undoubtedly suspect my connection to U.S. intelligence. If correct, he therefore has his own motives for continuing the relationship.

The restaurant Krüger selected was new to Fraser. A small modest restaurant on a side street.

"The best schnitzel and dumplings in Bern," Krüger said.

Enjoying a good bottle of wine before ordering, Fraser got down to business. The assassination attempt nothing more than an excuse.

"I have spent the last two days gathering all the information I could about this failed coup attempt. Looks like an army revolt. Well planned. Failed only because Hitler miraculously survived. The entire political scene altered had he died. The ending of this war likely shortened. So that is not to be."

Krüger made no comment preferring to take another sip of wine and wait for Fraser to make his point.

"Hitler will undoubtedly take control of every military detail in prosecuting the war. We both know that will lead only to disaster for Germany. In the end, unconditional surrender. That includes surrender not only to the Western Allies but also the Soviets"

Krüger replied, "Unfortunately that is likely. I can do little to alter that course of events except help Germany economically recover once this is over. Fortunate to be established in neutral Switzerland where I might be useful in cultivating international business opportunities."

Still not acknowledging his precarious circumstances.

"Perhaps there is something more immediate, Manfred. We both agree that Germany will suffer defeat. Undoubtedly by surrender. No armistice like the Great War. Germany's larger problem therefore becomes the Soviet Union. They will not only consume Eastern Europe into their sphere of control but potentially much of Germany. The Allies will occupy a defeated Germany. How that plays out is impossible to predict. Do you believe the Soviets will ever allow Germany to recover economically? I believe it is time to make a choice, Manfred."

Krüger set down his wine glass. Gone was his congenial expression, replaced with his bland lawyer demeanor. "Please explain what you are getting at, Marc."

"While I am an American journalist, I am also an American patriot. I am not neutral. Our countries are enemies, but that does not make you and me enemies. However, both of us must act according to circumstances neither of us can change.

"Let me be candid, Manfred. American Intelligence informs me you are more than just a lawyer facilitating international trade deals for the Third Reich. According to sources in Swiss Intelligence, you are an officer in the *Schutzstaffel*. A Nazi SS officer with the rank of *Obersturmbannführer*. The equivalent of *Oberstleutnant* in the *Wehrmacht*. In Western armies, a lieutenant colonel."

Krüger sat impassive and took another sip of wine before responding. "In these times we all have affiliations that position us to carry out our duties more effectively. Shall I assume you are more than just a journalist?"

"Let us concede that both of us are more than the roles we portray."

"Since that is out of the way, what is it you are after?" Krüger said.

"An arrangement hopefully you will find beneficial, Manfred. You must be aware that you will face certain...difficulties after the war. I propose an arrangement I believe you will find advantageous. The Western Allies also see the

Soviets as an immediate threat to postwar Europe. But let's order lunch before discussing particulars."

Krüger only picked at his food preferring to drink the wine, anxious to hear Fraser's proposal.

Fraser could see the crack in Krüger's self-assurance. Although well aware of the German military situation, his isolation in neutral Switzerland provided a sense of security. Fraser just damaged that complacency purposely stretching out articulating his proposition to aggravate Krüger's anxiety.

Fraser order brandies and coffee without asking Krüger.

"Here is the deal the American's are offering. They are not asking you to betray Germany. They are asking you to assist in confronting the Soviets. Who might be useful in providing counterintelligence against the Soviets? Especially in the postwar period. With your extensive knowledge of international German trade agreements, you personally might be a vital resource."

"And why should I even consider providing assistance to the Americans?"

"Because they will be victorious. You shall need a benefactor. After all, you are a high-ranking officer in the SS. The SS will be held responsible for its many humanitarian crimes."

Krüger vigorously shook his head. "I never played any role in these alleged crimes. My association with the *Schutzstaffel* was simply an organizational expediency."

"Perhaps. However, can you imagine the environment of revenge that will exist after Germany's defeat? The horrors of the concentration camps exposed. The extermination of the tens of thousands in your extermination camps. Lurid photographs shown to the world. All the work of the *Schutzstaffel.*

"I am told you are part of the SS-WVHA. Headquartered on Unter den Eichen in the Lichterfelde sector of Berlin."

"You must understand. The SS-WVHA is a large organization responsible for a broad range of financial matters. My responsibilities are associated with foreign trade matters."

"What about the economic output of the concentration slave labor? Is that not used to purchase foreign war materials?"

Fraser caught himself from taking too harsh a tone. He needed to maintain the social connection with Krüger.

"I am sorry, Manfred. I know you are not responsible for those crimes. However, you are indirectly involved. Part of the same brutal organization of torturers and murderers. You can see how things may go for you after the war. Every SS officer guilty by association. You will be among thousands of your *kameraden* professing your innocence. You cannot assume Switzerland is a safe haven."

Absorbing what Fraser said, Krüger considered the possible gravity of his situation. Taking more wine to fortify himself before proceeding, "And what are the American's offering?"

"If you can provide sufficiently useful assistance, the Americans will not pursue any prosecution for your involvement with the SS. They will also arrange for you to remain in Switzerland following German surrender. No trial for war crimes and you get to go about your life as an international dealmaker. The good German without the stain of Nazism."

Krüger just nodded. "And you are looking for information on persons useful for counterintelligence work against the Soviets?"

"Essentially, Yes. And any information you might consider useful that could shorten the war."

That brought an expression of concern to Krüger's face. "I will not become a spy for the Americans."

"Of course not, Manfred. I meant that only with your high-level access you might find certain information useful in shortening further destruction to your homeland. That of course shall be at your discretion."

Krüger understood precisely the bargain he was entering into. An opportunist and dealmaker, he knew deals were about timing. This time not of his choosing but he realized Fraser's offer came at an opportune time. When German defeat came, it would be too late to negotiate. This afforded the opportunity to begin a double role to ensure his future. He was confident he could manage the American's intelligence expectations sufficiently to satisfy the bargain. He did not intend to sacrifice himself by association with those brutal elements of the SS. The *Final Solution*, a madman's obsession.

Krüger nodded in an expression of agreement. "But I shall deal only with you. Is that agreeable?"

Fraser smiled. "Absolutely, Manfred. And just because the circumstances of war intrude, I see no reason not to remain friends."

Fraser understood the calculus Manfred Krüger just exercised. Fraser's experience accurately assessing journalistic sources served him well. Find the motivating wedge then lead the source to the conclusion you want. Easier when it is about self-preservation and the target of questionable character.

A month later, Krüger produced his first intelligence. Again at lunch at what was becoming Krüger's favored meeting routine. He did not want Fraser seen at his office, certainly not by his secretary/mistress. He also liked the benefits of fine dining and expensive wine. This time a different restaurant selected by Fraser.

As Fraser began the routine of ordering a good French wine, Krüger said, "I believe I have some useful information."

"What kind of information?"

"People that might be useful in combating the Soviets. The OKW general staff's own intelligence agency, the FHO."

The OKW, the *Oberkommando der Wehrmacht*, was the supreme high command of the German military. The FHO, *Fremende Heere Ost*, the Foreign Armies East, engaged in intelligence gathering in the Soviet Union and those Eastern European countries overrun by Soviet advances west.

"This is a different intelligence organization from the *Abwehr*?" Fraser asked.

"Yes."

"Are they also now part of the SS?"

"Not exactly. By a directive from the Führer, the Reichsführer-SS Heinrich Himmler and the Chief of the OKW share command responsibilities."

"How is this shared arrangement working out?"

Krüger smiled. "Not particularly well as you might image. Himmler wants to control everything. SS-Brigadeführer Schellenberg, head of the foreign intelligence service Section VI of the RSHA, is equally ambitious."

"Is the FHO in danger of Himmler reorganizing its leadership?"

"Possibly. However, I understand there is something of a standoff. The situation in the East continues to deteriorate. FHO provides the only source of intelligence on the Eastern Front. Therefore, for the present the FHO remains in place."

"Who heads the FHO?"

"A colonel by the name of Reinhard Gehlen. Career soldier. Graduate of the Prussian Staff College. Highly regarded by Schellenberg. Apparently rebuilt the FHO after taking command in early 1942. Dismissed all the department heads and brought in new expertise. Field Marshals Kittel and Guderian rely completely on his intelligence in conducting operations in the East. Gehlen supposedly has agents inside Russia, including the Red Army."

"Very good, Manfred. That is very useful. Do you have more? Specifics on Gehlen's senior staff perhaps?"

Krüger looked deflated. "I am afraid not. I do not have access to such information."

Fraser leaned forward and smiled. "You are a senior SS officer. I am sure you can find a way."

"You do not understand. The SS is a vast organization with many departments. I am involved only with financial matters. I have no access to personnel files, much less intelligence operations."

"I believe you underestimate your capabilities, Manfred. You are a skilled lawyer. A dealmaker you say. You negotiate international agreements with foreign officials and banks. Entrusted with wide powers."

Fraser sat back, his smile gone. After a few moments of silence, the smile returned and he said, "Well, you perhaps will think of something, Manfred. These things are important. Now let us enjoy our wine and order something special for lunch."

After their usual brandies and coffee, ready to leave, Fraser said. "One more thing that could be helpful, Manfred. A show of good faith if you will. These international financial deals you put together. We want to know the details. To understand which industrial firms are doing business outside Germany. Are these simply commercial interests or part of a larger postwar strategy?"

A look of surprise came to Krüger. "I cannot do that. That would be spying. I thought our arrangement included only advancing Americans anti-Soviet interests."

"Just part of understanding what Germany might look like once hostilities cease. Everything is interconnected. At the center is economics. I was also thinking it might be useful in broadening your usefulness to American postwar occupation authorities.

"Think about it, Manfred. Time is running out on the Third Reich. The Allies are pressing eastward in France. Adding to that, they just landed in the south of France. They will soon consolidate then invade Germany. In Italy, Rome has fallen and German forces pushed to the Gothic Line, the last German line of defense. The Soviets have pushed into Eastern Prussia. The end is very near."

# CHAPTER 10

ROME, ITALY | AUGUST 1944

---

Fiona Marchand arrived in Rome a week following its liberation. She immediately sought out Monsignor Rodrigo Donati, Curator of the Vatican Museum. Monsignor Rinaldi of Naples conveyed a warm message citing her assistance in the restoration of valuable oil paintings suffering damage in the bombings. Marchand knew Donati very well from a restoration project before the war and carried a letter of recommendation from Archbishop Bernardini in Bern.

"My dear, you have returned to the Eternal City. Praise to God's blessing for preserving the Holy Vatican and all its treasures. Now he brings us you again. "Donati said in greeting when Marchand stepped into his office.

In his sixties, Donati was a soft spoken, warm academic. As managing director of the many departments including the highly secured historical archives for over twenty years, he was a revered fixture. Not only well liked by staff and senior clerics, but also academically respected throughout the world. With his long tenure and affable personality, he possessed an eclectic range of relationships within the Vatican Curia, the central administrative body of the Roman Catholic Church.

Marchand knew him to be politically progressive. From her prior work in 1937-38, his indirect comments suggested his feelings. Living under Italian Fascist rule was an affront to his dignity as a priest and Italian. Yet he did not forcefully proclaim his political views to those conservative clerics that found justifications in Fascism as a counter to the threat of Communism. Although appalled by the lack of condemnation of the excesses of the Nazi regime by so many Catholic prelates, he remained silent.

For the next hour, Marchand recounted her personal experiences since last in Rome.

"I am so glad you found a life-partner. I am obviously no expert in romantic affairs, but as you relate falling in love with your husband, I truly see the hand of God at work. A woman with your beauty is like a flame to the male moth. When you were here years ago, there was no shortage of men orbiting around you. You often deflected their advances harshly."

"You are most observant, Monsignor. I confess to being what men call… excuse the expression, a bitch. Finding Marc hopefully has softened me."

"Perhaps in your personal interactions, but clearly not in your choice of endeavors. Never would have guessed you pursuing those dangerous activities you described with the French Resistance. Now continuing to fight the Nazis by coming to Italy."

"Both Marc and I lost people close to us by the Nazis. His mother being Jewish, Marc feels a personal calling to see justice delivered on those responsible for murdering of thousands of Jews. We do nothing more than every person rising up against these criminals."

"So true in these dreadful times. The second great conflict to consume Europe in my lifetime. Nonetheless, your sacrifices in this call for justice are laudable. From Archbishop Bernardini's letter, I believe your work here in the Vatican collection of 15th and 16th century oils you call a *cover* in intelligence work. Will there be time to devote to restoration work?"

Marchand smiled. "Of course, Monsignor. I shall make time. That work is at the core of my soul. Being a spy is only a temporary responsibility."

"Excellent. Then let us turn to more practical matters. Would it be convenient for you to stay here at the Vatican?"

"Most definitely. Safer I would think while closer to my restoration work which I can therefore indulge even at unusual hours. My physical as well as emotional refuge."

"Very well. I will introduce you to the appropriate staff and the Swiss Guard security. I am afraid the war caused many staff changes since your last time here, Fiona. Yet through the diplomatic efforts of his Holiness, the Vatican retained its sovereignty and remains unchanged.

"Perhaps you might introduce me to Monsignor Dell'Acqua. I have a separate letter of introduction for him from Archbishop Bernardini. I believe he is also expecting me."

"Ah, yes. The essential reason you are here of course. I shall contact his office at once."

"Archbishop Bernardini made a wonderful impression. A man of the world, yet compassionate. Credited for saving the lives of hundreds of Jews fleeing the Nazis. Is Monsignor Dell'Acqua a friend of Bernardini?"

Surprised by the question, he said, "I do not know. Monsignor Dell'Acqua is the nominal head of Santa Alleanza, the Vatican's clandestine intelligence service. In that capacity, he is on close terms with all senior Vatican diplomatic staff."

"How would you describe him, his political perspective I mean?"

Pausing for a moment to select his words carefully. "I know him only by reputation. My work focuses on the past where his involves the world's secular turmoil. He is outspoken. Known for his virulent, often strident views on Communism. Of course that is not uncommon in the Church given the atheistic underpinning of Communism."

"What about conservative and far-right ideologies?"

"I am afraid I do not have an opinion on what other views he holds. The Vatican and the Church leadership is a microcosm of the world. While the clergy stand in spiritual unity, views on secular aspects of culture vary as widely as among any population."

Marchand did not press the matter. Donati obviously did not share Dell'Acqua's views.

Before leaving Switzerland, Marchand researched Santa Alleanza. Dell'Acqua was ambitious and competed for influence with Pope Pius XII. After the death of the Secretary of State in 1944, Pius XII did not replace the position. As a career diplomat and secretary of state to his predecessor Pius XI, he assumed the role himself. Monsignors Tardini, Montini, and Dell'Acqua, all close confidants to the Pope, divided the duties of the powerful Secretariat.

Speculation points to the establishment of Santa Alleanza in the later sixteenth century to gather intelligence from the English court of Elizabeth I, with the intent to overthrow her rule. Regardless, it is the oldest intelligence service, originating hundreds of years before the Romanoff Tsars' Okhrana, Stalin's NKVD, the British Secret Service, the *Wehrmacht*'s *Abwehr*, or the Nazi *Schutzstaffel*'s RHSA.

It is an organization where the members hide their clandestine duties while functioning in plain sight. Every member of the Vatican Diplomatic Corps is an intelligence source. An organization bound by rigid hierarchy with every member committed to a life of obedience to the Church. Like any intelligence service, their mission is to understand circumstances that pose threats to the Church, and to exercise countermeasures to exploit circumstances favorable to Church interests.

Marchand's mission was to obtain intelligence useful to understanding the expected chaotic political environment of Italy once Germany is defeated in Northern Italy. Santa Alleanza was just one source. The other being the many partisan groups holding political power once hostilities ended. Italy was a Fascist state since 1922, surrendering to the Allies less than a year ago.

In that sense, repressed political ideologies lay dormant for decades. Everything ranging from a return to a monarchy, to a democratic republic, to different leftist ideologies of Socialism and Communism.

The outcome remained the question. Largely a matter of who established political dominance with an inclusive moderate position sufficient to form a coalition and attract international support and foreign aid. That meant the United States and given this most Catholic of European countries, the Vatican.

The following morning, Marchand made a telephone call to Fraser from the Vatican. It was only her third telephone call to him since leaving Bern two months ago. After the expressions of missing each other began the carefully crafted discussion of what each was doing. All under the guise of their respective cover legends of journalist and art restorer.

"I am working again with Monsignor Donati. He arranged for accommodations within Vatican City at a convent."

"Excellent. That means you are safe. What is Rome like?"

"Coming back to normalcy. Still an undercurrent of latent hostilities. Families torn apart now with this civil war. Lots of bad blood. Understandable I guess after twenty years of Fascist rule and half the country still an active war zone. Will France suffer the same fate once the Germans are gone?"

"Maybe. Collaborators will be in real danger. And just like in Italy, few functioning government institutions."

"Good to be doing some meaningful work. Going to try to link up with your distant cousin I ran into in Naples. I believe he is also now in Rome."

"Wonderful. When this is all over, I would very much like to meet him. Even though Rome sounds secure enough, does your work take you outside the city?"

"Possibly. Rome suffered little war damage since the Germans declared it an open city, but many surrounding towns sustained widespread destruction. I may be called on to assist in recovering works of art from damaged church property as I did in Naples. Must do what I volunteered for in the war effort."

"Nothing new here in Bern. Plenty of expatriate Germans to interview, all willing to profess their anti-Nazi views."

"Will Paris be liberated soon, Marc?"

"The retreating Germans are putting up a fierce resistance but it is still a rear guard action supporting retreat back toward Germany."

"I so miss Paris, Marc."

"More than Paris, I miss you, Fiona."

Over the next six weeks, Marchand scarcely found time to devote to restoration work. No shortage of masterpieces in need of work after years of neglect during the war years. What time she found was usually at night. It proved a restorative to her loneliness. The subtle details of the intricate work so absorbing she felt a sense of the artist's purpose in the brush strokes.

Monsignor Angelo Dell'Acqua proved to be a real piece of work. His arrogance only aggravated by his clear displeasure in Allen Dulles sending a woman as the OSS liaison to the Vatican. Nonetheless, he offered his full support to provide useful information gathered by the vast network of Italian clergy throughout Italy. Pointing out, all in accordance with the wishes of the Holy See.

In Marchand's report, she cited Dell'Acqua's strong ultra-right political views.

"I will say this, Signora Marchand, the Western Allies are ignoring the threat of Communism in its vilest form, the Soviet Union under the anti-Christ Josef Stalin. To consider the Soviets an ally is an obscenity. A regrettable alliance of expediency that America and Britain will come to regret. The Church believes the time has come for the West to recognize this threat."

"What change in policy does the Holy See suggest?" Marchand said. Another indirect rebuff of Dell'Acqua by the inference that he was only a messenger reflecting the Pontiff's position.

"His Holiness has been consistently clear about the threat of Communism on Christianity and Western civilization."

"I assure you the OSS is also very much concerned by the Soviet threat."

"Signora, intelligence is only part of combating the Communist threat. When Germany finally capitulates, the eastern half of Europe will remain under Soviet domination. The vast Red Army enforcing an occupation of equal brutality to that of the Nazis. That will become the geopolitical situation transcending all else. From such a position, Soviet ambitions will covet even more territory. The world struggle is soon to become the contest of Christianity against Godless Communism."

Marchand replied, "I would frame the struggle as one between dictatorships whether right-wing or left-wing. Where the unchallenged rule by a dictator and an elite few people subjugate the people. This in contrast to democracies where the people choose how to be governed."

Marchand suspected Dell'Acqua might find her comments insulting. The indirect implication also condemning of the Church as an autocratic institution ruled by an elitist hierarchy.

Dell'Acqua understood her insinuation and simply glared. "I will appoint one of my secretaries, Father Čirjak, to be your point of contact with my office."

As this signaled the meeting was over, Marchand abruptly stood as if dismissing him. Why not goad this arrogant ass. "Thank you, Monsignor Dell'Acqua. Might I then introduce myself to Father Čirjak before leaving?"

Soon after entering Rome, Marchand looked up Carla 'Elena' Capponi using her business card for the address of her food distribution business.

Capponi turned in her desk chair as Marchand entered the produce warehouse office.

"Oh my god, Fiona!" Capponi said.

After embracing, Fiona said, "Glad to see you survived to return home, Elena. Are you still active with your partisan group?"

"No. I no longer kill Germans. Married my commander, Rosario, and I am now pregnant. Unfortunately, life has yet to return to normal. Rosario is soon to head north and continue to fight the Germans in Yugoslavia. I shall run our small business and pray for his safe return."

A peaceful interlude for Marchand as she and Capponi spent the afternoon telling each other about their lives and sharing war experiences while sharing a bottle of wine and a meal of cheese and bread.

Capponi's description of participation on the front lines of fighting in Rome made a deep impression on Marchand. After joining the Central Gap Carlo Pisacane partisan group, she was denied a weapon. Women of the group typically relegated only to supporting roles. Taking the initiative, she stole a gun from a gendarme on a crowded bus. After that, she engaged in killing scores of Germans around Rome.

Marchand felt her exploits in the French Resistance paled in comparison. As a member of the Italian Communist Party, Capponi also suffered the oppression and fear of living her entire life under the yoke of Mussolini's Fascist dictatorship. Now the continued pain of seeing her country ravaged by a continuing war between Germany and the Allies while Italians fell into a parallel civil war after switching sides. Her only peace her unborn child and a resumption of life in Rome having escaped destruction.

"I understand most of the Italian resistance groups have loosely organized under an umbrella organization. Is that correct?" Marchand asked.

"Yes. The *Comitato di Liberazione Nationale*, the CLN," Capponi said. "Necessary to coordinate resistance activities with the Allied military."

"Does it include more than just the Communists like your group?"

"Oh yes. The CLN represents all the major political parties. Socialists, Christian Democrats, Labor, even Monarchists. Divided into three main groups along political affiliations then further broken down into brigades."

As Capponi elaborated in more detail, it became clear the CLN represented the core of Italian political activism. The only other partisan groups were the former military groups that remained unaligned with political ideology, particularly in the northwest province of Piedmont. It also became clear that adherence to left-wing ideologies represented a significant segment of the population. Explains the dire concerns of the Vatican. Much the same climate of fear of Communism that brought Mussolini and his Fascist Party to power twenty years earlier.

"Can you connect me with the CLN, Elena?"

"Certainly. In fact, I will introduce you myself. I shall start with the leader of the Italian Communist Party, Palmiro Togliatti."

Her political ideology notwithstanding, Marchand found a kindred spirit in Carla Capponi. Days later, Capponi escorted Marchand to the office of Palmiro Togliatti.

The distinguished looking Togliatti did not seem to fit the role of political subversive. Yet his background provided by Capponi was sufficient to raise concerns for anyone promoting representative democracy. Togliatti was a founding member of the Communist Party of Italy, *Partito Comunista d'Italia*, PCI. In 1930, he became a citizen of the Soviet Union.

Known to be on close terms with Josef Stalin alone made Togliatti's independence from Moscow suspect. With the Soviet advances into the Balkans on Italy's border, the Communist Party of Italy became more than just another political faction. Heavily represented in Italian armed resistance against the Germans, only worsened fears of a Communist dominated postwar Italy.

Marchand met with each of the other five political leaders constituting the CLN leadership. She realized after meeting separately with each of these men, they collectively represented the immediate political future of Italy. All graciously allocated extensive interviews, anxious to establish favorable relations with the United States and Britain.

Even though heavily tilted to the political left, these leaders represented a defacto coalition Italian government to the yet not fully liberated country.

Marchand reiterated the positions espoused by each of the CLN coalition leaders adding her impressions. Combined with her report on Monsignor Dell'Acqua speaking from the position of the Vatican Secretary of State's office, and the senior official of Vatican intelligence, it provided a snapshot of the Italian political landscape. Dulles responded with a complimentary communication pressing her to continue to widen her sources and make continuing reports on this important soft intelligence.

Interviews with the various political leaders of the CLN provided a sense of the diversity of the political landscape of postwar Italy from the top down. Marchand sought additional sources closer to the populace for anecdotal information to shape the picture. People risking their lives fighting the Germans. People like Carla Capponi. These partisans represented the immediate face of postwar Italian politics.

Receiving a message from Captain Trakonitz provided just that opportunity.

Arriving within hours at British headquarters, Trakonitz walked her to Major Rothschild's office. "Sorry to summon you on such short notice, but you may be interested in joining me on a new mission. I will let Major Rothschild explain."

Another man sitting across Rothschild's desk rose as she and Trakonitz entered.

"Fiona, let me introduce Lieutenant Ronald Atherton, SOE. Recently reassigned from France.

Britain created the Special Operations Executive, the SOE, following the occupation of France and the Low Countries by Germany. Their mission similar to the American OSS included espionage, sabotage, reconnaissance, and assisting partisans in occupied Europe. As Winston Churchill said, "To set Europe ablaze."

"Lieutenant, Fiona Marchand, American OSS. Recently recruited from the French Resistance."

"*Bonjour, Madame,*" Atherton said in French, extending his hand.

"To the business at hand," Rothschild said. "Lieutenant Atherton's orders involve a major weapons resupply mission to a partisan group known as the Maiella Brigade. A group formed in the southern area of Abruzzo immediately following the Italian surrender last September.

A motivated group of former Italian soldiers and young men avoiding German conscription into the forced labor brigades. Led by former Italian Army officers. They have seen terrible brutality with widespread reprisals by German *Wehrmacht* and *Waffen-SS* forces following the Italian surrender. Easy to understand why the Maiellas do not take German prisoners.

"A source of valuable intelligence working behind the German lines. Helped us punch through the eastern end of the Gustav Line. The German's are now falling back to their hardened defensive positions along the Gothic Line. The Maiellas have units already deployed north of the Gothic Line in the rear of the German positions.

"The Maiellas can be useful for sabotage and disruption of German supply lines. They have a history of working closely with British forces."

Rothschild turned to Atherton, "Lieutenant."

"Thank you, Sir. I am here to infiltrate with them along with supplying a large cache of weapons. We feel the type and quantity of weapons involved is better suited to movement on the ground rather than the uncertainty of airborne parachute drops. Particularly the heavy ordinance. Mortars, heavy machine guns, grenades, and C4 plastique explosives."

Marchand said with a critical inflection, "How is that, Lieutenant? You expect the partisans to sneak the ordinance through the German's last line of hardened defense? Is that not more risky?"

Trakonitz said, "Very observant, Fiona. I made the same argument. Someone much higher than my rank believes there is a better chance of the weapons arriving by dividing the risk into several small infiltration units."

Trakonitz shook his head and made an expression of disagreement. "Professionally speaking, the mission decision maker has never done this sort of thing. Better to risk weapons in a misplaced airdrop than risking committed Italian fighters."

Atherton did not comment. He understood the dangers of being SOE. However, Trakonitz's comments only highlighted the risk of this mission.

Rothschild said, "Captain Trakonitz has worked with these partisans and will command the transport of weapons to a location vacated by the Germans after their first line of retreat to the Trasimene Line. Atherton will then accompany the weapons north and remain imbedded with the partisans.

To Fiona, Rothschild said, "Given your brief, this is a preliminary move to a major offensive of the Eighth Army against the eastern end of the Gothic line. Want to join these gentlemen?"

"Absolutely. When do we leave?"

Trakonitz answered, "We leave the day after tomorrow at 0500 hours. Escorted by an infantry company in a convoy of lorries. Five or six hours journey north of here climbing into the mountains. Outside the town of Citta de Castello in Umbria, east of Arezzo. A small village named San Giustino about twenty kilometers south of the Gothic Line."

"That means close to the front lines, Fiona," Rothschild said.

"I understand. Like the rest of you, I have a job to do."

Trakonitz nodded. He genuinely liked this woman. Obviously talented and trusted by American intelligence, yet she did not seem suited for the violence of fieldwork like Carla Capponi.

"You will come armed of course, Fiona?" Trakonitz said.

"Of course."

Trakonitz thankfully did not ask specifics about her firearms experience. Contrary to Marc's instructions, this situation called for going armed with the heavy .38 caliber Smith & Weston revolver. In her jacket pocket the small caliber pistol Marc gave her for close quarter protection. If her circumstances became desperate, the switchblade strapped to her ankle as a last resort. She would also wear the .38 in a shoulder holster given her by the OSS instructor in Switzerland. Even without any real shooting experience, might as well look the part since she was flirting with danger that near the combat lines.

Glad she did not have to explain the danger to Marc ahead of time. Laughing to herself, armed to the teeth with field jacket, canvas satchel, and camera, she looked the part of a real wartime photojournalist heading into battle.

A glorious sunny summer day. Riding in the open jeep with Trakonitz and Atherton made the heat bearable. A convoy of five lorries followed behind, two with the weapons, the other three with British infantry.

"What is the plan after reaching the rendezvous?" Marchand asked.

Atherton explained. "After connecting with the partisans, we will organize into smaller groups to make the trek north. The Maiellas have scouted the German Gothic line in this sector and selected infiltration points. The terrain of steep hills and valleys offers opportunities for partisans familiar with this region."

"And our British infantry escort?"

"They will move on and join British forces for the upcoming offensive. They are not part of this mission other than delivering us to the rendezvous."

Outside the small village of San Giustino, Trakonitz directed the convoy down a dirt road into a small depression between two hills. Sitting in the front passenger seat, Trakonitz directed the driver as the radio crackled and he made brief exchanges in Italian with the partisans.

Turning to Marchand and Atherton in the back of the jeep, "The rendezvous site is secure. The partisans posted pickets two kilometers to the north. They have also monitored our approach for the last twenty minutes. These chaps know what they are doing."

"We will offload and prepare the loads for transport," Atherton said. "Did they muster enough donkeys with load saddles, Captain?"

"We shall find out shortly."

The plan called for loading the heavier mortars, machine guns, and ammunition onto the donkeys. The men would carry the C4 and grenades.

A single partisan appeared from behind a tree, directing the lorries with the ordinance to a spot designated by another fighter approaching the jeep with a broad smile.

*"Benvenuto, Capitano."*

*"Buon pomeriggio, Fabio,"* Trakonitz said as he leaped out of the jeep. *"Dov'e il Capitano Bianchi?*

After a brief exchange, Trakonitz said to Marchand and Atherton, "This is Fabio. In command of this operation is Captain Bianchi. A competent officer. He will be arriving from behind the German line with the remainder of the unit testing the infiltration routes."

Late in the afternoon, the first of the remaining partisans trudged into the encampment. Two hours later Captain Lorenzo Bianchi arrived.

Bianchi embraced Trakonitz and shook hands with Marchand and Atherton. The four went off to a secluded spot under a large tree.

Bianchi immediately related events since departing from north of the German lines starting at midnight.

"Four groups started at points approximately three kilometers apart. Places scouted to avoid hardened German positions. Unfortunately, the four-man group furthest to the west is long overdue," Bianchi said.

"If they do not show up, will you abort the mission?" Atherton said.

Bianchi gave him a hard stare. "No. We shall proceed using the other three routes. My men feel confident they can successfully traverse these routes with the weapons. The German line relies on fixed defensive positions using the mountainous geography of this region. Designed to repel a massed attack. Gaps exist between these hardened points, sufficient for small groups with knowledge of the terrain to slip through without detection.

"The weapons are vital, Lieutenant. We shall break the back of the German line in the east. If the British can then punch through, they can turn the German's left flank. We shall do our part by killing many Germans with these weapons."

Several women partisans prepared coffee and food over campfires. They would camp here for the night. The plan called for departing north with the weapons at dawn the next day. This would allow time to reach the outer positions of the Gothic Line by nightfall.

Marchand took the opportunity to observe and talk with individual partisans before returning to Rome with Trakonitz the next morning. Unlike Marc, her participation in the French Resistance afforded little opportunity to interact with fighters on the ground. Talking to these Italians painted an even grimmer side to German occupation than she experienced in France.

These brave young people witnessed the terrible scorched earth rampage of German forces once Italy surrendered to the Allies. Hitler felt betrayed by his southern ally for the second time after the loss of North Africa, which he blamed on inferior performance of Italian forces. The situation forced a massive re-deployment of German forces to Italy numbering twenty-seven divisions by July 1944.

Forced to commit massive numbers of German forces to shore up Italy, affected the war effort elsewhere. The Germans also had to contend with disbanding Italian military forces, now largely hostile to Germany. The feasible move to return Mussolini to power in a German puppet government in Northern Italy only increased the brutalization of the populace now treated as conquered people. The Germans responded to acts by partisan resistance with similar barbarity as meted out in their Eastern Europe conquests. Collective terror by murder, rape, and destruction.

Not sure how to form that into a useful intelligence report, but their stories profoundly moved her. Emotionally jarring, it added further antidotal justification to why she was doing this.

The notorious *16th SS-Panzergrenadier-Division "Reichsführer SS"* was a motorized formation of the *Waffen-SS* fighting in Italy since May 1944. The division already responsible for the massacres of 560 civilians in Sant'Anna di Stazzema, 159 in San Terenzo Monti, and 173 in Vinca in Northern Tuscany. Then the largest massacre of 770 Italian civilians in Marzabotto, south of Bologna.

The principle instrument of these atrocities was the *SS-Panzer-Aufklärungsabteilung 16,* Reconnaissance Battalion 16, commanded by Major Walter Reder. The battalion's mission was to search and destroy Italian partisan groups. Mass murder of civilians part of the cycle of reprisals and terror.

Captain Bianchi's missing fourth infiltration group stumbled into a newly created machinegun bunker in the early morning darkness not long after setting out. Two of the four men died in the firefight and the other two unfortunately captured. Capture meant death but frequently a more unpleasant death. Worse for these two after the *Wehrmacht* turned them over to the butchers of Major Reder's SS 16th Reconnaissance Battalion.

While witnessing the brutal torture of his companion, the other partisan gave up the plan, including the location of the weapons staging area south of the Gothic Line.

With wide latitude for independent action, Reder determined the partisan jumping off position was between known concentrations of British forces. A three-hour trip with his mechanized force even without roads. The partisans would not be able to flee with the stockpiled ordinance. Sufficient time to destroy the weapons then retreat back to German lines before British troops could converge on the area. To avoid Allied aerial reconnaissance, they would leave in the predawn darkness to attack at first light.

The first indication something was wrong was the crackle of small arms fire as SS panzers reached the outlying partisan pickets. Then came the rattle of heavy caliber machinegun fire.

Trakonitz grabbed Marchand roughly by the arm. "To the jeep!"

The entire encampment suddenly came alive in a state of chaos. The partisans began deploying in a skirmish line to defend against the approaching attack. Several began setting up machine guns. Others hurried to unpack mortars from the crates.

As Trakonitz and Marchand raced for the jeep, a German Panzer crested a slight hill only a hundred yards distant. Seconds later, it fired a round destroying the jeep in a ball of fire.

"Run to the village!" Trakonitz said.

Marchand followed Trakonitz on the run as he took a route using as much natural cover as possible. They had little time to make their escape. This was a mechanized German unit advancing rapidly. Mechanized infantry would accompanying the panzers. Exposed, the partisans stood no chance.

After fifteen minutes, Trakonitz and Marchand reached the village.

With the radio destroyed in the jeep, there was no way to alert British forces to the attack. Thinking rid of German occupation months ago, confused villagers appeared in small groups trying to decide what to do. Within minutes, retreating partisans began arriving. Setting up defensive positions using the village buildings as cover likely ineffective against German panzers.

Trakonitz and Marchand took up positions in a barn. Armed only with a Sten submachine gun and two Webley revolvers left them vulnerable with inadequate firepower.

"What happened, Pavel?" she asked as they both peered through the weathered cracks of the barn door slats. Trakonitz positioned them here because of the stone walls of the barn.

"My guess it has something to do with Captain Bianchi's missing fourth infiltration group. Captured probably. Forced under torture to reveal the plan and our location.

"The Germans would know this to be a lightly defended sector by the British. Some aggressive commander took the initiative to make an attack well south of their lines. Maybe a mobile SS unit charged with suppressing Italian partisans."

"You never liked this plan."

"No. Bad enough trying to infiltrate the German lines. Never would have guessed this jumping off point this far south to be a risk though. Sorry I enticed you to come along, Fiona."

"Not your fault. Like you, part of my job. Do you have a plan for getting us out of this?"

"Not really. Find the best defensive position possible. Fight it out to buy time. The Germans are overexposed and cannot engage for long before help arrives. Hopefully the partisans have radioed our situation to British forces."

Minutes later a panzer came up the main road into the village. Coming to a stop, it traversed its gun turret searching for a target for its short-barreled 75mm gun. Minutes later, German infantry arrived behind the panzer, which then resumed its slow forward motion.

From the loft of the barn, they heard movement. Seconds later, several small arms reports from a rifle rang out from overhead. Trakonitz knew immediately it was a partisan using the height of the barn loft as a sniper position. Suicide facing panzer artillery.

Little they could do except shield themselves as best possible behind a small tractor. Trakonitz pulled Marchand face down on the earthen floor. Seconds later, the roof of the barn exploded.

Fortunately, the panzer elevated its gun to take out the sniper in the loft. Nonetheless, the collapse of the roof tore the barn doors off their hinges twisting the remnants inward.

The entire wooden structure of the barn loft and roof collapsed, burying them under debris. Trakonitz pushed away shattered pieces of wood freeing his legs. Uninjured, he turned his attention to Marchand.

Moving a large beam trapping her, he whispered close to her ear, "Fiona. Can you hear me?"

Receiving no reply, he began carefully moving debris covering her while looking for wounds. As he touched a long splinter, it did not budge. Changing his position, he saw the reason as she groaned loudly. The end of a foot-long splinter protruded from Marchand's lower back.

"Quiet, Fiona. Do not move. You are injured. Germans are moving about. Stay absolutely still. Play dead. I am going to cover you with pieces of the roof to hide you. I must move to find a hiding place, but I promise I will not leave you."

Through another gasp of pain she whispered, "I understand. Give me my revolver."

Trakonitz extracted the Webley from her shoulder holster and placed it in her hand.

Where to hide was a problem. If lucky, the Germans might not see Marchand under the pile of rubble. Immobilized by her injury left him no choice. The Germans would undoubtedly check the barn even though it appeared destroyed. Trakonitz had no intention of risking playing dead and dying with a bullet in the back.

There simply was no place to hide. Rubble consumed the entire floor area.

A remaining hanging portion of one of the barn doors created a small dark space in the shadows. As a hiding place, it was only temporarily useful as a place of ambush. If the Germans entered while spraying everything with machinegun fire, or tossing in a grenade, it mattered little. Yet he had no choice.

A quick look through a crack showed the panzer by now advanced beyond the barn with sounds of continued small arms fire. He extracted his double-sided commando knife from his boot and set down his Sten submachine gun. If a German entered the barn, a silent kill or he was dead.

A minute later, the crunch of a jackboot on the gravel. His only hope just a single German.

The soldier entered far enough that Trakonitz knew he was inside the damaged barn door. Yet probably not far enough inside to avoiding alerting other Germans if Trakonitz attacked him. That meant waiting to allow the German to enter further into the shadows of the barn's interior.

Seconds later the German began stepping on the pile of debris to look around.

The distance sufficient for Trakonitz to grab the German's chin in his left hand to silence him while plunging the knife deep into his neck. The German remained standing for a couple of seconds until collapsing as his blood pumped out in an arch when Trakonitz removed the knife.

Pulling the German back further into the shadows, nothing more to do but wait. Would the Germans discover the soldier missing? Would his *kameraden* search the barn?

He took up a position with his Sten, circumstances now beyond his control.

After the sound of firing died away. He went to check on Marchand. She was conscious but in great pain. Turning her head she coughed and blood trickled from her mouth. The piece of wood protruding from her back looked ugly. Her shirt was soaked with blood around the entry wound but not bleeding profusely. Unfortunately, the blood from her mouth indicted internal bleeding. The wood shard probably penetrating a lung.

"Can you move, Fiona?"

"I don't know. My back. What is wrong?" she asked in a raspy whisper accompanied with more coughing while reaching behind with her left hand.

"Don't, Fiona. A piece of wood pierced your back. Still imbedded there."

"Oh God! And the Germans?"

"Outside. Can't tell what is going on. All we can do is wait. They cannot risk staying here very long."

Trakonitz hoped he was correct. This looked like a surgical attack to take out the partisans. However, if British forces caught the Germans here, they could find themselves in the middle a fully engaged battle.

He managed to pull Marchand from under the debris. Propping her against the end of an animal pen of some sort allowed the impaled piece of wood to stick through the slats of the pen. Awkward but better than lying face down in the dirt.

She saw the body of the German in the corner.

"You killed him?"

He nodded without turning his head from watching the scene outside.

"What are they doing?" She asked hearing shouts in German.

"My guess they are about to execute inhabitants of this village. Reprisal for supporting the partisans. The chap lying in the corner is SS. Insignia of the *16th SS-Panzergrenadier Division.* Also known as the *Reichsführer SS Division. Waffen-SS.* Himmler's own. Notorious for conducting massacres in reprisal for Italian partisan activity.

While in considerable pain, Marchand insisted Trakonitz move her closer to observe. Even with a limited field of vision, they watched as a machinegun cut down a group of villagers comprised of women with several children and a couple of old men. The continued rattle of machinegun fire in the distance probably more victims.

Even through the pain and coughing up blood, tears flowed down Marchand's cheeks. Witnessing mass murder by the SS made vivid the reports of roving *Einsatzgruppen-SS* murder battalions operating in Eastern Europe.

Twenty minutes later the panzers and mechanized personnel carriers left the village. Chance again favored Marchand and Trakonitz. No search of the destroyed barn for the SS soldier killed by Trakonitz.

For all the death and blood of combat he experienced witnessing this act of butchery profoundly disturbedTrakonitz. The SS were simply not human. Perhaps Himmler's *Schutzstaffel* simply released latent sadistic traits of its members. Regardless, they must destroyed.

Marchand remained his immediate concern. She would not survive her wound unless he found a way to contact the Army and get her medical help soon. For the moment, all he could do was get her into an abandoned house and place her face down on a bed with the wood splinter impaled in her back.

# CHAPTER 11

ROME, ITALY | SEPTEMBER 1944

---

Marc Fraser arrived in Rome two days after receiving a telephone call from his distant cousin Edmund de Rothschild. With no commercial service yet established to liberated Rome, he had to make a roundabout route via military transport. The journey a hell knowing so little of Fiona's condition. Rothschild knew only of wounds from an artillery shell, then undergoing surgery once transported back to Rome. She was alive but in serious condition.

Rothschild met his plane when it landed in Rome. "Edmund de Rothschild, but call me Eddy, cousin," he said shaking Fraser's hand."

"Glad to meet you, Eddy. How is Fiona?"

"Doctor says the surgery went fine. He removed a twelve-inch splinter of wood driven into her back. Penetrated her left lung but fortunately missed other organs. Says the danger now is infection."

"A piece of wood? How did that happen?"

"I will let Captain Trakonitz fill you in on the details. He was with her at the time. A rendezvous with partisans close to the German defensive line. Trakonitz saved Fiona."

American and British Army surgeons treated the most serious combat causalities at Rome's largest hospital. Rothschild led

Fraser to a ward full of female civilian patients. Seeing Marchand in the last bed, he rushed to her side. Touching her hand, he bent down and kissed her forehead. An instant wave of relief passed through him. Although pale and weak, she was alert and appeared resting comfortably.

"Marc, this is Pavel Trakonitz. He saved my life."

Fraser turned to the British officer that was sitting at Fiona's side, now sanding back allowing Fraser access to the bedside.

Offering his hand, Fraser said, "Words of thanks can never be enough, Captain. Can you tell me what happened? I didn't know my wife's mission took her behind enemy lines."

"We were not behind German lines. Actually twenty kilometers south of the German's defensive Gothic Line in this mountainous region. Learning of your wife's mission to contact Italian partisan groups, I offered to take her up to a location in Abruzzo, hours north of here.

"I was escorting loads of weapons and a British SOE agent to a rendezvous with a particular partisan group. Knowing the terrain, the plan called for the partisans to infiltrate the ordinance through the German line to arm a larger partisan force in the German rear area. The partisans would attack German positions in support of the forthcoming Allied offensive.

"But this is war. Like in chess, your opponent may make an unexpected move. When the partisans infiltrated the German lines to test the routes in various places, one group never showed up. Undoubtedly captured and someone talked since the Germans knew our location. A mechanized SS unit attacked the partisan encampment in the early morning hours.

"Total disaster. Caught by surprise, we retreated into the village of San Giustino. Your wife and I hid in a barn. Seems a partisan sniper also took up a position in the barn loft. An SS panzer tank rolled down the street ahead of the infantry. A blast of the tank's artillery destroyed the roof of the barn.

"Both of us buried under the debris of the barn roof. When I found Fiona, she had this large piece of wood sticking out of her back." He reached to his own back pointing to the entry location with his thumb. "Not bleeding badly, but a nasty sight."

"How did you get her out of there?"

"Good fortune. With the SS well south of their lines and risking exposure, they withdrew in short order. One of the partisans must have radioed British forces close by since a battalion of infantry arrived within the hour.

"We loaded the wounded including your wife in a lorry and transported them to a British field hospital. They did what they could, but the field surgeon determined it better to remove the piece of wood under better surgical conditions. They administered morphine and I commandeered a driver and jeep to make the long ride back to Rome. Good thing she was almost out with the morphine because it was a rough ride on these back roads."

"Thank you again, Captain. I appreciate you staying by her side until I got here. Can you help me find the doctor? I want to understand the details of her condition."

They found the doctor resting with a cup of coffee. He looked exhausted. Severely wounded casualties continued to pour into this hospital from the front overwhelming the medical staff.

Fraser approached the doctor, "Doctor, I believe you are treating my wife, Fiona Marchand? The patient pierced by a piece of wood. I am Marc Fraser."

The doctor remained seated while extending his hand.

"What is her condition?"

"I operated. The only organ damage was to the left lung. The repair I believe will prove successful. The most difficult procedure was debridement of the wound to remove any contaminants."

"I'm sorry. What does that mean?"

"Removal of all the damaged tissue and foreign material from the wound. You see this was not just a wood splinter. Badly decayed with age it came out in pieces leaving fine debris in the wound. I removed every fragment I could find and as much of the damaged tissue in the wound cavity as possible. Then I extensively irrigated the wound with antiseptic. All we can do now is keep her on a regimen of antibacterial drugs."

"You mean the danger is infection?"

The doctor nodded. "The fear is sepsis. The next few days will be critical."

Trakonitz understood the doctor's diagnosis. Sepsis killed the SS number two officer Reinhard Heydrich following a failed assassination in Prague by two SOE agents. A small bit of uniform fragment contaminated the shrapnel wound from a grenade. He recalled celebrating the death of the creator of the *Final Solution* in 1942. The doctor commented that Fiona's wound was far worse than typical contamination by uniform fabric.

Trakonitz's concern was well founded. Four days later Marchand experienced a severe rise in temperature. Soon after, with efforts to stem the infection unsuccessful, she lapsed into a coma. The same surgeon opened up the wound searching for any evidence of missed foreign material that might be the source of the infection.

Fraser was beside himself. For three days as she lay unresponsive, he maintained an around the clock vigil at her bedside.

Only once did he leave the hospital ward with urging by Rothschild and Trakonitz. A good meal at a restaurant, accompanied by a fair amount of whisky with the company of these two men, served to restore at least his physical well-being.

"Marc, Fiona is a strong woman. The doctor is guardedly optimistic," Rothschild said.

Trakonitz said, "I have seen a lot of death, Mr. Fraser. I feel in my heart that Fiona will recover."

"Thank you, Captain," Fraser said. "Please call me, Marc. Fiona calls you Pavel therefore we should also be on a first name basis. Especially with all you have done."

"Fiona did not tell you everything about her terrible experience," Trakonitz said.

Fraser's face immediately reflected concern. "There's more?"

"I am afraid so. Trapped inside the destroyed barn when the SS entered the village, we both witnessed the SS gathering together the local inhabitants. Then came the machine-gunning. The SS murdered forty-two people. Fiona witnessed the atrocity. Many children were among the victims. You cannot witness such a thing without it leaving a disturbing memory."

Fraser nodded trying to absorb what that must have been like.

Rothschild said, "I am also afraid Pavel and I must leave Rome within the week. The British High Command finally relented to allow Palestinian Jews to fight the Nazis. The Army is forming a Jewish Brigade. The officers are all Anglo-Jewish including our Brigadier. I am to become chief of intelligence. Given Pavel's unique talents, he will command a reconnaissance company.

"We leave Rome assigned to the Northern Italian Theater. Threatened on three fronts and suffering continual bombing, Germany cannot hold out much longer."

Fraser said, "I shall miss your companionship. Both of you. I will keep you informed about Fiona's condition. Here is our address and OSS headquarters in Bern."

"And when this war is over, we must get together, Marc. After all, we are family no matter how distantly related. Fiona told me a little of your background. Enough to appreciate you and Pavel share much in common with your past adventures."

"And I too shall hope to visit you and Fiona under better conditions." Trakonitz said then grabbed Fraser's shoulder. "She will survive this, Marc. I know it. For her, the war is over. Return to a normal life and take good care of your special lady."

The following day, Monsignor Donati and the young Croatian priest Father Čirjak appeared at Marchand's bedside.

Fraser stood as the two priests introduced themselves.

"Thank you for coming, Monsignor Donati. Fiona speaks fondly of working with you at the Museum." Turning to the younger handsome priest, Fraser said, "Do you also work with my wife, Father?"

Father Čirjak replied, "In a different capacity you might say. I work in the office of the Papal Secretary of State. Signora Marchand's other more secretive work brought us together."

Apparently Fiona's contact with Vatican Intelligence.

"I understand perfectly. I also work for American intelligence. I appreciate your kindness in visiting."

"I just learned of her situation from the mother superior after she did not return to her residence at the convent. What happened, Signore Fraser?" Donati asked.

"She received a wound in an attack near the front lines up north. Unfortunately, infection set in. A virulent form known as sepsis. She lapsed into coma two days ago. Candidly, the doctor told me she has only an even chance for surviving."

Donati placed his hand on Fraser's shoulder, "She is now in the hands of God. I shall pray for her recovery."

Donati and Father Čirjak prayed while Fraser bowed his head. A non-believer yet absorbed with all his being in willing Fiona's recovery.

Donati concluded with anointing Fiona's forehead with holy water.

"I shall leave you to your vigil, my son. God bless you. Trust in His mercy. I shall continue my prayers for Fiona."

Čirjak made the sign of the cross over Fiona's face and shook Fraser's hand before leaving with Donati.

Late the following evening in the darkened ward, Fraser awoke from a troubled sleep in the chair next to Fiona's bed. A groan, followed by another, and then stirring from the bed.

Jumping up he looked at Fiona in the dim light. Her eyes opened trying to focus.

Grabbing her cheeks in both hands, he spoke her name softly "Fiona, Fiona. You are back, my love."

He wept uncontrollably with joy having almost lost her a second time to the Nazis SS.

Within a week, Fiona made remarkable progress. The fever receded and the drainage tube removed from the wound. With the wound surgically closed, she could stand with assistance.

For the first time, Fraser lifted the bandage to examine the three-inch incision in the middle of her back. "Doesn't look bad. Does it still hurt?"

"Very tender. I still sleep on my right side. Doctor says the scar will not be too bad."

He was guiding her slowly down the hospital ward. "What troubles me now is recurring nightmares. Did Pavel tell you what happened?"

Fraser nodded and hugged her shoulders.

"Hearing accounts of atrocities is nothing like witnessing mass murder firsthand. Marc, I saw children butchered. There was this little girl about ten holding the hand of a small boy of five. A woman holding the boy's other hand. A mother and her children.

"Then the indescribable sight of machinegun bullets ripping them apart. Those small bodies exploding in blood and tissue. A scene I relive in recurring nightmares."

Fiona wept against Fraser's shoulder as he tried to ease her distress.

Recovering her composure, she said, "After the war, will the Allies bring these murderers to justice?"

Fraser sighed. "Some probably. Certainly not all. Thousands of SS murderers by all accounts."

At her insistence, Fraser reluctantly left her to return to Bern a week later. She was out of danger but still required weeks of rest and recovery before travel. He must return to work and she was in good hands, cared for by the Benedictine nuns at the Vatican, with daily visits by Monsignor Donati.

Returning to Bern, Fraser decided to turn up the heat on SS lawyer Manfred Krüger. Out of touch for weeks while in Rome, Krüger readily accepted Fraser's lunch invitation at his favorite restaurant.

Seated at a secluded table in the back, Krüger stood to shake hands as Fraser entered the restaurant. "Good to see you, Fraser. You have been away?"

"Yes. Rome actually. Doing a piece on the Italians now that they have switched sides. Things are going downhill quickly for the Reich, Manfred. Paris is liberated. Soon the Western Allies will cross into Germany.

"Germany cannot hold back the Soviet hordes on the Eastern Front. The Italian Southern Front will not hold for long. These new rocket bombs directed on London are a pathetic last-ditch effort by your demented Führer."

Krüger sat in glum silence not even reaching for his glass of wine.

"Sorry to be so frank, Manfred but you know the situation as well as anyone. On a personal note, I am afraid I have more bad news. Seems American intelligence has taken a greater interest in you. Your connection into the highest ranks of the *Schutzstaffel* casts a spotlight on you."

"But I have shown good faith in providing information on potential counterintelligence assets against the Soviets."

"The FHO? Come now, Manfred. Our London headquarters claim the FHO is reduced to nothing more than a subordinate section of the SS-Reich Main Security Office. Purged experienced Wehrmacht officers. Replaced by incompetent SS with no background running operations against the Soviets. Everything is turning to focus on your history in the *Schutzstaffel*. The *Wehrmacht* will eventually surrender and eventually return to society. But the Allies will seek retribution on everyone in the *Schutzstaffel*."

Fraser was making this up. Dulles communicated no such particular interest in Krüger. "Manfred, you belong to the most reviled criminal organization in history. SS crimes go beyond anything in modern times. There will be nowhere to hide. Retribution will be harsh and widespread."

Krüger looked as if hit by a slap to the face. He suspected all this without Fraser reiterating the situation. Yet Fraser was his only lifeline. Facing criminal charges for his association with the SS seemed incomprehensible. He was a banker and a lawyer. While in denial over the prospect of prosecution and imprisonment, he understood the likely prospect of losing his privileged lifestyle and remaining in Switzerland.

"Criminal charges based solely on my affiliation with the *Schutzstaffel* are unreasonable. Totally unjust. What more can I do to convince the Americans of my cooperation, Fraser?"

"That is why I am here, Manfred."

"Unfortunately, there was little new in your information on FHO personnel. American intelligence was not impressed. In fact, they were very specific about their interests. My principal contact said, *"Tell the fucking kraut lawyer if he wants to save his ass, we want everything about SS financial dealings with Swiss banking."*

For the secretive Krüger it was like asking to sacrifice an eye. He rigorously shook his head no. "That is not possible. I told you, I will not become a traitor by spying for the Americans."

"I told them that, Manfred. The same guy said, *"That is his problem. Either that or he can hang. The Swiss will kick him out and he has nowhere to hide. Personally, I do not give a shit.*

"So that is where you stand, Manfred. Sorry to be the bearer of bad news. I suggest you consider the offer."

As the waiter approached, Fraser brushed him away. "I fear I have ruined your lunch. Think on it and if you reconsider get in touch with me." Fraser stood up and put his hat on. Goodbye, Manfred."

Fraser concocted everything. There was no OSS interest in Nazi financial information at this late stage. Bigger issues looming. Krüger just another SS functionary. With no further expectations for any internal coup against Hitler following the July assassination attempt failure, Allen Dulles' focus turned to post-war American intelligence issues in Europe. Following orders from Washington, he even abandoned pursuing the self-serving desperate armistice feelers emanating from Heinrich Himmler. Continuing interest remained only for identifying possible Soviet counterintelligence sources. Krüger's information on FHO personnel useless.

Dulles turned his attention instead to preliminary peace feelers from an unlikely new source, SS General Karl Wolff, former chief of staff to Himmler now commanding all *Waffen-SS* forces and SS policing functions in Italy. Wolff's proposal, a surrender of German forces in Italy thereby freeing Western Allied armies to invade Germany from the south. They could then link with their forces moving eastward across France to invade the German homeland. Such a scenario would thwart Soviet advances along the extensive Eastern Front giving the Western Allies sole occupation of a defeated Germany. The best bulwark against a postwar Soviet threat in Europe.

However, it was a vastly more complex issue since most of the German forces in Italy were regular *Wehrmacht* under command of Field Marshal Kesselring. Dulles faced the additional political hurdle of keeping this secret from the Soviets who distrusted possible western Allied considerations of a separate peace with Germany.

Only Fraser remained interested in Manfred Krüger. In fact, the information he was pressuring out of Krüger would only serve to condemn him to war crimes prosecution. Fine with Fraser. He loathed everything about the Nazi *Schutzstaffel.* Manfred Krüger was a participant to SS crimes. Fraser's relationship nothing more than an act. Fraser hoped to see Krüger one day sentenced at least to prison. Fraser's interest was retribution against the *Schutzstaffel.* All *Schutzstaffel* must pay a price commensurate with their crimes.

With the expression of a cornered animal, Krüger's demeanor immediately transformed into resignation. "Please sit back down, Fraser. We shall enjoy our lunch and then return to my office. I shall provide the information the Americans demand.

For this, can you assure me that I shall remain free at the end of the war?"

"Of course, Manfred."

Arriving at Krüger's office, Krüger said to his secretary, "You may take the afternoon off, Helga. Herr Fraser and I shall be occupied for the rest of the afternoon."

Once alone, a defeated Krüger said, "Where do you wish to begin?"

"Let's start with a list of all accounts under your management."

The secretary's office contained a row of file cabinets leaving Krüger's elegant office uncluttered. Fraser took a seat around a small table as Krüger went to a cabinet inset as part of the mahogany bookshelves lining one entire wall. Opening the cabinet revealed a safe.

Extracting several folders, Krüger took a seat across from Fraser. Removing several sheets of paper, sliding them over to Fraser.

Listed were details of over a hundred different entries. A summary sheet identified the account holder's name, the Swiss bank, and the account number.

"These account names of companies are fictitious I assume?" Fraser said.

Krüger nodded as he extracted several more papers from a different file folder and handed them to Fraser.

Cross-references. No expert on the organizational structure of the *Schutzstaffel,* Fraser recognized the names of individuals controlling certain accounts from intelligence reports. The names concealed behind a fictional legal entity with the controlling individual also a fictitious name. The real names those of the most senior *Schutzstaffel.*

At the top was *Reichsführer of the Schutzstaffel* Heinrich Himmler, the second most powerful Nazi figure. Ernst Kaltenbrunner, Chief of the Reich Main Security Office, the RSHA. Walter Schellenberg, chief of the *Sicherheitsdienst*, the SD, the Nazi intelligence wing, and now head of all foreign intelligence with the abolition of the *Abwehr*. Krüger's immediate superior, Oswald Pohl, head of the *SS-Wirtschafts-und Verwaltungshauptamt*, the SS-WVHA, the SS Main Economic and Administrative Office, which included management of the Nazi concentration camps. Heinrich Müller, chief of the *Gestapo*.

"Some of these appear to be personal accounts?"

"Yes."

"I see your name. How did you become included in this very selective list? Like the others, funding your life after Germany's defeat?"

Krüger made no reply.

"Guess the higher powers needed to include the fellow that makes this work. Understandable, Manfred. No point in going down with the sinking ship. I hardly think you should suffer pangs of conscience over what you are doing. The *Schutzstaffel* is not Germany. You just got caught up in Hitler's madness like so many others. You owe it to yourself and your family to survive.

"Tell you what I will do. Give me a revised list removing your name. If American intelligence finds this information of sufficient value, no need for you to suffer further. You shall have money to build a new life"

Krüger said with an expression of surprise, "You would do that for me, Fraser?"

"Of course, Manfred. I have come to like you. You deserve a break."

"Do you think this will get me off the hook?"

"Not my call, but it sure looks like material of exceptional interest."

Fraser smiled falsely having no sympathy for Krüger, thinking to himself, *the material will condemn this greedy SS bastard.*

"How do you manage these accounts? I am not familiar with Swiss banking other than its obsessive secrecy."

"A simple process. The account number identifies the account holder. The account opened under the name of a legal entity or individual. Nationality is irrelevant. The account application merely requires a name that remains confidential. There is no reporting by the bank required under Swiss law. Quite the contrary, laws restrict any identification of account holders. In fact, the account number itself remains highly secret since it controls all access. Even bank transactions conceal the account number."

"And your function?"

"I hold individual powers of attorney for each account, authorized and notarized by the account holder."

"The fictitious account holder's name of course?"

"Yes. I then execute transactions on behalf of the account holder."

"What kinds of transactions?"

"Principally transfer of funds from various German banks which in turn move the funds through the Reichbank, the Reich central bank, then to the designated Swiss bank account.

"My broader function is making investments. International investments. My expertise is useful in negotiating as well as concluding contracts and various legal agreements.

"And this much longer list of business names with authorization names I do not recognize?"

"Various *Schutzstaffel* revenue streams."

Revenue streams?

"Such as?"

"The *Schutzstaffel* is a vast organization. It owns property, conducts business, purchases equipment and goods. *Waffen-SS* divisions comprise a whole army."

"By conducting business, do I assume that includes profits from forced labor and stolen assets of concentration camp inmates?"

"I have no way of knowing the origin of the money. I simply manage the funds as directed."

Not productive for Fraser to display his disgust at the evasion. Krüger was divulging everything, therefore better to move on and continue to play the role of his benefactor.

"Where is the money invested?"

"Neutral countries of course. Switzerland, Sweden, Spain, Portugal, South America."

"I shall require copies of everything." Fraser said as he extracting a 35mm Leica camera from his briefcase. "I shall photograph everything."

Krüger said, "That will take hours."

"Perhaps, but necessary. Best we get to it then."

While Krüger began organizing the files, Fraser set up a makeshift setup for taking photographs of the hundreds of documents. Anticipating Krüger caving into pressure, he came prepared with a large quantity of film.

On Krüger's desk, he arranged two stacks of law books. Across the books, he placed a sturdy carpenter's folding ruler, opened to span the stack of books separated by the width necessary for the document. This would act as a position rest to hold the camera at a consistent distance and position from the document placed between the books. The desk lamp arranged to provide illumination without shadows.

Fraser was an accomplished photographer beginning from his early days in journalism in Los Angeles. In Spain during the civil war, he used those skills to produce microdot negatives to smuggle out photographs damaging to the Fascist rebels. Activities that almost cost him his life.

The tedious work took four hours. A depressed Manfred Krüger dropped into a chair and said, "That is everything."

Fraser nodded. "You did the right thing, Manfred. This is your ticket out while keeping your head and making a future. Now, let me buy you a drink."

It took Fraser a week to develop the rolls of film in his apartment bathroom rigged as a darkroom. He could have turned it over to OSS technicians for developing, but he had an ulterior motive. Making a duplicate set of prints, he intended to keep one set. Why? Not entirely certain, but if Swiss banking refused to cooperate on the subject of Nazi looted gold reserves, not likely they would acknowledge SS deposits. Nothing official ever resulting with the funds remaining secure in the Swiss banks.

He harbored the concern that going after the Nazi *Schutzstaffel* might become a secondary Allied priority following German defeat. Most SS guilty of crimes against humanity would undoubtedly escape punishment. The number of perpetrators was simply staggering. A practical legal difficulty of unprecedented scope. As a journalist, he could not reconcile great numbers of mass-murderers escaping justice. Personal experience made it a matter of vengeance. Although with no specific ideas, this SS money hidden in secret Swiss bank accounts must not find its way to postwar fugitive Nazis SS.

# CHAPTER 12

## END OF WWII EUROPE- BAVARIA, GERMANY | APRIL 1945

---

Fully recovered, Marchand remained in Rome to finish two restorations at the Vatican. Pleading for more recuperation time from Allen Dulles, this was really about avoiding returning to some tedious administrative function at OSS. Work at the museum was meaningful and restorative to her spirit. She was effectively done with intelligence work. So was Marc once Germany surrendered. She longed to return to Paris.

Returning to Bern in early December, she and Marc fell into a leisurely social routine. The Christmas season in Switzerland was unusually festive this year.

Although German forces executed a surprise winter offensive on the Western Front through the Ardennes, it could only forestall the inevitable. With Allied liberation of their encircled forces in the town of Bastogne, German forces fell into full retreat back into Germany.

On the Eastern Front, Soviet forces with their overwhelming numbers continued to push back retreating German forces. In Italy, U.S. and British forces continued to push German forces north hampered by relocations of divisions to support the Western Front.

Those months in postcard Switzerland in the winter of 1944-45, reprised the prior winter. Marchand again recovering from a brush with death. Now the end of the war was imminent. Life already normalizing for Fraser and Marchand. They made the most of the situation by socializing with friends, simply relaxing, and enjoying each other.

Fraser could even joke about her wound. After making love celebrating New Year's Day, he commented to Fiona as she left the bed naked.

"Come back here," he said.

She coyly said, "I doubt you can get it up again."

"I want to show you how good the wound looks. Hand me that mirror from the bureau."

Holding it to so she could see, "Just this narrow white line. No puckering of the skin. The doctor took special pains to use many sutures from the inside of the wound. The kind of imperfection that makes you sexier."

"Not sure about that, but I agree, it does not look particularly ugly." Turning to face him for full frontal effect, "Want me to return to bed?"

After the holidays, Dulles said to Fraser, "So glad that Fiona recovered fully. I did not intend for here to be in harm's way. Most regrettable."

"Understandable. A fluke circumstance. Nevertheless, she is tough. Grateful however to have her back with me in Bern and working a desk."

With social niceties out of the way, Dulles handed Fraser a three-page report. The heading read:

S E C R E T
SUPREME HEADQUARTERS
ALLIED EXPEDITIONARY FORCE
Office of Assistant Chief of Staff, G-2
7 November 1944
INTELLIGENCE REPORT NO. EW-Pa 128

```
Subject: Plans of German industrialists to engage in
underground activity after Germany's defeat and flow
of capital to neutral countries.

Source: Agent of French Deuxieme Bureau. This agent
is regarded as reliable and has worked for the
French on German problems since 1916.
```

Dulles said, "Just arrived by diplomatic pouch a few days ago. Take a few minutes to read it."

Finished, Fraser said, "Not surprising. If anything, the Germans are pragmatic."

Dulles said, "They are calling it the Red House Report. The alleged meeting taking place at the Maison Rouge Hotel in Strasbourg on August 10, 1944."

"Alleged?"

"Army intelligence is not entirely convinced. No way to corroborate. Neither American nor British intelligence have a track record for this French agent. Therefore, I would like you to press your SS lawyer source Krüger. He is involved with German international investments and intimate with Swiss banking. If corroborated, no doubt further instructions will follow. Krüger might prove crucial to corroborating the report."

Fraser said, "Krüger is scared shitless. Afraid Switzerland might expel him from the country after German surrender if the Allies pursue him for war crimes. Has money stashed in his own Swiss bank account along with the other highest-ranking SS as I reported. Wants to protect his hide as well as remain in Switzerland in style to pursue his international business career and keep his Swiss secretary as his mistress.

"I invoked the fear of Allied prosecution given his SS association. May I use this as another inducement if he can provide information?"

"Good idea. Afraid neither of us can fulfill any such promise however," Dulles said.

Fraser did not care. Krüger was just another SS criminal that must not escape justice.

The report bluntly stated the premise of the meeting as recognition of the imminent defeat of the Third Reich and post-war planning to assure the eventual rise of a Fourth Reich. The Nazi Party was encouraging major German industrial firms to make surreptitious foreign investments by moving capital out of Germany, a reversal of previous prohibitions. Also encouraging them to make alliances with foreign firms to facilitate access to sources of foreign capital.

The conference confirmed the Nazi Party recognized many within the industrial leadership might face charges for war crimes. Therefore, these firms must install less visible managers and engineers in strategic positions to ensure continuity of German corporate leadership.

"Note the names. Presiding over this meeting was Dr. Johann Friedrich Scheid, Director of Hermsdorf-Schönburg GMBH. Holds an honorary rank as an SS general. Rumored to be close to Martin Bormann. Everything comes back to the SS.

"Find out if Krüger can provide anything useful on these two mentioned banks, Basler Handelsbank and Schweizerische Kreditanstalt of Zurich.

"Representatives from the leading German industrial firms in attendance included Krupp, Rochling, Messerschmitt, Rheinmetall, Bussing, Volkswagenwerk, Drose, Yanchew and Co., Brown-Boveri, Herkuleswerke, Buschwerke, and Stadtwerke. What can Krüger offer about foreign investments of these firms?"

After Krüger shared his records of secret SS Swiss bank account management, Fraser kept him on the hook through the holidays. He falsely told him things looked promising as American intelligence examined the material provided. Dulles of course simply passed the photographed documents to Washington with little comment suggesting his lack of interest with weightier matters consuming his attention. Washington made no request to follow up.

It came as a surprise to Krüger when Fraser showed up at his office unannounced.

After shaking hands, Fraser closed the door to Krüger's private office. Sensing something amiss, Krüger said, "Good to see you, Fraser."

With an expression of regret, Fraser replied, "Unfortunately this is not a social visit, Manfred. My superiors are pressing me."

"I am not sure I understand."

"Well, Manfred, first of all, I must confess to not being entirely truthful with you. While I am a newspaper correspondent, I am more than just a go between for American intelligence."

Krüger smiled. "My friend. I have always suspected that. Perhaps that makes it easier to negotiate my unique circumstances."

"That is what brings me here today, Manfred. Good news and some not so good news. First the not so good news. Powers well above my pay grade have differing opinions about the material you provided on managing secret SS Swiss bank accounts. Some harbor the expectation maybe you can prove useful as a witness against your superiors. Others argue your complicity to war crimes should condemn you."

"I thought you said my information was of importance?" Krüger said with a stricken expression.

"Thought so too. However, I am not in London or Washington to gauge the waters. You know large bureaucracies. You work for one. However, let me give you some better news, and maybe a way out for you.

"We have information that many of the largest German industrial firms have been pursuing a similar approach to getting money out of Germany. Using Swiss banking secrecy to launder money through foreign investments. Investments in neutral countries. Countries sympathetic to the German Reich.

"What do you know of about a couple of Zurich banks, Basler Handelsbank and Schweizerische Kreditanstalt?"

"I know their names of course, but I do not conduct business with them."

By the photographed documents naming several Swiss banks, neither of these banks appeared in any of Krüger's SS transactions.

"Why not?"

"No particular reason. There are hundreds of Swiss banks. I developed my banking relationships based on my own criteria of required services."

"Well, this might be your get out of jail card, Manfred?" The analogy meant for affect. "Seems this has taken on heightened interest as American intelligence concerns turn to the postwar political climate. The Soviet threat is one thing, but the resurrection of another Nazi regime is intolerable. The *Schutzstaffel* is the only institution capable of carrying on Nazi ideology and international investments and finance are your expertise.

"At any rate, I suggest you begin making serious inquiries. Useful information might prove to be your life line."

Krüger's shook his head in resignation. "I have no idea of how to even go about finding out information on German involvement with these banks."

"Come now. You started your career with the Reichbank. You know all the players. You are also a clever lawyer with deep connections to Swiss banking. I will also add one further bit of information. Our intelligence suggests this parallel scheme to move money out of Germany is sanctioned within the highest circles of the *Schutzstaffel*. Start there."

Events slowed during the winter months everywhere. The 1944-45 European winter proved one of the coldest in history. In a practical sense, Allied advances on all three fronts came to a standstill. Resumption of offensives required waiting for spring.

Like everyone else, Fraser and Marchand planned for the end of the war. By all indications, the Germans could not hold out past summer. Unofficially, Allen Dulles was maneuvering to take control of American postwar intelligence in western occupied Europe, caught between competition of the War Department and State Department. His plan for sending in his *German Team* was not going well. Hedging his bets, Dulles planned to send selected OSS operatives into sensitive areas to maintain a presence until ordered otherwise.

To Fraser he assigned the unpleasant task of assessing the looming problem of tens of thousands of displaced persons. Survivors of the Nazi concentration camps being the most problematic. Mostly Jews where repatriation to their former homes becomes impossible given the prevailing anti-Semitic climate of their homelands. Therefore, Fraser would follow American and British forces as they liberated Nazi concentration camps. Fraser agreed as his last official act provided Fiona could accompany him. Dulles readily agreed wanting to hold his team together for as long as possible in a bid to head postwar American intelligence in Europe.

Fraser was thinking beyond the end of the war. Neither he nor Fiona had an interest in remaining in the OSS. Yet their access to OSS files and connections within American and British intelligence could prove useful. Fraser intended to pursue the remnants of the Nazi *Schutzstaffel* after the war through journalistic means. Many of the worse might even escape prosecution for war crimes. Likely large numbers of the hundreds of lesser-known murderers would escape justice. In some manner, Fraser intended to hound former SS unmercifully as a personal crusade.

With that plan, Marchand used her administrative role to access reports identifying SS personnel, their origins and records of misdeeds. Over many weeks, she secreted out reports for Fraser to photograph at the apartment.

By spring, Allied forces on all three fronts moved relentlessly against retreating German forces on every front. In the East, Soviet Red Army forces became the first to encounter Nazi concentration camps as they came to Majdanek followed by the mass killing centers of Belzec, Sobibor, and Treblinka located in Poland in the summer of 1944. The world suddenly saw the horrific images of stacks of unburied dead bodies and the ghostly images of the walking dead inmates with shaved heads, clothed in filthy striped rags. In January 1945, the Red Army arrived at the massive Auschwitz-Birkenau extermination camp. The site of 1.3 million deportees from 1940-45. The camp was now empty. The remaining 60,000 inmates forced in a winter death march westward weeks earlier.

As advancing American and British forces entered the German Fatherland in April, they too encountered concentration camps in Germany. The vast Nazi archipelago of forced labor camps, subcamps, and extermination camps numbered 1,200 by German Ministry of Justice records.

The end came as the Soviet Red Army closed off Berlin in a final siege. Having decided against fleeing, Adolf Hitler retreated to his *Führerbunker*. A dank concrete tomb of 18 self-sustaining rooms 55 feet below the Reich Chancellery. With the Red Army closing to within hundreds of yards of the location, Hitler committed suicide on 30 April 1945. Surrender of German forces in Italy took effect on 2 May, followed on 7 May by all German forces surrendering unconditionally to the Allies. The bloodletting ended leaving a destroyed Europe. The aftermath left problems of unprecedented scope, threatening to consume Europe in unrelenting crisis for the indefinite future.

Before Germany surrendered, Fraser and Marchand left Bern by automobile to link with American forces pushing eastward into Bavaria. Both dressed in American army uniforms without rank insignia. Close to the fighting, both were armed, Fraser with a Browning .45, Marchand with her Webley revolver carried in shoulder holsters. Along with identifications as American intelligence, they carried written authorization from Allied headquarters in London.

Their objective to be among the first to enter the Dachau concentration just north of Munich. Two weeks earlier, Allied forces liberated several concentration camps to the north, including

Buchenwald, Dora-Mittelbau, Bergen-Belsen, and Flossenbürg. Fraser knew from his time in Germany in 1933 that Dachau was the prototype for all camps that followed during the twelve-year Nazi reign of terror. As such, it also became the training ground for the most diabolical of the *Schutzstaffel* formations.

The *SS-Totenkopfverbände*, the SS-TV, literally translated as Death's Head Units, were responsible for administering the concentration camps and the later extermination camps as the means to fulfill the genocidal objective of the *Jewish Final Solution*. While all SS wore the absurd *Totenkopf* skull insignia on their caps, the SS-TV also wore it proudly on the right collar tab. The SS-TV disproportionally represented the largest number of Nazi war criminals.

Fraser recalled his first visit to the early political internment camp in Oranienburg near Berlin as a foreign correspondent reporting from Germany in 1933. That disturbing experience nothing compared to the horrors of seeing Dachau. No description, no matter how vivid, could adequately prepare him or Marchand for the nightmarish reality they entered.

Ditching their car, Fraser and Marchand rode into Dachau in an Army staff jeep behind Brigadier General Linden, commanding the American 42nd Infantry Division. Nearing the camp, the convoy stopped after being flagging down by an American officer. He pointed to a long line of boxcars sitting on a rail siding a short distance away.

Fraser was close enough to hear the officer speak to the General's jeep ahead of them.

"Sir, Captain Williams, Baker Company, 2nd Battalion. You've got to see this, General."

The General and other officers from four jeeps followed the Captain on foot.

A hundred yards away a putrid smell assailed everyone. Marchand turned her head gagging as she pulled a handkerchief to her nose. Fraser reacted as did all the officers. The unmistakable stench of bodies in varying stages of decomposition.

Venturing closer, the open doors of the rail cars revealed stacks of bodies. Still a very cold late spring day, the flies had not yet descended in mass. However, Fraser noted a stream of disgusting-looking fluid seeping from the bottom of the closest car. After snapping a series of photos, he grabbed Marchand by the arm and pulled her back to the jeep.

"My God, Marc. What will we find at the camp?"

Approaching the main Dachau camp, the convoy of jeeps followed by trucks loaded with infantry stopped at the camp entrance. Again, all those in the forward jeeps got out. Ahead of them behind double rows of barbed wire stood thousands of inmates. Dressed in striped uniforms, standing in silence.

Orders rang out and the trucks emptied of troops. The soldiers also stood in silence trying to process the sight. Moments later came a spontaneous roar from the inmates. *Liberation!* Somehow, these pathetic-looking creatures survived their ordeals.

Entering the camp brought new visions of horror. More bodies heaped in large piles. Many inmates living skeletons devoid of muscle tissue. Starvation victims close to death. Army doctors warned of communicable diseases like tuberculosis and typhoid likely rampant.

As Fraser and Marchand entered the camp headquarters building, small arms firing erupted outside. Fraser told Marchand to stay put as he rushed out following soldiers with rifles at the ready.

Following the sounds of sporadic gunfire, they came to a large square surrounded by barracks. A number of SS guards lay dead on the ground, obviously executed by American GIs.

Fraser spent the following day interviewing camp survivors as Fiona made notes. Accompanying the division's G-2 unit, he photographed endless SS documents.

Before leaving Dachau, the initial assessment reported the liberation of 30,000 Jews, political prisoners, clergy, and Roma from Dachau and its approximately 100 subcamps. According to inmate statements, the daily death toll was 200 a day in the months preceding liberation. Yet reports suggested the notorious Mauthausen-Gusen complex of camps in northern Austria was worse.

Distinct from the extermination camps located in Poland using gas chambers, the design of Mauthausen-Gusen and Dachau like many others, worked inmates to death while extracting economic value. Death here was a protracted ordeal of misery with no hope of survival. Established to exploit political prisoners through slave labor as a renewable resource, inmate mortality was irrelevant.

After Dachau, difficult to imagine worse depravity. The Nazi *Schutzstaffel* at its malignant core. Impossible to conceive how an organization could spawn thousands of its members to engage systemically in torture and murder for no strategic purpose. Those like Manfred Krüger were equally guilty as the sadists directly running these death camps.

Getting to Mauthausen might prove questionable since the Soviet Red Army might get there first. However, seeing reports of the rapidly advancing U.S. Third Army commanded by the aggressive General George Patton provided an opportunity as they continued to press east toward Austria.

Fraser and Marchand attached themselves to the 222nd Infantry Regiment outside Schweinfurt, Germany as they rolled eastward. Using their orders, they commandeered military transportation to allow them to accompany the rapidly moving Third Army.

"Why are we doing this, Marc? The war is over. Why not just return to Paris?"

"Because I need to see what the SS has done firsthand not just read of their crimes. Even photos cannot convey the depth of their crimes. Just like you witnessing the murders in that Italian village.

"I have the obsession of a journalist. The crimes of the SS should be the story of the twentieth century not simply relegated to history as just a part of this war. What the Nazis did is something entirely different."

# CHAPTER 13

MAUTHAUSEN, AUSTRIA | MAY 1945

---

In a jeep driven by an American sergeant, Fraser and Marchand eventually caught up with the rear elements of Patton's Third Army. Trying to pass the endless convoy of tanks and trucks made progress slow going. They spent a cold night in a requisitioned German barn eating field rations and sleeping on blankets spread over hay. They arrived at the main Mauthausen-Gusen concentration camp complex ten days after its liberation by the Americans.

Even after Dachau, Mauthausen revealed new levels of barbarity.

The main camp sat on a hill above the town of Mauthausen twelve miles east of Linz where Adolf Hitler lived as a youth. Three other large camps around the village of Gusen just a few miles from the main Mauthausen camp together comprised one of the largest forced labor complexes in German occupied Europe. Like Dachau, a hundred subcamps spread throughout Austria and Southern Germany.

At three times the number of inmates as Dachau, it was not only the size of Mauthausen-Gusen that staggered the imagination. If Dachau was the prototype concentration camp then Mauthausen was the industrial model. The range of sadistic measures inflicted on inmates reached new levels of inhumanity designed to extract maximum value before causing death. Details related to Fraser and Marchand from interviews with survivors provided personalized details of SS crimes more compelling than incomprehensible numbers of those murdered.

Checking in with the American officer in charge at the former camp headquarters building after presenting their orders, the colonel said, "OSS. Just missed one of your own. A Navy lieutenant. A commando captured with a group of partisans. Took him out of here for medical treatment. Should have seen the poor fellow. This is an unbelievable shithole of misery. Rather than killing more *krauts*, I'm stuck with dealing with this human catastrophe.

"Christ, there are thousands of these poor wretches spread over God knows how many different subcamps. All starving. We are bringing in massive quantities of food and special medical units but the number of survivors is overwhelming. Some are not going to make it."

"I appreciate what you are up against, Colonel. We just came from the Dachau camp. Same thing. Decomposing piles of the dead and emaciated survivors."

"Not so many bodies lying about here. These bastards had their own crematorium. But here we also have the quarry."

"Quarry?" Fraser said.

"Yeah. Full of bodies. Inmates thrown from the above cliff. A disgusting sight. I will put you with one of the inmates helping us sort out this mess. He can explain firsthand what went on here. Sergeant!"

Appearing at the Colonel's door, the sergeant responded, "Yes, Sir?"

"Take these people to that fellow Wiesenthal."

Marchand said, "We understand there is a complex of outlying camps. We need to make a full assessment."

"Very well. Take them around to see the whole ugly mess, Sergeant."

The sergeant escorted them to a windowless room at the other end of the building. Each wall of the room lined with file cabinets. Seated at a table covered with piles of paper in the center of the room was a small man. Hard to determine his age with the shorn hair and the gaunt look of someone suffering malnutrition.

He looked up from examining records as the sergeant said, "Colonel told me to bring these people to you. They're from American intelligence."

As Wiesenthal still dressed in his stripped inmate uniform stood up, he set aside his glasses and came around the table to shake hands. Marchand reacted at his appearance with a tightening of her face. He could not weigh more than a hundred pounds. The uniform far too large. The pants held at the waist by a length of cord. The shoes so badly falling apart they seemed hardly functional.

"My name is Simon Wiesenthal. And you are?" He said in accented, but good English while extending his hand.

"I am Fiona Marchand and this is my husband, Marc Fraser."

"I apologize for my appearance Madam Marchand. Something of a shock by your expression."

"It is I who should apologize. You have obviously suffered greatly."

"Not as much as others you will see. Although rescued, a good many are beyond help and will soon die. Now at least they will die with some dignity."

"How long have you been here?"

"If you mean this camp, just three months. That is the only reason I am still alive. Any longer, I would be dead. However, the Nazis have imprisoned me since late 1941. Because I am a Jew."

"You mean you have been in other camps?"

Wiesenthal nodded giving a weak smile. "Most of the time at Janowska concentration camp in Poland from 1941 to September 1943. You see I am Austrian, born in Galicia in the north bordering Poland. I was an architect living and working at the outbreak of war in Lwów, Poland with my wife."

"Has your wife also survived?"

With his eyes tearing, "I do not yet know if Cyla is alive. They of course separated us. To have survived is largely a matter of chance. Some say the will of God.

"By chance I narrowly escaped being shot as one of 54 Jewish intellectuals in a tribute to Hitler's 54th birthday. All this the idea of a lowly SS officer. Months later, with rumors the Germans intended to liquidate the camp inmates before liberation by the Soviet Red Army, I escaped. Hidden by someone I knew, but eventually arrested and returned to the Janowska camp. Soon after, they sent me and a few other surviving inmates to Kraków-Plaszów.

"Evacuated again to the Gross-Rosen camp, I lost a toe after it was crushed by a rock working in the quarry. Amputated without anesthetic, infection fortunately avoided. The Germans then marched us on foot to Chemnitz as the Red Army continued advancing.

"From Chemnitz we boarded open freight cars to Buchenwald. From there to here by truck. This was early February. Because of the cold, half of those making the journey did not survive. Already close to death and unfit for labor, they placed me in a death ward for the terminally ill. Rations of only 200 calories a day to hurry death. I therefore remain alive against the odds.

"Even surviving the terrible journey to come to this place of death proved fortuitous. Only by chance did I avoid the alternative of the gas chambers in one of the many extermination camps in Poland.

"My story shows how capricious life can be. Philosophically, a game of chance where even against long odds, unlikely events may occur unpredictably."

Fraser and Marchand stood transfixed, silently listening to Wiesenthal recite his personal ordeal. They would hear many other such tales as they spoke with survivors. Thinking about the magnitude of Nazi concentration camps, Fraser saw reports naming two dozen main camps, with associated subcamps numbering over a thousand. Unlike the tens of thousands of refugees fleeing the ravages of war, these camp survivors could never return to their former locations. East Europeans fleeing west to escape subjugation under Stalin's brutal Soviet dictatorship added thousands more displaced persons unwilling to return to their homeland. An intractable problem confronting the victorious Western Allies.

U.S. Army 2 ½-ton trucks began pulling into the vicinity of the camp kitchen. Long planks set on makeshift trestles became serving tables. Soldiers unloaded tons of crates and barrels. Immediately the emaciated inmates converged on the area. Time for the midday meal. A cool yet mild spring day. All remained orderly, most kept silent.

For these unfortunate retches, life must still look bleak. Stuck in the same cramped barracks, inadequate sanitation and hygiene facilities, dressed in the same stigmatizing uniforms now disintegrated into little more than rags. Their only relief, adequate food and the expectation of medical care. The scope of dealing with these camp survivors seemed insurmountable for an army equipped only for combat.

Fraser and Marchand ate with the inmates. Predominately field rations but a special effort made by certain enterprising army cooks. In makeshift ovens they baked loaves of fresh bread and creatively cooked nourishing soup in the large pots of the former camp kitchen using scavenged vegetables. The eyes of these young American soldiers reflected the anguish of seeing these pathetic victims.

Following the meal, they requisitioned a jeep to tour the main Mauthausen camp and the nearby three principal Gusen camps with Wiesenthal as their guide.

Before setting out, Wiesenthal said, "Before going further afield, let me show you something truly grotesque. Known as the *Stairs of Death*. See there in the distance a wide staircase cut into the hill?"

"Its purpose?" Marchand asked.

"To torture and kill the inmates while providing sport for the guards. Prisoners forced to carry stone blocks weighing as much as 50 kilos up those 186 steps leading to the top of a cliff overlooking a quarry pit. Prisoners already exhausted by twelve hours of hard labor. Sometimes an entire line of prisoners collapsed from the top down with a domino-like effect.

"If the prisoner made it to the top he could either push the fellow in front of him off the cliff or get shot in the head."

Fraser pulled to a stop a short distance from the hill.

Fraser got out and said, "I am going to walk up to get photographs."

Wiesenthal said, "I believe I shall remain here. It is not something I wish to experience."

"Care to come with me, Fiona?"

"I will stay with Herr Wiesenthal."

After Fraser ascended the stairs, Marchand said to Wiesenthal, "I do not fully understand the seemingly contradictory motivations of exterminating prisoners through harsh labor and starvation, yet needing a workforce to produce war materials."

"Nazi efficiency. Accomplish two objectives simultaneously. The supply of fresh victims almost inexhaustible. Extract every ounce of value before discarding in favor of fresh replacements while continuing the genocide of Jews.

"Nazis methods evolved. While starvation and the threat of beatings made camp life a constant risk, the value of specific work skills became increasingly recognized. Labor in the quarries became reserved as punishment for camp infractions. No one survived working the quarries for long."

"Mauthausen operated for years. I assume great numbers of prisoners have died. Where are they buried?"

"That I do not know. Throughout the countryside I imagine. Many perhaps sent off to the extermination camps in Poland in the later years. However, Mauthausen has its own gas chamber and crematorium. When your husband returns I will show you. Camp records reveal the ability to murder 120 people at one time."

Fraser returned with a grim set to his expression. He said only, "Another scene of horror. Let's move on."

Following a tour of the gas chamber and crematoria, they left for the close by three main Gusen camps.

Seated in the passenger seat of the jeep while Fraser drove, Wiesenthal said, "Originally this entire complex of camps provided slave labor for the local quarries. A perfect form of excessively hard forced labor to serve the cause of exterminating the growing inmate population. By the end of the war however, the majority of the 100 camps and subcamps became largely devoted to producing war materials therefore inmate skills became more important."

"How is it you know this history having been here such a short time?" Marchand asked.

"I have been assisting the U.S. Army investigators. Understandably, there is a shortage of those fluent in German. And the Germans kept precise records of everything."

Within minutes, they arrived at designated Gusen I.

"Underneath here are large tunnels, 29,000 square meters of space devoted to small-arms manufacturing. Gusen II has twice that underground space. Just before the war ended, Messerschmitt ran a factory here with the capacity of eventually producing over 1,000 Me262 jet-power fighter aircraft a month. Fortunately, the Nazis were too late. Many companies producing war materials used slave labor from Mauthausen-Gusen."

"Can you provide us with a list including details?" Fraser said. He began to understand the scope of the *Schutzstaffel* economic engine and the origin of funds secreted in the Swiss bank accounts under the control of Manfred Krüger.

"Certainly. I already compiled a report for the American colonel in charge here."

Over the next three days, Fraser and Marchand interviewed a cross section of the various categories of inmates. Ethnicities ranging across Europe, including even Soviet prisoners of war.

Before leaving Mauthausen, Wiesenthal declared to Fraser and Marchand, "I hope to find my beloved Cyla and resume life. The odds do not favor her survival but I shall remain optimistic until I see evidence of her death.

"Regardless if our reuniting comes to pass, we can never again share a normal life. How can any of us? All of us must find reason to continue living. For me, I shall dedicate my life to avenging those that died at the hands of the Nazis."

"Fiona and I share your vision of bringing these criminals to justice. All those in the Nazi *Schutzstaffel* are guilty of war crimes. It is my sincere belief the victorious Allies will bring those Nazi leaders before some tribunal to face accountability. I worry about the thousands of SS that might escape justice. The direct perpetrators of murder and of torture. The concentration camp guards. The roving battalion units of the *Einsatzgruppen*. The *Gestapo* who sent them to the camps. These murders must not remain free."

Wiesenthal nodded. "More than a lifetime of work I fear. However, this exceptional catastrophe of genocide of perhaps millions of Jews cannot be allowed to pass into history as simply a footnote."

"Fiona and I shall soon leave American intelligence. We shall return to our former home in Paris before the end of the year. Before the war, I spent most of my life as a journalist. Like you, I must find a way to continue seeking justice for the victims of the SS. German surrender did not settle the issue of war crimes.

"I believe you also will continue your own struggle to seek justice. We do not yet know our address in Paris since we fled to Switzerland in 1943. However, we do wish to stay in touch with you, Herr Wiesenthal. We can be contacted through the United States embassy in Paris."

Marchand added, "Please write to us with how we can stay in contact with you once you … leave here. Marc and I sincerely hope Cyla has survived. May those odds again favor you, Simon."

Marchand hugged the frail little man, kissing him on both cheeks in the French manner.

Fraser also embraced Wiesenthal. "Fiona and I will never forget. I never mentioned that my mother and her parents were also Jewish."

# CHAPTER 14

TARVISIO, ITALY | MAY 1945

---

Fraser and Marchand prepared to leave Mauthausen-Gusen and its ghosts. The experience of Dachau compounded by Mauthausen and Simon Wiesenthal's recital of his ordeal left a profound impact. Not only shaken, both filled with an enduring anger for the magnitude of Nazi crimes. Fraser took this further as a personal affront to his humanity. Fighting against criminals his entire career, the Holocaust of European Jews cried out for retribution. Forget reliance on formal judicial processes. The Nazi *Schutzstaffel* was a disease.

"How about we take a long way back to Bern?" He said to Fiona. "Before leaving Switzerland, I learned the Jewish Brigade is now in Tarvisio, Italy on the Austrian border. I estimate maybe a six-hour drive.

"I feel compelled to share our experience seeing these camps with my cousin Edmund and Pavel Trakonitz. Not sure why, perhaps just identifying with my Jewish heritage."

Without explaining, he had an ill-defined sense that he must do something to target SS war criminals. He could not ignore the sight of SS barbarity firsthand and knowing SS blood money sat in secret Swiss bank accounts. Compiling a bullshit report about displaced persons as his final task with the OSS meant nothing.

"Fine with me, Marc. I would love to see Edmund and Pavel. All of us can now return to our former lives. Though I doubt any of our lives will be ever the same after our wartime experiences. After what Pavel did to save my life, I do want to keep in touch."

Once recovered from the infection, she shared the details of Pavel looking after her when the Germans attacked the partisans. Staying behind in the San Giustino barn to look after her. Killing the Nazi soldier silently with a knife to keep them hidden.

Fraser put his arm around her waist. "I do as well. We have much to share. They are true friends. I hope all of us can find a measure of joy in renewing our personal lives."

Requisitioning transportation, the Colonel generously provided a confiscated German staff car repainted with the American five-point star on each side. Fraser then sent a message through Army communications to Rothschild informing him of their arrival in Tarvisio in two days.

"After Tarvisio?" Fiona said.

"Take a train to Bern. If necessary we drive to Milan where the trains should be working again."

"Can we wrap up work with the OSS?"

"Better yet, I will wrap things up. I will write the report on our concentration camp inspections. Doubt it will make any impact on decision making in Washington. You resign and return to Paris. Like that?"

She embraced him giving him a long kiss. "I love that."

"I will be along in a few weeks after settling our affairs in Bern."

The following day they set off in the German staff car with a cautionary admonishment from the American colonel, "Watch yourself as you motor south. Although the car has an American star, a soldier might recognize it as a kraut car. This is where we met up with the Red Army coming from the east. This portion of Austria may well fall within the fucking Communist occupation zone once things are sorted out. Be careful."

Located on the borders of Italy, Austria, and Slovenia, Tarvisio is a small picturesque Alpine town situated in a valley at an elevation of 2,500 feet. The British high command posted the Jewish Brigade here as a seemingly backwater location. From its inception, the Jewish Brigade became problematic for the British. Eighth Army Headquarters withdrew the volatile and aggressive Jewish soldiers from the forward lines of the Italian front in the last weeks of the war. Fear of criticism should a Jewish formation suffer heavy causalities in the final stages of war given as the reason.

Resentment among the dedicated soldiers ran high. They accused the High Command of purposely diminishing the contribution of the Jewish Brigade in defeating the Germans.

For these battle-hardened Palestinian Jews, Britain became the new enemy as the obstacle for Zionist aspirations to establish a Jewish homeland. With World War Two ended, their new battleground became Palestine.

Restricting Jewish immigration to Palestine became policy in 1939 with the British government declaration known as the White Paper of 1939. A typical British colonialist-style solution that served only to inflame both Arabs and Jews.

In response to years of Arab revolt, the White Paper limited Jewish immigration to 75,000 over five years. Further immigration becoming subject to Palestinian Arab approval. The policy also added restrictions on the rights of Jews to purchase Arab property. Understandably, both Arabs and Jews rejected the policy.

For the militant Haganah, Britain prevented the most assessable escape route from the anti-Semitic Nazis onslaught across Europe. Pavel Trakonitz therefore cast the blame for the death of countless thousands of Jew during the war years on the British. With the surrender of Germany, there was no reason to believe the British would alter their position. There was surprisingly little compassion for survivors of the Holocaust. Few countries accepted Jewish immigration in significant numbers. Anti-Semitism existed across the globe. With the defeat of Germany, Britain now represented the enemy to Jewish Holocaust survivors and the paramilitary Haganah in Palestine.

The posting to Tarvisio turned out not to be that remote. Not only located at the convergence of three borders, it was a natural gateway for refugees fleeing previously German occupied countries. Territory now under threat of subjugation into Josef Stalin's alternative repressive dictatorship. *Liberation* by undisciplined Soviet Red Army soldiers pillaging and raping across Eastern Europe was often as vicious as the Nazis.

With a two-lane paved highway and rail line through the Brenner Pass, Tarvisio was the natural conduit south through the Alps to liberated Italy now aligned with the victorious Western Allies. Only miles from an Austrian bridge that separated British from Soviet occupation forces, the Jewish Brigade was at the front line of a new uneasy peace.

As Fraser and Marchand motored toward Tarvisio, they passed groups of refugees also headed south. Some with wheeled carts stacked with possessions. Others carrying nothing presented an even more depressing sight. Dressed in filthy clothes and well-worn shoes, all appeared gaunt an exhausted. As Fraser and Marchand drove slowly past, few even turned their heads.

Descending into Tarvisio, they could see the small town now dominated by a large expanse of tents. Drawing closer, they approached a roadblock with a flagpole flying the British Union Jack with a Star of David flag underneath. Despite driving a German staff car, their identifications and orders proved satisfactory. For good measure, a corporal accompanied them to the large headquarters tent.

After a warm welcome by Edmund Rothschild and Pavel Trakonitz and a generous bribe to the clerk, Fraser got a room at one of the two small hotels in town. That evening, they all celebrated together at the hotel restaurant.

"So good to see you have fully recovered, Fiona, No lasting effects I trust?" Rothschild said as they shared a bottle of Scotch.

"None. Doing fine. All thanks to Pavel's heroism."

She reached over and squeezed Trakonitz hand. The tough guy expression melted into a pronounced blush.

"What were you and Fiona doing in the occupation zones?" Rothschild said.

"Our last mission," Fraser said. "We just came from the Mauthausen-Gusen concentration camp complex. Before that Dachau outside Munich. Compiling a report for the OSS on the problem of displaced persons. No intelligence value in the assignment. I believe our boss Allen Dulles is just trying to hold together his team since he has ambitions to head American intelligence in the occupied territories. Not for Fiona and me. We are done with intelligence work.

"The days we spent at each of these sites proved emotionally wrenching. The experience will haunt us forever. Better than attempting to describe these horrors, I have photographs better conveying the indescribable. If I can get developing chemicals, I will show you tomorrow."

Marchand said, "But even with photos you have to experience it firsthand by talking to the survivors to emotionally absorb the horrors of these places."

Fraser said, "Fiona does not exaggerate. Early intelligence reports we read during the war of incorrectly categorized this Nazi genocide as Jewish pogroms. Later came fragmented reports about Nazi concentration camps. Then towards the end, the Soviet reports and photographs as the Red Army liberated the extermination camps in Poland.

"Yet these concentration camps we visited were also extermination camps. Just different from the gas chambers of an Auschwitz. At these forced labor camps, ultimately killing the inmates through brutalized labor and starvation remained the intent, but only after first extracting economic value. Worse than a quick death. It released unchecked sadism difficult to imagine until you confront the aftermath."

Rothschild and Trakonitz remained silent processing what Fraser and Marchand felt inadequate to describe.

Trakonitz in particular had a sense of conditions in the Nazi concentration camps. It was his job to interrogate refugees as they passed through the choke point of Tarvisio. With each recounted horror story, he envisioned the suffering of his parents and sister after he left Prague so many years ago.

Trakonitz said, "We have a photographer with the necessary developing equipment. Tomorrow morning I will enlist his help developing these photographs. I must see what you find so troubling."

Rothschild said, "What will you and Fiona do now, Marc?"

Marchand said, "We shall return home to Paris. I will resume my work at the Louvre and enjoy life once again. Before the war, Marc left journalism to devote himself to writing fiction. A way to take his experiences and make his opinions assessable to a wide range of readers. Yet I sense he intends to pursue remnants of the Nazis SS in some manner."

Fraser nodded. "Fiona is correct. I am an investigative journalist at heart. Feel both the challenge and the obligation to expose criminality. The Nazis certainly fit that label. However, their creation of the *Schutzstaffel* transcends criminality to become institutionalized murder on a mass scale.

"Working within the American OSS, I learned things not generally known about the *Schutzstaffel.* Fearing retribution for their crimes *Waffen-SS* units rarely surrendered like the *Wehrmacht.* Other components of *Schutzstaffel* like the *Gestapo* just melted away into hiding. Like cockroaches, they scurried into dark places. Impossible to eradicate because of their numbers.

"At Yalta, Roosevelt, Churchill, and Stalin agreed to prosecute the Nazis leadership for crimes against humanity. That is likely to happen. Victors execute or imprison the leadership of the defeated. But what of the thousands of SS mass murders and torturers? I guess I still want to play a role in seeing justice meted out to all those SS guilty of murder."

Trakonitz said, "How do you intend to go about that?"

"Not sure I have a good answer, Pavel. However, let me share some insider knowledge with you and Edmund. Classified information so do not repeat it.

"It is generally known that the Swiss financed Nazi Germany throughout the war. Raw materials, food supplies, vital war materials. Concealed under their claim of neutrality by engaging in commerce with both sides of the warring parties. Not only financed, but the Swiss laundered looted treasuries of the countries invaded by the Nazis. The current balances of these secret Swiss bank accounts remain unknown. The Swiss refuse to acknowledge the very existence of these accounts.

"Beyond those disputed funds, there are hundreds of other Nazi Swiss bank accounts. German industrial corporations exporting currency before the fall of the Third Reich. Profits made from selling war materials often produced using slave labor. Looted assets and personal belongings of Jews sent to the camps. Reports even of gold fillings removed from the teeth of those murdered.

"I even have personal knowledge of certain secret SS accounts. The *Schutzstaffel* was a large economic enterprise. They produced goods at their own factories using slave labor and supplied corporations with slave labor for a price. The most senior of the SS leadership have personal Swiss bank accounts of money diverted from already illicit SS profits. Somehow, that cannot be allowed to serve those SS escaping prosecution."

Trakonitz uttered an expletive in Hebrew.

"None of these funds will be recovered. The Swiss simply refuse to cooperate. I know all this because of American intelligence reports. I possess detailed knowledge of certain SS Swiss bank accounts from an asset I ran in Bern. An SS officer trying to save his skin. He allowed me access to all his banking files. The OSS found little intelligence value in these secret SS funds and will likely do nothing."

"Why not go after the Swiss?" Trakonitz said.

"Swiss neutrality makes the standoff complicated. For differing reasons, the U.S. and Britain do not even agree on how to confront the Swiss. Switzerland is vital to postwar European reconstruction, therefore European stability. Everything is now viewed through the lens of the Soviet Union threat."

"What about you, Pavel? What next?" Marchand asked to change the subject.

"Return to Palestine. Someday to become the State of Israel. Probably a career in the Israeli Army. That is all I know. Like Marc, my war is not over. I will help displaced European Jews come to Palestine despite the British position."

Rothschild said, "Although I am British, not Palestinian, I differ with my government's position restricting Jewish immigration. The mass murder of perhaps millions of European Jews changes the imperative for a Jewish state to save those Jews refused immigration by the entire world.

"However, for me, the war is over. I spent five years in Her Majesty's military service, but I am not a career soldier. I shall return to banking."

Wishing to lighten the mood, Rothschild said, "This is bloody marvelous seeing my distant cousin and his beautiful wife. We must remain in contact. London and Paris are not that distant."

Marchand said, "We shall. Now let us enjoy this evening with special friends."

The following morning, Trakonitz connected Fraser with the Brigade photographer. Sergeant Sandor Herczeg looked nothing like a soldier. No more than five foot three inches, prematurely balding, clearly nearsighted wearing glasses with thick-lens, he was soft-spoken, probably in his late forties yet looking older.

Once Fraser described what was on the rolls of films, Herczeg became animated and eager to begin the work. After Fraser explained his photographic training, Herczeg took charge to expedite the developing process using Fraser's help.

As the first images immerged from the developing bath, Herczeg began questioning Fraser on what the camps were like. Like so many in the Brigade, this was deeply personal. He narrowly escaped Hungary before the Nazis invaded sending Jews to concentration camps. Like Trakonitz, he too lost his entire family.

Fraser wanted two sets of each photograph. One set for Trakonitz. The Jewish soldiers of the Brigade should see the visual evidence of what befell the millions of European Jews in the Nazi concentration camps.

Developing took the entire day. Long before completing the work, Fraser could see Herczeg's increasing distress as he looked at the drying enlargements. Even in the glow of the dim red light of the darkroom, Fraser saw his tears.

"What is to happen now?" Herczeg said.

"Let the world see and understand this horror."

"What I meant, what is be done about this? Those that did this must answer for their crimes?"

"I have no answers to those questions, Sandor. Those of us that feel strongly must find ways of taking action. Mankind must attempt to balance the ledger.

"I shall leave one set of these prints with Captain Trakonitz. I trust he will share with the Brigade. I shall see these published throughout the world. There will be many other photographers also capturing images. The world will not be able to deny Nazi crimes."

That evening, Fraser and Marchand joined Pavel Trakonitz at the same Tarvisio restaurant.

"Major Rothschild cannot join us. Called to a senior staff meeting."

"Afraid I could not find any more Scotch," Trakonitz said setting a bottle on the table. "Best I could do was a bottle of Russian vodka. Got it from a Yugoslav partisan passing through here last week."

"You may need it after I show you these disturbing photographs, Pavel. Herczeg and I developed two sets. This set is for you to share with your fellow soldiers."

From a leather satchel, Fraser extracted the bundle of prints enlarged to 8x10. Sorted in some order of visual impact, the image on top was sufficiently jarring.

Trakonitz looked at the hundreds of inmates starring into the camera with vacant expressions. Beyond their untold physical suffering, all of these starving survivors likely suffered the emotional loss of family and friends. Their pasts erased. Suffering unimaginable grief, their futures uncertain and devoid of hope.

For the next twenty minutes, Trakonitz methodically went through the photos, pausing longer as certain images consumed him. Fraser and Marchand could see the subtle facial expressions to the usually stoic Trakonitz. Later he would ask for explanations of what he was seeing, but this first pass was simply to absorb the horror of something beyond comprehension.

Eventually looking up, Trakonitz said nothing, instead pouring a stiff measure of vodka into his glass. Fraser and Marchand did likewise, waiting for him to speak first.

After draining the vodka and several moments of silence, Trakonitz said, "There are no words for this. I cannot let this pass into history without doing something."

"Fiona and I share your feelings. Not clear how any of us can do something meaningful. I can publish these images as others will, but what exactly will that accomplish?"

"That is your job as a journalist, Marc. For me, my thoughts are with the victims. For those surviving the Nazi Final Solution, their only hope remains a new life in Palestine. A new Jewish State of Israel."

Trakonitz chose not to articulate his darker thoughts of seeking revenge on the perpetrators.

"Our thoughts also, Pavel," Marchand said.

The conversation passed back and forth, as they emptied the bottle of vodka. The effects of the alcohol did not lessen their collective distress. In better condition, Marchand ordered a large bowl of spaghetti and bottle of wine trying to deflect the anger of her husband and Trakonitz.

Although they all ate in silence, it had at a calming effect. Marc had not eaten all day and now looked better. Finishing their simple meal, Fraser said, "In my earlier years, I investigated crime and corruption. An obsession to go after bad guys. I have an idea how to do something to strike back at the SS. Something that might help Jewish survivors languishing in displaced persons camps.

"Last night I told you about an intelligence source I cultivated in Bern. A German lawyer. Also a lieutenant colonel in the SS. Obersturmbannführer Manfred Krüger.

"My OSS assignment was to develop German sources useful in postwar counterintelligence against the Soviets. Krüger manages all sorts of funds concealed in secret Swiss bank accounts. SS accounts. You see, Pavel, those terrible images are the evidence of the Nazi Schutzstaffel's economic enterprise."

Trakonitz said, "And you say the Swiss know this?"

"The Swiss are neutral in name only. Throughout the war, they financed the Nazi war machine by laundering looted gold and converting German Reichsmarks into Swiss francs. The Swiss made a lot of money financing the Third Reich. Even the Allies have not been able to penetrate the absolute secrecy of Swiss banking regulations. Goes way beyond these SS funds I am speaking about."

Trakonitz said, "Well the war is over. If the SS has money stashed away in Switzerland, what is your idea?"

"Steal the money. More money than you can imagine. Some of the money in personal bank accounts of SS officials. One of which is Heinrich Himmler. Use the money to finance smuggling Jews into Palestine."

This caught Trakonitz and Marchand off guard.

"What are you talking about, Marc?" Marchand said.

"Well I don't have all the details worked out, but hear me out. First, let me share the circumstances. Herr Krüger believes he is in jeopardy of prosecution for war crimes for his involvement with the SS. Probably true, however I have exaggerated his fears to pressure him to cooperate. Thinks the Americans will force the Swiss to deport him back to Germany to face arrest for war crimes. Loses his comfortable lifestyle, a postwar career in international business services, and his sexy secretary/mistress.

"I have steadily increased the pressure demanding more in the way of cooperation with American intelligence in exchange for no prosecution and to remain in Switzerland. We have developed a relationship. Typical between a source and his control officer. The information provided so far is of relatively useless intelligence value. However, in his desperation he finally showed me his entire file on Nazi SS Swiss bank accounts under his management. Everything. The account numbers, the false account holder names, cross-reference to the actual account holder names or SS section, transactional records, and his power of attorney authorizations. Krüger exercises full control for eleven different bank accounts and a hell of lot of money. I photographed the whole lot."

"Did you turn this material over to the OSS?" Marchand asked, concerned her husband breached his oath to the OSS.

"Of course. But just like these," He said patting the stack of concentration camps photos, "I made a second set."

Trakonitz said, "So American intelligence is going to go after this fellow and confiscate the money."

Fraser shook his head. "It does not work that way. The Swiss will balk, claiming sovereignty and neutrality. Beyond that, the sanctity of Swiss banking laws ensuring absolute secrecy. For years, they have successfully blocked American efforts to give up Third Reich deposits clearly originating with looted treasuries of the countries they invaded. This will be no different. I also believe there is little interest in pursuing this separate issue of secret SS funds. Allen Dulles, the OSS boss in Europe, expressed no enthusiasm when I presented the photographic evidence. It will just go into a diplomatic black hole."

"You cannot be serious about stealing these funds can you, Marc?" Marchand said. "No matter how you plan it, too many people will know."

"I do not think so. We will not withdraw the funds. That would raise red flags with the Swiss banks. Instead, we transfer the funds to other bank accounts under fictitious shell companies then further launder the money through subsequent transactions. Eventually, the money leaks into so many different channels, it becomes an impossible trail to follow."

Trakonitz said, "What about the Americans? Will they not eventually come after the money in these SS accounts?"

Fraser shook his head. "Doubtful U.S. intelligence will know the money is gone. Even if they did, they would encounter the same wall of Swiss banking secrecy. This is not bank robbery. Even if the Swiss suspected anything, by their own secrecy rules it would be difficult to trace. And the Swiss would never admit to a breach of their celebrated banking system through fraud."

"So how do you pull this off, Marc?" Marchand said.

"Like I said, I have not figured that out exactly. Obviously, it centers on Krüger. He receives instructions or acts on a prearranged plan. He alone has the power of attorney to authorize all transactions. They deposit funds in these accounts from German banks including the Reichbank. Krüger then moves funds to other bank accounts, mostly outside Switzerland, all under fictitious business names. Presumably investments, mostly in neutral countries. Countries sympathetic to Fascism. Spain, Portugal, Argentina, and other South American countries. Since these are SS funds, it stands to reason they would find it desirable for future access in places where they could openly operate."

"So you stick a gun to Krüger's head and force him to authorize payments to accounts under your control," Trakonitz offered.

"Not that simple. Leaves an obvious paper trail in neutral Switzerland. What I need is to replace Krüger as the controlling party of these various accounts with power of attorney authorized by the principle account holders. More than that, I need

Krüger to make the handoff in personal meetings with each bank by vouching for my credentials. Cannot expect Krüger to take part in such a charade. He is a respected businessman. Swiss intelligence knows of his SS background, but it has no bearing when it comes to financial commerce and profits."

"The only threat is Krüger's fear of what the Allies will do to him for his SS affiliation. That is why he is cooperating. Tell him if he gives up these SS bank accounts, he gets to stay in Switzerland rather than a prison. He will assume U.S. intelligence is behind this." Trakonitz said.

"Even if Krüger agrees, there is the matter of the power of attorney documentation. I must get personal control to manage these accounts. I have no way to create false documents. This cannot be done if Krüger is still in the picture."

"Do you know what these documents look like?"

"Yes. I have photographs."

"I know someone who can reproduce most any document and any signature."

Fraser leaned forward eagerly. "How do you know he could reproduce what I need?"

"Because I have seen his work. While sitting up here in this mountain pass with no official duties, many of us are finding meaningful alternatives."

"Such as?"

Trakonitz thought for a moment before deciding to reveal more.

"What I am about to say you must not repeat to your cousin Major Rothschild. A fine officer, passionate about the plight of Jews, but still thoroughly British. For many of us, the British are now the enemy.

"We call ourselves TTG. The acronym is an Arabic obscene phrase. We have found it convenient to assist Jewish refugees by issuing false identity papers. Red Cross passports. New names. Backgrounds obscuring their Jewish identities. The ability to relocate most anywhere."

Trakonitz was not completely candid. Select TTG led by Trakonitz also made forays into occupied Austrian territory using fake military orders, passes, requisitions, even British uniforms with unit insignia. Using American and British intelligence information accessed by Trakonitz, they sought SS hiding in Austria. To those located, they delivered summary justice in the form of a bullet to the back of the head.

"You have met my forger, Marc. Sandor Herczeg possesses many skills other than photography. Like me, he is Haganah. Before joining the Brigade, he refined his forgery skills by producing all sorts of documents to confound British authorities in Palestine."

Fraser nodded. "Okay. Then Herczeg produces a set of documents providing me with power of attorney for these accounts. Can he also provide me with a German passport?"

Trakonitz nodded with a smile. "Do you prefer civilian or SS?"

"Civilian will do. Now it is not likely I can just substitute myself in Krüger's place without raising suspicion. Therefore, I become his partner. Part of the deal I make requires him to introduce me personally to the various banks."

"What does Krüger get for his cooperation?" Marchand said.

"The Americans will not pursue him meaning he gets to remain in Switzerland. One of these secret Swiss bank accounts is his. Under a fictitious Swiss business name of course. He gets to keep his blood money. He continues to live a privileged lifestyle and pursue his lucrative business services practice. Life goes forward uninterrupted, including keeping his mistress."

"But you cannot leave it like that, Marc," Marchand said. "He knows your real identity."

"Yes. I know. That is troubling. I cited the above as the inducement for Krüger. He thinks this is an OSS scheme to gain access to the SS funds. Of course I cannot leave it at that."

"The answer is simple," Trakonitz said. "Eliminate Krüger."

"Kill him you mean?" Marchand said.

Fraser responded, "Not necessarily. What about forcing him to go to South America? I tell him the Americans might double cross him and pressure the Swiss to deport him. He upheld his side of the bargain, I feel obligated that we do the same. He will have money and can continue life out of reach of his past."

Trakonitz said, "You are making this too complicated. He is SS scum. Deserves nothing more than a bullet."

Fraser said, "I understand your feelings, Pavel. However, not easily done in Switzerland without raising suspicions. Both the OSS and Swiss intelligence know of my association with Krüger. If I do this, I want no trail leading back to me. Swiss banking secrecy will conceal the subterfuge even from Swiss investigators. Violence complicates that. Better to get Krüger out of Switzerland and out of reach of American intelligence where he cannot do damage."

"Are you ready to do this?" Trakonitz said looking to both Fraser and Marchand.

Fraser looked at Marchand before answering. "Yes. We are both leaving the OSS and returning to Paris. I cannot leave Bern with Krüger controlling millions in secret SS money."

Trakonitz nodded. "Very well. Here is what I suggest. Herczeg will accompany you on your return by train to Bern. He will have real orders, issued by Major Rothschild to deliver these photographs to a Haganah representative waiting in Bern. It is vital these images get to Palestine. Herczeg will then work on creating these powers of attorney documents."

"Why will Rothschild issue such orders?"

"The Major sides with Jewish aspirations for a State of Israel. He knows I am Haganah as are many others in the Brigade. He provides cover for unauthorized TTG actions better left unexplained. "

"Okay. Once I gain control to the Swiss accounts, I empty them into new accounts I create under fictitious business names. I am the principal of these firms based on a fictitious identity backed by French identity papers I used in my activities for the French Resistance. From these accounts, money is then distributed disguised as normal business transactions from these shell companies to fund Jewish refugee relocation. Your part of the operation, Pavel."

"Yes, I see. A very clever plan, Marc. All Sandor needs is to see Krüger's power of attorney documents to create a set with your name. Your fictitious name. He has even developed a technique to duplicate official stamps. A true artist in forgery. Tomorrow we shall begin. I know he can produce the German passport immediately. Everything else he can produce in Switzerland."

# CHAPTER 15

BERN, SWITZERLAND | JUNE 1945

---

Two days after the conversation with Pavel Trakonitz, Fraser, Marchand, and Sandor Herczeg boarded a train heading south from Tarvisio to Udine. From there to Milan, then changing trains again to proceed to Bern. A sixteen-hour journey. To satisfy Herczeg's absence, Major Rothschild armed him with orders reading *to secure photographic intelligence of importance to the British Army Jewish Brigade from an American OSS agent in Switzerland.*

Although Rothschild looked at Fraser's photographs of Dachau and Mauthausen, he understood the subterfuge of Herczeg's mission was a broader Haganah operation. Not the first time he blindly assisted Trakonitz and his TTG group. Best he did not know details in order to establish plausible deniability. He would simply keep the photos until Herczeg's return before making them available to brigade commander Brigadier Benjamin.

Fraser now had a German passport. A genuine Deutsches Reich passport in the name of Otto Albrecht. Nothing more than a well-executed substitution of Fraser's photograph, complete with the black stamp of the Nazi eagle.

"Do I assume there is a real Otto Albrecht?" Fraser asked Herczeg.

"Was. He is dead. But it does not matter since you will not be using it in Germany."

Although a civilian passport, Herczeg did not reveal that Albrecht was also a SS officer executed by the TTG therefore the name likely false.

Saying goodbye at the train station, Edmund Rothschild hugged Fiona and kissed her cheek. Turning to Fraser, "Wonderful meeting a distant relative. I look forward to getting together once I am relieved of this uniform and back at the bank."

"We shall certainly stay in touch, Edmund."

"I purposely do not know the details of what Trakonitz is about, but stay cautious. Pavel certainly is not. An exceptional soldier but a bit of a pirate. Obsessed with creating a State of Israel in Palestine."

Marchand thoughtfully brought along bread, cheese, and sausage for the three of them. Fraser brought along two bottles of wine.

A solitary and somber person, Sandor Herczeg succumbed to Fiona Marchand's charms. Responding to Herczeg's question about her life prior to the war, her recounting of various restoration projects of oil paintings struck a chord with him. As one artist to another, they enthusiastically engaged in discussing the fine details of each other's work.

Well into the journey and after much wine, Marchand asked about how he came to be a forger.

"In Budapest, I had a prosperous jewelry and watch repair business. Having a strong creative side from an early age, photography became a passion. Apprenticing in the jewelry trade, I discovered a new artistic talent. In addition to creating jewelry, I ventured further into creating larger artistic pieces, principally vases, silver, pewter, crystal, which I elaborately engraved.

"Once in Palestine, I needed work. With my language skills, I found a clerical position in the British administration's immigration department. Eventually someone from the Haganah approached me. Too old and too small to be useful with guns, my skills performed an even more important service. Working every day with all sorts of identity papers and with access to British official documents, my various prewar skills naturally combined into creating false documents. Everything imaginable and necessary to wage the struggle against British resistance to Jewish immigration."

Trakonitz told Marchand the story of Herczeg's journey to Palestine. An eight-month trek through the Balkans during winter. Although losing his wife to pneumonia he managed to survive. No different a story from those thousands of survivors of the concentration camps. Childless, his remaining family all lost to the Holocaust. This small bookish man possessed a formidable core of strength.

It was late at night when the train pulled into Bern. Fortunately, a single taxi remained on duty. Arriving at the apartment, Herczeg said, "Please show me these photographs of the documents I am to reproduce."

Marchand went off to prepare the spare bedroom. Fraser retrieved the photos and a large magnifying glass.

After studying the photos for several minutes, Fraser said, "Can you reproduce these?"

"Yes. I would prefer to see the originals. Fine details of the signatures and stamps are lost in the photographs probably owing to inadequate light."

Fraser examined one of the photos. "I was trying to capture the content on a large volume of documents in Krüger's office. I brought a lamp close but I see what you mean. The signatures and the stamps are not all that clear."

"Can you bring me the originals?"

Fraser thought for a minute. "I believe so. How long for you to reproduce these?"

"Two days, three at most. Duplicating the stamps is the most time consuming. I will need to buy proper paper after I see the originals. A good stationery store should have what I need. The other materials I brought with me."

"Very well. I will confront Krüger tomorrow. Fiona will escort you to buy the necessary materials."

Marchand returned to the room. "What does that mean, Marc?"

"Means we are leaving Bern sooner than planned. Once Sandor provides me with the power of attorney documents, I will present my credentials to the various banks accompanied by Krüger. That will take a few days. Except for one bank, the others are in Zürich and Basel.

"Once we ship Krüger off to Argentina from Genoa, I return to Switzerland and set up new Swiss bank accounts in Geneva then empty the SS accounts."

"What if Krüger refuses to cooperate?"

"Then I turn on him. Tell him I have done everything I can to help but he is on his own. He either caves in or stands firm. If he refuses then I tell him I will make it my objective to see him hang. Doubt Krüger has the backbone to risk making an enemy of an OSS agent."

"I understand. Regardless, I am to leave for Paris soon?" Marchand asked realizing what this meant.

"By the end of this week. We both see Allen and submit our resignations. I show him the photographs. The war is over for us. The photographs go to New York for publication. I explain there is no need for our report on displaced persons. The problem is simply overwhelming. Our brief visits to Dachau and Mauthausen cannot begin to describe the problem. Whatever their circumstances, the problem of all displaced persons is the inability to return to the place they came from. This is a humanitarian problem, not something for an intelligences service."

Not told of the entire scope of the operation, Sandor Herczeg asked, "Once these funds leave Switzerland, what happens?"

Fraser and Marchand looked at each other. Marchand was the first to speak. "Pavel did not tell you?"

Herczeg displayed a blank expression.

Fraser said, "Once I empty the Swiss SS accounts to new bank accounts under my control, I become the paymaster to fund TTG operations. Helping Jewish refugees emigrate to Palestine. Pavel said that is what you have been doing in Tarvisio."

Herczeg said, "What about money for weapons to build an Israeli army?"

Fraser nodded. "That too."

"Even if it means using the weapons against the British?"

After pausing for a moment, Fraser said. "The surviving European Jews of the Nazi genocide have no recourse other than Palestine. The British must bend. Unfortunately, violence may become necessary to force that political decision. So yes, the money needs to serve the objective of Jewish resettlement in whatever form necessary."

The next morning, Marchand prepared breakfast. Sandor Herczeg dressed in a civilian suit said, "Even in the dark last night, Bern reminded me of Budapest. Budapest before the war. Different architecture of course, but with the feel of hundreds of years of history."

"Then you shall have a splendid day, Sandor. Fiona will show you about. We live here in the picturesque medieval quarter. Find the materials you will need. As for me, I shall spend an unpleasant day pressuring Manfred Krüger into how he can save his miserable skin."

"I have some important news, Manfred. Goods news. I just returned from London. I shall come to your office first then we will celebrate with a special lunch.

Fraser entered Krüger's office at eleven o'clock. Fräulein Helga looked exceptionally enticing. Fifteen years younger than Krüger. Attractive face, good legs, and large breasts displayed in a tight-fitting blouse exposing cleavage. Helga could pose an obstacle into forcing Krüger to leave Switzerland. Fraser must first find out what Krüger planned for the wife and children in Germany before confronting him with the demand to leave Switzerland.

Once seated in Krüger's office, Fraser launched into his pitch. "Let me get right to it, Manfred. Good news as I told you on the telephone. I attended several meetings discussing the subject of war crimes. Intelligence people from OSS London and British MI6. As expected, former SS officers are chief among their targets for arrest on charges of war crimes. Your high-ranking *kameraden* have not fared well.

"Heinrich Himmler is dead. Captured after trying to pass as a common soldier. Committed suicide with a concealed cyanide capsule. Your boss Oswald Pohl arrested. Ernst Kaltenbrunner and Walter Schellenberg arrested. *Gestapo* chief Heinrich Müller presumed dead after last seen in the Führerbunker the day after Adolf Hitler took his own life.

"Those that participated in the killings in Reinhard Heydrich's *Final Solution* for the Jews are high on the wanted list. Heydrich's protégé Adolf Eichmann, members of the *Einsatzgruppen* mobile execution units, and anyone involved in running the concentration and extermination camps. So the hunt is on, Manfred. Orders exist for the occupying forces to detain any member of the *Schutzstaffel.* Those of officer rank will undoubtedly face prosecution."

Krüger appeared almost physically ill as he weakly uttered, "But you said you have good news for me?"

"That I do. Your name of course came up. The management of secret SS Swiss bank accounts gives you some negotiating strength. I returned to Bern with a banking expert and orders to explore how the Allies might use the information you possess.

"The good news, Manfred, you are not on a target list provided you cooperate."

"Cooperate? How?"

"Easy enough. I need all your files connected with the SS accounts. I have photographic copies but for some reason, they want to have the originals."

Krüger pursed his lips. "Those never leave my possession. It is the foundation from which I conduct business."

Fraser shook his head. "Manfred, you do not understand. All your clients are out of business. You must make other plans. Your most important concern is to survive given your SS past. If the Allies want you, they will easily pressure the Swiss to deport you. They are the victors and if anything, the Swiss are practical."

Krüger breathed deeply with a sigh of uncertainty saying nothing.

"Manfred. There is more. To show good faith, my superiors have agreed to allow you to keep your Swiss bank account. Sufficient resources to maintain your lifestyle while you build new business. The end of the war opens up new investment opportunities throughout the world. The rebuilding process in Europe alone will require state underwritten financing creating a boom in every type of commercial venture. With your international experience, you should have no problem acquiring new clients."

Appearing somewhat relieved, Krüger said, "What are your superiors going to do with these accounts?"

"I do not know. I am just following orders. My guess is to use your files to pressure the Swiss in some way. Switzerland represents a dilemma for the Allies. They resent the role Switzerland played in financing the war for the Nazis. Yet Switzerland is vital to the rebuilding of Europe. The Swiss franc is the strongest currency. I also know there are differing opinions between the Americans, the French, and the British with how to deal with Switzerland. It is complicated.

"Consider yourself lucky, Manfred. These files of yours save you from prison or the hangman. Look what has happened to your high-ranking SS *kameraden.* Likely all will hang."

After reinforcing the danger Krüger faces, Fraser needed to bolster his resolve by expanding on the benefits for cooperating. "Now let us celebrate over a good lunch. Tell Helga she can have the afternoon off. No need for her to become suspicious. If she does not know of your SS background, best it stays that way. Your SS past is a liability for promoting postwar business. After lunch, I will collect the files.

Later that afternoon Fraser carried two boxes containing Krüger's files into the apartment.

Fiona greeted him. "Sandor and I were just having tea. Care to join us?"

"How about some coffee instead. Need to counter the effects of too much wine over lunch."

"How did it go?"

"Difficult, but successful. These are his files. Once he came to terms with the finality of his circumstances and relieved that the Allies will not be coming after him, he saw no choice. I painted a reassuring outlook for his future."

"None of which is true. The Allies might come after him." Marchand said.

"Not if he is in Argentina."

"He agreed to relocate there?"

"I did not yet tell him that part. That comes later. He needs to assimilate this in steps."

"Um," Marchand said in a way implying her discomfort.

"You feel sorry for this piece of Nazi shit, Fiona? Pavel had it right. He deserves a bullet. I am giving him a life he does not deserve."

She laid a hand on his arm. "I know. I just dislike the inherent cruelty even for someone like Krüger."

Sandor Herczeg entered the room. "These are the files? Please show me see the documents I need to duplicate."

Herczeg took the power of attorney documents to the dining table for a closer examination with a magnifying glass. Eleven documents. Five for the personal accounts of ranking SS and six others.

"I can produce new documents with your name easily. I found good quality paper today. There is nothing special about these documents. Just need to duplicate the stamps."

"Excellent. All I need then is Krüger's cooperation to introduce me to the banks. He becomes corroboration to the documents authenticity you will create. From there on, the rigorous and secret Swiss banking system will conceal everything I do to empty these accounts."

Three days later, Fraser telephoned Krüger. "Manfred, I must see you this morning. A matter of some urgency. At your office. I have someone from London with me. I prefer Helga is not there."

With concern in his voice, Krüger said, "Of course. Is something wrong?"

"No. But a change in plans. A necessary arrangement that will ensure avoidance of difficulties with your past. It is a good deal, Manfred. Allows you get on with your life without looking over your shoulder."

Disconnecting the call, Fraser turned to Herczeg. "Up to playing your part as an American OSS agent."

Herczeg nodded. "The troubling part is coming face to face with one of these monsters."

"The real troubling part is that Krüger appears so ordinary. Does not even attempt to justify his involvement as part of the *Schutzstaffel.* I suspect that most SS appear ordinary because they are ordinary. That is the frightening reality. How are thousands of ordinary individuals seduced into committing torture and murder?"

Fraser and Herczeg entered Krüger's outer office. As arranged, Helga was absent.

At the sound of the door opening, Krüger came out of his personal office. "Herr Fraser," extending his hand then turning to Herczeg, "I am Manfred Krüger."

By arrangement, Herczeg did not shake hands or greet Krüger.

"This is Mr. Jones, Manfred. From our headquarters in London."

"Yes. Please come in and be seated. Can I offer you anything?"

Herczeg answered in German, "*Nein,* Herr Krüger. This will not take long. Let me get directly to the point of our visit."

Fraser wanted Herczeg to present the details of what Krüger must do to save himself. This allowed Fraser to play the good cop to Herczeg's bad cop as the voice of American intelligence.

Extracting documents from his briefcase, Herczeg launched into his delivery.

"These are power of attorney documents created to match your originals giving Otto Albrecht equal management authority over the Swiss bank accounts in question. Note the authenticity of the signatures and notarizations.

"Your signature on multiple copies of this document also confirms Otto Albrecht as your partner managing a new branch office in Geneva. As your cover story, you are looking for reconstruction investments in the former occupied countries of Western Europe making Geneva's proximity ideal for travel to the former western occupied countries. Herr Albrecht is fluent in French supporting that cover."

"Albrecht? Who is Otto Albrecht?"

Fraser said, "Manfred. I am Otto Albrecht. Educated in America to account for my accented German," Fraser said and reached into his suit pocket to extract his German passport. "More than that, you must also accompany me to each of these banks to present my credentials and authenticate my position as your partner."

"Under Swiss banking procedures, will that be sufficient, Herr Krüger?" Herczeg said.

Ignoring the question, Krüger responded, "What is to be done with these bank accounts? I have a fiduciary responsibility."

Herczeg slammed his palm down onto Krüger's desk. "Fiduciary responsibilities for stolen money and profits from slave labor? You are fortunate not to be facing the gallows.

"Even allowed to keep your personal Swiss bank account. For that, you have Herr Fraser to thank. Now there shall be no more wrangling. Are you willing to execute transfer of control over these accounts, Herr Krüger?"

Totally deflated, Krüger weakly answered, "Yes."

"Smart choice, Manfred," Fraser said. "Now there is one final matter. I argued against it, but my superiors are insistent."

Krüger's eyes widened with deepening anxiety. His whole world coming apart.

"You must leave Switzerland. In fact, leave Europe," Fraser said.

"No! That is not possible. Where am I to go?"

"Buenos Aires, Argentina."

Herczeg interjected, "Among your own kind. A large German expatriate population. A Fascist state governed by Juan Peron with close ties to Nazi Germany."

Krüger's head slumped forward. "Why must I leave Switzerland?"

"Because you are SS and a Nazi," Herczeg said. "You cannot be trusted. An undesirable. Eventually, the Swiss will deport you to Germany. Not a good ending for you. That means you will face arrest and trial by an American military tribunal. The occupying American Army knows nothing our arrangement with you. We prefer our arrangement remains confidential."

"I must have some time to think this through."

"That is not possible," Herczeg said. "My orders are to execute this immediately or terminate the arrangement. Frankly, I hope you refuse. You should pay for your crimes not rewarded."

Krüger looked at Fraser looking for an avenue of appeal.

"That is the offer, Manfred. Do not be a fool, take it."

Krüger took a deep breath. "Very well. When must we go to the banks?"

"Starting tomorrow. Kaufmann& Huber here in Bern. Make appointments for the following day in Zürich. Vontobell AG, Rahn & Bodmer, and Johann Wehrli. The day after, in Basel with Sturzenegger and Swiss Bank Corporation.

"Two days after that, you leave by train for Genoa, Italy to board a freighter bound for Buenos Aires as a passenger. You will have safe passage to Genoa. Mr. Jones and I will accompany you."

"That does not allow sufficient time."

"If you face arrest you will not be given time to get your affairs in order," Herczeg said. "How much time did Jews have before locked inside cattle cars without food or water for transport to your *Konzentrationslager* camps?"

"Manfred, you simply need to pack your clothing and personal effects. You assign someone to sell your household goods. Your legal services business is portable. I will arrange for your family in Germany to follow once you are settled in Buenos Aires."

"What about, Helga?"

"Let me be frank, Manfred. We are aware that Helga is more than just your secretary. If she is willing to go to Buenos Aires, I can see to that also. However, you must not yet tell her until you have handed over control to me or you threaten everything, including your own life."

Helga remained the problem. Unlikely she would follow Krüger to Buenos Aires. Krüger therefore faced giving up his way of life and sexual companionship with his younger mistress.

Herczeg said, "Now that everything is settled, I require your signatures on these documents. You are signing as a witness to the power of attorney documents. Note these new powers of attorney have the same authorizing signatures of your clients as your originals. These other documents are notarized copies of an affidavit attesting to Otto Albrecht as a partner in your legal services firm of *MK Internationale Dienstleistungen GmbH.*

Having set the stage of the fictional Mr. Jones' antagonism toward Krüger. Herczeg would join Fraser and Krüger on the train trips to Zürich and Basel to reinforce Krüger's position. Today's visit to Kaufmann& Huber would test Krüger's resolve. If all went well, Fraser would take him to lunch and reinforce the bond of controller to his source.

Returning to the apartment mid-afternoon, Fraser kissed Fiona and shook Herczeg hand. "Worked without a hitch. We were there less than an hour. I now have full control over three SS bank accounts."

"Which accounts are these?" Herczeg asked.

"According to Krüger's cross reference, one was the *Reichssicherheitshauptamt,* the Reich Main Security Office, or RSHA. Another named the *Persönlicher Stab Reichsführer-SS Hauptamt,* the Personal Staff of the Reich Leader SS. My guess Himmler's slush fund. The third was Heinrich Himmler's personal account according to Krüger's information.

"All the accounts held in Swiss francs. I assume the other accounts are also in Swiss francs or currencies other than Reichsmarks."

"Why is that, Marc?" Fiona said.

"Because the SS depositors knew for some time that Germany would lose the war. Reichsmarks therefore rendered almost valueless. Just like a fence's commission to buy stolen goods, the Swiss bankers undoubtedly demand an enormous commission to launder the money. They would not take payment for their services in Reichsmarks.

"Most likely the Swiss dealt only in gold or something of known value such as diamonds or art. Remember, the Nazis looted national treasuries and confiscated Jewish wealth. No telling the origin of these SS deposits.

"Even the profits gained from slave labor at the camps must undergo a circuitous transformation before becoming tangible value outside the Third Reich. The SS probably demanded payment from German firms using slave labor in the form of neutral country currencies. Not surprising the reach of the SS given Heinrich Himmler's vast power as Hitler's most trusted subordinate."

"How much money is in just these three accounts?" Herczeg asked.

"Over 11 million Swiss francs. About 2.5 million US dollars."

"*Isten áldjon.* God bless you. That will relocate many survivors of the camps to a new life in the future State of Israel," Herczeg said then embraced both Fraser and Marchand.

"Tomorrow you will join me, Sandor. From my early years in Hollywood, your performance the other day was award winning. Scared the shit out of Krüger. You can reinforce that as we travel to Zürich and Basel should Krüger waver."

Turning to Fiona, "Here is the plan. The schedule is tight. Saturday, Sandor and I will escort Krüger to Genoa by train. I already booked his passage to Buenos Aires. No visa necessary since he has a diplomatic passport. We spend the night in Genoa and ensure Krüger departs Sunday on his ship. Both of us then train to Milan where Sandor returns to Tarvisio and I return to Bern. Tuesday you depart by train for Paris. I will follow after I conclude affairs in Switzerland."

Marchand's eyes brightened." For good, Marc?"

"Yes. Your task is to make our old apartment ready. Repairs? The condition of the furniture? Do whatever necessary to make it our home again."

After the liberation of Paris, Marchand telephoned their apartment building manager. After she and Marc fled France in 1943, the *Gestapo* searched the apartment. Shortly after, a German *Wehrmacht* colonel took up residence. Once he left with the retreating Germans, his French mistress mistakenly stayed on in the apartment before being dragged into the street then stripped to the waist and her long hair sheared down to stubble. Since then, the apartment remained vacant. No telling the condition after eighteen months of neglect.

"While you work on the apartment and arrange to rejoin the staff at the Louvre, I will open new Swiss bank accounts in Geneva then liquidate the SS accounts. The names of the accounts to be fictional legal entities under my control using my alternative wartime false identity. From these new Geneva accounts, I can hold the funds in Swiss francs and draw from them as necessary to fund Pavel's refugee ventures through French bank accounts."

The name Louis Perrault came complete with a French passport Fraser used during his Resistance activities. Money routinely transferred to various corporate-named French bank accounts appears as normal business activity controlled by Monsieur Perrault. The theft of SS funds laundered through layers of channels appearing as normal business transactions. All transactions involving the Swiss accounts concealed from scrutiny under the protection of rigid Swiss banking secrecy. On the French side I construct legitimate business records."

Fraser continued, "Pack for thirty days in case the apartment needs more time for refurbishing. When I return to Bern, I will settle our affairs and ship our remaining personal items to Paris."

She hugged him. "I am so happy, Marc. Finally going home."

The following day, Fraser and Herczeg met Krüger at the train station for the short trip to Zürich. Resigned to his fate, Krüger said nothing once he saw Herczeg.

Before entering the Vontobell bank, Fraser said to Krüger, "You did well yesterday, Manfred. I expect the same today. This is nearly over. Soon you can get on with your life without fear."

"In a backwater like Buenos Aires?"

Herczeg responded, "Consider yourself lucky, Krüger. Others of your SS rank are under arrest or wanted fugitives. They face far worse than a comfortable life in South America. I shall wait here in the lobby."

Less than an hour later, Fraser and Krüger immerged from the office of the bank manager and collected Herczeg waiting in the lobby.

"Went as planned," Fraser said to Herczeg. "The manager made little reference to the Germans losing the war. More interested in how the changed circumstances might affect the business enterprises of Krüger's clients.

"You see, Manfred, not that difficult."

After lunch came Rahn & Bodmer. Again everything went smoothly. The manager congratulating Krüger and his new partner Otto Albrecht on looking toward new opportunities once this disastrous war ends.

Johann Wehrli & Company proved a different experience. Johann Wehrli came from a prominent German family, forming the bank in 1920. In semi-retirement during WWII, he left operations in the hands of longtime employee Karl Kessler, a fervent Swiss Nazi.

"A most unfortunate outcome for Germany," Kessler began after introductions. "Adolf Hitler accomplished so much to restore Germany economically following the Great War. Unfortunately, his political ambitions and lack of military skills proved disastrous. Difficult times ahead for your German clients, Herr Krüger. Fortunate to have someone with your understanding of international commerce and finance managing their business interests from Switzerland.

Krüger responded, "Yes. All Germans must look to the future. Yet the problems are so vast. Every major German city reduced to rubble. German industry and infrastructure destroyed. That is why Herr Albrecht has joined the firm as I look for opportunities to help in Germany's recovery. Please provide Herr Kessler with your credentials, Otto."

Fraser said, "Born in Germany, I grew up in the United States. Took a degree in economics. However, my father lost his professorship during the Great Depression and returned to Munich. I entered law school and took a political interest in National Socialism. I spent the war years working in the Reich Economics Ministry."

"I believe Otto will bring new capabilities to *MK Internationale Dienstleistungen*. He will manage our new branch office in Geneva."

Fraser said, "We must look beyond the disaster to the many economic opportunities offered by the reconstruction of Europe."

"Financing will come largely from the United States and Switzerland," Krüger said.

Kessler said, "You must also find new clients I should think, Herr Krüger. Your two accounts have ceased any transactions since Germany's surrender. I hope they can regroup.

"As to the Americans, unlike the British they think differently than Europeans. Their resources and wealth make them feel superior. A country run by Jews. They have exerted continuing pressure on the Swiss banking system to turn over deposits they claim stem from German looting of national treasuries. They even demand Switzerland deliver deposits not even ours to compensate the Jews. Compensation for what? To finance a Jewish resurgence now that their influence is removed from Europe?"

The visits the following day to Sturzenegger Bank and Swiss Bank Corporation in Basel went off without any hitches. On returning to Bern, Fraser turned to Krüger as they walked out of the train station. "The day after tomorrow, Saturday, Manfred. Eight o'clock in the morning at your apartment. You will be ready?"

Unhappily, Krüger replied, "Yes."

"Limit yourself to no more than three bags. Tell Helga an unexpected business trip. You can take care of affairs once relocated."

"We shall uphold our side of the bargain provided you leave Switzerland. Do not be foolish and change your mind. You will not get a second chance," Herczeg said.

# CHAPTER 16

BERN, SWITZERLAND | JUNE 1945

---

Saturday morning Fraser, Marchand, and Herczeg breakfasted on coffee and croissants. Today would complete the elaborate deception to steal SS deposits with Swiss banks. Once Manfred Krüger left Europe, he could do no harm. He could not risk contacting Swiss authorities. He was party to the fraud. His professional stature in Switzerland destroyed. Now wanted for war crimes by the Americans. Trapped in Switzerland until American intelligence persuaded the Swiss to give him up.

"There are 26 million Swiss francs now under our control," Fraser said. "When you return to Italy, tell Pavel to contact me through this number. An old neighbor and our building manager, Claude Bellamy and his wife Annette. They will contact us since we are staying at a hotel until our old apartment is ready.

"We shall be in Paris and much closer to the Brigade's new posting in northwestern Germany. These funds should finance whatever schemes he and the TTG plan. I shall act as paymaster. Transactions will be disguised to appear normal commercial payments."

Marchand hugged Herczeg. "I hope to see you and Pavel soon. I never liked this crazy plan of Marc's but now that we have come this far, it feels right to do something meaningful to help many Jewish victims."

Fraser drove his car to Krüger's address. He would leave it at the train station for his return tomorrow evening.

He never visited Krüger at his home. Could not stomach the idea of taking the relationship with Krüger that far. The three-story townhouse in the best neighborhood overlooking the river was no more than a mile from Allen Dulles' residence.

Both Fraser and Herczeg went to the front door. They rang the doorbell and stood outside for over a minute without a response. Fraser knocked on the door then rang the bell again. Concern spread over his face. Had Krüger decided to make a run for it?

Herczeg became agitated. "I will try the rear door."

Herczeg had taken only a few steps when the front door opened. There stood Krüger dressed as if going to the office.

"Ready, Manfred?" Fraser said with relief.

Krüger turned without saying a word and walked into his study. A magnificent room with expensive wood panel and bookshelves very much like his office. The furniture and appointments all high quality. Little wonder Krüger struggled to reconcile giving up his stylish urbane lifestyle in cosmopolitan Switzerland for the unknowns in remote Buenos Aires. He did not even speak Spanish.

Abruptly Krüger sat down in a leather chair. "I am not leaving, Fraser. I have considered everything. I shall take my risks staying here. According to you, the Swiss know of my background and yet have done nothing toward me since the war ended weeks ago. I doubt the Americans have sufficient leverage to pressure the Swiss. The Swiss are pragmatic. They shall be at the center of European reconstruction financing. As I will also. I am a respected businessman. A client that brings them profits."

Dumbfounded, Fraser realized he badly miscalculated. Too great a risk to make a move on the bank accounts while Krüger remained in Switzerland.

Standing next to Fraser, Sandor Herczeg came to the same conclusion. Trakonitz preferred a different solution and prepared Herczeg with alternative instructions and the means to carry them out if dictated by circumstances.

Herczeg did not hesitate. Thinking of the photographs of victims of Dachau and Mauthausen steeled his resolve. Reaching inside his suit coat to the rear of his waist, he extracted a compact Beretta .38 pistol.

Krüger's eyes widened as the small man took several steps coming close enough to put the barrel of the pistol tightly against his chest over the heart.

"You think you can ..." Krüger said before cut off in mid-sentence as Herczeg fired a single bullet into his heart.

Stunned by Herczeg's unexpected act, Fraser's immediate concern was the sound. Although muffled by discharging against Krüger's chest, it still sounded loud.

"Why the fuck did you do that for?"

The small man stood with his arms at his side still holding the gun while staring at Krüger exhale his final breath. Trying to calm himself, Herczeg said nothing.

"Shit!" Fraser took the gun from his hand and sat him in a chair. "Just sit there until I think of what to do. Sonofabitch!"

Checking for a pulse with two fingers to Krüger's neck confirmed he was dead. Although despising what Krüger represented, he was not prepared to kill him. However, suffering no remorse for Krüger, Fraser turned his thoughts to adapting to the changed circumstances.

In his early days in Los Angeles, Fraser had been to several murder scenes as a reporter. First thing, search and see if Krüger left anything that could incriminate him.

As he searched Krüger's desk, Herczeg said, "Make this look like a suicide."

"What?"

Herczeg got up, repeating, "Make it look like suicide. I shot him with the gun against his chest. That is how I would shot myself. Give me back my gun."

Fraser looked over at Herczeg emotionally recovered from having just killed Krüger.

Handing Herczeg the pistol, "Did Pavel order you to kill Krüger?"

"Only if you were successful in the deception with the banks and Krüger threatened the mission. Pavel never trusted your idea to send him to Argentina. If Krüger remained in Switzerland, he might do something foolish to ruin the plan."

Subduing his anger over Herczeg's unexpected action, Fraser understood it resolved the problem. To hell with Krüger. His arrogant stupidity cost him his life. A more fitting ending as a war criminal than escape to Argentina.

The new problem became liquidating the SS accounts before discovery of Krüger's death undoubtedly resulting in a police investigation.

Herczeg took the gun and wiped off his prints with a handkerchief. He then placed it in Krüger's right hand now resting in his lap. Blood slowly seeped from the wound soaking Krüger's white shirt and trousers.

"Place the ship passage ticket in a desk drawer. Look for anything that ties Krüger to the *Schutzstaffel*. Also something written in his own hand with a sample of his signature. I will draft a suicide note. It will include his Swiss bank account number. Since we cannot access it, the money might as well go to his wife. The expected gesture of someone committing suicide."

After an hour, Herczeg completed his forged suicide note. A short letter to his wife provided not only a sample of his handwriting, but added weight to the suicide note. Fraser also found Krüger's SS identification showing his rank with a photo in uniform.

Herczeg handed Fraser the note addressed to Krüger's wife.

*Dearest Adele,*

*Events have conspired against me leaving me no way to continue any sort of happy life. The Americans discovered by affiliation with the Schutzstaffel. At the time of joining, it became necessary to advance my career. I never participated in the terrible crimes attributed to the SS. Nonetheless, American agents have pressured me to spy against the Fatherland, threatening me with arrest for war crimes after Germany loses the war. I cooperated by providing information on my business dealings for the Third Reich. They now have no need of me and look only to take retribution on all Schutzstaffel officers.*

*With the war over, I expect any day for Swiss authorities to arrest and deport me to Germany under American occupation. Considering my important position in the Schutzstaffel, that means life in prison or possibly a worse fate. With the Allies victorious, the Swiss will likely yield to American pressure. Others have advised me to flee to Argentina. I went so far as to book passage.*

*I now realize I cannot do that, Adele. Cannot envision a life in such an alien place. What would I do? I cannot expect you to move to a place so foreign. What sort of life for our girls?*

*This is the only way out. I leave you with financial resources in the form a Swiss numbered bank account. Details are enclosed. Kiss the girls for me. Think fondly of our life together yet look to your future, Adele.*

*With deepest affection,*

*Manfred*

Fraser read the letter. "Nothing more to do here. Just hope no one saw us entering or sees us leaving."

While Herczeg created the suicide note, Fraser searched everything in Krüger's office and bedroom for anything else that might prove useful. Fortunately, Krüger possessed a second set of house keys. This allowed locking the deadbolt after leaving to reinforce the suicide scenario for the police investigation.

The surprise return of her husband and recounting the shooting of Krüger unsettled Marchand. Her initial concerns over this venture proving well founded, she now worried about the risk to her husband. This was no longer war. Krüger might be guilty of war crimes, but Marc was now an accessory to murder under Swiss law.

That the otherwise quiet Herczeg was capable of such violence came as a surprise. Yet the war changed everyone, including her. Every Jew in the world must feel the effect of history's greatest pogrom. Why should Sandor Herczeg not kill Krüger?

Absorbed in thought, Herczeg said nothing and took a seat in the living area, letting Fraser explain what came next.

"What now, Marc?"

"I go to Geneva to open new Swiss bank accounts. Fictitious French firms with Louis Perrault exercising control authority. You remember my alternative identity I used in the Resistance. The passport produced in London by the Free French is somewhat beat up from our ordeal in the waters of Lake Geneva, but good enough until I get a replacement in Paris. Sandor will draft the necessary paperwork. Not difficult since the Swiss do not scrutinize depositor's identities."

"Why the additional false name?" She said.

"Overly cautious. I do not totally trust Swiss banks therefore, I will avoid using my real name. Should they violate their own secrecy rules and compare names, then the names Perrault and Albrecht further obscure the trail. I liquidate the SS accounts by transferring to other Swiss bank accounts in Geneva. I use Swiss banking secrecy just like the SS to hide the money.

"Once back in Paris, I will create shell companies with bank accounts under my control, under my real name. I then transfer funds from the Swiss accounts to the new French accounts as needed, disguising the deposits as Swiss financing for the shell companies should they ever come under French scrutiny.

"From these accounts we fund Trakonitz's refugee operations. The entire money trail is obscured by fictitious names crossing sovereign boundaries and relying on Swiss banking secrecy as the ultimate safeguard."

Marchand said. "I think I follow. So when do you leave for Geneva?"

"Tomorrow by train. I want us out of Switzerland as quickly as possible. The following day, I go to Zürich. Execute the fund transfers to the new Geneva accounts. From there to Basel to do the same, and then return to Bern.

"We then leave Switzerland together for Paris. Three days from today. Since we are leaving together, we shall drive. We shall need a car in Paris.

"Think you can take care of that, Fiona?"

"Of course. Tomorrow."

"Good. With a car we can pack all our belongings. Also settle the rent with the leasing agent."

Fraser turned to Herczeg. "Did you get all that, Sandor?"

Herczeg merely nodded. "Can you produce these power of attorney documents today?"

"Yes. Just provide me the account names you wish to use. I will use the same notary stamps as for the Krüger documents.

"I believe I will return to Tarvisio tomorrow. Trakonitz will want a detailed report which I can only deliver in person."

To avoid suspicion, Fraser opened five separate accounts at different Geneva banks. Three of those with branches of banks already holding SS deposits. He appreciated the irony of cheating the Swiss right under their noses.

Marchand came to terms with her conflicted emotions. Although harboring concerns over Marc's bold scheme to steal SS money, its success presented them a perfect way to take part in helping Jewish survivors of Nazi genocide. The world was not going to help.

As for the killing of Krüger, why should that be troubling? An SS official managing profits from slave labor and stolen wealth of Jewish victims. What kind of a sentence for his crimes was appropriate? Considering millions of murdered Jews, a death sentence seemed fitting.

Returning to Paris and her artistic work would restore her after these years fighting Nazis. Yet it could never be the same as before the German occupation. Too many violent experiences. She would shape a more normal life around her art career, but one also embracing an active social purpose.

Given this opportunity, she must do her part to help victims of the Nazis Holocaust. Using illicit Nazi SS money seemed a righteous effort. Leaving it for remnants of the SS to access or remaining unclaimed and defaulting to Swiss bankers, dishonored Nazi victims.

Fraser's mission to Geneva proved uneventful. Opening accounts with a modest initial deposit of 5,000 Swiss francs each, about $1,000 USD, involved nothing more than filling out paperwork and providing identification to a clerk.

Somewhat different as he moved funds from the eleven SS accounts, leaving only token balances. In each case, the bank manager inquired if anything was wrong with the Bank's services.

Fraser delivered his rehearsed explanation to the question. "Not at all. MK Internationale remains most satisfied with your services. The transfer of funds simply represents payment into an account managed by a foreign investment firm. Our German client has suffered considerably as you can well imagine. Reichsmarks now valueless. Losses of capital equipment and inventories due to Allied bombing leaves recovery of German operations in question.

"While our client hopes for reconstruction financing, that is uncertain. Therefore, our client must creatively use its cash reserves in Swiss francs to sustain financial solvency. As these foreign investments return profits, they shall return here to your bank. Both our client and the foreign investment firm understand that deposit funds must remain in Swiss francs as the only currently stable European currency making your future services invaluable."

At Basel, Switzerland, Fraser and Marchand drove across the border into France. With over 500 kilometers to Paris, they decided to break up the journey. Both in great spirits having pulled off the audacious scheme to steal SS funds, they would stop for the night to break up the trip.

As Fraser drove, Marchand searched a Michelin Guide for a suitable place.

"Here is lovely place. Langres. An old fortified town in the Champagne region."

"Okay. Maybe it did not suffer destruction during the war."

"Even if it did, I am in the mood to celebrate. We are home in France, Marc. We also have had little time together in the last several weeks. I miss you if you understand my meaning."

Fraser grinned broadly and placed his hand on her thigh. "I understand perfectly."

Langres proved a delightfully scenic place. Unscarred by the war, they found a small hotel. Their comfortable room provided a picturesque view of vineyards in the valley below.

However, pleasure of a more carnal nature dominated their thoughts. After a quick wash in the toilet down the hall, Fraser returned to the room to find Fiona naked on the bed, propped on one elbow. She also delighted in watching her husband undress, aroused by the prospect of lovemaking. His full erection as he removed his underwear, elicited a smile from her as she beckoned him into bed.

As she caressed his erection, "I should capture this in oil sometime."

"Takes a long time to paint. You will have to find ways of sustaining my state of arousal."

"Like this perhaps?"

❖ ❖ ❖

Their first destination on arriving in Paris was their former apartment. As they drove down the Boulevard Saint-Germain on the Left Bank of the River Seine, they took in the familiar sights and feel of Paris. Turning southwest onto Rue Du Four, it became Rue De Sèvres then further on, Rue de Babylone. Turning right onto Rue Vaneau, they pulled in front of their apartment building at No. 27.

"Still looks the same. Hope the German officer left it in decent shape," Marchand said.

Pressing the buzzer to Claude Bellamy's flat, the older man exclaimed excitedly, "Monsieur Fraser, you have returned? And your lovely wife?"

As the outer door unlocked, Fraser said, "Right here by my side."

Bellamy and his wife Annette opened their first floor apartment door to embrace them with the customary kisses to each cheek. In their sixties, the Bellamys appeared aged with the ordeals of the years of German occupation.

"You must tell us what happened these last two years," Annette Bellamy said. "We feared the worse. However, I am sure you are anxious to see your apartment first.

"You will be pleasantly surprised. Needs a thorough cleaning, but nothing is damaged. We removed all the food once the German and his woman left. Claude and I check on everything every week. Come we will show you."

Except for no electricity or gas, the apartment was in remarkably good shape. After a thorough cleaning, immediately habitable. Even their books in the study remained undisturbed.

Both stood gazing out the windows that faced opposite from the street. Not only quiet, it afforded a view of trees and a large green area. The reason Fraser selected the apartment years ago in the heart of the 7th Arrondissement. Ideally located in the center of Paris on the Left Bank yet close enough to the Seine for Fiona to walk to the Louvre on the Right Bank.

They would spend a week at the Hôtel de Varenne a short distance away on Rue de Bourgogne while Marchand made the apartment ready. Fraser used the time to set up the last piece of the conduit to access the SS money as required to finance Trakonitz's smuggling of Jews into Palestine.

That night they treated the Bellamys to a fine dinner. A celebration for all.

Fraser's first order of business was to put his personal affairs in order by reopening his former bank Paris bank account and funding it by transferring funds from his U.S. account in New York. An all-day task. A year since the liberation of France, administrative functions in every aspect of everyday life still experienced rough spots after the years of German occupation. Yet the mundane process of reconnecting their daily life made him feel he was home.

The following day, Fraser met with different attorneys to set up three limited liability shell companies. Services required by Trakonitz and his TTG to smuggle Jewish displaced persons into Palestine likely centered on transportation. Accordingly, he created Logistique Maritime Internationale, Courtage en Services de Transportation, and Service d'Expédition.

Three days later he opened bank accounts at separate banks using newly acquired French tax identification numbers for the three companies. The accounts opened with minimum deposits arranged by the transfer of funds from the Geneva Swiss accounts under his control, converted into French francs.

# CHAPTER 17

TARVISIO, ITALY | JUNE 1945

---

Anxious to hear what happened, Trakonitz met Sandor Herczeg at the train station on his return to Tarvisio.

"What happened?" Trakonitz said.

"Fraser now has the necessary paperwork to access the SS bank accounts. He will proceed immediately. His plan calls for emptying the SS accounts into new Swiss bank accounts in Geneva under a false French name he used during the war. He and Fiona will then leave for Paris. There he will open French bank accounts under the names of shell companies."

"Why so complicated?"

"Fraser wants to both hide the money trail and optimize the resources. Says it is best to hold the funds in stable Swiss francs and convert to more volatile French francs or other currencies as needed. Not sure I followed everything, but he intends to arrange it such that you can exercise control over expenditures as needed."

"Pavel, we have access to 26 million Swiss francs."

Trakonitz expressed surprise. "Extraordinary. We shall make good use of the SS blood money. Now what about Krüger?"

Herczeg looked Trakonitz in the eye. "I shot him. He is dead."

"What happened?"

"He refused to leave Switzerland. I followed your orders. You made it clear not to allow him to jeopardize the mission. We made it appear a suicide. The evidence completely credible."

Placing his hand on Herczeg's shoulder, "I am impressed, Sandor. You are not a man of violence. It must have been difficult."

Herczeg made no reply.

"Violence has its place. While you were away, I led a recon team to this Mauthausen concentration camp. On Brigadier Benjamin's orders after Major Rothschild told him of his conversation with OSS agent Fraser. I chose TTG members to accompany me.

"Much worse than any pictures. Surrounding the main camp and the other three large camps known as Gusen I, II, and III, there are scores of satellite camps. Spread all over Austria. Nothing to do with war, Sandor. Constructed simply for exterminating Jews."

Once inside the staff car, Trakonitz confided, "For the last several weeks I have led a small group to deliver justice on these murderers."

Herczeg turned to look at Trakonitz.

"I avoided telling you since I did not know if you would agree. Perhaps I was wrong. Using intelligence reports, we locate former SS hiding among the population. Imagine the hundreds of guards running all these camps. They all went underground to hide their pasts."

"Once you locate them, what happens?" Herczeg asked, knowing the answer.

"Take them from their places of hiding and deliver a bullet to the head."

"How many have received such justice?"

"A great many. However, it is not possible to deliver justice on any meaningful percentage of the thousands of Nazi criminals. Yet it serves a purpose. No longer will Jews passively tolerate persecution. Let those perpetrators of this genocide feel the constant fear of our retribution."

"Now we need your expert services to forge orders, passes, and requisitions to carry on something of much greater importance. The reason you went to Switzerland."

"Smuggling Jewish survivors into Palestine?"

"Exactly. We visited several Jewish displaced persons camps on our return from Mauthausen. Thousands needing help. Jews still confined, waiting for the world to decide what to do with them. We must continue the effort to free them. Financed with the SS money, we can now do more.

"We still must not ignore these criminals within our grasp. Most will never be arrested and put on trial. As Fraser pointed out, simply too many of them. The world must understand Jews will kill their oppressors rather than ever again go quietly to their deaths."

Trakonitz realized his violent vendetta against Nazi SS represented an emotional imperative. Like himself, his TTG group was not willing to accept the loss of family to state-sponsored murder without taking revenge. He realized this hunt for Nazi SS was unsustainable, yet it provided some measure of outlet for his consuming hatred.

Not long after the Brigade's posting to Tarvisio, Trakonitz became friendly with American Army intelligence units working in Northern Italy as well as the American occupied sector of Austria. The Americans also recruited large numbers of displaced Jewish volunteers to assist in administration. The volunteers eagerly shared gathered intelligence files with these Jewish soldiers. They identified large numbers of SS probably hiding in Austria and northern Italy, often with links to relatives in the area. Always meticulous organizationally, the Nazi SS left extensive personnel staff records in their haste to evacuate many of the concentration camps. A defeated German populace was not anxious to assist Allied occupation forces. SS fugitives found ample sympathy from which to disappear into the population.

Practical suggestions included examining for blood group tattoos beneath the armpit of SS. Look for men too healthy, especially if overweight. Find a relative and coerce them. Catch a lower ranked SS and coerce by barter for giving up someone more important.

Trakonitz was a master at interrogation. From his years in service of the Haganah before the war, he fabricated endless stories to talk his way out of threatening situations in Palestine before the war. He knew how to lie therefore he knew what to look for. Hesitancy in answering a question, an ingratiating smile, a story too well composed and sounding memorized. As circumstances dictated, he could change his persona from empathetic to unemotionally terrifying.

This investigative activity to look for former SS did not originate as orders. Nor was it directed by Trakonitz superior, Major Rothschild as head of Brigade intelligence. However, Rothschild unofficially encouraged the effort. From the onset, there was the question of what to do with the information. Fraser's words of concern about the inability to arrest and try the many thousands of SS haunted him. Trakonitz chose the most direct course of action.

Forming a specialized unit, he intended to inflict summary justice on as many SS they could locate within striking distance from Tarvisio.

The initial group consisted of a dozen soldiers. Half were Haganah. All chosen from his battle-hardened reconnaissance company. Men he believed motivated enough to embark on this brutal work.

In a secluded grove of trees some distance from the Brigade encampment, he addressed the group after nightfall.

"I brought you here to explain a new mission. A strictly volunteer mission. Unofficial. Could result in disciplinary action if caught. I ask only for your oath to tell no one of this if you decline to participate. I shall also understand should anyone decline. What I have in mind is distasteful."

Looking around, none of the men said anything.

"Very well. What I propose is to go after former SS. Most worked at concentration and extermination camps in Austria. They are now hiding among the population."

One man said, "Once we find them, then what?"

"Execute them for crimes against the Jewish people."

None of the men said anything but several looked to their colleagues to gauge their reaction.

"We do this in uniform without orders. I have assigned a name for our unit. Among ourselves, we are *Tilhas Teezee Gesheften,* the acronym TTG. A composite expression of Arabic, Yiddish, and Hebrew slang. *You lick my ass business* in English. Anyone not willing to participate must now choose."

The man speaking earlier smiled.

It began in earnest with the interrogation of a *Wehrmacht* surgeon working at the local hospital. Paroled from a prisoner of war detention center near Tarvisio, someone looking to save his own skin reported him. Trakonitz conducted the interrogation.

After two hours, the surgeon confessed to allowing several SS to hide in his ward. Trakonitz already knew that. The doctor eventually confessed to assisting in their escape south into Italy as Austrian displaced persons with Red Cross passports. Like criminals the world over, he sought to strike a bargain in exchange for giving up more important criminals.

The doctor told of two SS camp guards he helped relating to him a story of a former *Gestapo* agent living in the town of Villach, Austria just over the border. The SS guards resented the *Gestapo* agent. Each week the agent picked up bags of confiscated money and jewelry from newly arrived Jews. Part of a collection circuit of many other camps. As these SS tried to escape arrest and prison, the *Gestapo* agent settled into a comfortable postwar life with his wife using a new identity, undoubtedly keeping much of the stolen Jewish wealth. The SS camp guards shared the *Gestapo* agent's new identity with the doctor.

Late one night, Trakonitz and two of the TTG knocked on the door of the provided address, a well-kept house on the outskirts of a small Austrian town. "Open up. British military intelligence."

A bleary-eyed man of fifty answered the door in a robe and pajamas. A jowly round face and ten kilos overweight suggested he did not miss many meals.

"What is this about? Do you know what time it is?"

Trakonitz pushed the man back into the house. The two well-armed soldiers followed, closing the door.

"You are under arrest."

"By what authority?"

"*Ich bin Jude,*" Trakonitz said pointing to the Star of David insignia on his shoulder.

The *Gestapo* agent turned pale and sat down in resignation.

"Where is your wife?"

"Upstairs."

Trakonitz motioned for one of his men to bring her down.

She came down the stairs glaring at the British soldiers and their Star of David insignia. A slender woman with a pinched face, displaying an expression of contempt and defiance.

With the couple seated, Trakonitz began the interrogation while his men began searching the house. He must verify the man was *Gestapo,* therefore they must find corroborating evidence. SS identification and this alleged stash of stolen Jewish jewelry.

The woman remained silent while the man continued to protest any association with official Germany. He was Austrian. He managed an insurance company in Vienna before moving to this second home owned by his family after Vienna suffered repeated bombings.

Too well rehearsed. After two hours, Trakonitz ended his questions. All this time, his men conducted a thorough search upstairs. Descending the stairs shaking their heads, In Hebrew, one soldier said. "Nothing incriminating in the office. We checked for false floorboards and wall panels"

Trakonitz said to the couple, "Move to the large room with the fireplace."

A massive fireplace of natural fieldstone dominated one wall of the room. The inside of the fireplace suitably blackened, but clean of ashes. Not unusual for summer. Three large logs sat on the two-meter long grate, ready for winter.

Trakonitz said to the soldiers, "Move the logs and check the fireplace floor stones."

While his men worked to remove the logs and the heavy cast iron grate, Trakonitz watched the couple. He caught the otherwise aloof wife casting furtive glances at the fireplace.

The soldiers squatted down examining the blackened joints, even probing with bayonets. "Looks normal, Sir."

To one of the soldiers, Trakonitz said, "Bring a large pot of water from the kitchen."

When the solder returned, "Pour the water into the fireplace."

Trakonitz walked over and looked down. The water drained away rapidly at the corner of one of the flooring stones.

The two soldiers understood. Using a bayonet to lift one corner while the other soldier levered the stone up with a poker, the heavy stone tilted to the back of the fireplace. Reaching down, Trakonitz lifted out a canvas satchel followed by another.

Inside the bags was a fortune in jewelry, loose diamonds, gold coins, and assorted currency.

Trakonitz grabbed the *Gestapo* agent by the throat pressing his Webley revolver against his chest while forcing him against the wall.

"Piotr, bring the woman over here."

"Please do not kill us! We are nothing," The man said. "I can give you names. Important SS officers."

"What good are names?" Trakonitz pulled back the hammer on the revolver. He intended to kill both of these Nazis. Perhaps right here. "This is to avenge Jewish blood."

"More than just names. I have records. *Gestapo* dossiers on SS personnel running the camps. Photographs. Addresses of relatives."

"Where is this information?"

"If I give you these names, you will not kill us?"

"Depends on the usefulness of the information."

Trakonitz looked at the loot of Jewish victims. Most now dead. Unless this SS pig produced something unusual, Trakonitz intended to execute him and his wife. His hatred ran high looking at tangible evidence of mass murder of Jews.

Accompanied by a soldier, the man brought down files hidden among piles of old magazines in the attic.

"This is what you have to offer?" Trakonitz said examining the *Gestapo* files.

"No. There is more. I know where many of these men are hiding. Here in Austria."

For four hours, the man complied page after page on his typewriter of specific information on specific duties of these SS and their current whereabouts. A remarkable memory if the information proved accurate.

As dawn broke, Trakonitz said. "We shall check some of these locations. If the men you name are not where you say, we will comeback. If you try to run, we will make it known you have informed on your SS kameraden to the Jews. Either way you and your wife will die.

"You will also continue to spy for us. Every week I expect new information."

Over the following weeks, Trakonitz's execution squads roamed across Austria, even crossing into U.S. and Soviet occupation zones. Now armed with false orders created by Herczeg and false requisitions for vehicles, gas, and gear, they ventured out to do their grisly work.

What struck this group of executioners was the pathetic nature of these once arrogant SS. Frightened men mouthing the repetitive excuse of soldiers just following orders. All the executioners lost loved ones to these murderers. Yet dispatching these pathetically ordinary appearing murderers as most fell to their knees crying and begging for their lives, took an emotional toll on the executioners.

Such were the final minutes of the *Gestapo* agent and his wife. Trakonitz saw the man's name posted on a wanted list distributed by the intelligence unit. He could not allow others to capture and interrogate him. The man served his purpose but now must pay the price for sending thousands of Jews to their deaths. His wife equally guilty of hording wealth stolen from the dead. Dragged from their house at gunpoint by two TTG wearing military police insignia, the couple did not struggle, retaining some hope after assisting these Jews.

The jeep drove only a quarter mile before pulling down a path into a stand of trees. Trakonitz was waiting. Suspecting what this was about, the *Gestapo* agent launched into a plea not to kill his wife.

"In the name of your Jewish victims, I sentence you both to death," Trakonitz said then shot both of them. After falling to the ground, he shot each in the head to finalize the executions.

Recognizing the increasing emotional toll on the TTG, Trakonitz conducted these executions as quickly as possible. Where possible, he delivered the bullet. Remove the accused from his home to a place out of sight and dispatch him with a bullet to the back of the head without preamble or warning. He alone seemed immune to the distress felt by his TTG colleagues.

He understood the process could never end. At best, a symbolic gesture. However transitory, he still felt satisfaction of Jews delivering justice to mass murderers.

Yet finding ways to relocate Jewish refugees to Palestine must become the principal purpose of the TTG. Redirect their anger to rescuing Jews while building a Jewish nation. The British restricting Jewish immigration to Palestine now became the enemy. With Fraser's theft of SS funds, they had financial means. In Palestine, Haganah also needed weapons. Eventually to defend against the Arabs, but first to bloody the British lion standing in the way of establishing the State of Israel.

While still part of the British Army, *requisitioning* small arms, grenades, and even mortars became possible. Before the Brigade relocated to the Rhineland, best to steal as much ordinance as possible from British stores while still in Italy. Sandor Herczeg's skills as a forger proved invaluable. The TTG infiltrated every aspect of the Jewish Brigade, so Herczeg had sources to provide official forms and stamps.

Generally, there was unofficial acceptance throughout the Brigade for the TTG's activities to assist Jewish displaced persons. Most of the officers, even those British-born, disagreed with British policy of restricting Jewish immigration to Palestine. Some even went so far as to express support of militant Zionist violent resistance to British Mandate rule.

Unconfirmed rumors eventually circulated of suspicious killings, missing weapons from British armories, and unaccounted numbers of missing Jewish displaced persons. The irregularities invariably implicated the Jewish Brigade. Never liking the political motivated establishment of a Jewish Brigade, British Army High Command chose to remove them from the more contentious Mediterranean theater.

None of this lessened TTG efforts to kill as many SS hiding in Austria as possible. Once the Brigade transferred to the Rhineland sector of Germany, those opportunities would end.

On 29 July, five thousand soldiers of the Jewish Brigade departed Tarvisio in six hundred lorries for the long journey across Austria and Germany to the British occupation sector in the Rhineland of northwestern Germany. The two-week journey proved an emotional experience for Jewish soldiers to be in the belly of the Nazi Fatherland. It was not without incident. Unavoidable confrontations occurred as anti-Semitic symbols or shouts from German civilians provoked violent responses from the Jewish soldiers.

# CHAPTER 18

MADRID, SPAIN | AUGUST 1945

---

Within a large estate surrounded by a wall located to the southwest of central Madrid just across the River Manzanares, two Germans sat in the richly appointed study. A former Catholic monastery, abandoned during the years of siege of Madrid by Nationalist rebel forces, restored and renovated with modern conveniences. This location near the southern corner of the vast park of Casa de Campo, a former royal hunting preserve, sat at the front lines during the years of the Spanish Civil War of 1936-1939.

As the capital, Madrid was the stronghold of the Republican government and the target of repeated assaults by Nationalist rebel forces commanded by General Francisco Franco. Adding to the Fascist Spanish Nationalist forces, Adolf Hitler provided German bombers to give Franco superior air power over Republican forces, and Mussolini provided ground troops. Following Nazi Germany's surrender in 1945, the ruling Franco regime made neutral Spain a safe haven for Nazis wishing to remain in Europe.

"What happened in Switzerland, Walkenhorst?"

"I do not yet know, Sir. According to Rothmund, the circumstances indicate Manfred Krüger committed suicide. Found at his home. Left a suicide note explaining American intelligence threatened him to act as a spy during the last few months or face postwar consequences for his SS service. When the war ended, he feared deportation from Switzerland and arrest for war crimes."

Heinrich Rothmund was the Swiss chief of police and ardent Nazi sympathizer.

The man questioning Walkenhorst was Henrich Möller, a former official of the Reichbank. A well-constructed false identity. His real identity was Heinrich Müller, former *SS-Gruppenführer* und *Generalleutnant der Polizei* of the *Geheime Staatspolizei*, the Nazi Secret State Police, abbreviated *Gestapo*. Only a few SS in Spain knew his real identity. Even the Spanish government knew him as Möller.

"It is essential we determine what happen to these accounts, Walkenhorst," Müller said. "Have our Swiss bankers changed sides? Violated their own secrecy laws? Or is this something else?"

"Other SS Swiss accounts not managed by Krüger remain unaffected, Sir. Perhaps this is an American intelligence operation?"

"Possibly an elaborate theft? Whatever the answer, it involved Krüger's complicity. You knew him. What is your opinion?"

Franz Walkenhorst was a former officer of the SS Main Economic and Administrative Office and Krüger's colleague. Abbreviated SS-WVHA, this was the sector responsible for SS finances, procurement, and business enterprises. Under the direction of their boss Oswald Pohl, only Walkenhorst, Krüger and a handful of others knew details of vast SS funds moved to Swiss bank accounts.

"Did not know him well, Sir. Might have been scared enough of what might happen to him if returned to Germany to face Allied arrest for war crimes."

Walkenhorst did not know that among the Swiss bank accounts in question, several were personal accounts of SS elite. Müller of course knew of those personal accounts, his included, because as chief of the *Gestapo* there was little he did not know. While concealing his personal financial loss, he intended to find out what happened.

"Yet multiple *Schutzstaffel* bank accounts are now emptied. Did the Americans do this, or was Krüger in league with others? Did some enterprising staffer at the *SS-Wirtschafts-und Verwaltungshauptamt* find the means to enrich himself? That is what you are to determine, Walkenhorst. Leave for Switzerland tomorrow. Take Voigt and Gerhardt."

"Yes, Sir."

Heinrich Müller did not project an imposing physical presence. Small in stature, with a rather dower face and thin lips, he usually appeared reserved with a guarded expression. Most notable were piercing gray-blue eyes conveying little expression other than menace.

While an ardent supporter of the Nazi regime, this was not from any ideological motivation. From an early career as a police officer, Müller joined the SS in 1934. In 1936 after Heydrich became head of the *Gestapo,* Müller became his operations chief. It was not until 1939 that he joined the Nazi Party, solely out of personal ambition as the necessary means for advancement.

His organizational skills and devotion to duty accompanied by a workaholic capacity for work brought him to the attention of Reinhard Heydrich, number-two in the SS hierarchy. Heydrich sought such functionaries like Müller, committed to their work and justifying any means to achieving success. Clever and ruthless, Müller was perfectly suited to secret police work and rose quickly in rank.

During the *Kristallnacht* Jewish pogrom of 9-10 November 1938, Müller ordered the arrest of between 20,000-30,000 Jews. During the summer of 1939, he created a centrally organized agency to deal with the eventual forced emigration of German Jews. After declaration of war, emigration ceased as a solution to the *Jewish problem,* evolving into the industrialized genocide of the extermination camps.

In September 1939, after *Gestapo* and other police organizations consolidated under Heydrich into the Reich Main Security Office, the RSHA. Müller continued his rise becoming chief of the RSHA Amt IV, the *Gestapo.*

His first high profile accomplishment was to create the false-flag covert action that was to act as the pretext for the invasion of Poland in 1939. Müller collected condemned men from concentration camps then dressed them as Polish saboteurs under the promise of gaining their freedom. Staged to support the fiction of Polish attacks on German positions, the combatants were actually Nazi SS dressed in Polish uniforms. First given lethal injections, the SS then shot the duped camp inmates leaving them as evidence of Polish aggression.

On that fabricated pretext, Germany then invaded Poland. This latest gamble by Adolf Hitler to seize new territory without serious consequences however failed. Two days later, the United Kingdom and France declared war on Germany.

Following Heydrich's assassination in 1942, Müller assumed command of the *Gestapo* reporting directly to Ernst Kaltenbrunner but remained closely involved with SS chief Heinrich Himmler.

In January 1942, he attended the Wannsee Conference at which Heydrich briefed senior officials from a number of government departments of the *Final Solution* for extermination of Jews. Once the conference concluded, Müller, Heydrich, and Eichmann remained to work on planning.

Müller played a leading role in the detection and suppression of all forms of resistance to the Nazi regime. Trusted by both Heydrich and Himmler, Müller was the organizational force in making the *Gestapo* the principal governmental organ of Nazi terror. No other Nazi war criminal bears greater direct responsibility for the Holocaust than Heinrich Müller.

After the assassination attempt against Adolf Hitler on 20 July 1944, Müller took charge of the arrest and interrogation of all those suspected of involvement in the resistance. Arresting 5,000 and executing 200, brought him into Hitler's narrowed circle of trusted subordinates.

Knowing the end was inevitable, Hitler refused to attempt escape from the *Führerbunker* even with his personal pilot standing by. He clung instead to the delusion that he still possessed the capacity to exercise authority as the Führer. This included ordering nonexistent armies to rescue Berlin, to seeking revenge.

During the last days of the war, Hitler dismissed Hermann Göring as head of the Luftwaffe, replacing him with Generaloberst Robert Ritter von Greim. Greim and his mistress the famous female test pilot Hanna Reitsch flew into embattled Berlin. Reitsch successfully landed on an improvised airstrip in the Tiergarten near the Brandenburg Gate to meet Hitler in the *Führerbunker*.

Feeling not only betrayed by longtime kamerad Hermann Göring, Hitler also discovered his principal henchman Heinrich Himmler engaging in unauthorized negotiations with the Western Allies. Enraged, Hitler replaced Himmler with Heinrich Müller thereby placing him in control over all elements of the Reich security apparatus. All was lost as Hitler descended deeper into psychosis.

A second aircraft followed Reitsch into Berlin on her the perilous flight. The situation however deteriorated over the next 48 hours as Soviet forces tightened the encirclement around central Berlin. The ability to fly out now was in serious question.

Neither General Greim nor Hanna Reitsch recognized the man in the unassuming black civilian suit and fedora. Hitler personally gave cyanide capsules to each of them. All three then hurriedly made their way up the stairs out of the Führerbunker.

At two o'clock in the morning of the 29 April, Reitsch at the controls of single engine *Arado Ar 96* trainer took off with General Greim from the same makeshift airstrip. With Müller at the controls of a *Fieseler Fi 156 Storch* reconnaissance aircraft, he followed her immediately climbing his slower aircraft into the night air.

The second aircraft was Müller's idea. As desperate as it seemed, better than using the cyanide capsule. He did not intend to risk capture by the Red Army. If successful, there were no witnesses to his escape from the Führerbunker. More importantly, he now inherited the mantel directly from Adolf Hitler to lead the remnants of the Nazis cause.

The *Storch* was a much slower but quieter aircraft than Reitsch's aircraft. It also possessed an extraordinary low stall speed of only 50kmph. Useful for making a landing in some field or back road if he successfully evaded Red Army small arms ground fire. With simple controls, he hoped it would more closely approximate the feel of earlier aircraft he piloted during the last year of the Great War. As an accomplished pilot serving with an artillery-spotting unit, Müller received several decorations for bravery including the Iron Cross 1st and 2nd class. Even after all these years, his concerns were not about his ability to pilot the aircraft but more about just getting off the ground.

Dressed as a civilian in a black suit, Müller possessed a unique false identification as a Roman Catholic priest. In addition to a German passport in a false name, he also possessed an official Vatican passport. If he could land successfully without being seen he would change into a clerical shirt and reverse collar of a Catholic priest, and become Father Hans Metzger, a member of the German Papal Nuncio's staff.

Although false, the identification was a genuine Vatican document secured through a sympathetic and virulent anti-communist bishop of the Church. If he successfully escaped the Führerbunker and evaded the Red Army, there was a fair chance he could make his way to Switzerland. From there to Spain where a year earlier he made arrangements as German defeat became certain. If captured, there was still the cyanide capsule in reserve. Better than a hangman's rope.

The small-engine reconnaissance aircraft made little noise. Flying very low at night should make it difficult for Red Army soldiers to direct accurate fire in the dark. Once in the air, Müller immediately turned southeast on a heading 90 degrees different to the noisier aircraft piloted by Reitsch. He hoped her plane might draw fire away from him. If he made it out of the Red Army encirclement, the next challenge became finding a suitable landing site.

Once beyond the encirclement of the Red Army, moonlight provided sufficient illumination for Müller to set the plane down gently in a field southwest of Berlin. Studying the latest intelligence maps, he determined a gap between the Red Army lines and the advancing American Army, north of Leipzig. Best not to fly over the American lines in daylight with American domination of the air. Land short in the path of advancing American forces if possible.

He made a rough but successful landing with the slow aircraft in a field with dawn breaking. With all identification disposed of in the ruins of Berlin after leaving the Führerbunker, Heinrich Müller became Father Hans Metzger. He walked southeast until he came to a road clogged with refugees fleeing Berlin.

Hitler committed suicide in the Führerbunker two days later in the afternoon of April 30th. Reports of Müller last seen in the Führerbunker on the following day proved mistaken in the confusion and recollections of others captured in the Führerbunker by the Red Army. No one ever mentioned a second plane departing, or a man in civilian dress. The capture of another SS general named Heinrich Müller elsewhere added to conflicting accounts.

Although traveling under false papers as Spanish nationals, there was a degree of risk for the three SS officers. No problem in their sanctuary in the sympathetic Spanish Franco regime or neutral Switzerland, however to reach Switzerland meant traveling through France or Italy.

Entering Switzerland presented no problem since they also possessed Swiss residency visas provided by Police Chief Heinrich Rothmund, their first point of contact.

Although Rothmund was anti-Semitic and pro-fascist, that was not universally the norm among Swiss officials. For example, Swiss intelligence generally favored bias toward the Western Allies. The reality however mixed, often according to individual views. As with any country, it was about Swiss national interests. For this reason, Rothmund chose to meet these Nazis in the restaurant of their hotel.

While Walkenhorst was the senior officer in charge, it was the former *Gestapo* agent Ulrich Voigt who questioned Rothmund.

After Rothmund explained the results of the investigation, Voigt said, "And your investigators are convinced this was suicide rather than murder?"

Rothmund appeared slightly surprised. "Yes. Absolutely."

"And this suicide note? You are positive Krüger wrote it?"

"Yes. There were extensive writing samples for forensic comparison."

"The gun was Krüger's?"

"No way to confirm that. He lived alone. The only other occasional visitor was his secretary and mistress. My people questioned her intensively."

Walkenhorst said. "Krüger's suicide note stated American intelligence was threatening him. Did the mistress know something about that?"

"Not really since she claimed learning of Krüger's affiliation with the *Schutzstaffel* only when told the reason he took his own life. However, Swiss intelligence was well aware of American OSS agents' activities, including frequent contact by an agent named Marc Fraser. The secretary-mistress confirmed that Krüger often lunched with Fraser."

"Do you have a photograph of this Fraser?" Voigt asked.

"I can arrange to provide you with that from his Swiss residency file."

"He still lives here?"

"No. He and his wife left Bern after the war ended. According to their immigration file, they lived in Paris before the war. Fraser is also a French citizen. Likely they returned there."

"They left before Krüger took his life?"

"I cannot verify the chronology of that precisely. We never questioned Fraser since he left Bern before discovering Krüger's body. However, medical people say Krüger was dead many days before the discovery of his body. The mistress said he told her he was leaving on a business trip."

"From your questions, gentlemen, are you speculating his death was possibly not suicide? Is there a reason you suspect murder?"

Walkenhorst answered, "Krüger possessed sensitive materials that I am not authorized to discuss. Materials of great value to the Allies. The shooting war may have ended yet the struggle against the underlying threat of Jewish Communism remains unresolved. I am told you share our sentiments along those lines Herr Rothmund."

Rothmund nodded in agreement. Walkenhorst had no intention of revealing their investigation of stolen SS assets from secret Swiss bank accounts. That would only complicate matters. To preserve their pretext of concern over sensitive materials, they asked permission to examine Krüger's residence and office.

"I will send a car and one of my officers to accompany you. The officer will also provide you with a photo of this American OSS agent Fraser.

After conducting the search and finding nothing of interest, and rid of the Swiss police officer, Voigt said to Walkenhorst and Gerhardt, "This search was enlightening."

Both men looked at Voigt with a quizzical expression, Voigt said, "Do you not think it odd finding no banking records in the large safe? Seems obvious someone took them. Someone in league with Krüger or American intelligence."

Walkenhorst said, "Possibly even the Swiss authorities. Perhaps they discovered someone violating their sacred banking secrecy. A scandal that could cost Swiss banking incalculable losses with client confidence. Perhaps Herr Rothmund was not entirely candid with us."

"Possibly. Everything comes down to how someone circumvented Swiss banking protocols. Whether the Swiss know something is amiss, unlikely they will be cooperative if we raise the subject. This is your area of expertise Herr Walkenhorst," Voigt said. "Any suggestions?"

"If any of the Swiss banks involved might prove helpful, it might be Johann Wehrli & Company in Zürich. Krüger once spoke to me about the managing director, Karl Kessler. A good friend to the Third Reich. Krüger learned that Hermann Göring began using them for his personal finances long before the *Schutzstaffel* began exporting assets to Switzerland."

Helmut Gerhardt spoke for the first time. This was within his particular expertise as a counterintelligence professional. Finding ways of turning sources. Money and fear being the preferred leverage. "Perhaps the financial threat of exposing his bank's lax security? A claim for restitution if not satisfactorily resolved. A major scandal ruining him personally?"

Speaking to Walkenhorst, "You understand banking protocols and the jargon. You also came armed with separate identification as the lawyer representing each of these clients. Voigt and I shall be private investigators. We should pay a visit to Herr Kessler in Zürich."

Traveling by train to Zürich two days later, the three SS arranged a meeting with managing director Karl Kessler of Johann Wehrli & Company. On the telephone, Walkenhorst stated he was an attorney representing a depositor of the bank. The issue involved certain *unexplained irregularities.* An alarmed Kessler pressed for more details however, Walkenhorst stated the information was sensitive and required discussion only in person.

"Let me get to the heart of the matter, Herr Kessler. Globale Unternehmen GmbH holds deposit account no. 345571324 at your bank. Is that correct?" Walkenhorst said.

"I am afraid I cannot discuss an account except with the account holder or a legally authorized representative."

"Of course. I believe this should satisfy my stature, Herr Kessler." Walkenhorst extracted a document from his leather portfolio. "As you see, I am corporate counsel for Globale Unternehmen GmbH, duly authorized to transact corporate business. Headquartered now in Madrid, Spain for obvious reasons following the occupation of the Fatherland. Therefore, the Spanish notary. Is that satisfactory?"

Looking at the document, Kessler said, "Yes, I believe that sufficiently establishes your credentials, Herr Weber. Now please, what are these irregularities you spoke about?"

Weber was the name on Walkenhorst's Spanish passport. Voigt and Gerhardt also possessed Spanish passports, all courtesy of Generalissimo Franco.

"My associates are investigators retained by Globale Unternehmen. They have many questions. However, let me explain the problem. In attempting to make a large transaction recently, your bank informed us there were insufficient funds to honor the transaction. We initiated the transfer of funds through our Madrid bank then received the reply from your bank a week ago.

"Normally we would conduct such business directly through our authorized agent in Bern, an attorney by the name of Manfred Krüger. Unfortunately, Herr Krüger died unexpectedly."

Kessler shook his head. "I am aware of his death from reports in the newspaper. I knew Herr Krüger for several years when he came to Switzerland to establish his legal services firm. In fact I met with him here just weeks ago with one of his associates.

"The newspaper cited the cause of death as suicide. I found that unusual since I knew Manfred Krüger. He did not seem the type to take his own life. The newspaper gave no reason. I even contacted the police but they refused to comment beyond the press release."

Gerhardt took over. "Frankly, there are questions concerning Krüger's death according to Swiss police. Considering the unauthorized removal of the majority of funds in the account at your bank, you can understand why we suspect wrongdoing."

"Unauthorized? You mean stolen?" Kessler said nearly coming out of his seat.

"There seems no other explanation, Herr Kessler." Gerhardt said.

"Are you suggesting the Bank might be involved?" Kessler said.

"We hope no one at your bank is implicated. However, I am sure you understand why we are here," Gerhardt said. "Herr Kessler. Let me reassure you. We have no reason to believe any of your staff are complicit. In exchange for your full cooperation in our investigation, we shall keep your name and that of Johann Wehrli & Company confidential. We understand the damage such a scandal would cause to business."

"Yes, of course. I understand completely. I shall do all …"

Gerhardt interrupted, "You just mentioned that Krüger was recently here with another person?"

"Yes. A new colleague with his firm. I believe his name was Albrecht. Let me check the account records."

As Kessler was about to ring the intercom for his secretary, Gerhardt handed him the photograph of Fraser. "Do you recognize this man?"

Kessler took the photo and responded immediately, "Yes. That is Herr Albrecht."

"What was the nature of your meeting with Krüger and Albrecht?"

Kessler's bearing sank as he grasped what took place. "Krüger introduced Albrecht as his new associate. Setting up a branch office of Kruger's firm MK Internationale Dienstleistungen GmbH in Geneva."

"And the purpose of their visit?"

Kessler sighed realizing he was the victim of some sort of fraud. "Krüger presented a notarized corporate document vesting Otto Albrecht with the same power of attorney authority under which Krüger conducted business for Globale Unternehmen.

"How did Krüger seem during this meeting, Herr Kessler?"

"Now that I think about it, he seemed unusually reserved. I would characterize Krüger as normally friendly, even gregarious." Pausing, he continued, "I believe I see where this is going, gentlemen. Let me examine the recent account transactions.

After the secretary brought the account file from the vault, Kessler said, "As I feared, Herr Albrecht was the one initiating the transfer of the major portion of the account balance to Altermatt Genève SA in Geneva. Perhaps Albrecht simply moved your funds to this bank closer to his base of operation. Yet he has not informed you?"

Walkenhorst replied, "Unfortunately not. However, I was not even aware that Krüger acquired an associate in which we invested power of attorney. With the chaos since the surrender, communications with Germany are unreliable. It may be that Herr Albrecht does not know to communicate to our Madrid offices rather than Munich.

"The problem seems to now be in our hands, Herr Kessler. We have no cause to believe your bank did anything irregular. Perhaps there is a logical explanation for the movement of our funds resulting from the upheaval in Germany."

Outside the bank, Gerhardt asked Walkenhorst, "Now to Geneva?"

Walkenhorst shook his head. "No point. That Swiss bank will not reveal anything. Kessler did reveal the account number. To do so would be a serious violation of Swiss banking law causing Kessler an even a greater problem. Even revealing the name of the bank was a violation. Depositor secrecy is sacrosanct to Swiss banking. They care nothing about the origin of money they receive in deposits. Without the account number, we have no stature at Altermatt Genève. Kessler only cooperated as much as he did because he was scared of a scandal."

"What about the other bank accounts emptied by this American Fraser?" Voigt asked.

"Unlikely they would be as helpful as Kessler. What more is there to learn? Fraser obviously did the same at these other banks. The question remains, was Fraser acting as an agent for American intelligence, or engineering theft? Fraser had Krüger killed after gaining control of the bank accounts.

"We return to Madrid. Fraser is the key. He is no longer in Switzerland according to Rothmund. The *Kameraden* must track him down."

# CHAPTER 19

## BELGIUM & OCCUPIED GERMANY | SEPTEMBER 1945

---

The apartment on Rue Vaneau took little more than a week to refurbish. A good cleaning put everything back into good order. The view overlooking the green area offered both quiet and a tranquil atmosphere. Even during the winter, the snow on the barren trees set a tranquil scene.

During the week at the hotel between activities to make the apartment ready, he and Fiona took time to relax. The first time in years. With Paris liberated over a year ago, life in the City of Light returned quickly to prewar vibrancy. The principle change was the return of bustling cafés and restaurants. Stocks of food finally returned to a semblance of adequacy. Following liberation in June 1944, Paris continued to suffered severe food shortages until the end of the war. The French rail system sustained extensive damage before the German retreat back across their border hampering food distribution. However, by the end of summer 1945, wines, cheeses, and French cuisine once again became the center of Parisian daily life.

The political situation remained in a state of flux. With the demise of the wartime discredited collaborative Vichy French government, General Charles de Gaulle's provisional government struggled to regain stability. Unorganized random acts of vengeance for collaboration with the German occupiers resulted in the execution of thousands of French citizens. Although the provisional government soon curtailed vigilante justice, official pursuit of collaborators eventually led to thousands more judicially ordered executions.

Yet to Fraser and Marchand, Paris felt like a return to home. Days after moving into the apartment Trakonitz telephoned.

"The Brigade is now relocated. Headquartered in Brussels but spread out from Eastern Belgium to the German Rhineland. The British high command believes they have removed us from assisting Jewish displaced persons from our former location closer to the Eastern Mediterranean. However, there are just as many displaced persons camps here in Germany as in Italy and Austria."

"Things are set on this end. Can you come to Paris to work out the details?" Fraser said.

"Yes. I will be there in three days. Major Rothschild has prepared my orders. Told me to give you and Fiona his fondest regards. Says he commends your assistance to help these unfortunate people."

"Does he know what we are about, Pavel?"

"Not everything. He knows of our efforts to get Jewish camp survivors to Palestine back in Tarvisio. I am sure he suspected what else the TTG was about but never confronted me. Now relocated, he has agreed to assist where he can. As head of Brigade intelligence and my superior, that is very useful. Allows me freedom of movement to organize efforts and even cross into the American zone.

"As to our source of funding, Rothschild believes the Haganah provides financial resources from American Jewish organizations. You contribute by laundering the source of the money then secretly distributing the money to purchase services and supplies. No need for him to know the real origin of the money."

"Very good. My cousin seems an honorable chap but he may have trouble reconciling stealing SS money from Swiss banks no matter the cause. After all, he is a British banker."

"Much less condoning killing Krüger," Trakonitz added.

The curator of the Louvre was thrilled to have Marchand return to her former position. As for Fraser, he resigned from Hearst Publications by telegram weeks ago. Since Hearst's avowed sympathy for Franco's fascist rebellion in the Spanish Civil War, Fraser severed the relationship in 1937. His reassociation with Hearst in 1943 became just a useful cover and source of income until the war ended.

There was talk within the print media of war crimes trials of the Nazi leadership. The idea that remnants of the Nazi SS possibly remained functional in neutral countries presented a personal challenge. He might perhaps seek a position with La Monde or one of the international news services to cover the proceedings. The idea of Nazis escaping justice offended his sensibilities. What particularly haunted him was the specter of sadistic monsters like Klaus Barbie remaining free. Barbie remained his personal demon. He regretted his failed attempts to kill Barbie. He could never rest until Barbie paid for his crimes. Barbie was emblematic of the underlying disease represented by the Nazi SS.

Aiding Trakonitz in rescuing Jewish refugees by smuggling them into Palestine did not satisfy Fraser's sense of vengeance toward the Nazis. Covering the trials was a start. A basis from which to justify asking uncomfortable questions and gaining information from proximity to the prosecutors. Information perhaps useful for exposing fugitive SS. This is how he started his journalism career. Exposing criminals. What originally brought him to Europe to witness the early stages of what became Adolf Hitler's twelve-year reign of madness.

When Trakonitz arrived at the apartment days later, he immediately wanted to launch into the plans for his first rescue. Marchand insisted they go to dinner first.

Trakonitz could not contain himself. After Fraser poured him a glass of wine at a good restaurant in the 7th arrondissement, he said, "We will smuggle 300 people out of a displaced persons camps. Transport them by lorry to Marseille. From there by ship to Palestine."

"Marseille? Are you serious, Pavel? "Marchand said. "The French are not going to let you do that. They will know what you are planning. France will not want to get involved with contributing to an international incident with the British."

"They will not know they are Jews."

"That is ridiculous. How do you hide 300 refugees travelling through France?" Fraser said.

"The only real danger is crossing the border into France. We are British soldiers relocating German POWs to a camp in North Africa. According to my fake orders."

"So they look inside the lorries and see refugees."

"In the rear of the lorries are men that could pass as POWs."

"Once in Marseille, then what?"

"We hire a small freighter. It is waiting for immediate boarding when we arrive. Bound for Tripoli."

"How do you offload the refugees in Palestine without the British seizing the ship?"

"The freighter runs without lights to evade the British naval blockade. If successful, we ferry the refugees to shore at a deserted sector of coastline using small local fishing boats. The Haganah stations people strategically and communicates by code with one of my people on board the freighter to identify an unpatrolled location. Once on shore, they will transport the refugees to various kibbutzes. Absorbed into the Jewish agricultural community."

Fraser and Marchand looked at each other.

"Marc, Fiona, what option do we have? Where is the risk? If we fail, these Jews are no worse off than the disgusting camps currently housing them. Apart from adequate food, the sanitation and medical services are appalling. Many are dying.

"If the British capture them, it means just another camp. If they make it far enough, Cyprus usually according to my information. Not only closer to Palestine but now they become a larger problem for the British."

"You are bound to do this aren't you, Pavel?"

Trakonitz nodded.

"Very well. We shall enjoy a good dinner and get down to work. I will show you how we pay for all this. Where to lease a fleet of lorries not to mention finding a ship will take some doing," Fraser said.

"I can manage that. Did that sort of thing in Italy."

"How are you going to sneak three hundred people out of these camps? I assume the British guard them?" Marchand said.

Trakonitz smiled. "That is the easy part. Done it many times when posted in Tarvisio. The camps are usually makeshift with few guards. Create a diversion. A fight breaks out or a fire in the kitchen facility. The guards are preoccupied while inmates escape through holes cut in any perimeter fence to waiting lorries. Inmate counts only roughly verified. Bad as these places are, they do not run with the efficiently of a Nazi concentration camp."

With Trakonitz spending the night at the apartment, they stayed up late. Over cognac, Fraser explained how to make use of the SS money.

Handing Trakonitz three small boxes, Fraser said, "These are business cards. All with different names and different companies."

As Trakonitz examined the cards, Fraser continued, "All French incorporated companies with proper French tax identification numbers. Logistique Maritime Internationale, Courtage en Services de Transportation, and Service d'Expédition. Names suggesting shipping or logistics services.

"Different names for you, two with vaguely German names, one Italian. Both languages you speak and it goes to explaining your position with a French company. One side of the card in French, the reverse side in either German or Italian. You can claim to be German, perhaps Belgian, or Italian. Not sure where you are going to operate.

"The titles on the card are suitably vague. I also have printed purchase orders for each firm. You simply sign and give the supplier a purchase order. If a bribe or something else illegal, just pay in cash. Here is a starting amount of French francs, British pounds, and American dollars. When you need more, wire me and I will arrange a transfer to a bank of your choosing.

"On this end, I keep company books just like these are real companies. All you need to do is telegram me supplier orders, or cash expenditures and amounts. I pay the suppliers just as any legitimate business and create fake business records. I replenish the operating capital for each shell company in a different French bank from the Swiss bank accounts. I record the deposits from the Swiss accounts as loan advances or revenue. Whatever is necessary to balance revenue and expenses providing the appearance of legitimate business. Since the money flows from secret Swiss bank accounts, records there are not subject to scrutiny by France."

"Why such an elaborate scheme?"

"Perhaps unnecessary but we are controlling large amounts of money. Stolen money under Swiss law. We do not want the French or anyone else digging deeper. I keep the majority of the funds in the Swiss bank accounts. Not the original SS accounts, but new ones under my control, using a false name of course. The bulk of the reserves are therefore held in stable Swiss francs rather than the uncertain exchange rate of the French franc. It also conceals explaining the origin of the money.

"The process is called money laundering. Obscure the origin of illegal money. That is how American gangsters avoid taxes." Displaying a smug smile, "But we shall even pay French taxes on what we show to be very modest profits."

Trakonitz nodded smiling, "You are very good at this, Marc." Turning to Fiona, "This is wonderful seeing you, Fiona. I am happy for you and Marc returning to Paris. Resuming your life."

"And you, Pavel?" Marchand said. "What about you?"

"What do you mean?"

"You never told me much about your life once you came to Palestine. No wife or woman back home?"

"Home? My home was Prague. Palestine is just a refuge. Since arriving there, I have been at war. First against the British, than the Germans in North Africa and Italy. Now once again the British. The Haganah needed to prepare for resuming its fight to expel the British from Palestine. Create a Jewish state. Experienced fighters needed so they encouraged many of us to join the British Army to acquire military experience.

"The Nazis represented the more immediate problem. Yet no one could imagine the scale of the Jewish genocide. That transformed everything. European displaced Jews have nowhere left as refuge other than Palestine. Once the British leave then we face certain war with the surrounding Arab states. There can be no capitulation. Either some of us survive or we all perish.

"There is no one waiting for me, Fiona. I have been at war now for seven years. Not likely to end soon. A romantic relationship impossible. Consumed as I am what kind of life could I offer?"

Marchand reached over from her chair and rested her hand on his forearm. Saddened by the lonely words of this strange man that saved her life in Italy, tears streamed freely down her face. What could she possibly say?

In two weeks, telegrams flowed in from Trakonitz. Mostly just names and amounts, several held more details where suppliers demanded down payments requiring bank drafts. . The largest of these being a three-month charter for a small Panamanian flagged freighter working the Mediterranean.

Trakonitz called Fraser to describe their first mission. "We are going to free several hundred Jews interned at Bergen-Belsen in the British occupation zone of Germany. I have been there. The place is a hellhole. There are still thousands kept just two kilometers from the former Nazi concentration camp. Housed in former German Army barracks and other repurposed buildings. Completely inadequate for the number of inmates. Over 10,000 Jews. You can still smell the former camp, which was rampant with disease when liberated in April. So bad, the British burned the former inmate housing.

"The British Army and Red Cross are doing what they can, but it is not enough. Food is adequate but sanitation is not sufficient for this many people. Except for serious medical conditions, basic care is non-existent."

"What is your plan, Pavel?"

"I have located a suitable ship. A thirty-year old freighter working the Mediterranean. It can accommodate several hundred people."

"That is why I called. The broker wants 15,000£ for the three month charter. Fifty percent down."

"I will wire the money tomorrow. The name of this ship?"

"The *Bruja de Mar*. Here is the name of the broker and the routing for wiring the money."

"Spanish for the *Sea Witch*. Are you sure it is sea worthy?"

"I have never seen it. Perhaps another desperate act. Yet everything we do is desperate. Having suffered so much, every Jewish survivor of the Nazi horror must seize any chance for life. Palestine is their only hope."

Prior to rescuing three hundred Jewish refugees from Bergen-Belsen Displaced Persons Camp, Trakonitz and a team of TTG canvassed the detainees. They needed to select leaders to which they could entrust instructions once the freighter left Marseille. As an intelligence officer armed with orders from Major Rothschild, entry into the camps presented no obstacles. Executing the escape required detailed planning from within the camp.

Within three days, his team selected several leaders. The first task for those selected would prove the most difficult. They must choose the three hundred for escape from thousands. Trakonitz laid down the criteria. No one sick or too weak to make the arduous thirty-hour drive to Marseille followed by as many as ten days at sea. No children under twelve. Equal numbers of men and women.

With detailed planning in place, they set the escape time for a dark moonless night the following week.

Trakonitz would also smuggle weapons for the Haganah on this voyage of the *Sea Witch*. With fake orders and requisitions created by Sandor Herczeg, they planned to steal a cache of small arms and mortars from a British Army Armory. Sealed inside 55-gallon drums marked *Red Cross Emergency Supplies*.

A week before the breakout, Trakonitz received a major setback. The marine broker told him French authorities demanded the *Sea Witch* leave Marseille within three days. Everything must advance by days.

Seems the British suspected something suspicious and pressured the French. With the end of the war, every logical places of resettlement for European Jewish refugees imposed restrictive limits on immigration. These included the United States, Britain, and the Commonwealth countries of Canada and Australia where anti-Semitism remained strong. With all of Eastern Europe now under Soviet occupation, Palestine remained the only place of refuge. Yet the British closed off Jewish immigration under the British Mandate to avoid angering Palestinian Arabs and the surrounding Arab states. The only means of reaching Palestine was by ship. British agents and informants throughout Mediterranean ports were on heightened alert.

The problem made worse since this now became the only possible voyage from Marseille for the *Sea Witch*. Trakonitz expected more sailings if the first trip evaded the British blockade.

After hearing the deadline for the Sea Witch to sail, Trakonitz telephoned the camp office requesting to speak to a specific detainee. The chosen leader of the refugees was a former Polish partisan, a battle-hardened survivor of several concentration camps.

On the designated night, the partisan arranged a fire in one of the camp kitchens. The selected escapees made their way quickly to an escape staging location some distance away from the diversion. The surrounding chain link fence easily breached. No guards patrolled the perimeter.

On hand to supervise the escape, Trakonitz became alarmed as he watched the line of escapees. Clearly more than 300 people. The last escapee through the fence was the former partisan.

Trakonitz said in a harsh whisper, "Zieliński, how many?"

"Something more than 400 I believe."

Trakonitz shook his head in frustration. "Why? I said to limit it to 300."

"We created a committee of six to choose. Difficult to do anything by committee, but choosing who may have a chance for life is a terrible burden. Moving up the deadline made the situation more difficult."

"We do not have sufficient trucks for that many."

"Then we shall just crowd together more tightly. Having survived standing room only for days in Nazi railroad carriages without food or water, we can manage the journey."

Trakonitz quickly gathered his TTG, all wearing their British uniforms.

To a subordinate, a sergeant by the name of Erdheim he said, "Take the truck with the weapons and Geschke along with four of the strongest refugees. Return to that old warehouse we used to park the rented lorries. Offload the barrels of weapons there. You are to stay with the weapons until we return from Marseille." Turning to Geschke, "You drive with the four men to this location."

Armed with multiple copies of the same maps, Trakonitz pointed to a location and gave Geschke the map. "Rendezvous with the convoy here. You should be able to catch up carrying no load. We need those trucks for the additional people. The weapons must wait."

To the other soldiers and Zieliński, "Empty the other truck containing the Red Cross food drums. Disperse the drums among all the other trucks. That will provide us one more truck. Do this quickly. I want to be rolling in ten minutes. Follow my jeep and keep close together."

The journey proceeded without incident across Germany and into Belgium before reaching the French border.

Stopped at the manned border crossing, Trakonitz got out of the jeep with his driver who spoke passible French. As the TTG driver explained their mission of transporting German POWs to the two border guards, Trakonitz handed them a copy of his orders.

The conversation continued for several minutes. Translating for Trakonitz, "They say they have no authorization. They cannot even read our orders in English."

"Tell them we are behind schedule. We must make a ship sailing from Marseille to a prisoner of war camp in Tripoli, or we will be stuck with these *krauts* and everyone will be in big trouble." Putting his hand on the driver's shoulder, "Hold on. Try offering the case of brandy in the back of the jeep."

The ploy worked. The French guards did not even inspect the trucks with the closed canvas flaps in the rear, waving them through after shaking hands with the TTG translator.

All went well until they reached higher country south of Lyon. Driving through the night, a dense fog set in. To minimize raising suspicions of the long convoy, they taped over the lorry headlamps.

Descending a grade at no more than fifteen kilometers per hour, the unavoidable still happened. Trakonitz heard crunching of metal. After stopping the jeep came another distant sound of collision further back of the convoy.

Working his way on foot up the road, Trakonitz encountered the drivers outside the trucks. Not only was there substantial damage to two trucks, but one man badly injured. A terrible wound to his head bleeding profusely after his head struck the windscreen.

Eventually they found someone with medical training among the refugees. Unfortunately, two lorries were damaged enough not to continue.

"Redistribute everyone into the other trucks. Place Pulaski in the back of the jeep and have the medical fellow ride with him. Remove the tape from the headlamps. We leave in ten minutes."

The convoy arrived on the designated Marseille dock in the early morning darkness a day before the French-imposed departure deadline.

Trakonitz and the partisan Zieliński boarded the freighter. Even in the dim moonlight, rust stains streaked the hull, and every surface was long overdue for painting. After finding a sleeping crewmember on the bridge maintaining the watch, Trakonitz forced him to wake the captain.

Even the interior of the bridge looked derelict. When the captain entered, he did nothing to dispel concern. This was a desperate undertaking.

With a several-day growth of beard, dressed in pajama bottoms and a dirty sweater smoking a cigarette, the captain said in badly accented English, "What the fuck is this?"

"Delivering cargo as arranged. We are early," Trakonitz said.

"You are the English soldier? What is the cargo?"

"400 people. Jewish refugees. You are to take them to Palestine."

The captain suspected this was a rogue operation seeing the Star of David insignia on Trakonitz's shoulder. "You are crazy. That is not possible. British warships blockade Palestine."

"You will attempt to evade the blockade. For that you will be paid a great deal of money?"

"How much?"

"Three thousand British pounds."

The captain thought about it for a moment. "If we are caught, the ship will be confiscated."

"That is not your problem."

"I will not get another command. Cost you more money."

"How much?"

"I will do this for five thousand pounds."

Trakonitz replied, "Very well. Three thousand now the other two when you reach Palestine. You get the two thousand if you deliver the refugees."

"What is plan once I reach Palestine? How are refugees offloaded?"

"Mr. Zieliński here will explain once you are out to sea. He will also have your additional fee."

The captain nodded and extended his hand to Trakonitz.

Trakonitz said, "Now I suggest we load the passengers while it is still dark. We have food also to be loaded. Make way at first light. Possibly avoiding the attention of British spies."

Descending to the wharf, Trakonitz turned to Zieliński handing him a revolver. "Here take this. I do not trust the captain. I will also give your colleagues arms. Use them if necessary."

"Yes. We shall not be taken."

"No. These weapons are to keep the captain and crew in line. Do not fire on the British if facing capture. You will hang if you kill a British soldier. Best to disable the ship if facing capture. Destroy the engines. They cannot then force it to sail back to Europe. You will end up at a camp in Cyprus. At least you will be closer to Palestine. The British must eventually concede and allow Jews into Palestine."

The two men embraced. As the *Sea Witch* left port the convoy of trucks left to return north.

It was nerve racking not knowing the fate of the *Sea Witch.* The only contact was by telephone to a Haganah contact in Haifa. If the *Sea Witch* successfully evaded British patrolling warships, the captain was to radio on a specific frequency. Using Morse code, he was to signal success by a code word, followed by a string of numbers providing his position. The Haganah operative would relay receipt of the message to Trakonitz by telephone.

This was to happen at nighttime with the ship dead in the water a mile off shore, darkened and silent. Small fishing vessels would come along side to offload the refugees. The gangway rigged alongside the hull to the water level to allow the refugees to descend rapidly into the waiting boats.

Once on shore, Haganah operatives would take charge of the refugees.

Things did not go as planned.

By sheer chance, the *Sea Witch* avoided discovery by British warships in route for most of the journey. Even with increased British coastal patrols off Palestine, the captain brought his darkened ship to the prescribed coordinates without incident. Thirty minutes after transmitting the radio signal, several fishing trawlers pulled up quietly alongside.

As the first fishing boat loaded and pulled away, the unmistakable intermittent wail of sirens shattered the quiet. Two fast British torpedo patrol boats armed with machine guns converged with beams of searchlights fixing on the fishing boats.

Believing they were close to stepping into the Promised Land of Israel, the former partisan Zieliński realized the escape failed. His duty now to destroy the engines and the seaworthiness of the *Sea Witch.*

Zieliński mustered his six armed squad of men to follow him. Forcing the captain and two crewmen at gunpoint, the group descended below.

"Captain, I need to destroy your ship," Zieliński said.

"Sink it?" The captain said."

"I do not think that possible. We instead destroy the engine. I know something of sabotage. I need a welding rig and any flammable liquids, gasoline, turpentine, or kerosene. Also something combustible. Where do we find these things, Captain?"

The Captain remained silent.

Pressing the revolver under the Captain's chin, "I have no time, Captain. Help us or die."

The Captain directed two crewmen to the ship's maintenance storeroom.

"The crew's quarters are next to the engine room. The mattresses will burn if saturated with flammable liquid." The Captain said. "Are you going to burn the ship?"

As Zieliński entered the engine room, he made a quick survey. A startled engineering crewman backed away seeing the revolver. Trying several languages, "Where is the fuel intake line?"

Eventually the man went to the engine and put his hand on the small diameter pipe.

Zieliński examined the fuel line. Clear what he needed to do.

"Where is the water pump for the fire suppression system?"

The crewman pointed to a corner of the engine room.

Grabbing a fire ax from the wall, Zieliński severed the electrical wiring to the pump then with the spiked end of the ax, destroyed the pump casting.

A crewman returned with a ten-liter can of kerosene and two smaller cans of turpentine, another pulled an oxyacetylene welding cart with gas cylinders and welding visor.

"Get me mattresses from the crew quarters."

Zieliński was not a welder but understood the basics. Cutting required no particular technique other than the gas settings. He attached a cutting torch.

To his armed colleagues, Zieliński said, "I will destroy one of the main bearings to the propeller driveshaft. Damage the engine as much as possible then set fire to the engine room. Stack those mattresses around the engine. One of you go up two levels and close the access door to the engine room. Stand guard. Prevent any crew coming down. Shoot as a warning but do not shoot any British."

With the torch, Zieliński attacked the casing of the large bearing supporting the propeller shaft closest to the engine and the transmission case. After several minutes, he cut away a large section of the casting, exposing the outer race of the large roller bearing. Minutes later, the outer bearing race split open. Flames curled up from the ignited bearing grease.

Seeing a bucket of sand in the corner used for absorbing oil spills, he poured sand into the bearing to add further damage.

Shutting down the idling engine, he then preceded to cut away the control box, lubrication lines, and anything else to make repairs difficult if the fire did not prove sufficiently destructive.

A shot rang out from the above level. "British soldiers!" The armed refugee shouted.

Lastly, he turned off the diesel fuel with the shutoff valve. After cutting the line with the torch, he reopened the value. Diesel fuel poured onto the floor.

"Pour the kerosene and turpentine on those mattresses then everyone out."

The last thing Zieliński did was ignite the mattresses with the torch. Eventually the heat of the burning mattresses would ignite the growing pool of diesel fuel. With no working fire hoses, the heat should destroy the engine room. Given enough time, the fuel tank might explode destroying the vessel.

He carried out what was necessary. Yet for Zieliński to have come so far to wind up in another stinking camp in Cyprus proved too much.

After offloading the refugees and ferrying them to shore to a waiting company of British infantry, smoke began rising out of vents on the deck of the *Sea Witch.*

The last of the ship's crew and armed refugees surrendered from below.

The ship captain said to the officer in charge, "These Jews hijacked my ship. The engine room is on fire. Their leader is still down there."

With increasing smoke now exhausting from the vents, the British officer became concerned for the safety of his boarding party. "Then we shall let the bastard die down there."

# CHAPTER 20

PARIS, FRANCE | SEPTEMBER 1945

---

A beautiful late summer day in Paris. After lunch outside at Les Deux Magots on Boulevard Saint-Germain, Fraser and Marchand spent the afternoon walking and looking at art galleries. After crossing over the river to Île Saint-Louis, they returned to the Left Bank walking down the Rue de Seine with its many galleries. The telephone was ringing as Fraser unlocked the door to the apartment.

With no preamble, "This is Pavel." Sounding tired and upset, "The mission failed. The *Sea Witch* did not land its cargo. Four hundred camp survivors are now on their way to Cyprus to another British camp. The ship suffered a fire. A total loss. Lost one good man."

"Sorry to hear that, Pavel. You will try again?"

"Of course. We must. However, I need to find a better way. The French route is too long. The sea voyage too long with too many British warships patrolling. I believe camps in Southern Germany and Austria present better possibilities for rescue. So many refugees flowing into Italy makes for better opportunities. More ports to use. A shorter distance to Palestine.

"A game of percentages. The British blockade has holes. We must keep trying. Even getting to Cyprus is better for these people than stuck in Germany. The world has turned its back on the surviving European Jews. Palestine is their only hope. Having survived the Nazi Holocaust, Jews must not suffer a protracted genocide by world indifference.

"So what do you plan to do differently?"

"The problem is not on the front end helping these people escape the displaced persons camps. The key is finding ways to circumvent British barriers into Palestine. I can do that only from Palestine. I will resign my commission immediately. Continue to smuggle in Jews and weapons. Participate in harassing British military and police. Anything necessary to establish the State of Israel.

"Within a few weeks, I expect to be back in Palestine. Probably work out of Haifa. I can be of more use to Haganah smuggling efforts working from there."

"I understand. Let me know if you need new arrangements for funding future *investments*. Good luck. Keep your head down, Pavel."

Fraser understood Trakonitz's anger at the British position restricting Jewish immigration into Palestine. He also understood Trakonitz history with the Haganah. Violence was ratcheting up against the British in Palestine. Haganah focused on Jewish immigration and building an army as their means of forging a Jewish state. Eventually the British must relent and leave Palestine.

The more militant groups of Irgun and Lehi engaged in terrorist acts of bombings and assassinations of British personnel. Advocating for a Jewish State of Israel by the Jewish population in Palestine became increasingly strident and violent. With tens of thousands of European Jewish displaced persons denied any other option for resettlement, the pressure mounted.

Having served in the British Army, Trakonitz refused to participate in killing British soldiers. Whitehall in London was the problem. His contribution was active subversion by bringing more Jews and weapons into Palestine preparing for war with the Arabs.

❖ ❖ ❖

In his villa in Madrid, Henrich Müller sat at his large desk in his study. Having just returned from Switzerland, Walkenhorst, Gerhardt, and Voigt explained their findings.

Walkenhorst summarized, "Krüger's suicide note stated he was blackmailed by American intelligence. Swiss Chief of Police Rothmund confirmed that an American agent named Marc Fraser had frequent contact with Krüger. Swiss intelligence reported multiple occasions seen dining together. Rothmund provided a photograph of Fraser."

Walkenhorst handed the photo to Müller. "Once the banker Kessler confessed that Krüger introduced a new associate possessing a power of attorney document, it seemed obvious what happened. Kessler confirmed the photo of Fraser as that of the fictitious Otto Albrecht."

"What of the other accounts at other banks?"

"We did not pursue inquiries with any other banks after meeting with Johann Wehrli. Unlikely those other banks would discuss anything except to the registered account holder of the closely held account number. Better this not appear a widespread attack on Swiss banking. Kessler was only cooperative because he was particularly friendly to the Third Reich."

"Kessler also wanted to avoid a scandal," Voigt the former *Gestapo* agent said.

"Safe to assume, Fraser is responsible for emptying those accounts using Krüger then getting rid of him," Walkenhorst said.

"Is this an American intelligence operation or did Fraser simply steal the money?" Müller said.

"No way to know. We need to get to Fraser to determine that," Voigt said. "He is no longer living in Switzerland. Rothmund suggested he might be in Paris where he lived before the war. Married to a French woman named Marchand. An art restorer. Previously worked at the Louvre."

Turning to Gerhardt, the former SS intelligence officer, Müller said, "Since you served in Paris and speak French, find out everything you can about Fraser. Do we have any assets in Paris?"

Gerhardt answered, "I have a source I ran in Paris during the war. A woman. A clerical worker in the Paris Police Department."

"Go to Paris if necessary, Gerhardt. Find Fraser," Müller said.

Gerhardt remained in contact with a number of former colleagues within the Reich Main Security Office, the RSHA. The RSHA absorbed the functions of the former *Abwehr*. Fearing infiltration by anti-Nazi elements, Hitler dissolved the *Abwehr*, reassigning their functions to Himmler's RSHA.

For 25 years, the *Abwehr* proved a highly effective foreign intelligence organization led by the capable Admiral Wilhelm Canaris. Compiling extensive files on foreign intelligence operations, most of those files went into concealment as the war ended. Any officer involved with German intelligence knew these files were as good as gold for personal barter after Germany's defeat. Therefore, files existed in countless secret locations.

It was to these sources, Gerhardt turned. From his background in the *Sicherheitsdienst,* the SD, part of the Reich Main Security Office, he knew many officers still in hiding in Germany. One in particular was a specialist in United States foreign intelligence. That meant the OSS, created at the start of the war. Gerhardt personally confronted the OSS and their British counterparts the SOE as they mounted missions into German occupied France during his service in Paris.

Helmut Gerhardt grew up in Saarbrücken, Germany near the French border. Following the Armistice of 1919 ending WWI, it became part the Territory of the Saar Basin, an area administered by the French and British under a League of Nations Mandate. The coal-rich Saar Basin became part of the punitive reparations imposed on defeated Germany from 1920 to 1935. It was here the young Gerhardt learned to speak French and English while fostering a lifelong resentment against the French and British occupation.

Two days later, Gerhardt received a telephone call. He and the other former SS working with Müller maintained offices in central Madrid under the factious company name *Empresas de Fénix S.L.* This was not about hiding since the Spanish Fascist regime condoned their presence, but rather a cover for secretly coordinating with other groups of former Nazis in Europe and South America. Their principal mission was enabling former SS hiding in Europe to avoid arrest by the Allies. Among the chaos following German surrender, they reorganized outside Germany. Dispersing funds to further postwar SS ambitions using secret SS Swiss bank accounts became their principal function. Significant funds now stolen.

"Sturmbannführer Gerhardt. I believe I have the information you requested," The caller said.

"This man Fraser has a large dossier. Full name, Marc Douglas Fraser. Born 1903 in New York. American father, a financial executive with a Hollywood movie studio. Mother was French and part of the Rothschild banking family. Jewish."

"So Fraser is a Jew? Perhaps also understanding something of finance?"

"Probably. Educated in Paris and New York. Early career as a journalist in Los Angeles. Came to Europe in the early 1930s as a correspondent for Hearst Publications. Covered the Spanish Civil War.

"It is here his background becomes interesting. Fraser covered the war from Franco's Fascist Nationalist side. They discovered Fraser spying for the Americans. An accomplished photographer, he produced microfilm negatives that he mailed hidden under postage stamps.

"After interrogation, he and a woman accomplice escaped while waiting execution."

"How did he escape Spain?"

"No record of that, Sir. However, his name resurfaces in France two years ago. Seems Fraser joined the French Resistance. Implicated in murders in Lyon of an SS officer serving previously as a Reich liaison officer in Spain, and a Spanish Falange officer. The two officers involved with uncovering Fraser's spying activities in Spain. Those murders occurred simultaneous with a failed attempt on the *Gestapo* chief of Lyon.

"The next dossier entry places Fraser and his wife in Bern, Switzerland working for American OSS intelligence."

"Excellent work. Are you safe?"

"I think so. Hard to say. At least I am in the American zone of occupation, not the Soviet zone."

"Very good. If you need anything, call this number," Gerhardt said.

After reporting his information, Müller said, "I believe you must go to Paris, Gerhardt. Do you have proper identification?"

"Yes. I have a set of French papers I used before leaving in '44. A lawyer. My cover as residing in Spain until the German defeat therefore explaining my lack of newly instituted French documentation."

"Locate Fraser. I suspect he is now residing in Paris. If still with the OSS, he might be operating anywhere in Europe, but likely his wife is in Paris."

"If Fraser is in Paris, what are my orders, Sir?"

"Your mission is to determine what happened to the Swiss money. If not an American intelligence operation, then we must recover the funds."

"And Fraser?" Gerhardt asked.

Müller looked at Gerhardt with his cold expressionless eyes. "Take Schmidt and Voigt with you. Fraser is the source of this problem. Use the wife to get Fraser to talk. Whatever he reveals, eliminate the Jew."

Gerhardt, Schmidt, a fellow SD officer, and Voigt the *Gestapo* agent arrived at Paris Gare Lyon train station after the long trip from Madrid. While Gerhardt was fluent in French, Schmidt and Voigt spoke only German. Therefore, they traveled under false papers identifying them as Belgian since German was one of that country's three official languages. Businessmen having fled to Spain in 1940, helped by their lawyer Gerhardt.

Although no Francophile, Gerhardt enjoyed his three years in Paris. What better place to serve out the war. A magnificent city. The food, the wine, the women. As a mid-ranking SS intelligence officer the posting to Paris was a choice assignment compared to serving in Berlin or the Eastern Front. Not only refined, Paris did not suffer continual Allied bombing.

Eleanor Pascal lived in an inexpensive modest apartment in Montmartre in the 18th Arrondissement. She held a good job in the records department of the Prefecture of Police on the Île de la Cité since 1937. She married a French army officer in the summer of 1939 just before France declared war on Germany following Hitler's invasion of Poland.

In May of 1940, Hitler invaded the Netherlands and Belgium then made a daring push through the wooded Ardennes. The maneuver outflanked British and French forces to the north while bypassing the heavily fortified French Maginot Line to the south. France fell in June. Taken prisoner, Eleanor's husband became one of 1.8 million French POWs. Within a year, he was among those POWs transferred to camps in Eastern Europe.

Her collaboration with the Germans began out of desperation over the fate of her husband. Hauptsturmführer Helmut Gerhardt was anxious to establish himself in the *Sicherheitsdienst*, the SD, the intelligence service of the Nazi SS. Developing useful French sources of information was key to promotion.

On a tour of the Paris Police Prefecture, it was the attractive clerk with the auburn hair in records that drew his attention. A casual question to his French police escort provided a name to the face. Further inquiries established her marital status and address.

Days later, following her as she left work, he created an excuse for greeting her as they waited for the Metro. Both traveling to Montmartre. Gerhardt deftly escalated that first introduction. After she revealed her husband was a POW, he offered assistance. He advanced the recruitment by arranging her to send and receive letters along with her husband to receive Red Cross packages. In exchange, she would provide information from within police headquarters.

Six months later the husband died of an illness. Trapped, she could not break off the relationship without risking exposure as a Nazi collaborator. A possible death sentence. Already committed to betrayal, she succumbed to the inducement of decent food and even wine, leading to a sexual relationship of convenience.

Gerhardt therefore knew her address and the nearest Metro station. He last visited Eleanor eighteen months ago before hastily departing Paris ahead of the Allied liberation. Best to meet at her apartment. Difficult to predict her reaction. She would still fear exposure as a Nazi collaborator, worse yet a spy for the Nazi SS. Treason meant death by guillotine. However, if she became unhinged and exposed him as a Nazi SS officer, he could find himself in real danger. If arrested, the French courts might even give him a death sentence for his wartime activities while in Paris.

As Eleanor Pascal trudged up the stairway to her third floor apartment, Gerhardt immerged from the shadows.

"Hello, Eleanor."

She jumped as he spoke. Seeing him brought a look of terror as she put her hand to her mouth.

He took the key from her trembling hand and inserted it into the lock. "Better we talk inside."

Closing the door, Pascal said, "Why are you here? What if the French arrest you?"

"I need you to do something, Eleanor."

Turning away from him, she said, "No! No more. I am done helping you. The war is over. Leave me alone!"

Gerhardt grabbed her arm gently turning her around to face him. "It is something very simple. Do this and your secret remains safe. You will never see me again."

"What is it you want?"

"An address. The name is Marc Fraser. Occupation journalist. Married. Wife's name is Fiona Marchand, employed at the Louvre. Address might be in either name."

"What does the SS want with these people?"

Gerhardt shook his head. "That does not concern you, Eleanor."'

Thoroughly shaken having thought the dark history of her collaboration buried, she sat down in a chair and wept.

"Come now, Eleanor, it is not as bad as all that. Just a simple task. In fact, I shall pay you for your troubles. I imagine circumstances are perhaps difficult for you.

Seeing no way to refuse, she said, "How am I to reach you?"

"I see you have a telephone. I will call you tomorrow evening. Can you get the address by then?"

"I will try."

"Do not disappoint me, Eleanor."

The following evening, she told Gerhardt on the telephone, "The address is 27 Rue Vaneau in the 7th."

"Well done, Eleanor. Tomorrow evening I shall come by to give you 1000 francs as I promised. And for old time's sake to say goodbye."

"Can you trust this woman not to reveal our presence in Paris, Gerhardt?" Voigt asked.

"Not entirely. She fears exposure for her collaboration. Not likely after all this time. She did a thorough job hiding our relationship. However, fear clouds rational thought.

"Therefore, we cannot trust fear alone to keep her quiet. Police perhaps waiting at her apartment? Instead, tomorrow Mademoiselle Pascal will meet with an accident. I shall intercept her as she leaves work from police headquarters with the excuse, *too far to go to your apartment, Eleanor. A coffee close by instead?*"

Gerhardt extracted a folded piece of paper. Inside was a standard SS issue cyanide capsule.

"I will choose an outdoor café. I go inside to the counter and order two espressos. I wait at the counter. When the first coffee arrives, I break open the capsule and pour it into the cup.

"Then I take it to her and return to the counter for my coffee. I simply wait inside until she sips the coffee. As you know, it takes only a matter of seconds. In the ensuing chaos, I slip out the rear entrance. You two watch from across the street and make sure she collapses.

"With Mademoiselle Pascal eliminated, we proceed to Fraser's residence. Walk across the river. I will meet here." Gerhardt said pointed out the Saint-Germain des Pres church on Boulevard Saint-Germain. "Take the map. I know the way."

After giving Gerhardt Fraser's address, Eleanor Pascal suffered a sleepless night. Her guilt over collaboration may have started to save her husband, but taking up with Gerhardt after his death was inexcusable. Now this. Perhaps this Fraser was a German spy. Maybe even SS. Since Gerhardt did not know his address, that appeared unlikely.

She could never live with herself if harm came to this man or his wife. Her conscience already bore too great a guilt. Therefore, once at work, she located the telephone number for Fraser. After procrastinating all morning, she placed the call in the early afternoon. Fiona Marchand answered. "*Bonjour*?"

"Is this the residence of Marc Fraser?"

"Yes. Who is calling?"

"You are his wife, Madame Marchand?"

"Has something happen to my husband?"

"No. Please just listen carefully. A former Nazi SS officer named Sturmbannführer Gerhardt is in Paris. His intentions are unknown. However, he now has your address."

"Who are you?"

"That is not important. Just someone who hates Nazis. Please heed the warning."

The call disconnected abruptly.

Deeply shaken, Marchand needed to contact Marc immediately. He was to meet with the managing editor of Le Monde. Frantically calling the newspaper, she learned that Marc left after lunching with the editor. Was he coming directly home?

How could the SS be in Paris? Why target Marc? Having been through many dangerous situations these last several years, her discipline helped to remain calm and think through the problem. The danger was coming here. Would someone be waiting outside for Marc to return? For what purpose? To kill him?

First, she must arm herself. No different from Italy during the war. Prepare for every contingency. She did not intend to hide in the apartment and let Marc walk into a trap. Meet the threat well armed. Her bulky .38 revolver went into her shoulder purse. She could hold it in her hand while concealed inside her shoulder bag. The small .25 caliber pistol she placed in her jacket pocket.

Over the initial shock of the telephone call, she was now thinking clearly. This must involve the theft of the SS funds from the Swiss banks for former SS to risk coming to Paris. Obviously, they planned to confront Marc as he left or returned to the residence. They would lay in wait outside. Clearly, that is where she must set up surveillance. With errands to run that morning, she used the car. With clear weather, Marc chose to walk. Returning from the other side of the river, Marc would walk south on their street. She would intercept him blocks from the apartment.

Prepared with a plan of action, Marchand cautiously opened the front door. Stepping into the hallway, she clutched the revolver in her shoulder bag and descended the three flights of stairs to the building foyer. Twisting the deadbolt with her left hand, she removed her right hand from the revolver in her shoulder bag to pull open the door.

As she started to open the door, it suddenly thrust open sending her backwards.

"*Excusez moi mademoiselle,*" A man dressed in a suit said as he continued to push forward. Before Marchand could utter anything, two other men came in behind him.

She reached inside her shoulder bag to extract the revolver but unfortunately fumbled its extraction. The man that spoke saw her weapon and immediately slammed his fist into her jaw. The heavy blow hard enough to send her to the floor dropping the revolver.

Gerhardt turned to Voigt and Schmidt. "*Sie abholen.*"

As Schmidt hoisted her over his shoulder, she began to protest weakly but unable to offer much resistance still dazed from the blow.

Voigt, the ex-*Gestapo*, withdrew a large folded knife. Opening the five-inch blade, he held it close to her face as a threat.

Gerhardt knew the apartment number from the outside mail drops and intercom. Extracting the apartment key from Marchand's purse, they all entered with Schmidt dropping Marchand to the floor followed by a hard slap to her face with his open hand as she tried to rise.

Giving Schmidt the outer door key, Gerhardt said, "Wait outside the building and watch for Fraser. Follow him up the stairs. Let him put his key in the apartment door then come in behind with your gun drawn."

Marchand got to her hands and knees disoriented.

"Sit her in that chair," Gerhardt ordered Voigt in German.

Drawing a 9mm Luger, he addressed Marchand in French, "You will remain silent. Call out and my colleague will cut your throat. You are expendable. I must speak with your husband. My associate is armed and waiting for him outside."

Voigt pulled up a chair close to Marchand. Gerhardt pulled a chair close to the front door.

"When your husband unlocks the door, make no sound and neither of you will be harmed."

An hour passed before Fraser turned his key in the lock. Opening the door, Gerhardt pointed his pistol in his face. Surveying the room, Fraser saw the man standing next to Fiona with a hand on her shoulder holding a knife to her throat with his other hand. From behind, someone pushed a gun into his back and pushed him forward into the apartment.

"*Qui diable étes-vous?*" Fraser said.

Gerhardt replied in German, "*Schutzstaffel, Herr Fraser.*"

In English, Fraser replied, "Fucking German pigs. What do you want?"

In English, Gerhardt said, "Our money of course. The money you stole in Switzerland. Now sit down over there, Fraser," pointing to a chair next to a round table with a lamp and a bronze bust of Victor Hugo.

"We shall now begin. This can be over quickly or become extremely unpleasant. In the end, I will get what I want. I suspect you will not talk without lengthy physical abuse. I do not have time for that. Therefore, my colleague will use his knife to inflict terrible damage to your beautiful wife.

"I know how you pulled this off. Clever but you left a trail. Was this an OSS operation?"

Fraser said nothing as he looked at Fiona trying to gauge her distress.

Gerhardt continued, "Did you empty all the accounts managed by Krüger? Where is the money now?"

Fraser remained silent.

"As I suspected. Stupid bravado in the face of obvious defeat. You know the questions so for the last time, will you cooperate?"

Fraser already made up his mind. If he provided them the information, or even lied saying it was an OSS operation, these SS still must kill both of them. Perhaps tortured first if this SS pig did not believe him. Therefore, his only recourse must be to take the initiative no matter how desperate.

"Very well. Schmidt, you hold her while Voigt cuts off her ear?"

Voigt repositioned himself, allowing Schmidt to grab her long hair pulling her toward him to expose her right ear while also holding her.

Resisting, Marchand fell to her knees in front of the chair as Schmidt fought to hold her Voigt maneuvered himself preparing for the sickening assignment to disfigure this beautiful woman.

Marchand reached into her jacket pocket. Gripping the small .25 automatic remembering to thumb the safety off. Pulling the pistol out of her jacket with her right hand, she looked up at Schmidt pulling her hair while standing on her left side. Pointing the weapon no more than twelve inches from Schmidt's face, she pulled the trigger twice. One round entered under his left eye, the other centered to his forehead.

She immediately turned the gun on a shocked Voigt standing there holding his knife. Without hesitation, she emptied the remaining rounds of the magazine into this vile creature about to disfigure her.

These seconds of violence provided all the opening Fraser needed. As Gerhardt bolted out of his chair, so did Fraser. Gerhardt switched his attention from watching Voigt go down to turn toward his right after peripherally seeing Fraser's movement. The turn exposed his torso as Fraser launched the heavy bronze bust of Victor Hugo catching Gerhardt square in the solar plexus.

Fraser immediately advanced a step and delivered a kick to Gerhardt's hand still gripping the Luger.

Dropping the weapon, Gerhardt fell to the floor on his knees holding his chest. Fraser advanced smashing his fist into Gerhardt's nose releasing a torrent of blood. Looking toward Fiona, she just stood transfixed looking at her attackers lying prone on the floor. Fraser returned his rage on Gerhardt reverting instinctively to his early boxing training to deliver rapid jabs with both fists repeatedly battering Gerhardt's face.

With his fury spent, Fraser picked up the Luger then knelt down placing his fingers on the neck of each assailant. Neither registered a pulse.

Hugging Fiona, "Are you okay?"

"I am not injured. I will be alright."

Fiona took in deep breathes trying to calm the effects of the adrenaline rush.

Fraser picked up Voigt's knife then recovered the handguns from the dead men handing them to Fiona.

Returning to the barely consciousness Gerhardt now rolled on his side on the floor clutching his chest, Fraser's rage only increased. "Who sent you? Who are you working for?"

Gerhardt said nothing. Understandable with the intense pain. His breathing labored. His sternum perhaps cracked, his nose badly broken, one eye already starting to close with swelling.

"What is your name?"

Gerhardt just groaned. The heavy bronze bust undoubtedly doing significant damage.

Fiona said, "The caller said his name was Gerhardt. SS Sturmbannführer Gerhardt."

"Just like you threatened, Gerhardt, you will tell me what I want to know or you will suffer before I kill you. Make no mistake, I will kill you unless you tell me everything. The French police could care less. Now again, who sent you?"

Gerhardt mustered enough strength to look up defiantly at Fraser.

Letting a couple of seconds past as they locked eyes, Fraser suddenly raised his left hand holding Voigt's knife and plunged it downward. With Gerhardt propped up with his right hand on the floor, the knife penetrated through his hand.

The knife sunk deep enough to imbed into the wood floor under Gerhardt's hand. Already in intense pain, Gerhardt managed only a large grunt. Gerhardt's eyes enlarged as he looked in horror at the knife impaling his hand to the floor.

Breathing with difficulty, he said in a raspy voice, "Yes, my name is Gerhardt. I was sent by a group of former *Schutzstaffel.* Our mission to discover what happened to SS funds stolen from Swiss banks."

"Who sent you?"

"The most senior officer is Henrich Möller. He gave the order."

"Who is this Möller?"

"I believe he was an aide to Himmler."

"Rank? Doing what?"

Sensing Gerhardt was withholding something, Fraser kicked Gerhardt in the chest with his shoe.

The pain so intense, Gerhardt screamed and convulsed in a spasm of pain.

Even Fiona gasped at Fraser's viciousness.

"Listen well you piece of shit. Tell me the truth or it gets worse."

Composing himself, Gerhardt answered, "His real name is Henrich Müller. Gruppenführer. Head of the *Geheime Staatspolizei*, Amt 4 of the RSHA."

Stunned, Fraser said, "*Gestapo* Müller? Reports say he died in the Führerbunker."

"No. It is him."

"Where are you based?"

"Madrid."

"What is the name of your group?"

"Name?"

"What do you call yourselves?"

"*Komeradenwerk.*"

"Is everyone in your group former SS?"

"Most, yes."

"Who else of importance is in your group?"

"I am told that Obersturmbannführer Otto Skorzeny established the Madrid location before the war ended.

"You mean the guy who rescued Mussolini?"

"Yes. A favorite of the Führer. He keeps in contact with Müller."

"Where is Skorzeny now?"

"I do not know."

"Who else?"

"SS-Obersturmbannführer Gerhard Rasch. A former paratroop commander. Franz Walkenhorst, a former officer in the SS Main Economic and Administrative Office. A colleague of Manfred Krüger in Bern.

"Standartenführer Walter Rauff, a former aide to Heydrich. In hiding somewhere in Northern Italy."

"And your two dead kameraden?"

"Schmidt was *Sicherheitsdienst* the same as me. Voigt was *Gestapo.*"

"How large is your *Komeradenwerk*?"

"You mean how many in Madrid?"

"Of course. I know there are thousands of SS in hiding. I am talking about assholes like you that have found safe haven and still intent on fighting the war."

"There are others in Madrid. Mostly junior officers. Many more in Buenos Aires but I do not know their numbers."

With each intake of breath, Gerhardt experienced a spasm of pain from the injury to his chest. Exhausted by the pain, he looked as if he might slip into unconsciousness. Every word a struggle. Unlikely to get much more out of him.

Fiona sat in a chair holding her head in both hands, staring at the two dead men. No emotional display, just allowing the shock subside. "You okay, Fiona? This is all over. I need you to telephone the police."

Shaking off the shock, she mustered control, "The police? They will question us why three former SS risked coming to Paris to attack us."

Fraser already thought about how to answer. "The answer is very simple. It involves intelligence work during the war when we were both part of the American OSS. We cannot discuss classified operations. Trust me, the French will take it no further."

"What about him?" Fiona asked referring to Gerhardt. Reverting to her learned survival instincts, her concern was about Marc's reaction to the attack. She recalled her husband's blind rage in Lyon that led to his killing the SS and Spanish officers forcing the need to escape the *Gestapo*. Would he now kill Gerhardt?

"Let the French deal with him. He does not know what happened in Switzerland. I ran Krüger as a source and turned all his financial files over to the OSS. If he talks about missing SS money, the Swiss banks will not cooperate with either French or U.S. investigators.

# CHAPTER 21

DACHAU WAR CRIMES TRIALS GERMANY | JANUARY-JULY 1946

---

The Paris police investigation of the SS killings went as Fraser predicted. Paris Police records documented Helmut Gerhardt from his years in Paris during the occupation. The same Vichy records confirmed Fraser and Marchand as having served in the French Resistance. A call to the U.S. Embassy confirmed their serving with American intelligence in Switzerland during the last years of the war.

The police determined the matter was self-defense homicide. They also had a former German SS officer in custody. Charged with attempted murder, he might also face charges on war crimes offenses. As a German, Gerhardt faced a very bad future incarcerated in a French prison.

The apartment building manager and his wife took charge of cleaning up the blood while Fraser and Marchand moved to a hotel for a couple of days. Although Fiona appeared under control when interviewed by Paris detectives, Fraser feared the trauma of killing the two assailants might have inflicted deeper emotional damage.

Unlike Fraser's rough and tumble professional background, Fiona was an intellectual and artist. He soon realized Fiona was much tougher than expected. While obviously supremely confident, he misjudged her deeper strength. Like so many others, the extreme experiences of the last five years of war changed people. In Fiona's case, what he originally saw as confidence was the outward expression of an extraordinary inner balance and adaptability. Looking back, he recalled her management of the continual fear as they worked for the Resistance under constant threat. That culminated with events in Lyon forcing their harrowing escape to Switzerland. Then went off by herself to Italy as an intelligence agent surviving a severe combat wound. A very tough woman.

After only two nights at the hotel, she said, "I want to go back home now, Marc."

She just killed two attackers in a very personal close encounter. Yet she never emotionally broke down. Following the shootings, she simply suffered the expected physiological effects of shock as the adrenalin subsided. Restless sleep seemed the only visible aftereffect.

"Sure you are up to it?"

"Marc, it is my place, my home, our home. Those bastards will not take that from me."

"Very well. I will call Claude and make sure everything is back to normal."

Fiona smiled and walked over to kiss his cheek. "For such a tough guy, you can be like an old woman. Let me tell you how I feel about what happened.

"Killing those two does not leave me with any lingering distress any more than how you must feel about killing Cabrera and Leitner. They deserved to die. So did these two.

"I feel nothing about their deaths. Why so callous? The answer is simple. I have only to recall the sight of that knife and what they were about to do to me. That horrific thought crowds out anything else."

Fraser embraced her then said, "But I cannot leave it that. This is not over. It is very personal. We spoke of getting back to normal. Life before the Nazi plague ravaged Europe. Not sure that is possible knowing organized remnants of the SS remain.

The former head of the *Gestapo* is safe in Spain. He tried to kill us. Not sure how, but I must go after these bastards, Fiona."

"I understand. I will do everything I can to help you. I may not share your motivations for revenge, but if we can do something to see these Nazi criminals face justice, we bear a responsibility.

He telephoned Pavel Trakonitz in Haifa, Palestine.

After a lengthy conversation, Trakonitz remarked, "Bloody fucking bastards. We had the right idea when the Brigade located to Tarvisio at the end of the war. Find SS in hiding and eliminate them. Wish I could offer to go after Müller with a team of former TTG.

"Unfortunately, that is not possible. Smuggling Jewish displaced persons remains my priority. That and preparing for war with the Arabs. Once the British Mandate terminates, the State of Israel will come under siege from the surrounding Arab states. This will happen soon. The British realize continued rule of Palestine is hopeless. So my other priority is running guns into Palestine."

"I appreciate the thought, Pavel. Not sure what I specifically intend to do, however I mean to pursue the SS. Cannot tell where that will lead but the starting point is gathering intelligence.

"Intelligence means sources. Fiona and I have many contacts in U.S. intelligence. My cousin Edmund Rothschild might prove a source with British intelligence. My Nazi hunting friend Simon Wiesenthal. I am also covering the upcoming war crimes trials in Nuremberg. Might develop new sources in the process."

Trakonitz said, "Perhaps I can contribute. Many within Haganah intelligence harbor the same thoughts about seeking vengeance on former Nazis. I have a close associate. A Spaniard. Emigrated to Palestine after Franco came to power in '39. Former Republican army intelligence officer by the name of Martel. He may have sources in Spain."

"Martel? Major Felix Martel?" Fraser said.

"Well a Colonel Felix Martel. You know him?"

"Must be him. How many Jews named Martel in Spain? Met him briefly in 1936 while covering the Spanish Civil War. He connected me with his cousin, Loretta Elizalde an anti-Fascist journalist. A long story. The short version is I collaborated with her to smuggle out my photos and reporting from the Fascist Nationalist side. Both of us caught and tortured. She and her husband saved my life. In France, they took up with the French Resistance like me.

"The *Gestapo* chief in Lyon, Klaus Barbie, tortured her. I took part in rescuing her but she died of her injuries. Fiona and I then helped her husband try to kill Barbie. The attempt failed forcing us to escape to Switzerland. So I guess you could say we have something of a shared background."

"Good. I will see what he can turn up about these SS in Madrid."

"Do not yet reveal we know that former *Gestapo* chief Henrich Müller is the principal in this Madrid SS group. If this becomes public, even for Franco that could prove to be too much unwanted pressure. Müller might flee to South America and disappear.

"Not sure how to use this knowledge but Müller is the highest ranking living Nazi not in custody awaiting trial. I did some research. Müller is thought to have died trying to escape the Führerbunker after Hitler committed suicide. Never confirmed by a body. Everyone would like to get their hands on him."

"Considering your confrontations with the *Gestapo,* I am sure you would like see Müller at the end of a rope."

Fraser replied, "Since he tried to kill me and Fiona, I would rather put a bullet in his head."

Fraser opted out of joining the French newspaper Le Monde. The assignment meant covering the major war criminal Nuremberg Trial continuously. The trial undoubtedly lasting many months. Twenty-four defendants represented the Nazi leadership in custody. Many others including the Führer Adolf Hitler, Reichsführer of the *Schutzstaffel* Heinrich Himmler, and Reich Minister of Propaganda Joseph Goebbels chose suicide rather than the degradation of hanging. Nonetheless, those on trial directed the war and the atrocities defined in the indictments as crimes against humanity.

Instead, he would freelance with accreditation from the Reuters news service allowing him to choose the timing and duration. Attending the trials as a journalist was largely a cover to ask probing questions of investigators. In this way, he could also write articles that could serve his objective to uncover the whereabouts of other fugitive SS.

Fraser was more interested in those directly responsible for executing Nazi policies of murder and torture, specifically Himmler's thousands of subordinates of the many facets of the *Schutzstaffel*. The vast SS organization consisted of the secret state police the *Geheime Staatspolizei,* abbreviated *Gestapo,* the state security service the *Sicherheitsdienst,* abbreviated SD, the administrators of the concentration camps and extermination camps, the *SS-Totenkopfverbände,* abbreviated SS-TV, and the combat troops of the *Waffen-SS*. The SS was the means by which Adolf Hitler exercised absolute power.

Many lesser Nazi SS currently awaited trial. The first of these trials would commence at the former concentration camp of Dachau in Bavaria by a U.S. military tribunal. Concurrently, the British would try SS defendants working in Auschwitz and Bergen-Belsen in Lüneburg, Lower Saxony Germany. Fraser was more interested in these defendants. Here he might gather information from interviewing the investigators. Perhaps even allowed to interview some of the defendants.

It was this secondary level of less infamous war criminals that interested Fraser. The lower SS ranks that executed policy. The sadistic psychopaths and sociopaths that reveled in inflicting pain. Those running the concentration camps issuing specific orders to torture and murder. The mobile murder units. Doctors conducting grotesque experiments. Those responsible for feeding the flow of victims into the Nazi genocide.

This element of the SS included the most wanted Nazi fugitives. Adolf Eichmann, organizer of the *Final Solution,* Alois Brunner, assistant to Eichmann, Josef Mengele, the *Angel of Death* of Auschwitz, Aribert Heim, *Dr. Death* and *Butcher of Mauthausen,* Franz Stangl, commandant of the Sobibór and Treblinka extermination camps, Walter Rauff, commander of mobile extermination units, and Klaus Barbie, the *Butcher of Lyon.*

These war criminals were among thousands of former SS in hiding, many planning their escape from Europe. Fraser had little interest in reporting on the trials. His interest was investigative. Exposing those SS *not yet arrested.* Deny them the means of hiding. Eliminate their means of escaping to safe havens. Destroy them by any means.

Marchand agreed to take over administering the SS funds to Trakonitz during Fraser's absence from Paris as he covered the war crimes trials. His first stop was the Belsen Trial convened before a British military tribunal. As the Soviets overran Auschwitz-Birkenau in Poland, many of the camp's SS personnel relocated to Bergen-Belsen in western Germany now within the British occupation zone.

Fraser arrived two weeks after the opening of the trial. Only Forty-five defendants consisting of concentration and extermination camp personnel of Auschwitz-Birkenau and Bergen-Belsen faced trial.

He expected to remain only for a couple of weeks in Lüneburg, near Hamburg before journeying south to the American Dachau Trials outside Munich. The experience provided him the first close-up look at these monsters.

Listening to the accusations was chilling. Fraser struggled to find words to describe acts of inhumanity. Witness testimony reciting torment difficult to comprehend proved even more disturbing when delivered unemotionally by victims. Conversely, testimony of the defendants was uniformly disgusting. The consistent theme of following orders with no other recourse. Some more revealing. A doctor serving at both Auschwitz and Bergen-Belsen testified to the question of how he ethically reconciled his actions as a physician. His reply, "My Hippocratic oath tells me to cut a gangrenous appendix out of the human body. The Jews are the gangrenous appendix of mankind. That is why I cut them out."

Like other journalists covering the proceedings, the consensus was a hasty and poorly prepared prosecution. For Fraser, he was at least gratified with the handing down of eleven death sentences by hanging that included three female camp guards.

The trial reinforced Fraser's view that overwhelming numbers of SS would escape justice. Although he held the view that just being a member of the Nazis *Schutzstaffel* was in itself criminal, the numbers of SS directly committing crimes must be staggering. Crimes by any standard of social norms. Hundreds of SS involved during the operational years of Auschwitz-Birkenau, Bergen-Belsen, and Mittelbau-Dora yet only 45 charged in this trial proved the limitations of judicial process.

Perhaps the American Army's Dachau Trials might prove different. The schedule called for successive proceedings to start in November 1945 for defendants serving at various concentration camps.

Before going to Dachau, Fraser returned to Paris for the holidays. The first Christmas in five years at home without suffering under Nazi occupation. Paris now returned to pre-German occupation normalcy. Although the aftermath of war still held their thoughts, Fraser and Marchand enjoyed three weeks of simply enjoying each other. What better place than their beloved Paris even in the chill of winter with snow.

Fraser arrived in Dachau in January 1946. Seeing the concentration camp brought back the horrific visions of his first visit with Fiona. The dead bodies spilling out of the railroad carriages, the thousands of emaciated surviving inmates. The indescribable stench.

Whereas a judicial panel representing the major Allied nations conducted the Nuremberg Trials, the Dachau Trials were proceedings held before a U.S. military tribunal. Dachau concentration camp chosen as the venue because of its intact facilities. It also provided a fitting emotional backdrop in which to try defendants serving at Nazi concentration and extermination camps. The cases would not only include defendants from Dachau, but also Buchenwald, Flossenburg, Mauthausen-Gusen, Muehldorf, Dora-Nordhausen, as well as crimes directed against U.S. prisoners of war.

Fraser's interest was the broader judicial reach to render justice rather than the antidotal stories of individual defendants. After interviewing prosecutors, he established the total number of camp defendants projected for the sequence of trials at Dachau at about 300. To add perspective, the British military Belsen Trials included only 45 defendants. Only 23 major Nazi war criminals faced the joint Allied military tribunal in Nuremberg. Following this would be a series of subsequent trials at Nuremberg for second-echelon Nazi leaders. Yet, collectively according to official sources, the expected number of these additional Nuremberg indictments probably would not exceed 150.

This meant that little more than 500 accused Nazi war criminals would face trial. None of the prosecutors interviewed by Fraser knew of plans for future war crimes trials other than anticipated show trials in the Soviet occupation zone. Those trials would likely see predominately collaborators rather than Nazi perpetrators as defendants since most escaped west to avoid capture by the Red Army.

Therefore, only high profile Nazis fugitives would face trial if ever arrested. The math supported Fraser's contention that thousands of former SS guilty of crimes against humanity would escape justice. Of these, a significant percentage conceivably guilty of committing multiple murders, torture, or hideous medical experiments. How many of the 3,000 SS *Einsatzgruppen* death squad members would never see justice? How many SS concentration camp personnel escaped by simply blending into the hordes of displaced persons? These former SS discarded their uniforms and identifications claiming to be refugees or stole identifications of German *Wehrmacht* soldiers, therefore becoming prisoners of war. With new identifications issued by the Red Cross in a new name, these criminals sought refuge in Germany and Austria, helped by family and a general sense of Germanic nationalistic unity among the populace. Rooting out former SS in significant numbers was unrealistic.

Within a week of arriving at Dachau, Fraser made the rounds of talking to other journalists to understand the landscape. The criminal acts of the worst of the defendants. Which prosecutors were approachable? Which of the investigators of the U.S. Army's Counterintelligence Corps most helpful? How did they track down the defendants? What efforts to go after more?

Since his earliest days as an investigative journalist in Los Angeles, Fraser relied on his talent to coax people into talking to him. A chameleon, he could call on a wide range of persona to suit the circumstance. He could charm, empathize, conspire, or threaten convincingly.

One particular source proved not only helpful but in developing a personal rapport, might prove greatly helpful.

Captain David Larson was a young army officer from New York. A lawyer graduated from Columbia Law in 1941. Fluency in German got him assigned to army intelligence in early 1942. As a fellow New Yorker having received a degree in journalism from Columbia, Fraser made an immediate connection. Quickly this developed into a relationship as Fraser related his wartime service with the French Resistance then with the OSS. Not only captivated by the older Fraser's exploits, but Fraser's telling of the attack in Paris by former SS cemented a quasi-professional bond with Larson.

Larson shared his eagerness to go after other war criminals. With his father a prosecutor in Brooklyn, Larson aspired to follow his father into law enforcement. With the rise of Adolf Hitler before the war, he recognized Hitler as the ultimate arch criminal. Obsessively inquisitive, Larson chose German as his undergraduate language to read and hear this rabid dictator in his own words. With this background, a natural assignment followed as an investigator for the Army's prosecution of Nazi war criminals at the end of the war.

"This attack on you and your wife in Paris, what is being done?" Larson asked as they shared a beer at a local cafe.

"Nothing as far as I know. No one from U.S. intelligence has followed up. Perhaps Washington did not want to acknowledge former Nazis presenting a continued threat. French police played down the incident. Never made the newspapers."

"Bad enough that hundreds of war criminals are still on the loose, but to think they might be mounting tactical operations is disturbing. Glad your wife was not harmed."

"Speaking of all those SS never arrested, what is the Army doing to hunt them down?"

Larson shook his head. "Very little I'm afraid. Oh, there are lists of those wanted but not particularly useful. Most do not have pictures. At the camps, the SS destroyed many records before the Allies moved in. You can image their own personnel records would be the first to go."

"Yet it looks like you captured various camp commandants. What about their immediate staff?"

"Most just slipped away. Blended into the civilian population. Some are in detention. A daunting task attempting to make cases. It is as if the police arrested every crook in Brooklyn all at once. Making a case requires evidence. Little evidence found among these ruins. Prosecution based almost entirely on witness testimony. That means multiple direct witnesses to the criminal acts of the defendant necessary to make a strong case. The scope is beyond the resources of the Army."

"Beyond the resources of the Army? You just defeated the Nazis, Captain. Perhaps there is a lack of will. Everything now shifted toward the Soviet threat? Before I left the OSS there was even talk about using former Nazis in that effort."

"More than just talk within the Counterintelligence Corps, Mr. Fraser. For the same classified restrictions you cannot discuss the attack in Paris, I am not at liberty to say more."

"Of course. However, I find using people guilty of war crimes is nothing more than a justification of any means to serve a desired end. Every dictator uses the same argument. It does not fit American values."

"Also troubles me," Larson said.

"Must be many junior SS officer war criminals not accounted for."

"Unfortunately, you are correct. The Army obviously did not round up the majority of SS serving at these camps. Little planning appears given to that mission. The American Army is not trained for police work."

"As a journalist, I have covered all sorts of criminals. Nothing approaches the level of depravity of the Nazis. As a European correspondent, I covered Hitler's rise to power in the early '30s. Had my first direct run-in with the SS in 1933." Two drunken officers accosted me outside a restaurant in Berlin."

"What happened?"

"It did not go well for them. Not sure if either of them survived our violent encounter. Fine by me if they did not. Anyway, I hastily left Berlin."

Larson wondered if Fraser exaggerated the incident. Fraser did not elaborate remarking, "I have seen enough of the *Schutzstaffel*'s crimes. I visited Dachau immediately following liberation. Piles of rotting corpses. The survivors suffering from starvation. By nature of just belonging to the SS, all its members are guilty of war crimes. These were not conscripts. The SS consisted of selected volunteers.

"I understand the social imperative of administering justice through a judicial process. However, the vast membership of the

SS makes that impossible. Yet the magnitude and nature of Nazi crimes demands a different solution. Remnants of the Nazi SS must be eradicated."

Taken back by Fraser's strident declaration, Larson remarked, "This is obviously very personal to you."

Fraser reflected on the deaths he caused. Cabrera, Leitner, Krüger, the two killed in Paris. Perhaps he might get the chance to execute Klaus Barbie and Heinrich Müller. Unlikely he would ever get the opportunity, but at least he knew Müller's location.

"Very personal. I could also add that under Nazi racial laws, I am a Jew."

Larson nodded then said, "Here is some news that might make good copy. I am working on investigating Otto Skorzeny on charges of war crimes. He was a favorite of Hitler. The SS commando who freed Mussolini held in the Italian mountains after being deposed."

"Why is he charged for war crimes?"

"Deployed English speaking SS soldiers wearing U.S. uniforms to disrupt U.S. supply movements in the Battle of the Bulge."

By midyear after traveling back and forth by train to Paris every other week, Fraser had enough of listening to testimony against SS war criminals. He chose to capture the testimony of witnesses to give his submittals to the news agency more compelling reading. Yet the words of the victims describing horrors so unspeakable could never impart the experience to others. Having experienced Dachau and Mauthausen close up, Fraser also found his words inadequate to communicate the indescribable.

While Captain Larson and others provided names of those sought based on their serving in these camps, it was not particularly helpful for his journalistic quest. The names represented just a small portion of the SS having perpetrated the worst atrocities of the Holocaust. Intelligence remained fragmented on SS serving in the camps in Poland now under Soviet occupation. Auschwitz-Berkenau, Treblinka, Majdanek, Sobibor, Belzec, and Chelmno, the principle extermination camps. Most of those SS camp personnel escaped west ahead of the advancing Red Army after destroying as much as possible of the evidence.

Then there were the thousands of members of the Nazi mobile killing units, the *Einsatzgruppen*. These units operated on the eastern front before the creation of the industrialized extermination camps. By nature of their function, every *Einsatzgruppen* was a war criminal.

Covering the war crimes trials as a means of networking investigative sources was not proving productive. Before aborting and returning to Paris, he convinced Fiona to join him in Linz. Having met Simon Wiesenthal the tough survivor of Nazi concentration camps, they continued a correspondence over the past year.

Wiesenthal's tenacity in pursuing Nazi war criminals as his life's work impressed them. From their correspondence, they knew Wiesenthal by now had an extensive archive of war criminals now running into the thousands. The whereabouts of these perpetrators of the Holocaust however remained elusive.

Fraser remembered Wiesenthal's comments before they parted after visiting Mauthausen: "*When the Germans first came to my city in Galicia, half the population was Jewish. One hundred fifty thousand Jews. When the Germans were gone, five hundred were alive. ... Many times I was thinking that everything in life has a price, so to stay alive must also have a price. And my price was always that, if I lived, I must be deputy for many people who are not alive.*

*Having survived is not enough. There must be an accounting to the other side of the ledger. Justice is a societal term. For the individual victim, retribution becomes the natural response.*"

Wiesenthal worked for the American Army's Counterintelligence Corps War Crimes office for a year collecting information on the perpetrators from victims. He relocated to Linz with the

American investigators when Mauthausen fell within the Soviet occupation zone.

Just twelve miles to the west of the Mauthausen main camp, Linz remained a somber place. Bombed during the war, life here seemed overshadowed by the proximity of the extensive Mauthausen-Gusen network of abandoned concentration camps.

A joyful reunion. Housed in a displaced persons camp, Wiesenthal was overwhelmed when we entered unannounced. That first evening, they left the camp to enjoy a modest dinner at one of the few functioning restaurants.

Marchand immediately asked, "Any word about your wife, Simon?"

Wiesenthal smiled as tears cascaded down his cheeks. "Wonderful news. She is alive. Unfortunately, her ordeal has left her with health problems. In a remarkable sequence of events, she returned to Lvov in Poland after the war ended. She found me through a message posted on the Jewish community's notice board. I saw her for the first time only two weeks ago."

Marchand reached over and grasped Wiesenthal's hand her own tears flowed.

"She hid in Warsaw with false papers and the help of the Polish underground. Unfortunately, it did not last. Discovered, the Nazis sent her west to a forced labor camp.

Fraser said, "We are so happy for you, Simon. You will be together soon?"

"Yes. Certainly not in Poland. I want nothing to do with the Soviets."

"You look remarkably recovered from when we first met, Simon," Fiona said.

Wiesenthal said, "Reuniting with my Cyla and the effects of receiving sufficient food. You look just as beautiful as I recall, Fiona. Your letters say you are again back at the Louvre. I hope your life in Paris has returned to some normalcy."

His comment touched a nerve sufficient to cause an expression noticed by the observant Wiesenthal. "What is it, Fiona? Is something wrong?"

"Something terrible happened in Paris, Simon," Fraser said. "Three former SS attacked us in our apartment."

After relating the details, Wiesenthal said, "Obviously thinking that SS have scattered into hiding from arrest is not entirely accurate. Not surprising given their arrogance of superiority."

Fraser said, "Therefore, like you, Fiona and I have our personal reasons for hunting these criminals. My endeavors as a journalist provide the means of sourcing information and exercising the power of the written word to try making some difference."

"But this attack? You say it related to an intelligence operation during the war? Why would they now risk coming after you?"

"Unfortunately certain circumstances during the war remain classified. Something I did damaging the *Schutzstaffel.* Perhaps they sought revenge. That is now what I am after, Simon. Call it justice, but it is really revenge. I have many reasons for wanting to destroy remnants of the *Schutzstaffel.* I want to collaborate with your efforts, Simon. Use your extensive files and do what I can to punish Nazi war criminals."

"Of course. I welcome any efforts directed against former Nazis. However, I am not sure of the resolve of the Allies in pursuing war criminals. The SS have assimilated into the populations of Germany and Austria. New identities. Helped by family and sympathizers. An impossible task to locate them much less bringing them to justice.

"Many of the worst are trying to leave Europe. As you know, I work closely with the American Army counterintelligence war crimes office. Some evidence exists of certain Roman Catholic clergy in Rome aiding war criminals to escape to South America."

"The Church? Why would they do such a thing?" Marchand said.

Wiesenthal said, "I do not know. Perhaps it is not true. Yet my sources were even more specific. They mentioned an Austrian bishop named Hudal and a Croatian priest named Draganović. Both apparently known to hold Fascist sympathies. Both work in Rome. They even coined the name *Catholic ratlines*.

Back in Paris, Fraser and Marchand considered what to do next. Fraser contacted two former OSS colleagues now with the successor agency the American Central Intelligence Group, the CIG. Both confirmed what Wiesenthal related. This now represented a new line of investigation. If true, adverse publicity might force the Church to suspend any efforts to assist escaping war criminals.

Broaching the idea of going to Rome, Marchand offered to go with him. She can arrange for a working leave from the Louvre. Monsignor Donati, Managing Director of the Vatican Museum, will gladly submit a request to the Louvre requesting her restoration assistance. Her only request is to enjoy the last two weeks of late autumn in Paris before going to Rome in December.

Fraser agreed. He would use the time to work his sources and probe this new lead of Catholic clergy involved with helping war criminals. Many critics of Pope Pius XII criticized the pontiff as harboring Fascist sympathies. Some even called him Hitler's pope. Fraser knew the circumstances to be far more complicated. Preserving the Vatican as a sovereign state within Mussolini's Fascist Italy, then surrounded by German troops in 1943, required a delicate balancing act. Yet aiding those charged with horrific crimes seemed unconscionable for His Holiness. If true, what could possibly be the motivation?

A letter arrived one afternoon that further inflamed Fraser's anger toward the remnants of the Nazi *Schutzstaffel*.

Old friend,

It has been ten years since we met in Madrid. So much has happen. Both our countries taken over by Fascists. Spain remains under the yoke of a Fascist dictator.

Once in France, my cousin Loretta wrote to me about the terrible ordeal in Bilbao and later about working together with you in the French Resistance. The last communication from my cousin was in 1943. I would be indebted for any information you could provide on her and her husband Rafael. You can reach me by post through our mutual friend here in Palestine.

He related what happened in Paris last year. Seems you have a knack for survival. We share your hatred for the Nazi *Schutzstaffel.* Sources I maintain in Madrid provided the following.

The perpetrators you described consist of former SS as well as other Nazi functionaries and collaborators. They keep a low profile but their backgrounds are known to the Franco government. They refer to themselves as the *Komeradenwerk.* There is also some reference to the name *Die Spinne.* All possess false identifications. We will endeavor to obtain photographs perhaps useful in establishing their actual identities.

Waffen-SS Obersturmbannführer Otto Skorzeny founded this Madrid base of operations in early 1944. You perhaps will know the name from the headlines of the rescue of Benito Mussolini. Madrid was to be part of broader contingency plans as Germany faced inevitable defeat. This included the creation of a paramilitary guerilla force called the *Werewolves*, and plans for elite German forces to ultimately retreat to an Alpine Redoubt in the south. Skorzeny was involved in these preparations that never materialized. He also participated in the last ditch German offensive in the Ardennes.

Madrid is a perfect operating base from within Europe, under the protection of a sympathetic Fascist dictator. Skorzeny met with many Nazi collaborators to create the underpinnings of this Nazi outpost. A base from which to conduct operations into the Fatherland. Also a way station for those seeking refuge in sympathetic Argentina.

The collection of Nazis consists primarily of former SS. The numbers are unknown. Among those are an unknown number of former *Fallschirmjäger,* SS paratroops. Skorzeny also set in place a Spanish company to channel funds into investments to provide a source of sustaining financial resources to this exiled group. The name of the company is *Empresas de Fénix S.L.*

The organization to which your friend and I belong share your interest in eradicating this collection of SS. Unfortunately, the only assistance we can offer at this time is intelligence. Survival of not only the *Yishuv* in Palestine but the Jewish survivors of the Nazi Holocaust take priority.

We recognized your unique contribution in this great struggle. As you have given to the cause of saving European Jews, we shall provide whatever assistance possible to bring Nazi war criminals to justice.

Shalom,

Felix Martel

# CHAPTER 22

## MENNINGEN GERMANY | MARCH 1947

---

Gerald Mayer their former OSS colleague from Bern contacted Fraser and Marchand as they prepared to go to Rome. Mayer also left American intelligence at the end of the war to pursue his civilian career. Before the war, he worked for the National Broadcasting Company. He obtained their address through former contacts in the OSS. Mayer was in the process of setting up an office in Paris as the new director of international operations of the Motion Picture Association of America.

The congenial Mayer took a liking to both Fraser and Marchand when they turned up in Switzerland. While he and Allen Dulles were armchair intelligence operatives, Fraser and Marchand came directly from dangerous work behind the lines in France. As in his case, they felt compelled to join the fight, now choosing to return to their former careers.

Born in Berlin of American parents, he like Fraser was as much European as American. With Fraser's involvement with the French film industry during the difficult years of German occupation, perhaps he might be helpful in Mayer's new international role promoting the American film industry.

Both Fraser and Marchand welcomed Mayer's visit, especially with the prospect of a friend taking up residence in Paris.

"I am delighted to hear you are back working at the Louvre," Mayer said. "I can imagine there are countless restoration projects here in France awaiting talented restorers like you. Italy too. Would you ever return to do work there?"

"Oh, of course. I always enjoyed Italy. My injury did not change that. In fact we are planning to return to Rome soon for a few weeks."

"Any physical aftereffects?"

"No. Only a scar. It was the infection that almost did me in."

"And you Marc? What are you now doing?"

"Briefly returned to journalism. Doing freelance work for Reuters. I plan to return to writing novels where I left off when the Germans invaded. I certainly have amassed enough new material. Right now, I am covering the various war crimes trials.

"However, my interest is not reporting on the trials. I hope to use it as a means of making contacts to investigate those Nazis that are not facing trials. The hundreds, perhaps thousands of SS directly carrying out the Holocaust. Guess you might call me a Nazi hunter."

"Interesting. So you have not entirely put the war behind you."

"I guess you do not know what happened over a year ago. I would think French authorities informed U.S. intelligence. Probably after you left the OSS."

Fraser was probing. Did Dulles send Mayer to look into the incident in Paris?

"What are you referring to, Marc?" Mayer said with a look of genuine concern.

"Not long after we returned to Paris, three former SS paid us a visit."

"Good lord! What happened?"

"It concerned the Krüger matter. You recall the report I filed about Krüger managing SS Swiss bank accounts? I assume the SS experienced difficulties with the accounts after Krüger killed himself. Somehow they learned I was running Krüger. Thought I might be involved with something that happened to the SS deposits.

"They never got far enough in their questioning for me to understand what they were after. In a hurry, they threatened to disfigure Fiona using a knife if I did not tell them everything I knew about Krüger. Always prepared after her experience in the field in Italy, Fiona continued to carry a small caliber pistol. When they moved toward her with that knife, she shot two of them. I disarmed the other one."

Mayer looked at Fiona, "Then what happened?"

With composure, Fiona answered, "The two I shot died. Marc badly injured the other. The Paris police arrested the injured man for attempted murder. An SD officer serving in Paris during the occupation. The incident never made the newspapers. With occupation experiences still raw with the Paris citizenry, the chief inspector said the thought of SS infiltrating Paris might cause unnecessary panic. The war record of the SD officer was also sufficient to try him on war crimes. Somewhat difficult to easily return to our prewar lives."

"That is remarkable. To think former SS would be bold enough to mount an attack suggested something of critical importance. One would think their concern was remaining in hiding."

"You would think," Fraser said. "But the SS are not only fanatical but pragmatic. Thousands have evaded detection. Not surprising that some refuse to remain fugitives. I suspect that many will attempt to escape Europe. Regroup out of reach of Allied retribution. These SS apparently came from Spain."

"Or some of the more opportunistic and enterprising will seek new careers with the Western Allies."

"What do you mean, Gerry?" Fraser said with a questioning expression.

"I assume you knew of the Army CIC Operation Paperclip to take German scientists and technicians to the United States. Even those that used slave labor in their work like the V-2 program. Of course the Soviets did the same."

Fraser said. "To be expected even though some should face trial for war crimes."

"I agree. However, you may not know how far things have gone concerning using former Nazis for intelligence purposes."

Fraser said, "All of us in the OSS were tasked to seek out sources. Krüger even tried to provide names of officers in Gehlen's Foreign Armies East military intelligence."

"Yes. *Wehrmacht* officers. However, I have it on good authority that our Army colleagues in the Counterintelligence Corps are becoming less discriminating. Actively recruiting former *Schutzstaffel*. Not only the intelligence branch, the *Sicherheitsdienst*, but even former *Gestapo*."

"That is disgusting. Are we that desperate to employ war criminals?"

"Troubled me enough to poll my former contacts in American intelligence. One former OSS agent, still on the payroll with the Central Intelligence Group willingly confided to me something particularly disturbing. This agent worked undercover in France with the French Resistance and the British SOE. Now works out of the Paris embassy. What I repeat, he told me just two days ago.

"Being so close to the French, he was not only angry but feels betrayed. Knowing your experience in France, I suspect you will find it even more disturbing. As a journalist, you must promise not to publicize this, Marc."

"What? Is it that bad?"

"You be the judge. I must protect the source. Promise not to print this?"

"Fine. I won't make it public."

"It concerns Hauptsturmführer Klaus Barbie. *Gestapo* chief for Lyon. Your old nemesis, the *Butcher of Lyon*."

"What about him?" Fraser said raising his voice.

"The Army CIC recruited him."

"That can't be true. How can he be of any counterintelligence use against the Soviets?"

"My CIG source says the information is solid. He will not reveal his source but is certain of its reliability. Said demobilization decimated Army CIC operations on the ground in Europe by the loss of most experienced officers. His opinion is many of those remaining in Europe stayed on because of poor prospects back in the States. The Soviet scare has unleashed a reactionary response by an understaffed and inferior CIC. Conflicting missions of policing German denazification while pursuing the Soviet threat. Barbie may be an example.

"Case in point, I know also the U.S. is working closely with General Gehlen. After his debriefing, the United States set him up in Germany to assemble a counterintelligence organization to penetrate the Soviet Union. Gehlen is recruiting not only former *Abwehr* operatives, but also former SS. So not that farfetched that some ambitious CIC army officers are doing the same."

"Shit. Barbie is not just any SS war criminal. He must be on CIC lists to arrest on sight. The French have already sentenced him to death in absentia for war crimes."

"My source said much the same thing."

"I would like to talk with him."

"Thought you might. He agreed to telephone you tomorrow evening. As I also warned him, tread carefully. Don't get crossways with competing American intelligence missions."

The following evening, the CIG man called. "Our mutual friend told me of your interest in knowing more about a former official in Lyon."

"Yes. A very personal interest."

"Would tomorrow evening, seven o'clock be convenient?"

"Excellent."

"I suggest the English Bar at the Regina Hotel across from the Louvre. Close to your wife's work. Feel free to bring her since all of us worked for the same company. Recognize me by a red scarf and gray swede gloves. I have seen your personnel file so I will recognize you"

❖ ❖ ❖

The English Bar at the Regina Hotel is decorated in Victorian era styled dark wood paneling with red upholstered chairs around small tables spaced to provide reasonable conversational privacy. Arriving early, Fraser and Marchand sat at a table with a view of the entrance from the hotel lobby. After ordering drinks, they saw their man entering. Tall in his thirties, he approached their table immediately offering in perfect French, "I am Hugh Granger. Preferred not to use my name on the telephone."

Fraser stood and shook hands Granger's hand. "My wife, Fiona Marchand."

They exchanged pleasantries including Granger briefly sharing his wartime experiences operating in occupied France.

"From your file, I know quite a bit of your background, Mr. Fraser. A fascinating read. I met Jean Moulin briefly once in London. You on the other hand actually escorted him around to meet with Resistance leaders using your cover in the film industry. A clever but dangerous undertaking.

"Moulin was an extraordinary man. That my own government is harboring a monster like Klaus Barbie is an affront. If I can disrupt those assholes in the CIC, I will do what I can. Pardon my language, Madame Marchand."

Marchand smiled, "Marc's language can be far worse."

After the waiter brought Granger a Scotch, Fraser launched into his questioning. "Do you have more specific details concerning the whereabouts of Barbie?"

"Oh, yes. Made a point of digging deeper. When Truman dissolved the OSS, it became the Central Intelligence group. Placed under the War Department just like the Army's CIC therefore, more connected than during the war.

"The CIC in Europe is now a disorganized collection of incompetents with all the best experienced officers mustering out and returned stateside. Fair amount of infighting. Poor command structure. Security leaks like a sieve. Easy enough as part of the War Department larger intelligence apparatus for me to get information.

"You see, American intelligence has no eyes or ears into the Soviet Communists. The Reds now control all of Eastern Europe. Everyone paranoid about Soviet influence with the Communist parties of France and Italy. Using Gehlen and his cadre of former *Abwehr* and Nazis as our surrogate counterintelligence arm is an act of desperation.

"However, back to your specific question, Mr. Fraser. A former *Abwehr* agent named Joseph 'Kurt" Merk, working for the CIC, recruited Barbie. Merk worked out of Dijon during the occupation. He and Barbie jointly ran successful penetrations into French Resistance networks. CIC Region IV in Bavaria recruited Merk last year. Merk brings along his former comrade, Lyon *Gestapo* chief Klaus Barbie. Somehow sells these clowns on his usefulness to the Americans.

"Rumor has it there is a running disagreement between Region IV and the 7970 CIC detachment command in Frankfurt about continuing to use Barbie as an informer or to arrest him. Yet Barbie remains on the payroll, safe in the American occupation zone. Works out of an office at 36 Kaiser Promenade in Memmingen. Stays at a rooming house in the town. "

Fraser retreated into a moment of thought before looking at Marchand then back to Granger. "Got any bodyguards around him?"

"I couldn't say. No reason though for physical protection. Who is going to come after him?" Granger said as he saw the hardened expression on Fraser's face. "Remember, this is no longer wartime, Mr. Fraser."

Fraser smiled. "Much as I would like to put a bullet his head, I understand the limits of taking extrajudicial action. However, knowing his location does suggest other possibilities. After all, France has already convicted him of war crimes and sentenced him to death. The problem seems to be a bunch of American cowboys going off the reservation."

Granger said, "Obviously I am in no position to assist in any official capacity. Best you do not ask for more details. I need to maintain plausible deniability for any help I provide. Sounds like I came to the right person though. Someone who hates Barbie more than I do. I will continue to provide whatever intelligence I can. Here is my direct line at the embassy.

"Now let me treat you and your lovely wife to dinner. Expense account you know, Plus I like the company."

Later, back at the apartment, Fraser was in a high state of agitation. "Can you imagine, the Americans harboring Barbie. Hypocritical bastards."

Marchand said, "According to Granger, it sounds like either a rogue operation by some CIC officers, or broader mission confusion within the Army."

"The fact remains, Barbie has avoided arrest. Even if the CIC changes their mind, they will face some very awkward explaining. Barbie is in the same class of war criminal as Eichmann and Mengele."

Hesitantly, Marchand asked, "So what do you want to do?"

"Go after him."

"To do what?" She was afraid he intended to kill Barbie.

"Capture him. Drive him to France. Strasbourg is a four-hour drive. He is under sentence of death in France. Shooting him would be more satisfying but better to see him go to the guillotine. Besides, it is a better way to fuck the Americans when I make public what they were doing."

"God damn it, Marc. Will you ever stop?"

Fraser looked at her defiantly. "It is what I do, Fiona. My whole life I have been chasing bad guys. None as bad as Barbie. He deserves to die. So does Heinrich Müller. Both are enjoying freedom. What am I to do? Write my exposés and expect the wheels of justice to take its course?"

"And why not? Why must you risk your life?"

Fraser paused trying to articulate something fundamental in his makeup, "It is just the way I am, Fiona. I have no faith in government institutions doing the right thing. Look what the American Army is doing with Barbie. Probably others. So I push the boundaries to make things happen."

Marchand shook her head in resignation then embraced him. "I understand. At least I understand that is who you are. But I insist on being part of whatever you are planning. If you are going to risk your life, I must be at your side. Agreed?"

Fraser nodded agreement and kissed her.

"So what do we do next?" She said.

Pursuing Catholic ratlines in Rome must wait. Klaus Barbie was too important. However, attempting to capture Barbie in occupied Germany while under the protection of the American Army presented an insurmountable feat without help. What better than the assistance of an Army counterintelligence officer investigating war criminals? If he could manipulate Captain Larson, it might afford the necessary protection if circumstances went badly.

Larson appeared properly motivated working to make prosecution cases of SS currently in detention. Why not a major war criminal like Barbie? Granger provided proof that Barbie's name remained prominent on all arrest lists distributed to military, intelligence, and diplomatic U.S. government branches. The fact these CIC buccaneers in Bavaria were ignoring that suggested they might be running their own game.

Best to share with Captain Larson the cover story of uncovering the information through a source as a journalist he could not name. Needed someone within the CIC he could trust to arrest Barbie.

If successful in capturing Barbie, the problem remains to alter Larson's expectation of turning Barbie over to his own CIC commander. How does he convince Larson to interfere in another CIC unit's operation? A delicate maneuver to which Fraser had not yet devised a clear plan.

However, the opportunity to capture Barbie was too good to pass up. Simply publicizing the sordid story would result in Barbie disappearing. The Army forced to cover up the incident and quietly reassign the involved army offices. Harboring a major Nazi fugitive while war crimes trials were taking place would cause a major scandal ruining military careers. Why the Army saw any Soviet counterintelligence value in a notorious middle-level *Gestapo* officer serving only in Western Europe remained incomprehensible.

Armed with his press credentials, Fraser and Marchand left Paris Gare Est for Stuttgart then changed trains for Munich. Fraser wired ahead for a rental car. The plan called for making an unannounced visit to Captain Larson. They must convince Larson to accompany them immediately to Memmingen or miss participating in a spectacular arrest.

Arriving in Dachau, Fraser registered at the same hotel he used for covering the trials. After getting a good night's rest, he telephoned Larson's office the following morning.

Larson appeared at the café where he previously shared drinks with Fraser. Pleasantly surprised when he saw the attractive woman sitting at Fraser's table.

Fraser rose and greeted him with a handshake.

"This is my wife Fiona Marchand, Captain."

Larson beamed a wide smile. "Captain David Larson, ma'am. What brings you to Germany?"

As Larson sat down, Fraser pulled out the copy of the Army's most wanted list of war criminal fugitives provided by Hugh Granger the American CIG agent. "This," He said handing Larson a packet of papers."

"I am familiar with this wanted list, Mr. Fraser. Circulated among every American headquarters in our occupied zone. Problem is we do not know the names these people are using. No pictures even. Not particularly helpful."

"Look at these pictures," Fraser said passing Larson two photographs. "Look at page two. Does the name Klaus Barbie mean anything?"

"Not really. The offenses the same for most of these monsters."

"Barbie is known as the *Butcher of Lyon* for good reason. Worse than most. A mass murderer who also personally liked to torture his victims. The French already convicted him and sentenced him to death in absentia. That is his picture. I also know where he is?"

Shocked, Larson said, "You came here to see that the Army arrests him?"

"Something like that. Unfortunately, more complicated. There are those protecting him."

"Not a problem. I can muster a squad of military police. Where is Barbie?"

"You don't understand, Captain. Barbie is under U.S. Army counterintelligence protection."

Larson's jaw clenched but he remained silence for several moments. "How do you know this?"

Surprised Larson did not refute the allegation as ridiculous, Fraser said. "You are not surprised?"

Larson sighed. "Disappointed. As I mentioned when we first met, there is talk about using former Nazis. Never would imagine someone on the most wanted list though. You sure about this?"

"Came from a reliable source in American intelligence, not the Army."

"Makes no sense. Why publish a wanted list and then hide someone as notorious as this?"

"Mixed signals to the occupying forces. It is less about denazification now than confronting Communism. Here you are prosecuting Nazis while others employ known war criminals.

"Who do you work for, Captain?"

"The commander of the investigative team. A lieutenant colonel."

"If you brought him Barbie, would he arrest him?"

"I'm sure he would. He's a former police captain. Worked as an investigator for Tom Dewey when Dewey was a special prosecutor pursuing organized crime and corruption in New York."

"Okay. Here is the deal, Captain. I want Barbie's head. It is personal. Goes back to my time fighting with the French Resistance. He tortured and murdered a friend. I need your help but obviously cannot trust the Army unit using Barbie. So the three of us will arrest Barbie and bring him back here. We will trust your colonel to do the right thing and seek an indictment on Barbie. It will not be difficult to make a case against this monster. I took the opportunity to add research information further detailing his crimes and listing potential witnesses, including me."

"Barbie is close by?"

"A few hours' drive."

"Where?"

"I would rather not say, Captain. I do not care to risk you feeling compelled to inform your superiors. Too much chance of this getting back to those in the CIC hiding Barbie. We bag Barbie and drive him back here. You get credit for the arrest, I get my revenge and a front-page story."

Larson said, "No offense, ma'am, but have you ever done anything like this?"

Marchand said calmly, "I actively served in the French Resistance. I was also an OSS agent in Italy. Wounded in combat. I can handle a gun. I have killed two men. Is that satisfactory?"

With a look of surprise, Larson said, "Yes, of course." Pondering his choices for a moment, "Very well. Count me in. When do we leave?"

"Immediately. If we are successful then we should be back here tomorrow.

Less than a two-hour drive, they arrived in the small Bavarian town of Memmingen. On the drive into Memmingen, they passed a displaced persons camp. 36 Kaiser Promenade was a modest four story building in the main square. The town retained the vestiges of a picturesque town in spite of Allied bombings damaging parts of the old town and surrounding industrial sites.

As they drove past the building, an American flag and an Army unit flag flew above the building entrance guarded by two American soldiers.

"Jesus Christ," Larson uttered. "Your source says Barbie works out of the local Army headquarters?"

"Apparently. The problem is surveillance of the building until Barbie appears. We need to remain inconspicuous. Need to catch him alone walking to the rooming house where he lives. The cover of darkness preferable but it will also make identifying Barbie more difficult from a distance."

Marchand dressed that morning in a green kaki field outfit similar to what she wore in Italy during the war. Borrowing Fraser's cameras satisfied her cover as his photographer with her wartime false OSS press credentials. Fitted with a long lens, it provided magnification to examine faces from a distance.

"What's my cover for being here?" Larson asked.

"How about that displaced persons camp we passed? Interviewing camp survivors as witnesses for the Dachau trials. Accompanying these journalists," Fraser suggested. Considering that Barbie might be working out of the local American Army headquarters, Larson in uniform added the perfect cover for their presence.

"Okay," Larson said halfheartedly, uneasy about this venture. Was he getting himself into real trouble? Yet justice mattered. That was what he was doing. Investigating wanted war criminals like Barbie.

"That café over there," Fraser said. "Let's have a long lunch. We can see the entrance to number 36."

After two hours, they decided they must move or become obvious. Asking the café proprietor about hotel accommodations, he directed them to a small hotel down the street.

Fraser said, "I will get us a room. If possible, one with a window facing the street. In which case we can use the telephoto camera lens to watch the entrance to number 36. Otherwise we will have to manage from the hotel lobby and take turns walking about outside waiting for Barbie to emerge."

"What happens when we spot Barbie?" Larson said.

"You and I follow him on foot. Fiona will drive the car following slowly at a distance. If Barbie is alone we seize him assuming we can do so without witnesses. Best if it is dark but if given the opportunity, we take it. Otherwise, we figure a way once he is at the rooming house. That's where you in your uniform will come in, Captain."

"I brought handcuffs," Larson said.

"Excellent. Once we grab him, we gag him with a handkerchief to keep him quiet. Then march or drag him quickly to the car. Any witnesses at this point will just see your uniform escorting a prisoner in handcuffs.

"Wedge him between us in the backseat of the car. He is small in stature so we can handle him. Fiona, you drive. Get us out of town as quickly as possible without drawing attention. I will navigate."

Should they get that far, it was not to be a return to Dachau but instead to Strasbourg, France. Considering Larson's assistance, Fraser regretted the deception. However, he could not trust the U.S. Army bureaucracy to do the right thing. Most likely, they would opt to avoid a scandal.

A room at the front of the building on the second floor was available. The window afforded a view to the front door of number 36. With the telephoto camera lens set on a tripod, a perfect surveillance point as long as they had daylight. If Barbie did not show by dusk, then each would take turns making rounds outside in the cold to avoid being obvious.

Should Barbie not show, then a long night in the cramped room before resuming efforts the next day.

As daylight began fading, it was Marchand's turn at the camera lens. "Marc, come here."

Fraser jumped up and looked. "Could be. Hard to be certain with that hat, but let's go. Get the car ready, Fiona. The Captain and I will approach him on foot.

"Captain, I will do a walk-by heading in the opposite direction. You stay in the background then fall in beside me. If it is Barbie, he is with someone. We will see what develops."

As Fraser walked toward the approaching two men, he purposely stopped in front of them to ask directions to the American Army local headquarters in German. The shorter man looked at him while the other man answered and pointed behind.

Fraser held the gaze of the shorter man for as long as he dared. Enough to confirm he was Klaus Barbie.

Fraser responded with *dankeschön* and moved on to join up with Larson. "It's him. Let's follow from the other side of the street. If the other guy leaves Barbie, we take him."

Looking behind, Fraser could see Marchand inching the car along the street at a distance with the headlamps off.

They walked several blocks before Barbie and the other man arrived at a large house. A rooming house by the sign. The other man left and Barbie entered the house.

"Here is the plan, Captain. We go in together. You take charge. Show whomever comes to the door Barbie's photo. Demand to see him. Play it with arrogance.

"Once we confront Barbie, draw your sidearm. Tell him he is under arrest. Give me the handcuffs. Do not discuss anything with him. Just move him outside quickly and push him into the backseat. If he resists, I will smash him in the head with my gun and we stuff him in the trunk. Ready?"

Larson nodded taking the steps to the porch and knocked loudly.

Moments later a middle-aged woman answered the door. "Yes?"

Larson thrust the photograph in front of her face. In German, "Do you know this man?"

"Yes. That is Herr Altmann. What is this about?"

"Where is he?"

"The first room on the left up the stairs."

Fraser motioned with his head for both of them to go up. In case of trouble, he gripped his .45 automatic inside his overcoat pocket with the handcuffs in his other pocket.

Larson knocked. Moments later Barbie opened the door. He immediately looked at Fraser recognizing him as the man that stopped him outside. Something was clearly wrong.

"Nikolaus Barbie, you are under arrest," Larson said.

Barbie shook his head vigorously. "My name is Altmann. You are mistaken. I work for you Americans.

Fraser reached around Larson and grabbed Barbie by his shirt drawing Barbie closer. In German he said, "No, you are Klaus Barbie. Former *Gestapo*. A murderer. The Butcher of Lyon."

Barbie tried to pull away from Fraser but Larson stuck his .45 pistol in his face. "Or die here if you prefer."

Fraser roughly pushed Barbie against the door then turned him to place the handcuffs on his wrists behind his back.

Grabbing Barbie's overcoat, Fraser said, "Let's get moving, Captain."

Larson held Barbie by the arm and guided him towards the stairs. As all three looked down, an American Army military police lieutenant and another man in civilian clothing looked up from the bottom of the stairs.

In German, Barbie yelled, "Kurt, help me!" Shaking free of Larson's grasp, he tried to retreat backwards but Fraser stood in his way.

Fraser leveled his .45 toward the lieutenant as the officer opened his overcoat trying to reach his sidearm. "Don't be stupid, lieutenant. This man is under arrest."

"Who are you?" The lieutenant said.

Barbie dropped to his knees. Larson tried to lift him to his feet but Barbie resisted. The distraction allowed the lieutenant to unclasp his holster flap, but hesitated with Fraser still pointing his Browning.

Fraser shouted, "Remove your weapon and place it on the floor. Now!"

Once the lieutenant complied, "Hands on top of your head. Both of you."

With Larson unable to get Barbie to his feet. Fraser swiped the barrel of his pistol across Barbie's forehead over his left eye. Filled with rage this close to Barbie, the blow was much harder than intended. Barbie fell forward slipping down several steps.

Larson tried again to lift Barbie to his feet. Barely conscious, Barbie just groaned while remaining on his knees leaning against the staircase railing as blood streamed down his face. He knew his fate if taken away. Something terribly gone wrong circumventing his protective arrangement with American Army counterintelligence.

Fraser realized he and Larson could not carry Barbie while at the same time contending with the Army officer and the other man. The situation compounded when two male occupants of the rooming house joined the landlady in the foyer.

Not willing to concede failure, shooting Barbie passed as a fleeting thought for Fraser. However, rational assessment overruled emotion. Too many witnesses. Still under American military marshal law, he was also clearly upsetting some American intelligence arrangement. Fiona was equally at risk, and he could not betray young Captain Larson to a court martial.

Yet facing this sadistic murdering pig, his rage provoked some means of outlet.

With no other recourse as Barbie looked up defiantly at him, Fraser smashed him across the head repeatedly making no effort to moderate the force. Not finished, he delivered several brutal kicks to Barbie's abdomen. Bleeding profusely, Barbie lay in a fetal position making no sound.

As everyone looked aghast including Larson, Fraser said in German to the man in civilian attire accompanying the lieutenant, "Your name?"

"Merk."

"Joseph 'Kurt' Merk. Former *Abwehr*. Operated in Dijon according to your dossier. Working now with U.S. Army Counterintelligence. Correct?"

Fearing what Fraser intended to do, he answered simply, "*Ja.*"

Fraser said, "Outside. You too, Lieutenant." Turning to Larson, "Captain?"

Larson appeared bewildered by these unexpected events, trying to think ahead about getting out of this mess.

Fraser forced Merk and the lieutenant into the trunk at the point of his gun. "I will let you out an hour's drive from here. Cannot risk you raising an alarm until we are far away from here.

Fraser got into the passenger seat, Larson in the back seat.

To Marchand, Fraser said, "Drive to the train station. No time to explain. The whole thing fell apart. Had to leave Barbie behind. That is not Barbie in the trunk. Two guys that interrupted. One is an American Army officer so we need to get the hell out of Germany after we dump them somewhere remote."

Marchand said nothing. Time enough for questions later.

Arriving at the Memmingen train station, Fraser stepped out of the car followed by Larson. Both were careful not to talk during the drive to prevent those in the trunk overhearing.

Moving away from the car, Fraser said, "Sorry this turned to shit, Captain. Take the train to Munich then back to Dachau. Stick with your cover story if ever challenged. You came to Memmingen to interview concentration camp survivors at the DP camp. Make up enough believable detail to sound convincing. We did the right thing, but like the saying goes, no good deed goes unpunished.

"By the way, I am going to publically expose this entire affair of the U.S. Army employing a wanted war criminal. Barbie is not the typical concentration camp guard Nazi war criminal. The Army will be doing serious damage control. Having convicted Barbie, the French will make an international stink. I will say nothing about your involvement. Suggest you also keep it that way."

Making no attempt to shake hands, Larson said sarcastically. "Rest assured. This never happened."

# CHAPTER 23

BERN, SWITZERLAND | MARCH 1947

---

After letting the two men out of the trunk on a secluded country road, Fraser directed Marchand to backtrack to the main road. They would head south and eventually skirt the eastern end of Lake Constance to enter Switzerland at Saint Margrethen. A two-hour drive. Having just interfered with American Army counterintelligence, best to be out of Germany.

"What happened?" Marchand said.

"We had Barbie in handcuffs when a U.S. Army officer with a colleague of Barbie's stopped us on the stairs. Barbie fell down and refused to walk. No way for Larson and I to carry him out with spectators gathering. All of us are now at risk of arrest by Army counterintelligence."

"So you just left Barbie?" Knowing he wanted Barbie dead after the failed attempt in 1943, Marchand could not see him just walking away.

Fraser hesitated before answering. "No choice. Too many people and only Larson and I. So I smashed Barbie in the head with my gun. Repeatedly. Lots of blood but he will probably survive. Not likely to forget me though."

They arrived at the small Swiss border town of St. Margrethen. To obscure the trail placing him in Memmingen, Fraser paid a local car hire firm to return the car to Munich giving a change in plans as the reason plus a generous tip. From St. Margrethen they took a train to Zurich. From there to Basel at the border with France.

Fraser remained silent brooding over the failed mission.

"Since we are in Switzerland, we should take the opportunity to visit Jacob and Ruth," Marchand said referring to their friends the Ausfelders.

"Very well." Silent for several moments, before he said, "Someone else we should see then in Bern. Archbishop Bernardini."

Knowing the answer, she said, "Really? You have a particular reason for seeing the Archbishop?"

Fraser said, "The rumors Wiesenthal related about Catholic clergy in Rome assisting war criminals to escape justice by leaving Europe for South America. The Archbishop might shed some light on that."

Marchand shook her head. "You are the most tenaciously driven man I ever met. I understand this business with Barbie is troubling. Wiesenthal is making hunting Nazis his life's work. I do not want that to be our life."

"Neither do I, Fiona. However, I share Wiesenthal's concerns that war crimes will quickly fade from world attention. I feel compelled to keep attention focused on these war criminals escaping justice. I can do that journalistically while still enjoying a normal life."

"I do understand. I hope you can keep your crusade limited to investigative reporting and not operational missions like Memmingen. I had enough of that in France and Italy. I want to go back to museum life." Marchand touched his face. "It may be selfish but I want a normal life with you, Marc."

After an enjoyable visit with the Ausfelders, the following day they lunched with Archbishop Bernardini.

Bernardini was his usual convivial self. Enthusiastic about the prospects for his beloved Italy now free of both Mussolini and the Germans.

After an Italian lunch served with Tuscan wine, Marchand touched on the reason for their visit. "Your Excellency, we met a remarkable concentration camp survivor when we toured Mauthausen-Gusen concentration camp just weeks following its liberation. He worked with the Americans for some time following Germany's surrender. Helped them by translating confiscated SS records. Also cataloged endless interviews with camp survivors, and even a few suspected Nazis trying to hide as refugees.

"Herr Wiesenthal is committed to avenging the Holocaust by becoming a self-styled Nazi hunter. We stay in touch since we share the same interest in seeing Nazi war criminals brought to justice. He related some troubling rumors. Considering his range of sources, perhaps more than rumors. Unfortunately, it involves the Church.

"Do you know an Austrian bishop named Hudal or a Croatian priest, Father Krunoslav Draganović? Both apparently working in Rome."

Bernardini's expression suggested the names as an unpleasant subject. "I am familiar with Bishop Hudal. Never personally met him however. He is well known to those of us working closely with the Vatican. Unfortunately, he carries the reputation of being overly sympathetic to Nazi ideology. A fervent enemy of Communism but also of democracy. A conservative with the negative traits often associated with the political far right.

"He is head of the Austrian-German congregation of Santa Maria dell'Anima in Rome. Until 1937, very influential in Austrian Catholic affairs."

"What happened?" Marchand asked.

"He published a disgusting tract titled *The Foundations of National Socialism.* Praising Adolf Hitler and much of his policies. Argued National Socialism's good and bad aspects. In so doing, he indirectly attacked Vatican policies. Hudal is an avowed anti-

Semite. His fanatical pronouncements on Jews little different from Hitler's *Mein Kampf.*

"His published extreme views caused the Vatican to ostracize him. An embarrassment to the Holy Father. You see Hudal was consecrated a titular bishop by then Cardinal Eugenio Pacelli, now his holiness Pius XII. Pacelli at the time was cardinal protector of the German national church."

Fraser interjected. "Meaning no disrespect or placing you in an awkward situation, Your Excellency, but speaking of the Pope, could there be any sympathy on his part for those accused of war crimes?"

"Not at all. I realize that there are many critics of the His Holiness. Some have even used the label, *Hitler's Pope.* I feel that is an unfair characterization. However, I can understand the origin of such slander. Germany represents a large part of the background of His Holiness. Yet what his critics ignore is the delicate circumstances that threatened the sovereignty of the Vatican. Any public criticism of Hitler's Final Solution by the Vatican would arguably not have had any substantive impact. What did Hitler have to fear from Vatican condemnation?

"It is unthinkable to imagine the Vatican occupied by the Nazis."

Fraser and Marchand understood the history of Pope Pius XII, Eugenio Maria Giuseppe Giovanni Pacelli. From his earliest official duties, Pacelli became involved in Vatican affairs of state. A year prior to the Armistice of the WWI, Pope Benedict XV consecrated him titular Archbishop and appointed him Apostolic Nuncio to Bavaria. In 1920, Pacelli became Apostolic Nuncio to Germany at large.

In December 1929, then Pope Pius XI consecrated Pacelli as cardinal-priest. Two months later, he elevated him to Cardinal Secretary of State, the second most powerful position within the Roman Catholic Church. After negotiating concordats with the various German states, Pacelli achieved his singular accomplishment in 1933 by concluding a Reich Concordat with Germany as a whole.

The Church-State treaty with the German government of Adolf Hitler provided the Vatican with increased control of dissident German bishops. The concordat sanctioned the Vatican to impose Church law on German Catholics. It provided assurances of Church control over Catholics schools and privileges for the clergy. The quid pro quo was for German clergy to cease any political activity. This meant dismantling the powerful Catholic Centre Party. The many Catholic associations and publications must also discontinue all social and political activity. A one-sided bargain that played into Hitler's political ambitions.

While this centralized control of German Catholicism within the Vatican, it was a pact with the devil incarnate. It left no collective voice in Germany to oppose Hitler's genocidal policies against Jews. Once in force, the Reich immediately began ignoring the privileges for German Catholicism granted in the concordat.

"How do you justify the current Pope stifling German Catholic decent with his signing the *Reichskonkordat* with Hitler in 1933 when he was Secretary of State?" Fraser said.

Bernardini sighed, "The short answer is I cannot. History will clearly declare it a bad deal. Like so many great endeavors, the pursuit of a purposeful objective distorted over time by unintended consequences. Remember, the Holy See not only functions as the spiritual leader for hundreds of millions of people, but also the head of state of a sovereign nation, the Vatican. In practice, governance falls to a select group as with any government. In the case of the Vatican, that is the Curia.

"Remember also the Vatican became a state in modern times only in 1929 with a deal struck with Mussolini. Pius XI was then Pope. The *Reichskonkordat* following only a few years later.

"I offer that observation only to illustrate the Vatican was interested in consolidating power in the tumultuous times during the intervening years between the two world wars.

"Forgotten in these attacks on His Holiness Pius XII are the many Jewish lives saved by Vatican efforts. Failure to publicly censor Nazi excesses undoubtedly a matter of preservation of the Church weighed against the uncertain benefit of directly confronting Hitler.

"But enough of my reciting history and sounding like a diplomat. Is there real evidence supporting these allegations about Bishop Hudal and this Father Draganović assisting war criminals?"

Fraser replied, "I do not yet know, but I am going to find out. What do you know of Father Draganović?"

"Very little. I know his name through conversations with Monsignor Dell'Acqua the recognized head of Santa Alleanza. If you consider that an intelligence organization, then Draganović might be said to head the Croatian desk. Works out of the Monastery next to San Girolamo dei Croati on Via Tomacelli."

"So you are saying conceivably Draganović might be assisting war criminals to escape Europe?" Marchand said.

"No, I have no basis from which to make that assertion. However, consider this. Forgive me again for digressing with historical background but it may be important if Draganović is playing some role in helping war criminals.

"Following the Axis powers invasion of Yugoslavia in 1941, the Ustaše counterrevolutionary Fascists created the Axis puppet state of the Independent State of Croatia. As a punitive measure to the Austrian-Hungarian Empire in World War One, Yugoslavia was assembled from the historically antagonistic Balkan states of Serbia, Croatia, Slovenia, and heavily Muslim Bosnia and Herzegovina. Croatia became a vicious ultranationalist fascist state fully as demented as the Nazis. The atrocities committed by the Ustaše as barbaric as the Nazis. Their targets Serbs, Roma, and Jews.

"Croatia is overwhelming Roman Catholic. A Christian bastion in the Balkans. Mussolini and Ustaše leader Ante Pavelić had close relations prior to the war. With the advancing Red Army, the Ustaše retreated west to Austria eventually surrendering to the British at the end of the war. The British promptly repatriated tens of thousands to Tito's now Communist Yugoslavia. Another round of atrocities, this time with the Communists executing Ustaše soldiers.

"If there are unholy conspiracies in Rome, these factors undoubtedly figure in the mix."

"Your relating of that history is most helpful, Your Excellency," Fraser said.

"You are a journalist, Mr. Fraser. What do you intend to do with these rumors?"

"Investigate them of course. If true, publish what I find."

"I sincerely hope there is no involvement of Roman Catholic clergy in such a despicable act as aiding those guilty of crimes against humanity. If however true, you should make it known to the world. The Church must also atone for its lapses."

Fraser silently thought, rather than atone more likely to obfuscate, deflect, and resolutely ignore the shit storm until the crisis runs its course. The Catholic Church has an exceptionally dark history as a religious institution, yet survives after almost two millennia.

"I assume from your questions, you will go to Rome to find answers. And what about you, Fiona?"

Equally practiced at diplomatic evasion, "Marc is the journalist. I am anxious though to see Rome again. Returning to my artistic work. Perhaps consult with Monsignor Donati about restoration projects postponed during the war years."

"So you are still intent on going to Rome I presume?" Marchand said.

"I must see if there is any basis of Catholic clergy ratlines, using Wiesenthal's term, to help war criminals escape to safe havens. If true then I will do my best to make trouble."

Marchand said, "Tell you what. We are half way to Rome. Both of us go there now for a couple of weeks instead of returning straightaway to Paris. I will take the opportunity to see my old friend Monsignor Donati. Probe him on these rumors. Besides, he might have an interesting restoration project providing an excuse to return to Rome. You also need an interrupter."

He leaned over and kissed her passionately as they walked into the hotel lobby. You are a perfect partner. How about catching a train tomorrow?"

"I like that."

"We shall enjoy a good dinner this evening. And speaking of a partnering, interested in enjoying the carnal aspects of our partnership in bed before dinner?"

"I like that too."

Still being in the hunt mitigated the failure to capture Barbie and the near disaster in Memmingen. More encouraging was Fiona's participation even though her convictions did not propel her into his brand of action. With that mix, the previous night celebrated each other.

Arriving at Rome Termini rail station, Fraser picked up a map of Rome. Might as well stay close to their targets. Locating Santa Maria dell'Anima and San Girolamo dei Croati, he asked Fiona, "Here are the locations for Hudal and Draganović. Both not far from the Vatican. Any suggestion where best to stay?"

"Before the war I stayed close to the Vatican when doing work there. More interesting is a warren of narrow streets across the Tiber in the older area west of the Piazza Navona. I like old things, and Santa Maria dell'Anima is located there. Not sure about decent hotels though."

Marchand directed the taxi driver in Italian, "Campo dei Fiori. Show us a couple of good hotels in that area, *per favore*."

After quizzing the taxi driver, she settled on the Hotel Farnese in the quieter Piazza Farnese a block south of the Piazza Campo dei Fiori. Their simple but attractive spacious room looked across the piazza to the renaissance Palazzo Farnese.

She said, "I did not realize the Palazzo Farnese is the French Embassy. Might prove useful should you get us into trouble, my dear."

Over coffee the following morning, Fraser said, "The first thing I want to do is get a look at Hudal's Collegio Santa Maria dell'Anima and Draganović's San Girolamo dei Croati."

Marchand said, "Perhaps I can get an audience with Monsignor Donati. A wonderful man. I want you to meet him. Although guarded in his opinions, he clearly does not share the far-right conservative views of those like Hudal, Dell'Acqua, and certain cardinals. As a journalist, please be considerate with your questions. He would be highly wary of even implying critical remarks directed at those powerful in the Church hierarchy."

"Of course. Not an institution that looks kindly on rebels within its ranks. So I will not embarrass you," Fraser responded with a wry smile.

"Seriously, how will you go about investigating these two priests?"

"Not sure. Any investigation is a process that builds on itself. As you discover bits and pieces, this usually points to avenues to explore. In this case, starting with other clergy, particularly those with different political views is a first step. This is an issue of politics not Church doctrine so it might be surprising what they might reveal.

"Approaching the Italian police a possibility. Not sure where the Italian government stands given the conflicted wartime history of Italy. Yet the Nazis committed atrocities in Italy.

"Then there are people loosely associated with these two suspicious Church institutions. Suppliers of goods and services."

Marchand said, "Sounds labor-intensive. We could be at it for a considerable time with little prospect for results. Obviously you need me as interpreter."

"Well, I feel compelled to at least make a stab at it. Will see what we can find in the next couple of weeks. Then I promise we return to Paris and reassess what we have before considering returning to Rome."

Marchand took a sip of coffee. "What about surveillance? If these priests are trafficking in war criminals, these locations might be the pinch point."

"What do you mean?"

"I mean, these Nazis are fugitives traveling under false identities. They need papers to get passage out of Italy. Those undoubtedly originate in Rome meaning the fugitives may actually come through the Collegio Anima or the Collegio or San Girolamo dei Croati."

"I see what you mean. Certainly hope that is the case."

"The primary problem remains not having photographs of these Nazis except for a few of the most notorious. Otherwise there is no way to distinguish them from whoever they claim to be."

She was right. He neglected to acknowledge any pursuit of fugitive war criminals rested entirely on photographs.

He nodded. "Of course you are correct. That means we need Wiesenthal's help. His files are the best source. Even our contacts within American intelligence will not be able to provide us a wholesale catalog of photographs of all wanted Nazis. Guess I need to place a call to Simon."

"Yes. Regardless what comes of this investigation into Church assistance, the photographs will be necessary for anything you publish. Without a picture, these monsters are just obscure names. Once you assemble a catalog of photographs, doesn't this suggest mounting surveillance at some point?"

"Of course. But unlike the situation looking specifically for Barbie, here we are looking for anyone of hundreds of wanted Nazis."

"I realize that. But what if you photographed everyone coming and going from both locations?"

"Fiona, how is that possible? We would need teams of people with cameras working shifts."

"Yes, I know. What if we could find people willing to participate?"

"What are you suggesting?"

"What about enlisting former Italian partisans? I can contact Capponi or maybe Pavel. He must still have contacts. Those that may still want to exact revenge against the Nazis. We would have to pay them of course. But then, what better use for the SS funds we control?"

"Brilliant! I wish Trakonitz and his band of Jewish Brigade cutthroats were with us. Think any of these former partisans might go for the idea?"

"Worth a try. Yet it still requires collecting photographs of these fugitives. Without that, not likely surveillance photos will lead to any discoveries. With photos, still a difficult process to separate former SS from all the people involved in normal activity."

"I will place a call to Simon today."

Marchand still wondered what Marc intended if he successfully identified any wanted SS. Given his inclinations and hatred for everything SS, he might want to do more than merely publish their faces and raise a scandal involving the Church. A real issue to confront if things progressed that far.

Marchand telephoned Monsignor Donati's office. "Hello, Fiona, so good to hear from you." After an exchange of small talk, "Delighted to hear you are in Rome. Of course I can make time to see you. What about today say two o'clock?"

Fraser followed with a call to Simon Wiesenthal in Linz, Austria. "Simon, I am here in Rome. I intend to follow up on those rumors related to Catholic clergy running ratlines to help escaping war criminals. Starting with Bishop Hudal and Father Draganović.

"The ability to identify Nazi fugitives is essential to the investigation. Do your files include photographs?"

"Yes. At least of the most wanted. Bear in mind, my work is largely a collection process. Material continues to pour in. As you recognize, putting a face to these names is essential, therefore further research is usually required."

"There are thousands of former SS of all types, SD, *Gestapo, Einsatzgruppen,* and the *Totenkopfverbände* from the camps. For those accused of war crimes, have you ever classified according to seriousness of their crimes?"

"In a manner of speaking."

"Is it possible for you to assemble a list of those accused of war crimes? Those with serious blood on their hands. Including particulars as to date and place of birth and alleged crimes. With photographs of course."

"I already have a great deal of material gathered. A continuing work in process. Been compiling material since the end of the war. Largely through interviews of camp survivors and German POWs. Then we research the seized SS archives to add background and search for a photograph. Are you looking to publish such a list?"

"Maybe eventually, but I want it now for a more immediate use. How long to put something like this together?"

"Depends on how comprehensive a list you are looking for. Beyond the more obvious names are those guilty of a multiple acts of murder or maltreatment compared to the thousands of the better-known names. Not sure the extent of what you have in mind. I have volunteers, other camp survivors helping to run our modest research center. Perhaps a few weeks to expand into a larger list."

"Excellent. I have certain funds at my disposal. When I see you in Linz, I will provide a generous donation for your efforts, Simon. By the way, include every important SS not confirmed dead or already in custody. That means even those thought dead but unconfirmed."

If Heinrich Müller actually escaped, then possibly others exist. He still withheld his knowledge that it was Müller behind the attack in Paris.

Fraser and Marchand set off on foot to scout the target locations. First to the Collegio Anima, Bishop Hudal's base of operation at his Pontifico Istituto Teutonic, only a ten-minute walk. From there, following the River Tiber a half mile north to the Via Tomacelli, to visit Father Draganović's Croatian Catholic enclave, the Collegio San Girolamo dei Croati and Monastery. Following lunch, they would make their way across the river to the Vatican.

Just a reconnaissance mission to get the lay of the land. Determine if a protracted surveillance might yield identifiable photographs. He took along his Leica to capture the target buildings from different perspectives that could serve as observation locations.

Scouting first Bishop Hudal's Collegio S. Maria dell'Anima housing his Pontifico Istituto Teutonic less than a half mile from their hotel, it became apparent surveillance logistics presented real challenges. The Collegio occupied an entire block, two sides bounded by narrow streets. Many points of entry. It would require reducing down probable points of entry and exit likely frequented by Nazis fugitives in transit.

The location of San Girolamo dei Croati proved just as challenging in a different way. Via Tomacelli was a broad thoroughfare leading west across the River Tiber to the Vatican one mile away. To the east, it crossed the Via del Corso where it became the Via Condotti leading to the Spanish Steps.

Spending thirty minutes at each site, they walked the perimeter observing relatively few people entering and exiting. That was encouraging when it came to sifting through surveillance photos looking to match with wanted Nazis.

They must position the watchers to get close up facial shots while remaining unobtrusive. Fraser took photographs for later study and sketched a diagram of possibilities at each site. Telephoto lens determined as necessary to capture sufficient facial detail of the subject.

Far more difficult then he anticipated. However, if these locations were pinch points in the Nazis fugitives' journey on the ratlines, the opportunity was too good to pass up.

An outline of the operation began forming in his mind. Buy the necessary camera equipment to outfit a surveillance team. Train them in basic camera technology. Locate a trusted photographic studio to develop and enlarge the photos. Perhaps an analytical team to compare the harvested images against SS photographs. That will be the toughest part. The quality of photographs Wiesenthal had might be questionable. Many perhaps dated. Probably in SS uniform with caps. In essence, this must become a full-blown intelligence operation if they had any chance for success. A daunting endeavor with uncertain prospects for success.

Everything therefore became contingent on a usable catalog with photographs. That and recruiting the necessary surveillance manpower. Difficult to keep secret with so many involved, but no risk involved other than scaring off the prey. If discovered, they were not breaking Italian laws. The Church unlikely to register a complaint with Italian authorities.

A productive morning. A workable plan if they can bring all the elements into play. Still difficult to believe senior priests might be running smuggling conduits of war criminals. If true, did the perpetrators conceal these activities from the Vatican, or was the Vatican Curia turning a blind eye?

After lunch, they passed through layers of Vatican security arriving at the museum office of Director Monsignor Rodrigo Donati. Fraser did not expect much but they must start somewhere. From an intelligence standpoint, reintroducing Fiona inside the Vatican made sense.

On the walk to the Vatican, Marchand said, "There was a Croatian priest I dealt with briefly before my injury. Father Čirjak. Works in the Vatican Secretary of State office. Specifically works in Monsignor Dell'Acqua's office. Dell'Acqua is the recognized head of Vatican intelligence, *Santa Alleanza.*

"Never provided anything of value but I sensed the handsome young Father Čirjak had something of a crush on me."

"Yes, I remember him. He was with Donati at the hospital after you lapsed into coma. Being Croatian, he must know of Father Draganović. Since he was fond of you, might be worth you talking to him."

Jokingly she said, "Spin my feminine charms on a sexually frustrated celibate priest?"

Fraser laughed. "Expected tradecraft for any good female spy."

Donati greeted them effusively, clearly delighted to see Fiona Marchand.

After much small talk, Donati conducted a guided tour of the Vatican Museum backrooms, not only for Fraser's benefit, but also to show Marchand two 16th century oils in need of restorations. Impressive to watch Marchand engage in technical discussions with Donati. Without her even raising the question, Donati was anxious to pitch the possibility of her possibly returning to Rome to work on these paintings.

Concluding the tour, Donati asked Fraser what he was doing since the war ended.

"Returned to journalism. Freelancing for Reuters news service. The war may be over but much remains unresolved. The Nazis genocide against the Jews continues to trouble me. I covered some of the war crimes trials. Mostly those of Nazi SS defendants running the concentration and extermination camps.

"My interest is exposing the hundreds of war criminals so far escaping justice. The vast majority of perpetrators by any estimate. That is now my mission. Expose them wherever possible. Force the world not to forget."

Donati nodded his understanding. "The world wants to move beyond those horrors. The threat of Communism now overshadows the crimes of the Nazis and their collaborators."

"I agree. However, that very real threat should remain separate to dealing with Nazi war criminals."

"Certainly. The Church itself struggles with these same issues. The Soviet Union persecutes Catholics in Eastern Europe. Little wonder that anti-Communism sentiment runs strong within the Church."

"Understandable. Josef Stalin is fully as evil as Adolf Hitler. The Soviet regime the next threat to world order. However, that should in no way ignore Nazi war crimes. In my investigations, reliable sources claim that certain Catholic clergy in Rome are knowingly assisting escaping war criminals."

"My God, that cannot be true. There are thousands of refugees in Italy. Most from territories overrun by the Red Army. A great many without papers. The Church works in close cooperation with the International Red Cross. Certainly possible that some former Nazis have escaped by masquerading as stateless refugees. Do these sources cite names?"

"One that is mentioned is an Austrian bishop named Hudal. Known to be sympathetic to Nazi ideology."

Donati scowled. "Everyone knows of Bishop Hudal's unacceptable views. His book, *The Foundations of National Socialism* openly questioned Vatican policy. Pope Pius XI with the collaboration of then Secretary of State Cardinal Pacelli, now our Holy Father, responded with the encyclical *Mit brennender Sorge*, directly attacking National Socialism. The Vatican sanctioned Bishop Hudal. Restricted his work only to affairs of the Collegio S. Maria dell'Anima. An embarrassment for His Holiness."

"Could he be sufficiently sympathetic to National Socialism to knowingly provide aid to fugitive war criminal fugitives escaping Europe?" Fraser said.

Donati shook his head as if disgusted with any discussion of Hudal. "I hope that a fellow priest would not allow his political beliefs to compromise his morals."

Donati said no more on the subject. He might be somewhat naïve, but Fraser sensed that Hudal's reputation suggested to Donati that his extremist views might allow for such conduct.

"Yet certain priests have participated in this war well beyond their spiritual duties. I speak of course about the Ultranationalist Fascist Croatian Ustaše. Evidence reveals that certain Croatian Catholic priests held officer rank in the Croatian Ustaše. In fact there is talk not only of Bishop Hudal assisting fugitive war criminals but a priest by the name of Father Krunoslav Draganovic, also based here in Rome."

"Rumors concerning the Ustaše exist within the Vatican as well. Priests gossip as much as any other group. Personally, I have no direct knowledge to venture an opinion. Within these ancient walls, the misdeeds of history tend to occupy me more than the swirl of current events."

Fraser took the queue from Donati as well as Fiona's cautionary expression to let the line of inquiry drop. Not likely Donati could or would be a source of further value.

Once outside, Marchand said, "Thought you said you would behave yourself?"

"I doubt Donati felt offended. I see why you like him. My sense the subject disturbed his moral sense as a churchman. He knows bad things go on everywhere, including within the Church. Also knows I am a journalist and naturally inclined to asking direct questions."

"Just the same, I will see Father Čirjak alone. Make up some excuse about my reporter husband working on a piece about displaced persons flooding into Italy looking to escape Soviet occupation of Eastern Europe.

Marchand's overtures to Father Čirjak as a backdoor to gain an audience with Father Draganovic failed at the onset. Čirjak sidestepped her request for lunch for old time's sake. He stating the reason bluntly, "It has come to Monsignor Dell'Acqua's attention that a senior U.S. Embassy official in Rome communicated a confidential damaging report to Washington. It reads *The Vatican is the largest single organization involved in the illegal movement of emigrants. The justification of the Vatican for its participation in this illegal traffic is to propagate the Faith. It is the Vatican's desire to assist any person, regardless of nationality or political beliefs, as long as that person can prove to be a Catholic. The Vatican further justifies its participation by its desire to infiltrate not only European countries but also Latin American countries with people of all political beliefs as long as they are anti-Communist and pro-Roman Catholic Church."*

Not surprising since Vatican intelligence had good sources with in Western intelligence.

"My sincere regrets, Signora Marchand. Under the circumstances, my instructions are to avoid interaction with the American press. I believe your husband is not only an American journalist, but like you, perhaps still involved with American intelligence."

Recounting the conversation to Fraser, he said, "Very well. Then the Church becomes fair game. What remains clear is the greatest migration of displaced persons comes through Italy. Vatican assistance is substantial. They work in close cooperation with the International Red Cross. That means Italy and Vatican refugee humanitarian services represent the best method for fugitive war criminals to escape Europe. Whether Catholic clergy knowingly facilitate these ratlines for war criminals remains to be proven."

# CHAPTER 24

LINZ, GERMANY | SEPTEMBER 1947

---

Fraser said to Marchand, "Little more we can accomplish in Rome without a wanted list with photos. How about we join Simon in Linz? Maybe help him and his volunteers. Eager to see if we can put this together."

"I agree. The list provides a tangible symbol of what we are after. Easier to sell the idea to those we try to convince for help. I still want to return to Paris before returning to Rome at the end of the year. I suspect we might be in Rome for some time."

"Possibly. I also need to get things in order to manage the SS funds easily from Rome. Want to meet with Pavel if possible. The last money requested was that operation involving another packet steamer the Haganah recommissioned as the *Exodus 1947.*"

"Sadly, another failed attempt," Marchand said.

"Not necessarily. The Haganah must have clearly known by this time there was little hope of running the British blockade of Palestine. A political maneuver is my guess. A staged event to inflame condemnation against the British for continued persecution of the Jews. Made worse when the British forcibly returned the 4500 Jewish concentration camp survivors to Germany.

Three days later Fraser and Marchand arrived by train in Linz. The picturesque city remained in reasonably good condition in spite of Allied bombing of nearby industrial targets in the last years of the war. Fraser gave the taxi driver the address to Wiesenthal's Jewish Historical Documentation Centre.

The center occupied office space on the second floor of a modest office building. After knocking on the door, a woman answered the door. "Yes?"

"We are here to see Herr Wiesenthal. I am Marc Fraser and this is my wife Fiona Marchand."

From behind the woman came the excited voice of Simon Wiesenthal, "Cyla, show them in."

Wiesenthal embraced Marchand then pumped Fraser's hand placing his other hand affectionately on his shoulder.

Cyla said, "Oh my, this is a surprise. Simon speaks often about you."

"Marc and I felt a great sense of joy when Simon told us of reuniting with you. I cannot imagine the ordeal both of you suffered," Marchand said.

"Yes, an unusual stroke of good fortune. Otherwise our circumstances are no different than so many other Holocaust survivors." Whereas Simon was lively with intensity in his eyes, Cyla appeared sad, the light gone from her eyes.

"What a surprise, Marc. Did not expect you so soon," Wiesenthal said.

"Well I am reasonably sure war criminals must be using Catholic relief efforts to escape Europe. Circumstantial evidence points to those two clergy you named. Whether knowingly or disinclined to question refugees too closely, is not certain. What is important is finding a way to disrupt the ratline machinery.

"To move forward everything depends on having a wanted list with photographs as the reference document."

Excitedly, Wiesenthal said, "Before we sit and chat, let me show what I have put together from my two years of research. I organized the material into categories. The first being the worst war criminals. Those responsible for mass murder. Including those presumed dead but without confirmation. Next, those directly guilty of committing many murders. Lastly, SS serving as camp guards and administrators but without direct testimony of crimes from witnesses. Because of their affiliation, any *SS-Totenkopfverbände* members must be suspect. A large incomplete list unfortunately lacking photographs."

File cabinets heaped with piles of files on top consumed all available space. Wiesenthal went to a file cabinet behind his cluttered desk and extracted a folder. Handing it to Fraser, "Take a look at this list. These I deem the worst of those still wanted."

Klaus Barbie | Born October 1913. SS no.272284. Rank: Hauptsturmführer. Sicherheitsdienst(SD), Gestapo chief Lyon, France. Known as the *Butcher of Lyon*. Wanted for torture and deaths of as many as 14,000.

Adolf Eichmann | Born March 1906. SS no. 45326. Rank: Obersturmbannführer. Administrative head of the *Final Solution*. Subordinate to Reinhard Heydrich. Wanted for organizing concentration and extermination camp system and the deaths of millions.

Josef Mengele | Born March 1911. SS no. 317885.Rank: Hauptsturmführer. Medical doctor at Auschwitz II (Birkenau). Known as the *Angel of Death*. Wanted for designating arriving deportees for death in the gas chambers and conducting sadistic medical experiments.

Aribert Heim | Born June 1914. SS no. 367744. Rank: Hauptsturmführer. Medical doctor. Known as *Dr. Death and Butcher of Mauthausen*. Wanted for conducting medical experimentation on camp inmates.

Alois Brunner | Born April 1912. SS no. 342767. Rank: Hauptsturmführer. Drancy Camp (France) commandant. Eichmann subordinate. Wanted for deportation of 100,000 European Jews to ghettos and concentration camps.

Martin Bormann | Born June 190. SS no. 555. Rank: Obergruppenführer. Head of Nazi Party Chancellery and private secretary to Adolf Hitler. Wanted for participation in genocidal crimes. Presumed killed fleeing Führerbunker.

Heinrich Müller | Born April 1900. SS no.107043. Rank: Gruppenführer und Generalleutnant der Polizei. Head of Gestapo. Wanted for directing murder and deportation of hundreds of thousands to concentration and extermination camps. Presumed dead after fleeing Führerbunker.

Franz Stangl | Born March 1908. SS no. 296569. Rank: Hauptsturmführer. Participated in Nazi T-4 Euthanasia Program and Commandant of the Sobibór and Treblinka. Wanted for genocidal crimes of thousands of victims.

Rudolf Lange | Born April 1910. SS no. 93501. Rank: Standartenführer. Sicherheitsdienst (SD). Einsatzgruppe A, Einsatzkommando 2. Wanted for murder of 35,000 Latvian Jews in less than six months. Presumed killed by Soviet forces.

Gustav Wagner | Born July 1911. SS no. 443217. Rank: Oberscharführer. Part of Action T4 euthanasia program. Deputy commander of Sobibór extermination camp. Known as *The Beast or The Wolf.* Wanted for genocidal crimes.

Walter Rauff | Born June 1906. SS no. 342945 Rank: Standartenführer Sicherheitsdienst (SD). Aide to Reinhard Heydrich. Instrumental in developing mobile gas chambers. Wanted for genocidal crimes of 100,000 victims.

Ante Pavelić | Born July 1889. Founder & leader of Croatian fascist ultranationalist Ustaše and Nazi ally. Wanted for directing murders of 300,000 Serbs, Jews, Romani, and anti-fascist Croats in Yugoslavia.

Erich Priebke | Born July 1913. SS no. 393766 Rank: Hauptsturmführer Gestapo. Wanted for participating in the murder of 335 Rome civilians in the Fosse Ardeatine caves in reprisal for a partisan attack on SS Police Regiment.

Lorenz Hackenholt | Born June 1914. SS no. 419387 Rank: Hauptsturmführer. Wanted for building and operating the gas chamber at the Bełżec extermination camp carrying out the murder of hundreds of thousands. Presumed dead.

Gerhard Bohne | Born July 1902. SS no. 407556 Rank: Hauptsturmführer. Instrumental in the creation of the Aktion T-4 euthanasia program at Grafeneck Euthanasia Centre. Wanted for genocidal crimes.

Joseph Schwammberger | Born February 1912. SS no.283499 Rank: Obersturnbannführer. Sicherheitsdienst (SD) Commander of three forced-labor camps in Krakőw, Poland sector. Wanted for murder of over 3000 people.

Herbert Cukurs | Born May 1900. Latvian aviator and member of Latvian Fascists Arajs Kommando led by Nazis SS. Known as the *Butcher of Riga*. Wanted for mass murder of Latvian Jews.

Eduard Roschmann | Born November 1908. SS no. 152681. Rank: Hauptsturmführer. Sicherheitsdienst(SD). Commander of Riga, Latvia ghetto. Wanted for participation in murder of 3740 Jews at Jungfernhof concentration camp.

Kurt Franz | Born January 1914. SS no. 269272 Rank: Untersturmführer. SS-Totenkopfverbände. Served at Bełżec extermination camp. Commandant of Treblinka extermination camp. Personally murdered unknown numbers of inmates.

"Outstanding, Simon. Just what we need. Look at this gallery of mass murderers, Fiona."

Wiesenthal added, "To accompany the list, my team of volunteers prepared brief dossiers of each perpetrator recounting the crimes and the sources supplying that information. A useful starting point for prosecution."

After scanning some of the entries, Marchand commented, "Reading the magnitude and wholesale barbarity of these crimes by so many staggers the imagination. Difficult to make the world comprehend the scale of Nazis institutionalized murder. The level of brutality something from medieval times."

Wiesenthal said, "And these are just the worse of those not yet captured. My team has also made good progress on assembling a long list of lower echelon murderers and sadists.

Fraser extracted an envelope from his jacket pocket. "As promised. A donation to keep up your work." He removed the check and handed it to Wiesenthal.

With a look of surprise after seeing the amount, "Very generous, Marc. Can you afford this?"

"Not my personal money, Simon. A benefactor that wishes to remain anonymous. Funding for going after these people and destroying their escape routes."

"You must tell me how you intend to go about this."

"Of course." Looking at his watch, Fraser said, "I could use a drink followed by a good dinner. How about all of us go to the best restaurant in Linz."

They told Wiesenthal about staying over in Linz for several days to review and help complete the Nazi wanted list materials. Before heading to the restaurant, Wiesenthal dropped them at a small hotel to make sure they secured a room with limited public accommodations available in war-damaged Linz.

At dinner, Wiesenthal asked, "So how do you intend to proceed in Rome?"

Fraser answered, "Armed now with your list, we station people at the locations from where Bishop Hudal and Father Draganović operate. We are betting that these Nazis actually come to these locations. Then we take photos of every male leaving and entering. After eliminating staff and service people, we compare the remainder against the photographs of your list."

"That is a major undertaking. You and Fiona cannot do this alone. Do you have others you can call on?"

"We hope to find them among former Italian partisans. Those that still harbor hatred for the Nazis. Fiona has contacts from her time in Italy with the American OSS. Another person we are well acquainted with, a former officer with the British Jewish Brigade also has connections in Italy. We have funds to pay for their services."

Wiesenthal said, "But the real task is in attempting to match your surveillance photos to names. Also quickly if these are fleeing Nazis. Who does that painstaking work?"

"From the same people hopefully, the former partisans. A major intelligence operation, Simon."

"Difficult work. I know from personal experience pouring over images trying to connect an old photo with a later one. Out of uniform, especially without a cap, faces appear different."

"Any suggestions, Simon?" Marchand said.

"Perhaps. One of my volunteers was a former photographer before the war. Survived the camps because of his skills. Produced portraits of officers and their families. Works now at a pawnshop not far from here."

"How might he be of help?" Marchand asked.

"Might be useful for developing your surveillance photos. Like most of us, Victor Kronberger lost his entire family in the Holocaust. I believe his work with our Nazis hunting efforts sustains him. Revenge can be a powerful motivation for survival.

"He is from Villach, Austria near the Italian and Slovenian borders. Speaks passable Italian. If your funds permit, you might entice him to join you in Rome."

"Does he have travel papers?" Fraser asked.

Wiesenthal laughed. "Like all of us from the camps, he has an International Red Cross passport."

"I would like to meet Herr Kronberger."

"I shall pick you up at the hotel tomorrow morning and take you to the pawnshop."

The bell on the door to the pawnshop tingled as they entered. Fraser immediately noticed a large display of cameras and lenses under a glass display case.

A small man in his early forties greeted Wiesenthal from behind the counter.

Wiesenthal responded, "Victor, I would like you to meet Herr Marc Fraser and his wife Fiona Marchand. It is their project we have been working on to assemble a catalog of war criminals."

After shaking hands, "I met them shortly after liberated from Mauthausen. At the time, they were with American intelligence. Like us, they now hunt down Nazi war criminals. I will let Herr Fraser explain what they have in mind."

Fraser explaining their mission and the energetic Kronberger interjected with a barrage of questions. After Fraser finished, Marchand interjected in Italian.

Kronberger's eyes brightened, responding in good Italian. She ended by asking, would you consider coming to Rome and working with us?"

Kronberger looked at Wiesenthal with an expression of surprise. "What you are intending to do is most interesting. I would willingly help to prevent Nazis escaping justice. Unfortunately, I do not have the financial means to go to Italy."

Marchand said, "But what if we can pay you as well as provide living expenses while in Rome?"

Taking an instant liking to Kronberger already emotionally invested in hunting Nazis, Fraser added, "Simon tells us you are a professional photographer. What if in exchange with helping us in this endeavor, after returning to Linz, or anywhere you desire, we also finance setting up your own photographic studio?"

Kronberger looked at Wiesenthal with a questioning expression. Wiesenthal nodded. "I can vouch for Herr Fraser. He also has access to enough money to embark on this project, Victor."

Kronberger simply nodded with a large smile extending his hand to Fraser then Marchand.

Fraser said, "Thank you, Herr Kronberger. Now perhaps I can help with the shop's sales today. Quite a collection of camera equipment you have. We will need first-rate equipment for our teams of watchers. Why do you have so many cameras?"

"The war. Years of hard times. The shop owner is good man. Takes in all this merchandise with little chance of the owner paying back the amount loaned and redeeming the item. Cameras being an expendable item of value we are exceedingly overstocked."

Given Fraser's photographic knowledge, within thirty minutes he and Kronberger selected half dozen good quality Leica cameras and several telephoto lenses.

Adding two tripods for good measure along with a large leather bag to transport the cameras and a large stock of film meant a very good day for the pawnshop. Had Fraser been able to tell them, Kronberger and Wiesenthal would appreciate the ironic justice of the project funded by SS money.

After a week working in Linz with Wiesenthal, Fraser and Marchand returned to Paris for two weeks. Fraser made arrangements to manage the SS funds from Rome. Marchand made utility and apartment maintenance arrangements for a possible extended stay in Rome. The next piece to implementing the operation rested with recruiting surveillance teams in Rome. A delicate undertaking falling to Marchand with her fluency in Italian.

With the help of Carla Capponi, could they find a team of former partisans willing to go after Nazis war criminals? Although they would employ them for wages, it required individuals sufficiently motivated for the undertaking rather than mercenaries.

Marchand successfully secured a restoration commission at the Vatican Museum providing the basis for a sabbatical leave from the Louvre. Something she did many times in the past. Typical reciprocity among the world's great museums. Necessary for her peace of mind. Although supportive of Marc's quest, she did not relish spending endless hours involved with fruitless surveillance followed by the laborious work examining photographs to see if they caught anybody on film. The undertaking perhaps never achieving results.

Once back in Rome, Marc must decide on a course of action should they identify any wanted Nazis. They must sell the former partisans on that as well. Capture the fugitives? Then what? Turn them over to Italian authorities? Will the Italians even detain the wanted men? Perhaps they had no appetite for prosecuting war crimes given their own Fascist experience under Mussolini.

Would the partisans deliver any captured Nazis to American occupation authorities over the border into Austria? Based on what happened in Memmingen, will the American Army detain them? Was public exposure in the press to pressure the Italian government and attacking the Church sufficient for the Vatican to shut down the ratlines the best outcome they could expect?

She hoped Marc's solution did not lean toward the more extreme. Trakonitz shared his solution with vague references when stationed in Tarvisio following the German surrender. Marc might summary justice expedient. American western frontier justice? Place a bounty on the heads of captured Nazi SS? Could he find former partisans willing to do the killing? She hoped it would not come to that. This was no longer war or self-defense. Civilized norms must replace Nazi barbarism.

It had been weeks since Fraser communicated with Pavel Trakonitz. News reports almost daily reported clashes in Palestine between Jewish militant insurgents of the Irgun and British security forces. Was Trakonitz directly involved in some way? He was Haganah not part of the breakaway violent Irgun. Then again, the Irgun might be a useful tool while Haganah engages in negotiations with the British while disavowing Irgun violence. Pavel Trakonitz would be the perfect liaison to play a double game.

They could use Trakonitz's considerable operational experience in this Rome undertaking. Trakonitz would welcome going after Nazis war criminals. However, his military experience was vital in preparation for war with the surrounding Arab states once the British relinquished rule.

No assurance of secure telephone communications presented a problem. With British control of the telephone exchanges, they undoubtedly monitored conversations of known Haganah. Fraser wanted to entice Trakonitz to Rome. His operational expertise invaluable. Help with finding an alternative for any captured SS other than taking them out to sea and disposing of the bodies. How best to wreck the ratlines?

"Pavel, this is the husband of the woman you saved in Rome near the end of the war. She is returning to work on a project in Rome. We have some matters that require your assistance. Matters of particular interest to you. Unfortunately, not able to get into details over the telephone. Might there be a possibility of you coming to Rome for a week sometime within the next month?"

"Good to hear from you. So glad your wife fully recovered. A remarkable woman. Given the situation here in Palestine, travel papers to renter Palestine come under rigorous scrutiny because of the political situation. Circumstances are under considerable stress as you probably know. My responsibilities demand constant attention. Would it be possible for you to come to Haifa?"

"Yes, I believe so. I will telephone again once I am in Rome and make arrangements."

Fraser understood the meaning of *circumstances.* The previous year the Irgun bombed the King David Hotel in Jerusalem killing 91 and injuring 46. On September 29 of this year, they blew up the Central Police HQ in Haifa killing 10 and injuring 70. The bombing in retaliation for British deportations back to Germany of the Jewish displaced persons arriving on the *Exodus 1947* ship.

Several weeks later, Fraser and Marchand set off again by train to Rome. She packed sufficient clothing for a three-month stay. Wiring ahead to the Hotel Farnese, she arranged for a small suite suitable for an extended stay.

"Three months, Marc. All I am committing too. I will help set up this operation in Rome but that is it. Paris is home. I wish to return to my work at the Louvre. Back in Paris by spring. I do hope you will return with me. Pursue your vendetta through words. You must finish with your running around Europe hunting Nazis."

Toward that objective, Fraser filed a piece with Reuters exposing the United States Army Counterintelligence Corps' employment of a major Nazi war criminal. In the piece, Fraser recounted Barbie's crimes in detail including graphic testimony by many victims to his personally inflicting horrific forms of torture. For impact, he also included his personal experience with Barbie in Lyon. Fraser never touched on events in Memmingen, or how he came by the information of U.S. Army CIC involvement with Barbie.

Although never contacted by any U.S. official, he nonetheless knew that U.S. intelligence suspected their former OSS agent of having inside sources. He must tread carefully if he uncovers further evidence of the U.S. assisting war criminals. The long article appeared in major newspapers throughout the world under his byline.

Having sentenced Klaus Barbie to death in absentia for war crimes, there was a public outcry in France. For reasons never made public, the U.S. High Commissioner for Germany, John J. McCloy, apparently refused to acknowledge U.S. complicity. The U.S. Army never handed Barbie over to the French. As nothing further happened, the story eventually lost traction and disappeared from interest.

So much for publicly exposing war criminals and relying on governments to arrest and prosecute.

Even compared to the escape from justice of other high value Nazi war criminals, Barbie's story was exceptional.

In 1947, with official approval of the U.S. Army's 430 CIC in Austria, a U.S. sponsored ratline developed in Austria. The principle purpose was to provide a conduit to help agents and those potentially useful to escape the Soviet occupation zone surrounding Vienna to Salzburg in the American zone. For whatever misguided reason and desperate for sources, certain U.S. Army counterintelligence officers in the Bavarian occupation sector considered Barbie useful. Exposure of the collusion now represented an international embarrassment.

An Army three-man escort team transported Barbie in an American uniform south by jeep to Bad Gastein, Austria. From there the four traveled by train through the Alps to the Italian border. With Barbie armed with fake identification papers there was no difficulty at the Italian border. Following a route from Bolzano to Verona to Milan, they arrived in Genoa on the Mediterranean coast.

Once in Genoa, Barbie's U.S. Army minders concluded arrangements with a Catholic run ratline operation. Secured in a safe location, Barbie awaited passage on freighter. This particular ratline was run from Rome by Father Krunoslav Draganović, a Croatia priest and former lieutenant colonel and chaplain for the Ustaše concentration camps. At the end of the war, Draganović fled to the Vatican. His ratline became the means of rescuing Fascist Croatian Ustaše fleeing the Red Army, and assisting fellow German Nazis Fascists.

Barbie ascended the gangplank as his minders turned him over to someone onboard representing the last link in the ratline. The Draganović operation provided Barbie money and entry visas in the name of Klaus Altmann, a mechanic by trade, allowing his entry into Buenos Aires, Argentina and subsequently Bolivia.

# CHAPTER 25

ROME, ITALY | NOVEMBER 1947

---

Several weeks later, Fraser and Marchand arrived in Rome. The larger room at the Hotel Farnese afforded a comfortable environment.

Fraser embraced Marchand as she began unpacking clothing along with a steamer trunk of art supplies used in her restoration work. "Thanks for agreeing to help. I realize this is my doing. Something I feel compelled to pursue."

She kissed him. "Doing this because I love you and because I want my own revenge on the Nazis. They took my brother. I watched them murder civilians in San Giustino. Heinrich Müller sent those SS to Paris to murder us.

"So I have my own personal reasons for going after these war criminals. I just refuse to make it my life's work. Remember our agreement."

"Of course. I want to get back to Paris as soon as possible. Just want to damage these ratlines and maybe catch some war criminals before we call it quits."

She said, "Then the next thing is seeing if we can recruit a team. Shall I contact Carla Capponi?"

"I would first like to discuss what we have in mind with Pavel. That means flying to Haifa. Let me do that first. Pavel may suggest former partisans he worked with and how to go about this. Will only take a couple of days. Then we can meet with Capponi."

"Very well. Then I will call on Monsignor Donati while you are gone. Have him show me the restorations I am to work on. Anxious to get back to my artistic work."

After obtaining an entry visa for Palestine from the British embassy, Fraser boarded a DC-3 commercial flight to Haifa. As he exited the aircraft making his way to the immigration desk, the high state of security was in clear evidence. British soldiers patrolled about the tarmac and inside the terminal building.

At the desk, he showed his American passport and entry visa.

"Business in Palestine?"

"I am a journalist. Reuters news agency," He replied showing his press credentials.

Within an hour of placing a call to Trakonitz, he sipped tea at a small café after a taxi deposited him at a small café following efforts to lose anyone tailing him. Dressed in the typical Middle East colonial style of white shirt and cotton trousers, Trakonitz came to the table enveloping him in an embrace.

"My friend, so good to see you. How have things been? I trust Fiona is well? Recovered from the ordeal in Paris?"

"Yes, she is fine. Amazing her strength. Shot those two bastards point blank. Held her composure while sticking to our cover story throughout the police questioning. Speaking of that, I have not forgotten about that group of SS operating out of Madrid. Eventually something must be done to eliminate them."

"Perhaps in due time. Your old friend from Spain, Felix Martel is obsessed with former SS finding a welcome haven in his country. He even raised the idea of the Haganah mounting some form of operation against them. Unlike South America, Spain is within easier striking distance."

"Really? Is that a possibility?"

"Maybe one day. Many of us agree with Martel. However, not possible at this time. Everything now is about establishing a State of Israel. The British will leave soon. The Mandate is untenable. That will of course mean immediate war with the Arabs."

"I understand. Still could use your help, Pavel. Something else happened recently. Could not tell you over the phone. I came damn close to getting Klaus Barbie. Know the name?"

"Of course. The *Butcher of Lyon*. Up there with Eichmann and Mengele. "You told me about what happened in France during the war."

Fraser recounted the story of the ill-fated venture in Memmingen.

Trakonitz shook his head. "You should have shot him, Marc. These bastards are never going to pay for their crimes. The Americans harbored him? Unbelievable."

"You and I see Nazis crimes in black and white. Many others find their own reasons to see things differently. That is why I am here. It is not only American intelligence but also the Catholic Church. Evidence points to certain Catholic priests operating what are called ratlines to assist Nazis fugitives escaping Europe."

"You know this to be true?"

"I intend to find out. Italy is the obvious escape route for refugees fleeing the Soviet occupation areas of Eastern Europe. The Vatican runs the largest relief organization in close cooperation with the international Red Cross. Fleeing Nazis simply infiltrate the thousands of refugees. The Vatican and IRC cooperate to provide travel documentation to allow refugee resettlement.

"The perfect means for SS to discard their former identities and become reborn with new names and histories. Provided the means to travel to safe havens if they choose. For the most wanted South America, Spain, and maybe your Arab neighboring states. Fascist-leaning countries.

"Now, whether the Church or some of its priests, is a willing conspirator, or just beyond their means to filter out the war criminals is not certain. I mean to find out. That is why Fiona and I are in Rome."

"What can I do to help?"

"I intend to set up a full scale intelligence operation. I have information on two priests operating from locations in Rome. With a team of watchers, we photograph everyone coming and going from these locations. Then we compare the photos with those of wanted Nazis SS. I have such a list prepared by a Nazi hunter I met. Even have a photographer volunteer camp survivor to develop the film and supervise the identification effort."

"Who makes up this surveillance team?"

"That is where I need your help, Pavel. Fiona suggested former Italian partisans. She knows Carla Capponi. You must know those that might be willing to participate. I will pay them from the SS funds.

"Amazing. You are certainly committed to going after the SS. Wish I could come to Rome and work this with you. Good idea about using former partisans. Capponi will help you find them, especially if you are paying for their service. What happens if you catch any SS?"

"That still presents a problem. I am not willing to turn them over to the Italians without being sure of prosecution somewhere. Unlike the Americans, they might only prosecute those wanted for crimes committed against Italians. Not doing this to simply publish the photos and give the Church a black eye."

"Now you sound like me, Marc. Up to doing what the TTG did right after the war?"

Fraser sighed. "That is what should happen, Pavel. As much as I want revenge, not in my nature to be an executioner."

He paused realizing that was not exactly true. Discounting those acts of self-defense while working stories, what about killing Cabrera and Leitner in Lyon? Regardless, he was not going there again. Nor was Fiona.

"I considered the idea of paying the partisans to capture any fugitives then transport them north into the American occupation zone in Austria. Yet after the experience in Memmingen with Barbie as a major fugitive on the U.S. Army wanted list, possibly nothing will happen."

With a sardonic smile, Trakonitz replied, "You are far more civilized than me, my friend. Are you prepared to go to all this trouble then if successful see these rats escape to live out their lives in South America?"

The answer clearly no. Since conceiving this, he wrestled with the problem.

"Perhaps the answer is not that complicated. Do you care what happens to Nazis war criminals? Does your conscience demand a particular form of judicial due process?"

"Not necessarily. Given the number of Nazi war criminals that is not possible."

Yet given the opportunity to get away without endangering Fiona, he would have shot Klaus Barbie in Lyon in 1943 or again in Memmingen. That however stemmed from personal vengeance. Extending execution to those known only from their criminal records created moral unease.

"Let me suggest a simpler alternative my civilized friend. There should be those Italian partisans willing to do more than kidnap former SS then turn them over for questionable prosecution. Many suffered greatly at the hands of the SS in Italy. Just let these former partisans deal with them like they did with Mussolini."

"Not going that route, Pavel. Yet I need several tough men capable of physical violence to seize any SS we uncover. Do you have specific individuals in mind?"

"A couple. Can you stay over for a couple of days? Give me a chance to see if I can make contact by telephone or wire. If not, I will at least provide you with names and last known addresses."

"Sure. By the way, I can still distribute funds for your refugee efforts from the Paris accounts from Rome. Fiona and I are staying at the Hotel Farnese if you need to reach me."

"What about weapons?"

"That too. Your struggle for a Jewish state is no different a cause from my effort to go after murderers of Jews."

❖ ❖ ❖

Once back in Rome, Marchand telephoned Carla Capponi. Two days later, they arrived at her apartment over the same food distribution cooperative in the old working class Trastevere district she managed during the war.

The last time Marchand saw Capponi was three years ago. Pregnant at the time with the war in Italy still raging. She married her former partisan Rosario Bentivegna who commanded the Central GAP Carlo Pisacane, part of the $4^{th}$ Italian Garibaldi Partisan Division. As an Italian Communist, Bentivegna left his pregnant wife after the Allied liberation of Rome to continue the fight alongside Tito's partisans in Yugoslavia.

The four spent an enjoyable afternoon along with their two-year old daughter Elena, recounting their respective adventures the last couple of years. Bentivegna returned to finish medical school, recently becoming a doctor. With Marchand translating, Fraser enthralled both Capponi and Bentivegna with his exploits in Europe covering the rise of Hitler and the Spanish Civil War. Their experiences resisting the Nazis created a shared bond.

After the conversation turned to their mutual war experiences fighting the Nazis, Marchand used the opportunity to segue into the reason for their return to Rome.

"After returning to Paris at the end of the war, we experienced a violent attack at our apartment. Three assailants. Former Nazis SS."

"Oh no!" Carla exclaimed. "What happened?"

"They wanted information. Something related to Marc's American intelligence work in Switzerland. To force Marc to provide the information, they threatened to disfigure me with a knife. Out of habit as an OSS agent, I still armed myself with a small caliber pistol.

"One man grabbed my hair as the other prepared to slice off my ear. From my jacket pocket, I extracted the pistol. Even a small caliber round at close range to the face can kill. I could not afford to miss. They would kill us once Marc gave them what they wanted.

"I killed both of them. With the third man distracted, Marc violently attacked and disarmed him. Threatened with death, the third man revealed their identities.

Both Capponi and Bentivegna asked a barrage of questions. Marc could generally follow the Italian since he spoke Spanish, with both languages having spelling and phonetic similarities.

Eventually Marchand resumed. "Because of that incident we reconnected with a concentration camp survivor we met at Mauthausen just after liberation. Simon Wiesenthal calls himself a Nazis hunter. Wants the world never to forget. His revenge is to hunt down, harass, expose, and force governments to prosecute fugitive war criminals.

"I lost my brother to the Nazis. The Nazis tortured and murdered a good friend that saved Marc's life in Spain. I witnessed a *Waffen-SS* battalion murder an entire Italian village. Then what happened in Paris. We decided we too must help destroy Nazis SS not yet brought to justice.

"Rome apparently is central for Nazis looking to escape to South America or other safe havens. We also have information that certain Catholic clergy are actively providing escape conduits called ratlines. Like rats escaping ships by coming down the mooring lines."

"The Church? Why?" Capponi said.

"We do not know. However, it presents an opportunity to possibly catch Nazi war criminals."

Fraser opened his briefcase and removed the list of the major fugitives. Knowing that Capponi spoke some English, he said, "Our Nazis hunter friend compiled this list. The worst of the wanted war criminals. We also have an even longer list of others, all wanted for mass murder or other crimes."

Capponi and Bentivegna began looking at the list. Bentivegna translated aloud in Italian the crimes of some of the worse war criminals.

Marchand translated after Bentivegna responded to a particular entry, "Rosario says both he and Carla participated in an attack on a unit of German police in the Via Rasella in March

1944. They killed 33 Germans and wounded more than 100. The Germans murdered 335 civilians in caves outside Rome. Known as the Fosse Ardeatine Massacre. It is referenced as the crime of Hauptsturmführer Erich Priebke."

"Tell them what we are planning, Fiona. Can they provide us the names of former partisans that might be willing to take part? Explain what the work entails. No financial hardship for giving their time since we will pay well for their services."

Marchand spent several minutes in back and forth conversation with Capponi and Bentivegna.

"They said they can easily find such former partisans. Many motivated by revenge against the Nazis. Carla serves on the executive committee of the National Association of Italian Partisans so she has a wide range of contacts."

Fraser said to Marchand, "Pavel gave me three names of partisans he worked with during the war. Do they know them?"

Both recognized two of the names. Marchand translated, "They recognize Giordano and Moretti by reputation although they never met them. Known to have worked as a team of assassins targeting German officers."

Understandable coming from a recommendation from Trakonitz.

"Rosario asks what happens if you identify any of these wanted men?"

"Tell him we kidnap them. Then transport them north. Turn them over to American authorities in occupied Austria. That is why we need determined people on the team. Am I correct that Italian authorities might not prosecute?"

After Marchand translated, and Bentivegna responded, she said, "He did not think the current government would prosecute war crimes unless the acts happened in Italy. Most of those wanted committed crimes outside Italy. He suggested transporting them instead to Yugoslavia as a surer solution."

"Ask him to explain."

Marchand said, "Yugoslavia suffered terribly under the Nazis and their Fascist Croatian partners the Ustaše. Tito's regime will deal harshly with former Nazis or Ustaše."

Fraser said, "That is an interesting alternative. One of the priests supposedly helping these war criminals was a lieutenant colonel in the Croatian Ustaše. A chaplain involved with their concentration camps."

Instantly Fraser realized this to be the solution. Let Communist Yugoslavia execute them. Perhaps after a show trial but that did not trouble him. Apart from the U.S. Army CIC harboring Klaus Barbie, Wiesenthal also pointed out a lack of American enthusiasm to pursue Nazis war criminals. Transport those captured to Trieste on the border with the bordering Yugoslav province of Slovenia. Since Bentivegna fought with Tito's partisans during the war, he could arrange the transfer. No conflicting agendas as experienced with the Americans in Bavaria.

Late that night after further discussions and a fine diner, Bentivegna drove them back to their hotel. He and his wife would support the project but could not directly participate. They parted agreeing to meet again the following week to finalize plans.

Together, Fraser and Marchand set about organizing the necessary infrastructure and operational planning. Find a working location for Victor Kronberger to develop the photos and supervise the difficult work of identification. Most importantly, fixing on where and how to post the watchers. The coverage needed to be comprehensive so as not to overlook any fugitives. That remained the most difficult challenge. No matter how well they staged the surveillance, at best they could only hope for limited success. Yet if they could seize even just one of the major war criminals then worth the effort.

Everything presumed fugitives physically came to these locations. Fraser rationalized if these clergy knowingly aided war criminals, they would probably supervise the process closely before moving them down the ratline. Minimize the number of those involved to preserve secrecy. What better place than established Church property under their immediate control?

No way to resolve that question before moving forward. Fraser felt the urgency. No telling how many Nazis may have already escaped Europe. Once in South America living in Fascist-sympathetic regimes, they became out of reach. Fraser and Marchand must proceed quickly with recruiting the partisans and bringing the photographer Victor Kronberger to Rome. The only risk in the venture was SS blood money.

If proven these priests were helping the escape of war criminals, difficult to believe the Pope sanctioning such acts. If limited to only certain clergy, public exposure might therefore destroy the ratlines. The only means toward that end was compromising the ratlines by capturing a wanted war criminal under their protection.

Each armed with a Leica 35mm camera, Fraser and Marchand set out for Hudal's Collegio Santa Maria dell'Anima. The objective to identify the principal entrance points and the best surveillance vantage locations.

On the walk, Marchand theorized aloud. "There is no reason former Nazi SS should sneak about if they are under the protection of these churchmen. Their faces are unknown to anyone in Rome. That means they would likely use normal entrances. Of course, if they are hiding among the mass of refugees elsewhere, then perhaps no reason to come to these locations or even Rome. There must be places where the Church or the Red Cross temporarily shelter displaced persons."

"In which case our mission fails," Fraser said.

"Not actually fails. That would just mean there is no practical way for us to intercede directly to stop them escaping Europe. The line of attack therefore becomes political persuasion rather than covert action."

With the Pontifico Istituto Teutonic, Fraser's fluency in German allowed working a cover as an American newspaper reporter. While inside, Marchand would traverse the outside perimeter of the complex determining points of entry and observation locations.

If these were Church-sponsored ratlines, Fraser doubted it to be a wide conspiracy involving the Vatican leadership. Maintaining secrecy exponentially degraded with more conspirators, elevating the risk of exposure. That logic suggested even within these two locations, knowledge of the backgrounds of Nazis fugitives was probably restricted to just the principal clergy and trusted subordinates.

As a German-American, Fraser's cover story was researching for a piece on the state of the Catholic Church in Germany and Catholics in territories overrun by the Soviets. Play on Germanic nationalism and anti-Communism.

He entered through the main entrance off the narrow Via Della Pace in front of the Church of Santa Maria. He wandered about the ground floor, finding another main door opening on the other side to the Via dell'Anima. On the second floor, a priest asked in Italian if he could be of help. In German, Fraser replied, "I would like to speak with Bishop Hudal?"

"Do you have an appointment?"

"No. I am an American journalist."

"His Excellency is not in today. I am his secretary. If you will follow me to my office, I will check the Bishop's calendar."

After giving the young priest his name and reason for the audience with Hudal, Fraser asked if the priest might show him around the Collegio in order to take photographs as background material for his newspaper article in the American press.

Armed with an appointment in three days and understanding the layout of the Collegio complex, he joined Marchand in front of the church.

He said, "This is the main entrance, the other is on the street backing the building on the eastside."

She immediately said to him, "I think I have the answer for how to deploy those doing the surveillance. Notice that street musician just down the street?"

Fraser nodded.

"Our surveillance team at each location should consist of a street musician and couples, a man and a woman, posing as tourists moving along the street. Armed with cameras, they will not raise suspicion. The magician can remain for hours. One team at each entrance."

Fraser thought for a moment. "Very good. Establishes the criteria for selecting our recruits."

As they walked north to Via Tomacelli, they passed a surveying crew. Fraser said, "Look at those workmen. That will be the perfect cover San Girolamo. We equip separate two-man crews each with a surveyor's transit. Arm them with cameras. Some sort of municipal public works project. Sewer system work maybe."

Unlike the dell"Anima tucked within narrow streets, Via Tomacelli was a wide boulevard. The ancient ruins of the Mausoleum of Augustus, surrounded by a park-like setting, occupied the area behind the church and monastery next to the River Tiber.

As Fraser entered the monastery, Marchand walked the perimeter making a diagram and taking photographs of possible surveillance positions. Wandering about inside, Fraser established the main points of entry. Since no one asked his business, he took his time. Whether noteworthy or not, he observed a number of men inside, obviously not clergy by their manner of dress. Exiting through the back, there were several more men walking around the circular ruins of the mausoleum. He took the opportunity to take photos appearing to be capturing the ancient monument in the background.

A productive day although many unknowns remained. Did fugitives actually move through either of these locations, or did Hudal and Draganović just direct activities from here? If they did, would they be able to identify any wanted war criminals by capturing photos or were the odds too long?

The only way to resolve those uncertainties was to move forward. The next step, reconnect with Capponi and Bentivegna to recruit the surveillance teams. Fraser wired money telling Simon Wiesenthal they were ready for Victor Kronberger. Same offer as described when they met. A salary for the duration of the project and accommodations while in Rome. Once his services concluded, funds provided for Kronberger to set up his own photographic studio.

Events moved quickly. Kronberger arrived within a week. Enthusiastic by the prospect of thwarting escaping Nazis war criminals, Capponi and Bentivegna assembled a group of former partisans willing to participate. In all cases those with personal reasons for seeking retribution. Not only tested by experience, but those known capable of violent measures. Several capable of acting as street musicians. Including the three recommended by Trakonitz, a tough capable bunch.

Among the volunteers were eight woman. Four would serve as part of the surveillance teams. The additional four to work under Kronberger's direction to assist in developing the film then the painstaking work looking for matches to the wanted list images.

None of the recruits seemed in this for the money. Marchand thanked them for their help. Since they must take time away from their jobs, they would be paid well. The funds came from a private source in America who lost relatives to the Nazis Holocaust. Economic times were difficult and they wished none of the volunteers to sacrifice financially.

After a meeting with all the volunteers gathered in Capponi's warehouse, they scheduled the operation to begin in one week. This was to be about identifying Nazis SS by taking photographs. Each field team received a camera and instructed in its use. The photos immediately developed into enlargements by Kronberger. Then another team took on the difficult task of searching for a match among the SS photos of wanted war criminals.

Marchand added her thoughts by explaining in Italian, "Look for subtle manner of dress that might distinguish the Nazis from locals or refugees. These are former SS officers. Use to privilege they may appear in ordinary clothing but look for those perhaps better dressed than typical refugees. Look for their bearing, erect and arrogant rather than fearful. Look for mannerisms that make them stand out. How they smoke their cigarettes."

One former partisan asked the question on everyone's mind, "What happens when we identify one of these *bastardi*?"

Marchand answered in Italian, "We abduct them then transport them north by car to Trieste. Deliver them to Yugoslav border police along with their identifications and crimes."

"Where does this information come from?"

"A Nazis hunter and former concentration camp survivor. He compiled the material from interviewing witnesses and working with the American Army following Germany's surrender. Marc and I met him after the Americans liberated Mauthausen concentration camp when we worked for American intelligence."

"Is this an American intelligence operation?"

Fraser understood the question and interjected, "No. Unfortunately, we cannot rely on the Americans to deal with these war criminals. The war crimes trials are almost over. The Americans worry more about the Soviet Union than cleaning up the mess from the war. The Yugoslavs will be more aggressive."

As Marchand translated, several of the partisans nodded.

Capponi and Bentivegna suggested the three men recommended by Trakonitz stay behind after everyone filed out.

Fraser spoke, stopping for Marchand to translate. "I believe you gentlemen know Pavel Trakonitz, the officer with the British Army's Jewish Brigade?"

All three nodded. "He is a good friend of both Fiona and I. He saved Fiona's life after a SS battalion attacked their group of partisans then took reprisals of the locals at the San Giustino Massacre. Pavel Trakonitz recommended you three specifically. High praise coming from someone like Trakonitz."

All three nodded in agreement.

"Should we be successful, we are looking for you three to make the abduction and deliver the packages to the Yugoslavs. Select any others you need to help."

The one known as Lorenz Giordano said in broken but understandable English, "You realize things may become violent? These SS will know their fate."

"Of course. That is the reason Trakonitz recommended you. The important outcome is serving justice on these murderers. Do whatever is necessary. It is of no importance to me how you accomplish that.

"You will have the most difficult job. For that, you will each receive the equivalent one thousand U.S. dollars as a bounty for every SS captured and transported."

Fraser understood the implication of the way he made the pronouncement. Why should these battle-hard partisans make such a long journey when a bullet proved more expedient? That would be Trakonitz's solution. Best he could do was offer a bounty for transporting them to the Yugoslavs.

Marchand scowled also understanding the implication. Not a solution she approved of, yet no other viable alternative remained. Transport to the Yugoslav border nothing more than a fig leaf to appease the conscience. Whether a bullet or a show trial, execution the assured outcome. That was Marc's intent.

# CHAPTER 26

ROME, ITALY | JANUARY 1948

---

At the scheduled meeting with Bishop Hudal, Fraser sought to gather an impression about his rumored reputation as overtly embracing Nazi ideology.

In response to Fraser's general question concerning the status of the Church in Germany, Hudal said, "As with everything in Germany, the Church has suffered immeasurably in this tragic war. The pressing problem is dislocation of the German people. Adding to this is the flood of refugees from Eastern Europe."

"Is that the reason for your personal involvement in relief efforts, Your Excellency?"

"Yes, of course. The victorious Allies have little regard for citizenry of Germany and Austria. They still see Germans as the enemy. The Church treats these poor souls as children of God. I am devoted to working closely with the International Red Cross to bring relief and assisting in resettlement of these displaced persons."

Sanctimonious bullshit. In preparation for the meeting, Fraser read Hudal's *The Foundations of National Socialism.* A tedious diatribe praising Germanic nationalism and much of Nazi ideology, particularly anti-Semitism.

"Does assisting displaced persons extend to Jews that survived the Nazi concentration camps?"

Hudal's expression stiffened as the little man stood to deliver emphasis as he paced about with hand gestures. "No it does not. The Jews are at the heart of this problem. In that, Hitler was correct. Aligned with the atheistic Communists of the Soviet Union and the financial centers of the West, the Jews have themselves to blame."

"Yet do you not condemn those guilty of the mass murder of millions of Jews?"

"That is for God to judge. I condemn injustice in whatever form. Those responsible already face trial before war crime tribunals."

"Only a handful of the Nazi leadership. Thousands more have fled justice. Some people suspect that many of the worst criminals are seeking to escape by blending into these masses of displaced persons. Does that concern you that your humanitarian efforts might also facilitate their avoiding justice?"

Hudal exhibited a condescending smile. "The Church is merely extending Christian charity. We remain blind to the histories of those in need. Impossible to investigate the circumstances of each of these poor souls. To those crying out for revenge, the Church does not believe in the eye for an eye of the Jew."

With that, Fraser had what he needed insofar as determining the likelihood of Hudal knowingly sheltering wanted war criminals. The motivations of Hudal and Draganović seemed all too clear. Both unrepentant anti-Semitic Fascists.

Why the Vatican Secretariat of State's office chose the most publicly avowed pro-Nazi bishop in Rome as the Spiritual Director of the German people resident in Italy remained suspicious. Where senior prelates perhaps in the Curia sponsoring the ratlines?

Surveillance preparations consumed the next few weeks. Following Victor Kronberger's arrival, they found a suitable place to set up the darkroom and working space to pour over photos looking for matches to the wanted list. Better yet, Kronberger could stay in the apartment above a former retail shop. Conveniently located only a half mile south of the Hotel Farnese.

Helping Kronberger purchase the necessary photographic processing equipment, Marchand suggested Kronberger actually establish a photographic studio. It made for a perfect cover. To Fraser she said, "He has little future in Linz. Perhaps he might decide to relocate permanently to Rome since he speaks Italian."

Fraser and Marchand spent Christmas at the Vatican as a guest of Monsignor Donati. Considering they would soon move against the Church ratlines, they felt like spies. Following the Christmas holiday, the team of recruited partisans would commence surveillance operations.

"I have done all I can to help with this crazy plan, Marc," Marchand said to Fraser. "I support what you are doing but I am going to now immerse myself in restoring the Caravaggio. I will be back to the hotel every evening. Make sure you leave some time for us while we are in Rome."

A total of twelve surveillance members taking part. All former partisans with combat experience. Building on Marchand's suggestion, the group included four musicians. Two playing concertinas and two others violins. None were professionals but adequate to impersonate street musicians. At each of the two locations, the plan called for a mobile surveillance team consisting of a man and woman couple working with a musician for a six-hour shift. Another musician and team would take over for another six hours. All trained and supplied with cameras with at least one telephoto lens for each team. No practical way to work after dark since the street lighting was inadequate for photographs.

Fraser selected the three former partisans recommended by Trakonitz to be the capture team. All spoke passable English because of their wartime work with the British Army. Necessary since Fraser would supervise capture should they identify any wanted Nazis. Selected for their wartime experience. Tough, battle-tested men and women, still harboring grudges against the Nazis.

If they did seize any wanted war criminals, Fraser suspected he might have to convince them not to simply shoot the Nazi rather than go to the trouble of transporting to Yugoslavia. That they worked with Trakonitz as assassins meant they undoubtedly shared Trakonitz's brand of justice. Uncertain if the financial inducement might dissuade them. If it came to that, so be it.

One of these men would also move about each location in case of immediate need of their skills. The third always available by telephone. These men always went about well armed. In their pockets, they carried rolls of adhesive tape suitable for binding the wrists and covering the mouths of those captured.

In the first week of surveillance, the amount of exposed film produced from both locations proved overwhelming. Kronberger and his team of women volunteers struggled to keeping up with the developing. The meticulous work searching for possible candidates with magnifying glasses took whatever time necessary depending on the quality of the photographed facial detail. This prompted adding two more volunteers to Kronberger's team. Producing enlargements of any potential matches constituted the final work product for more detailed study. Kronberger proved an able organizer shifting everyone's tasks periodically to reduce boredom.

Two weeks into the operation, their first success.

One of the women pouring over the previous day's batch of photos, asked her colleagues to look at photos of two men walking together. Several good photos taken of each. Later they found out the surveillance team taking the shots observed the two men acting suspiciously. They snapped several photographs as the subjects first entered the San Girolamo dei Croati church then again as they walked down the boulevard, circling the monastery before entering. During the twenty-minute observation, the men continually looked around, stopping to light cigarettes as an excuse to stop and look in every direction. With little place for concealment on the busy Via Tomacelli, using the cover of a surveying crew proved ingenious. It allowed for continuous long-range observation using the surveyor transit telescope without appearing obvious.

"One of these could be this man Hauptsturmführer Engel Zimmermann. What do you think?" A woman analyst said to a colleague.

The second woman picked up the surveillance photo, repeatedly comparing to the image on the wanted list using a magnifying glass. She then compared the other surveillance photos providing different angles of the face. "Yes. I believe it is."

With that discovery, they quickly identified the other man. The other women all agreed after examining the photos.

When Kronberger immerged from the darkroom, they excitedly showed him the find. After just a brief study, "You are right," He said.

The woman making the first identification added, "Now look closely at his companion. We believe him to be this Obersturmbannführer Walter Schumacher. "I do not read English, but does this not identify them as part of the same SS unit?"

Kronberger read the description of the alleged crimes, replying to the women, "Ah yes. Both served in *Einsatzgruppe E, Einsatzkommando 3*. A mobile SS death squad. They operated in Croatia. Accused of murdering several thousand Serbs, Jews, and gypsies. Makes sense why they came to San Girolamo dei Croati.

"They probably worked closely with the Croatian Ustaše. The priest that runs San Girolamo was himself an officer in the Ustaše. Schumacher is a big fish. I must telephone Signore Fraser immediately."

Events happened rapidly. Fraser collected copies of the photographs then drove his car to San Girolamo to distribute to the current surveillance team. Also on scene from the capture team, was Lorenz Giordano. Fraser dispatched one of the surveillance team members to alert Flavio Moretti and Raphael Pariatore to come immediately.

Should the two fugitives leave the monastery, the capture team would respond at the first opportunity. If the fugitives proceeded by foot, they would seize them quickly. A delivery lorry waited close within sight of Fraser's car for transport out of Rome. If spotted leaving by automobile, Fraser would follow in his car with the capture team close behind in the lorry.

Fraser instructed the team to seize anyone accompanying the SS fugitives. Unharmed if possible. Released later once the fugitives are securely out of Rome.

Giordano asked, "And if the SS are with priests or monks?"

"Seize them."

An hour later, two monks and a priest accompanied the two SS as they left the monastery. Too many to seize and transport without raising attention and drawing police. They could only follow hoping the Church minders deposited their charges somewhere more opportune before attempting the capture.

Fraser sent one of the surveillance team to collect the lorry and to follow his car. They would drive at a discrete distance while the capture team followed the fugitives and their entourage on foot.

The way this unfolded did not dismay Fraser. From the onset, any success in identifying fleeing war criminals required adapting to the circumstances. No way to anticipate every eventuality. Every step of the mission involved unknowns. Not surprising that priests and monks might escort the fugitives. After all, this was a clandestine ratline with the SS unlikely fluent in Italian. Moving about obviously required the assistance of local minders.

Of equal importance is disruption of these ratlines. Best if they could obscure the abductions to the extent possible by avoiding confrontation with the clergy and their methods then altered in response. If unavoidable, then perhaps the fear of public exposure might curtail future activity. Perhaps Draganović and Hudal operated independently. Therefore, possible Hudal might not know if the parallel San Girolamo operation became compromised. Endless unknowns. The objective remained to damage the ratline machinery and snare any war criminals in the process.

Although not among the major wanted Nazis, these two were still mass murderers. The equivalent to a lieutenant colonel and a captain. If captured at war's end, likely to have become defendants in the Nuremberg Einsatzgruppen Trial started back in September. Probably receiving death sentences. Surely facing execution if shipped off to Yugoslavia.

One way or the other, justice served. They could not escape his committed and well-armed partisans. Must however be careful to avoid the Italian police. Even if these two murderers are the only ones caught, the exercise was well worth the effort.

The fugitives and their clerical escort walked the mile and a half to Rome Termini rail station. Giordano, Moretti, and Pariatore followed closely.

Fraser parked his car. To the partisan driver pulling up with the lorry, he handed over his car keys and said, "Follow me inside. My guess, the fugitives are boarding a train. I will go with the capture team. Tell the others. Tell Kronberger to explain to my wife. I will contact him tomorrow by telephone. Take care of my car."

Fraser came alongside Giordano who said, "The priest bought tickets to Genoa for only the two SS."

"Excellent. We shall join them on the train." Handing over some money to Giordano, get all of us tickets including me. We will take them in route or when they get off."

The train crawled up the Mediterranean coast. During the eight-hour journey, the two subjects sat toward the front of the railway carriage only sparsely populated with other passengers. Fraser and his team remained at the back of the carriage.

The spectacular coastal scenery unappreciated while concentrating on how best to carry out the capture. Flushed with the success of their efforts, Fraser nonetheless realized the difficulties in concluding the mission.

They must accomplish the capture without drawing undue attention. What if the SS raised an alarm? They may not fear arrest in Italy. They undoubtedly possessed Red Cross travel documents in new names. Tickets on some freighter bound to South America. Entrance visas for the destination country. All while under protection of the Roman Catholic Church.

As the train rattled on, Fraser broke down the likely options. Take them by gunpoint as the train stopped in route. No one else therefore involved assisting them. They just disappear without explanation. However, should the suspects resist, this would attract police stationed at every rail stop platform.

Waiting until arrival in Genoa meant someone meeting the subjects to escort them through the remaining stations of the ratline conduit. That likely meant contending with Catholic clergy. A complication but unavoidable. Fraser held no regard for anyone helping war criminals escape. They could do nothing except raise an immediate alarm. The tactical challenge was finding transportation and getting away before any Italian police arrived.

The best option was to make their move in Genoa. Huddling with his three colleagues, he explained. "We take them in Genoa after they disembark. Too many unknowns if we make an attempt in route. Stops are only one or two minutes. At each railway station we must expect a police officer on duty. We must avoid any contact with the Italian police. None of you are to be connected with any crimes under Italian law."

"As the train pulls in Giordano and Pariatore will disembark immediately once the train comes to a stop. Take up positions walking ahead of the targets through the railway station to the street. Moretti and I will stay close behind the subjects. Keep your weapons hidden until ready to make our move."

"Someone will probably be on the platform to meet them. Perhaps a priest," Giordano said. Of the three, he was the defacto leader of the team. What then?"

"Take the priest or anyone else working with the subjects. These SS *bastardi* must not get away. Do not harm others helping them unless they interfere. I realize they will raise the alarm once released, but that is unavoidable. Just scare the hell out of them. By then it will not matter."

As the train pulled into the vast Genova Piazza Principe railway station, Giordano and Pariatore jumped off quickly then moved toward the station entrance taking up an observation position.

Once they seized the subjects, the problem remained transportation out of Genoa. At least they were closer to Trieste compared with Rome. Still a long journey. For six people plus whoever met the subjects. This required two cars or a lorry. Fraser anticipated that to be a major problem before they arrived in Genoa. Steal a car or lorry if necessary? If the situation deteriorated, shoot the SS and make their escape?

Giordano and Pariatore passed a priest walking toward the train platform. The priest immediately went up to the two SS having stepping down from the train car and shook hands.

The SS officers carried on a conversation with the priest walking between them. The priest even smiled.

Watching this friendly interaction particularly upset Lorenz Giordano. "Fucking priest."

Everyone exited the train station onto the busy Via Andrea Doria Boulevard. A steady flow of other passengers exited with them filing the broad sidewalk with people.

Fraser said to the team, "Stay close to them and be ready to move should they have a car waiting."

Seconds later, the priest waved his arm as a car pulled to the curb.

Realizing the transportation problem immediately resolved, Fraser said, "Now! Take them!"

Discretely reaching into to their coat pockets, the team came up behind the two subjects and the priest.

As Giordano approached to the back of the taller of the SS, Fraser said in German "Obersturmbannführer Schumacher that is a gun in your back. If you move or yell out, I will shoot you immediately. You too Hauptsturmführer Zimmermann."

Rafael Pariatore stood behind the other German pressing his revolver into the man's back.

Flavio Moretti faced the startled priest with his weapon thrust forward inside his coat pocket. In Italian, "You too priest. Make a sound and you are dead."

The priest protested, "Who are you? What is this about?"

Fraser said in German. "Shut up *padre*. Resist and we shoot everyone. Your driver is no longer needed. Tell him there is a change of plans. More people to transport. We need the car."

With a motion of his head toward Moretti, Fraser said in English, "Take the priest and make sure he does as instructed. You drive." To Giordano and Pariatore, "Wedge these two into the back seat between you."

Moretti ordered the driver to put the suitcases in the trunk then got behind the wheel. Fraser grabbed the priest roughly by the arm pushing him to the passenger side of the car.

Fraser starred menacingly at the priest just inches from his face. In German, "Get into the front seat. Direct us north out of Genoa."

Twenty minutes later, the signs read Milano 140 kilometers.

"Why are you doing this?" Schumacher said. "You have the wrong people."

"Really?" Fraser said. "Who do you claim to be?"

"We have papers. Please let us show you."

Schumacher slowly reached inside his suit coat and extracted his papers handing them to Fraser. Zimmermann followed with his.

"Ah. Herr Vogel and Schulte," Fraser said looking over the documents. "What did you do during the war?"

Schumacher answered, "*Wehrmacht*. Eastern Front. Separated from our unit after being overrun. Needed to avoid capture by the Red Army. Discarded our uniforms and sought refuge among the hordes of refugees."

"What rank?

Schumacher continued to do the talking. "I am a sergeant. Schulte was my corporal."

"What unit?"

"The German 17th Army."

"So two enlisted men traveled all the way to Rome and gained the help of the Catholic Church? Not only new Red Cross passports but even entry visas to Argentina. Also tickets for passage on the steamship *Río de la Plata.* All this for a mere sergeant and a corporal? What say you, Padre?"

Although frightened, the priest made a show of authority. In German, "I demand you release me and these men. You are committing a grave crime. These men are refugees under the protection of the Vatican."

"Who specifically? The Pope?" Fraser said. "Someone of lesser stature? Who in Rome engineered this?"

The priest remained silent.

Within an hour they were seventy kilometers north of Genoa. Consulting a map of the region inside the glove box, Fraser directed Moretti to turn off the main highway. Several miles further, they turned onto a rural dirt road with no farms in sight.

Pulling to a stop, Fraser said, "Everyone out."

Schumacher said in German, "What do you intend to do?"

Once everyone was out of the car Fraser said, "Now you and the corporal remove your shirts."

"*Nein.*"

Giordano with his limited German, said, "Do as you are told or I will shoot you in the knee. *Schnell, schnell!*"

The Germans began removing their jackets and shirts knowing their subterfuge about to be discovered. Under their left upper arm, *Waffen-SS* received a tattoo designating their blood type.

The younger Zimmermann fearing they were about to be shot, threw his overcoat over Pariatore's revolver then took off running down a grassy slope.

Giordano took chase. Closing to within only a few meters of the German, he stopped and shot him twice in the back. Pulling off the dying man's left sleeve of his suitcoat, he then ripped away the shirtsleeve revealing the incriminating tattoo.

Giordano then finished off the German with a shot to the head.

Trudging back up the hill, Fraser confronted him, "What the hell happened?"

Giordano did not answer. Instead, he walked up to Schumacher and fired a single round into his forehead.

With a look of horror on his face, the terrified priest made the sign of the cross expecting he was next.

Turning to Fraser and his stunned colleagues, Giordano said, "They are SS of course. Check this one's left arm and you will see the blood type tattoo." Turning to Fraser, "You are very clever finding these murders, Signore Fraser. You and Bentivegna however make this too difficult. It is a long dangerous journey transporting these men to Yugoslavia knowing they will still die.

"This is how Trakonitz and I dealt with SS after the war ended."

Fraser shook his head. Giordano was right, yet that was not his solution. It was not about these SS deserving of a quick bullet to the head. It was about him. He continued to tell himself his killing Cabrera and Leitner was different. Looking at the dead Schumacher ... was it? He would kill Barbie given another chance.

Giordano said, "What about the priest?"

"He goes free. He is not a murderer. We will be far away before he can report what happened. Remove his shoes. He needs to do penance for his sins."

Fraser and his team drove in silence to Milan. After parking the car, he bought tickets for Rome and sandwiches for the long return trip.

He then telephoned Marchand. A short conversation. "I am fine. So are the others. The packages unfortunately suffered damage. I will explain when I return to Rome. Love you."

Boarding the train, Giordano said, "I know you do not approve, Signore Fraser. Yugoslavia however was not worth the risk for just the one SS."

Fraser glared at him, not sure what to say. Why was it necessary to shoot the one fleeing? The answer simple. The most expedient solution. An excuse for Giordano. Turning them over to the Yugoslavs unnecessary. Certainly naïve to expect these former partisans to face the added risk even for extra money.

Giordano continued, "Your plan worked. We caught two SS murderers responsible for killing thousands. They belonged to units following the regular German Army for the purpose of murdering civilians."

With Fraser sitting in silence as the train departed Milan, Giordano asked, "Are we to continue our surveillance work?"

For a moment, Fraser was uncertain what he intended. His operation yielded results. Difficult to abandon the work because of this unintended outcome. The intent always to see these SS ultimately executed. Even though Father Draganović might suspect their ratline compromised, perhaps Bishop Hudal's operation was sufficiently separate not to know of events in Genoa.

"Yes, we shall continue. We will shift everyone to Santa Maria dell'Anima. They may not know what happened in Genoa. One stipulation, Giordano. No more executions. We catch anyone else, we take them to Yugoslavia. I will even go with you. Otherwise, we risk Italian police investigating. Agreed?"

Giordano nodded his agreement. "Let me suggest a minor variation. Trieste is out of the question. Too far travelling by lorry or car. Better a fishing boat. Transport the prisoners to Pescara on the Adriatic coast. From there by fishing boat across the Adriatic to Split on the Dalmatian coast of Croatia. Avoids detection while preventing escape of the fugitives."

"Very well," Fraser said. He needed Giordano and the others. "You will also be paid for doing what was necessary with these two."

❖ ❖ ❖

Back at the Hotel Farnese, Fiona embraced Marc with tears running down her cheeks fearing what might have happened.

After Fraser explained the events in Genoa, she composed her swirling emotions into a clear pronouncement. "I want out. I want you out. This is enough, Marc. Do you wish to live your life like this? I do not.

"I will complete the first restoration in a few weeks. I realize how important this is to you, but I will then return to Paris. Will you come with me?"

Disillusioned with the violent outcome of the venture, he agreed to wrap up the operation and return to Paris with her. He can never hope to seize more than a couple of fugitive Nazis SS with his small adhoc group. No reason to expect future successes will not end the same way. Working outside any legal structure cannot be sustainable. Better to use the gathered experience and expose the Catholic Church to scandal forcing the Vatican to shut down the ratlines. Work with Simon Wiesenthal to publicize his research to continual harass Nazi war criminals and attack those governments knowingly harboring war criminals.

"Yes. I will wrap this up. As much as I want to see former SS pay for their crimes, I do not relish being their executioner. Maybe I can at least find a way of crippling these established ratlines."

# CHAPTER 27

ROME, ITALY | FEBRUARY 1948

---

Rudolf Lange was born in 1910 in Prussian Silesia. From a middle class family with his father a railway construction supervisor, he was able to attend a university. Receiving a doctorate in law in 1933, he joined the *Gestapo* and the *Sturmabteilung,* the SA, the paramilitary wing of the National Socialist German Workers Party. To advance his career opportunities, he later joined the elite Nazi *Schutzstaffel,* the SS in 1936.

Lange rose rapidly in the *Gestapo,* enthusiastically embracing Nazi ideology, particularly extremist anti-Semitic positions. In 1939, Heinrich Müller became *Gestapo* Chief while Lange ran various *Gestapo* offices in Weimar, Erfurt, and Kassel. In 1940, Lange became deputy head of police for Berlin.

Recognizing Lange's anti-Semitic zeal, led to the command staff of *Einsatzgruppe A* as commander of the *Einsatzkommando 2, or EK2* detachment in 1941. Lange embraced the radical mission of the EK2 death squads to resolve the *Jewish Problem* by killing as many Jews as possible following German forces advancing through Eastern Europe.

Eventually he became area chief of the *Sicherheitsdienst* the SD, the Nazis Security Service for Latvia. Giving orders to not only *SS-Einsatzkommandos,* but also death squads comprised of Latvians such as the *Arajs Kommando,* Lange was responsible for the planning and carrying out of the murders of 35,000 Latvian Jews from the Riga ghetto and another 1,000 arriving German Jews shipped east.

Many personal accounts of survivors of the Riga ghetto attested to Lange's fanatical anti-Semitism by describing incidents of him personally shooting Jews with his pistol without provocation.

Lange attended the Wannsee Conference in 1942 hosted by Reinhard Heydrich. Attended also by Adolf Eichmann, the purpose was to put into practice the solution to the Jewish Problem.

Promoted to SS-Obersturmbannführer, equivalent to lieutenant colonel, Lange ordered the final killing of Jews remaining in the Latvian Daugavpils ghetto, the last of as many as 16,000 Jews to perish.

In early 1945, Lange became head of all SS in Poznań, Poland. Soon after his arrival, the Red Army surrounded the well-fortified city. Reported wounded, Hitler ordered Lange's promotion to SS-Standartenführer, equivalent to full colonel, to encourage his fanatical leadership, also awarding him the rare German Cross in Gold.

Two weeks later, the Red Army overwhelmed the remaining German Poznań garrison. Official information on Lange's fate never reliably confirmed. No documentation ever found explaining the nature of his wounds. Never identified among the captured Germans or the recovered dead. Given his command position, the Red Army undoubtedly made a thorough search. However, with the city center reduced to ruins in the final Soviet assault, substantial numbers of bodies were likely never recovered.

Lange escaped death in the siege of Poznań. In reality, the wound he received earlier was relatively minor. A piece of shrapnel imbedded into his left upper thigh. Painful but not life threatening and still able to walk after a medic removed the shrapnel.

Known as a fanatically driven SS commander, Lange was not ready to fall on his sword for the Fatherland. With the help of his driver, an experienced senior SS sergeant, he intended first to make a try at escaping. "We cannot prevail. Rather than commit suicide you and I shall try to escape the city. You must obtain suitable civilian German identifications for both of us."

Previous resettlement increased the population of ethnic Germans in the city of Riga to 95,000 by 1944. Many now refugees fleeing west in the wake of the advancing Red Army. From this population of relocated Germans both the SS and *Wehrmacht* pressed civilian personnel into service for administrative and other non-combat related functions to free up troops.

With the heavy Red Army shelling, plenty of dead German civilians. Lange dispatched his sergeant to the German military hospital. His mission to locate suitable new German identities from among casualties. Find two identifications with sufficient likenesses among the many German non-military staff injured or dead. Not a foolproof escape plan, yet better than other alternatives. If questioned, they could not pass scrutiny using Polish identification papers since neither spoke Polish. However, papers identifying them as part of the German occupation machinery as ordinary soldiers might still provoke a bullet by the revenge minded Red Army. Better than a protracted death if identified as an SS officer, but Lange sought a better chance than becoming a POW.

A tense wait for Lange as he studied the map for the best escape route waiting for his sergeant. Intelligence reports identified the principal refugee routes. The trick was slipping through the Red Army cordon around Poznań in civilian clothing with plausible stories to fit new identities. No way to know how much scrutiny the Red Army might devote to refugees.

The enterprising sergeant requested to see the identification papers of all the patients in the hospital along with those dead of their injuries. By orders of SS commandant Standartenführer Lange. Going through the piles of identification documents looking at pictures while separating military from the lesser number of German civilians, he eventually selected the most suitable choices.

Lange thought the likeness assigned to him questionable but it must do. Leading the sergeant to his quarters, he provided the sergeant with a change to civilian clothing as they both discarded their SS uniforms.

With all available troops distributed to defend against the main Red Army thrust from the east, they slipped away making their way through streets clogged with debris from collapsed buildings. Each carried a blanket-bundle containing a few meager necessities tied with a cord. Both kept a loaded Lugar in their jacket pocket. Little protection if they encountered Soviet soldiers, but necessary for a self-inflicted bullet to the head rather than capture.

As they approached the outskirts of the city, they saw a long line of refugees trudging westward on foot, some pulling carts or pushing wheelbarrows with possessions. Looking at the refugees from the remains of a collapsed house, Lange extracted his Lugar service pistol and shot the sergeant in the back of the head.

The lone shot attracted no notice. No one to identify him.

Once he looked at his new identity selected by the sergeant, Lange began rehearsing his cover story as Ernst Stroebel. His papers read, born in Stuttgart. Bookkeeper. Employed by XXXVIII Armeekorps of the German *Wehrmacht* in the quartermaster section of the 52$^{nd}$ Infantry Division. The likeness passible, especially without shaving for days and his hair in need of trimming.

He also appreciated the fact he never received the blood type tattoo under his left arm. Although a fanatical advocate of SS ideology, he thought the practice nothing more than ritualistic nonsense embraced by Heinrich Himmler. Same as the ridiculous *Totenkopf,* the deaths-head emblem on SS caps.

He must now get well west of the advancing Soviets once they overran Riga. Even hidden behind a false identity, remaining in Soviet occupied territory meant little chance for escape. He must find the means to leave Europe. To accomplish that meant somehow moving south to Italy. Five hundred miles as the crow flies, however the Red Army moved westward along that entire front. Avoiding landing in some Soviet detention facility became the first priority. He must reach American or British lines in Germany or Austria for any chance of getting to Italy. From the latest intelligence reports, that meant a longer journey.

As head of the *Sicherheitsdienst des Reichsführers-SS* in Latvia, Lange had access to the highest level of Nazis intelligence. In these waning days of war with Germany facing certain defeat, contingency options became a constant topic of discussion among all SS, particularly those serving on the Eastern Front. Surrender to the Soviets meant certain death. Even regular German army troops suffered harsh treatment at the hands of the Red Army. Imprisonment in a forced labor camp in Siberia with starvation rations and uncertain repatriation.

Rudolf Lange therefore knew that many Roman Catholic clergy in Germany and Austria were sympathetic to those serving in the military of the Third Reich. Sufficiently sympathetic and anti-Communist to avoid asking awkward questions about one's war service, particularly those claiming to be Catholic.

Toward the end of the war, Pope Pius XII made clear he wished to extend his mission of charity in favor of all victims of war without national or religious distinction. As Pro-Secretary of State for the Vatican, Giovanni Montini, the future Pope Paul VI, made the overture to the Americans and British. He proposed sending papal representatives to the internment camps housing tens of thousands of prisoners of war and civilian detainees in Italy.

When the Western Allies agreed, Monsignor Montini proposed Bishop Alois Hudal as the Vatican's Spiritual Director of the German people to head the effort. Inexplicably the most outspoken pro-Nazi in Rome for such a mission. Did the Holy See approve his appointment?

While the Allies knew of Hudal's views, they agreed to the request on diplomatic grounds. Therefore, Hudal gained access to the German internee camps with only vague limitations to administer only to the spiritual needs of the detainees. When war ended, Hudal's special travel credentials extended his access into the internment camps of Austria and Germany.

Escaping war criminals therefore had only to make their way to American or British occupied territory under false identities rather than all the way to Rome. In his elevated position in the SD, Lange knew of the rumors about help offered by the Vatican for Catholics fearing Allied prosecution. Hudal's name often mentioned.

Lange grew up in a religiously indifferent family but one with a Catholic heritage. He therefore knew enough of the dogmatic trappings to pass as Catholic.

Once Lange felt sufficiently out of reach of the Red Army, evading forced conscription into retreating *Wehrmacht* units became the next hurdle. Here his unhealed wound helped as evidence of his infirmity, aided by a pronounced limp using a discarded crutch as a prop when necessary.

Six weeks later, after attaching himself to a large refugee column, Lange encountered advance elements of the Twelfth United States Army Group. The Americans set up inspection stations, looking for escaping German military personnel disguised as civilians with specific interest in fleeing SS.

With his identification as a German civilian working for the *Wehrmacht* in Poland, they hauled Lange aside for secondary interrogation. His well-rehearsed cover story as a civilian accountant prior to the war passed his German-speaking interrogator. Exempted from military service because of severe asthma, his circumstances changed as the war went badly. Eventually conscripted into quartermaster work, this led to relocation to Latvia on the Eastern Front in 1943 as the German military situation became desperate. A victim of Adolf Hitler's disastrous ambitions.

No one questioned the poor likeness of the photograph on his papers. No telltale blood type tattoo under his armpit. No reason to suspect this German as a masquerading soldier. After several weeks at an internment camp, another interrogator however remained suspicious. Although possessing civilian identity papers, he was still part of the German military machine. A quasi-POW. Lange was then transported by truck further south to a different internment camp, one for detainees designated for closer investigation. The location to prove fortuitous for Lange. Just north of Salzburg, Austria, the camp was closer to Italy.

With his exceptional intellect, Lange by now reinforced his cover identity with sufficient detail to confidently engage interrogators. Once Poznań fell to the Red Army, he simply fell into the mass of survivors fleeing the destruction. Grateful to have served the Fatherland and equally grateful to not to be in uniform facing a Soviet POW camp. The Red Army largely ignored the refugees fleeing west since they still faced intense resistance of a rear guard action as the beleaguered *Wehrmacht* fell back.

Within a few weeks, Bishop Hudal entered the camp. Hudal spoke with a great many of the detainees. Engaging each personally, his message had little to do with spiritual issues. Instead, his message concerned the preservation of Germanic nationalism.

"Germany must not be allowed to become a second-class European nation. The greatest threat is Soviet occupation. The Soviet Union is the common enemy of western civilization. We must now join with other nations to not only confront Communism, but to restore Germany to its rightful stature. We Germans must band together and reject political differences."

His nationalistic message was clear. He justified German aggression of WWII as a response to the devastating punitive measures inflicted by the victorious Allies following WWI to subjugate Germany. He was here to assist Catholic Germans.

Hudal cared nothing of past allegations of Nazi war crimes. Nothing more than natural pogroms against the Jews or subjugation of the inferior Slavic populations of Eastern Europe and Russia. He was here to rehabilitate German Catholics.

In his conversation with Lange, Hudal quickly suspected Lange as someone of elevated rank. For Lange's part, he passed along subtle references designed to convey to Hudal his devotion to Nazi ideology and his fierce German nationalism.

"Perhaps someone of your stature and intellect could best find a new home among others sharing your views."

"Yes. Much remains to be done to resurrect Germany. I have nothing to return to in Germany yet the Fatherland must live on. I expect to someday be part of a new Reich. Best to begin that work in a safe haven outside Germany."

"Excellent Herr Stroebel. There is a large German community in Buenos Aires, Argentina. You will be among like-minded Germans in a Catholic country governed by a strongman sympathetic to National Socialism ideology."

Hudal knew full well Stroebel was a senior Nazi, probably SS, yet he never challenged his obviously fictitious identity.

Weeks later, a Catholic priest extricated Lange from the internment camp and accompanied him by train to Rome. From the train station, the priest then drove him to the Pontificio Collegio Teutonico di Santa Maria dell'Anima.

News of events in Genoa eventually reached the *Komeradenwerk* in Madrid. Madrid was an integral part of a wider loosely connected organization of former Nazis. Called by various names of ODESSA, the term coined by American intelligence, *Die Spinne* by some like Otto Skorzeny, they shared common objectives. Chiefly that of self-preservation to avoid capture and prosecution for war crimes. Additionally, they provided a support structure for those with like-minded ideological views of National Socialistic Germanic nationalism. Pathological anti-

Communism served as a unifying political ideology. That in turn engendered support from powerful forces in the Vatican and worldwide acceptance by sympathetic Fascist-like regimes with predominately Catholic populations.

The inexplicable murders of Zimmermann and Schumacher therefore spread concern through this *führungsring*, this Nazi Mafia. Once the priest escorting the two murdered SS reached the nearest Catholic Church, he alerted both the Italian police and Father Draganović in Rome. From there, word spread back to the postwar Nazi SS network through a series of indirect telephone communications.

Madrid served as the defacto headquarters of this Nazi *führungsring*. Not only assessable to all of Europe, Madrid was a safe haven under the protection of the Spanish Fascist government of Francisco Franco.

The city of Gmunden in Upper Austria served as the forward operating post. Like Madrid, this too was setup by the daring *Waffen-SS* commando leader, Otto Skorzeny. After acquittal at the Dachau war crimes trials for his part in the Battle of the Bulge, Skorzeny escaped from an American internment camp in July 1948, while awaiting a decision by a denazification court. Hiding out in Bavaria, Skorzeny closely directed a shadowy network of well-placed former German military intelligence operatives under the direction of former *Wehrmacht* Major General Reinhard Gehlen.

Unlike the flamboyant Skorzeny, Gehlen was a brilliant pragmatist who overhauled the *Fremde Heere Ost*, the FHO military intelligence operating on the Eastern Front in 1942. He was not SS but regular army. Unlike Skorzeny, he reviled Hitler to the extent he knew in advance the details of the July 1944 assassination plot on Hitler. While not participating, he provided protection for Colonel Claus von Stauffenberg and his fellow conspirators. Gehlen was sufficiently clever to avoid the wide raging purge following the failed attempt to kill Hitler. What he shared with Skorzeny was a fanatical German nationalism and a continuing duty to confront the Soviets.

The clever and opportunistic Gehlen sold himself to the Americans as the only viable intelligence organization available to confront the Soviets. In December 1946, Gehlen and his organization began spying for the United States from occupied Germany and Austria. Although never a Nazi, he nonetheless used his clandestine resources to aid in the escape of those Nazis that might prove militarily useful to a revived Germany. Skorzeny became part of Gehlen's organization.

A Croatian priest close to Draganović telephoned a designated number in Madrid. In guarded language, careful not to mention names, he said, "Something happened to two packages. Both shot in route outside Genoa."

"What happened?

"The assailants spared the priest that met them when they arrived from Rome. He said the gunmen were Italian but one spoke German. The same man then addressed the Italians in English."

"Not likely a Communist operation since they did not harm the priest. Perhaps an American intelligence operation?" The subordinate to Müller asked rhetorically. "Where did this happen?"

"Seized outside the Genoa railway station. Driven to a rural location then shot."

On hearing of this first incident directly compromising the escape system, Müller understood the *Komeradenwerk* must provide security to the critical focal point of the escape route. The two sympathetic senior Catholic priests in Rome provided an indispensable service. Essential to rescuing wanted SS was new identifications and travel documents. These priests provided the ability to secure unlimited Red Cross passports by their intercession and recommendations never questioned by the Red Cross.

Both the Hudal and Draganović escape routes used Catholic support structures in Genoa to shepherd the fugitives safely to arranged ship passages. Now all that could be in jeopardy. The *Komeradenwerk* must protect the Italian escape route.

This must be the work of American intelligence. Who else had the capacity to identify SS traveling under false identities? Yet why not move against these two SS while in Rome? The obvious answer was to snare more fugitives before closing down these Catholic operations.

Müller understood this meant more than just supplying security for escaping *komeraden*. The first priority was determining the nature of the threat. To do that, they must deploy teams not just for security but to confront the opposition.

Operational assets were limited in Madrid. He must avoid a repeat of the debacle in Paris attempting to seize the American OSS agent in 1946. The perfect assignment for Otto Skorzeny to lead personally. However, Skorzeny must remain in hiding from the Americans. Operating from a farm in Bavaria, he was further disinclined to leave the intimate company of the niece of Hitler's former finance minister looking after him. With Skorzeny's connection to Gehlen, they should be able to determine if this was an American intelligence operation. Regardless, give Skorzeny responsibility for securing the escape operations in Rome.

Only two weeks after returning to Rome following the killing of the two SS outside Genoa, Fraser received an early morning telephone call at the hotel. It was Victor Kronberger.

"You must come at once, Herr Fraser. I am looking at a photo of someone of much importance. Taken just yesterday outside the Santa Maria dell'Anima Pontifico Instituto."

"Who is it?"

"Rudolf Lange. Responsible for killing tens of thousands of Jews in Latvia."

"Are you sure?"

"Yes. All my team agrees this is Lange."

"Very well. Begin developing enough prints for everyone. I will be there within ten minutes."

Explaining to Fiona, "This will be the last, Fiona. I will tell the team. Lange is too important to let escape. I could not live with myself if I did not do something having come this close."

Fiona said, "I understand. Just get it over with and turn to exposing these Church ratlines. How are you planning to seize Lange?"

"Gather everyone at Carla's warehouse. I will explain on the way to Kronberger's studio. I can use your help."

Marchand nodded as she ran a brush through her hair. To Fraser's surprise, she slipped her revolver into her purse after seeing him take his .45 and spare magazines.

"My last battle against the Nazis," She said.

In route to Kronberger's, Fraser explained the rough outline of his plan.

Marchand said, "This must happen very quickly before the police descend on the area. We need to carefully plan escape routes."

Looking at the photos, no doubt this was Lange. The surveillance team captured him exiting a large Mercedes with Vatican diplomatic plates. The clever camera operator using his female partner as the reason for the photograph with her image appearing off to one side.

Fraser also took note of two tall men exiting the car with the shorter Lange. Several photos gave the impression they might be bodyguards as they clearly directed their attention to the surroundings. Because Lange was important, or possibly a response to the incident in Genoa?

After visiting the surveillance teams covering Santa Maria dell'Anima, Fraser issued specific contingency instructions should Lange exit. Of the capture team, Flavio Moretti was currently on duty stationed in a car.

Out of earshot to everyone, including Marchand, he said to Moretti, "If Lange leaves before we set up and surround this area, crash into their car. Shoot Lange if you can. Do not allow him to get away. Be careful, he may have bodyguards. See these two in this photo?"

"If he leaves by foot?"

"Better yet. Run him down with the car. And anyone with him."

Next, they alerted the team at San Girolamo to join them at Carla's warehouse and round up the remaining team off duty.

Two hours later, except for those already stationed at Santa Maria dell'Anima, Fraser addressed everyone with Fiona translating into Italian to be sure everyone understood the plan.

On the warehouse floor, Fraser placed crates of produce as a three-dimensional model of the block. Bottles of olive oil and wine represented cars and delivery lorries. With Marchand translating into Italian, he said, "He arrived on the main street Via di Santa Maria dell'Anima. If leaving by automobile, then that will be the most likely location rather than the narrow Via della Pace. However, we cover both.

"At each end of both streets, we station a car and a lorry here and here. Two teams of musicians and strolling couples will continue as usual. Except today, everyone goes armed. Those other two in the picture might be bodyguards and therefore armed."

Lorenz Giordano said, "We are to capture the target as he exits the building?"

"Yes. He is not to escape the area. Once spotted, the roving team signals by waving. The vehicles at either end of the street converge on the target. If Lange gets into a car, crash your own vehicle into the car. If caught on foot, box them in with guns drawn by everyone. A show of force with many guns may deter them from using their weapons."

"If fired on, what are we to do?" Giordano asked.

"Return fire. If this becomes a shootout, make it brief. The fear is the Italian police. Be careful not to shoot a priest. I do not want anyone getting into legal trouble."

"What about Lange?" Giordano asked.

"Capture him if possible of course. Making his capture public will have a greater overall impact. Possibly enough to shut down these ratlines. Force the Vatican to crack down. Maybe the International Red Cross will no longer accept Church recommendations without question when issuing passports. However, do not risk your own lives. If Lange must die here then so be it."

"The streets in question border the Collegio and the Pontifico on the east and west. Therefore, we set up additional people on the north and south sides to visually signal by relay into which street Lange exits. An armed raised high means Via della Pace on the west. A waving arm meaning Via di Santa Maria dell'Anima.

"We keep watch around the clock, signaling at night by flashlight. A series of long flashes meaning the west, short flashes the east."

Someone said, "At night, it will be difficult to identify Lange."

Fraser said, "Of course. After dark the roving teams on foot must station themselves very close to the possible exit locations."

Weapons were not an issue. All these former partisans kept their weapons from the war. Several even came armed with British Sten submachine guns. If this opened into a firefight, it could prove a bloody affair.

Against Marchand's wishes, Fraser chose to stand duty at night. Against Fraser's wishes, Marchand suspended work at the Vatican to do surveillance duty from a nearby café. She could not bear waiting somewhere to hear about what happened.

On the second night of surveillance, Fraser sat in his car with Giordano manning the northern position on Via di Santa Maria dell'Anima. The same entrance used by Lange. Streetlights afforded enough light to distinguish people, but not sufficient to make identification from a distance.

At ten o'clock, a car passed their parked car followed closely by a Mercedes with Vatican diplomatic plates.

At the glare of the headlamps, Fraser and Giordano ducked low so their car would appear empty.

After passing, the two vehicles came to a stop in front of the same entrance Lange previously used to enter the Pontifico.

Two men exited the building as the Mercedes pulled to the curb.

At the same time, the man and woman watchers standing close to the door recognized the shorter man as Lange. Realizing she must send the signal, the woman ran into the middle of the street waving her arms, clearly visible under the streetlight.

At the wheel, Fraser started the engine and slammed into first gear. At the same time, a lorry at the opposite far end of the street did the same.

What happened during the next few moments validated Fraser's tactical plan. The lorry crashed into the front of the car parked in front of the Mercedes pushing it back into the Mercedes. With his car, Fraser blocked the Mercedes from behind.

When the Mercedes pulled up a bodyguard, obvious by a weapon in his hand, exited the Mercedes holding the car door open as Rudolf Lange got into the backseat. Simultaneously, the bodyguard escorting Lange drew his weapon after seeing the woman run into the street obviously signaling. The male partisan watcher then drew his weapon. Within moments they exchanged gunfire striking each other repeatedly.

In the damaged car in front of the Mercedes, the driver and a second man took several moments to exit as they struggled with the doors jammed by the collision.

The partisan from the lorry saw guns in their hands as they exited the damaged lead car. Armed with a British Sten submachine gun, he cut down both Germans in bursts of fire before they could return fire.

As Giordano rushed toward the downed partisan, he confronted the bodyguard standing next to the Mercedes. A mismatched contest against the more powerfully armed bodyguard. The German's Mauser C96 machine pistol fired a burst hitting Giordano twice in the torso. A deadly weapon with its high velocity 7.63 rounds.

Fraser had the advantage on a second bodyguard exiting the left side of the Mercedes now standing outside the vehicle holding a weapon while surveying the scene. As the man turned, Fraser shot him twice in the chest with his .45 at close range.

Rushing toward the Mercedes, Fraser saw the driver was a Catholic priest in clerical attire. Assuming the priest no threat, Fraser tapped the barrel of his pistol on the rear seat window. In German, "Rudolf Lange. Get out with your hands up!"

When Lange did not immediately move, Fraser fired a round shattering the window purposely missing Lange.

Lange emerged quickly with hands raised.

Grabbing Lange by the collar, Fraser pulled him to the other side of the car to see about Giordano.

The two partisans from the lorry and the woman partisan converged toward their two wounded colleagues. The wail of police sirens began in the distance. Lights came on in windows down the street.

Fraser took charge. These loyal partisans remained his chief responsibility. In broken Italian, "Take Giordano and Bonetti out of here. Get them medical help. I will take Lange."

"Tell that fucking priest driving the Mercedes you will shoot him next time if he helps Nazis."

As two of their vehicles from the other street arrived, the scene quickly cleared. The entire episode lasted only three minutes.

Flavio Moretti drove the car with Fraser in the back seat with Lange.

"How bad was Lorenz wounded?" Moretti asked.

"I do not know, Flavio. Sorry. I know you two are close."

"Where to?"

"Just get us out of Rome. Somewhere quiet."

"Turning to Lange, Fraser said in German, "Who were those protecting you?"

Lange instead responded with arrogance. "You will not get away with this." Looking out the window, Lange could see by the moonlight they were leaving the city. "Where are you taking me?"

Fraser made up his mind. "Flavio, pull off this highway. Ten minutes later, he said, "Stop here."

After Moretti got out of the car also pointing his handgun at Lange, Fraser said to Lange, *"Aus! Schnell!"*

Lange exited slowly his eyes now registering fear as Fraser motioned with his .45 to walk into an alleyway off a narrow residential street.

In English Fraser said more as a pronouncement, "You have cost too many lives. I have no stomach to transport you hundreds of miles for trial. Instead, I shall leave you here as a warning."

With that, he shot Lange in the back of the head.

## CHAPTER 28

PARIS, FRANCE | SEPTEMBER 1950

---

The events in Genoa and Rome over two years earlier receded into memory. For both Marc Fraser and Fiona Marchand, a disturbing mixture of emotions. For them, the war did not end with German surrender in 1945. Due to Fraser's compulsion to pursue war criminals of the Nazi *Schutzstaffel*, their war ended in 1948 in Rome. A new normal life evolved after returning to their beloved Paris.

Whereas she easily slipped back into her artist career, readjustment for her husband came harder. His very nature since his early journalistic career in Los Angeles was crusading. His skill chasing down bad characters fostered both career and personal satisfaction.

He wrote and published a series of articles exposing the flow of Nazi war criminals fleeing justice. Particular condemning of the Catholic ratlines, the Red Cross tacit ignoring of the problem, and the complicity of American occupation forces using former Nazis to further U.S. interests in the Cold War. He relished the fierce counterattacks by the Vatican and the U.S. State Department, providing him added media exposure to his written attacks.

Returning to fictional writing as a means of using his wealth of experiences, the first draft of a novel about chasing former

Nazi SS neared completion. With real authenticity, it skirted as close as possible to real events without exposing those helping him. Stealing SS funds in Swiss bank accounts noticeably absent.

He took particular satisfaction of the impact of using those funds in helping Trakonitz smuggle displaced Jewish survivors of the Holocaust into the new State of Israel. Even the mixed results of the Rome mission worthwhile. Justice delivered to three mass murders. Satisfaction in depriving Heinrich Müller of money hidden in his personal Swiss bank account.

However, for the attempt on his and Fiona's life, only a bullet to Müller's head could ever appease Fraser's lust for revenge. For that matter, failing to get Klaus Barbie continued to trouble him. A great deal of the stolen SS money still remained. Perhaps to serve a future use for going after Müller or Barbie?

While he might continue to dwell on Nazi war criminals escaping justice, Fraser understood the world moved on. The real fear of a militant Soviet Union led by a murdering despot already a stark reality. The first act of confrontation in the Cold War came with Berlin blockaded by the Soviets. The unfortunate agreement establishing a jointly occupied Berlin of all the victorious Allies contained within the larger Soviet occupation zone of Germany invited confrontation from the onset.

U.S. President Harry Truman immediately called the bluff of Josef Stalin by supplying the entire needs of food and energy of Berlin by air for almost a year. The U.S. effectively staring down this new enemy of Western democracy. The world now living under constant threat of nuclear confrontation between two world superpowers. WWII war crimes became just a part of history.

Mindful of the new political realities of post-WWII, Jewish survivors of the Holocaust however never forgot Hitler's fanatical efforts of genocide. Nor had the Jewish State of Israel. What was formerly Palestine became the only safe haven for surviving displaced Jews of Europe, including continued Russian anti-Semitic persecution with its long history of Jewish pogroms. None of the Western powers allowed postwar immigration of significant numbers of Jews. This included the United States, Canada, Australia, and the United Kingdom. The entire world abandoned European Jews surviving the Holocaust. With their backs to the wall and British withdrawal from the United Nations Palestinian Mandate, war with the neighboring Arab states erupted in 1948 immediately following proclaiming of the State of Israel.

After prevailing against great odds in ten months of war, the Jews of Israel vowed never again to suffer subjugated. As part of that new worldview, many of those having suffered the loss of entire family members were not about to forget the perpetrators. Among those now in influential official positions was Pavel Trakonitz. He was now with the newly created *HaMossad leModi'in uleTafkidim Meyuḥadim,* the Institute for Intelligence and Special Operations, known simply as the Mossad. Trakonitz was both a natural in skills, experience, and temperament necessary to fulfill the ambitious role vital to the survival of the young nation.

For Trakonitz, time and events since the ending of WWII did not diminish the need to exact retribution against Nazi war criminals. Everything since WWII ended only validated his extra-judicial execution approach perpetrated by his fellow TTG members of the Jewish Brigade.

Trakonitz vigorously lobbied for the authorization to pursue Nazi war criminals. The worst of the mass murderers known to have escaped justice by the war crimes trials. Among the inherently aggressive Mossad, he had wide support. However, cooler heads in the current government headed by David Ben-Gurion prevailed.

Ben-Gurion personally counseled Trakonitz. "Pavel, you have been a rock in our efforts to win statehood. For a dangerous man of action, you are also a cunning pragmatic planner. One day you may become chief of Mossad. As much as our hearts cry out for justice, pursuit of these Nazis does not advance our stature in the world at such a precarious time."

Trakonitz replied, "I cannot argue that. However, Israel exists as much as a Jewish idea as a political entity. We just successfully beat back our Arab neighbors against much greater odds. It does not end there, Mister Prime Minister. There shall be future wars. For that reason, we must foster within our population this newly created Jewish self-awareness. The rhetoric of *never again* needs reinforcement with a new sense of what it means to be Jewish. The world needs to understand our resolve."

Ben-Gurion smiled his trademark crocodile smile. "Well spoken, Pavel. Worthy of a speech in the Knesset. However, what you suggest is premature. Counterproductive with respect to our international stature at this time. We must carefully cultivate our few friends by acting within international norms."

Expecting Ben-Gurion's refusal, Trakonitz proposed his alternative gambit before conceding defeat. "Perhaps a middle ground approach might satisfy both objectives.

"What if I assembled a team of skilled fighters but not of Mossad or the Israeli Defense Force? I have a confidential source of funds I accessed to smuggle refugees when I was with Haganah. Operations could therefore be subcontracted and funded with no money trail leading back to Israel."

"And the source of these funds?"

"I cannot say. Rather not say actually, Prime Minister. A matter of honor. The money controlled by a private individual, no other government involvement. I can say only that it came from a rogue operation during war. The source of the funds comes from confiscated secret Nazi bank accounts."

Ben-Gurion laughed heartily then came back with, "Very interesting. Yet any clandestine operation will still be blamed on Israel."

"We counter this with our own misinformation. This is a Soviet NKVD operation. To foster that, we use the Mossad to provide operational intelligence and disinformation. Only a couple of my Mossad colleagues will know the true nature of the operation. The others will know only that we are providing information on former Nazis to Soviet intelligence using former Spanish Communists dissidents."

Ben-Gurion remained silent for a moment digesting the ramifications. "You are a devious bastard, Pavel. "You have a target in mind in Spain?"

"Yes. We know of an organization calling itself *Komeradenwerk*. Headquartered in Madrid. These Nazis enjoy the security of Franco's Fascist Spain. We believe Madrid is instrumental in orchestrating the escape of prominent Nazis still fugitive in Europe. Perhaps with delusions of organizing a Fourth Reich in exile."

"Who else in Mossad have you discussed this with?"

"Only two others, Prime Minister. Felix Martel. Emigrated from Spain with the fall of the republican government. Former colonel of intelligence. It was his sources in Madrid that uncovered the existence of this Nazi *Komeradenwerk*. The other, my old colleague, and our best forger, Sandor Herczeg, necessary to provide false documents. "

"Very well, Pavel. You make an impassioned case. I shall take it up with the cabinet. You shall have an answer within a week."

Three days later Trakonitz received a partial answer. He was to appear before a meeting with the cabinet and plead his case directly. Tersely, Ben-Gurion told him, "You and Martel are to present the basics of a workable plan. I must first spell out certain ground rules.

"You must avoid anything connecting the operation to the Mossad. Only you and the other two must know the true nature of what you are doing along with Director Shiloah. If authorized, he will be in overall charge of the mission. Therefore, you must develop a sufficiently plausible cover to deflect Mossad staff curiosity.

Second, as you offered, the operational assets cannot be from the IDF. In fact, no Israeli national must be involved in Spain.

Financing of the operation must not be able to lead back to Israel as you explained. Obviously, we must therefore know the source and origin of the money. The money trail is possibly the most serious threat. Lastly, should circumstances go badly in Spain, your team is entirely on its own. The government of the State of Israel will disavow any knowledge of your actions.

"As this is intended to send a message not only to these diehard Nazis, but also to the rest of the world, you must be prepared to explain how we manage the aftermath. What becomes the plausible scenario to deflect responsibility away from Israel and how do we convincingly float that to the world?"

Ultimately, the decision fell to Ben-Gurion but the clever old lion wanting his cabinet to share in the decision after examining the feasibility of Trakonitz's plan.

Thumbing through his calendar, Ben-Gurion said, "Two weeks from today. Two o'clock in the cabinet room."

The *Komeradenwerk* recovered from the brief setbacks in 1948. Ratline operations continued with minor tactical changes. Negative media attacks by the American journalist Fraser never gained traction as the Berlin Crisis confrontation consumed world attention. The Vatican denied any Church organized effort to help war criminals. Any that did escape using the humanitarian efforts of the Church did so only because of the inability to investigate every refugee.

The *Komeradenwerk* never discovered the source of the two attacks on the ratlines in Rome. With secondary connections into American intelligence through Reinhard Gehlen's intelligence organization working for the American CIA, they ruled out the Americans. Possibly the Soviet NKVD perhaps working through former Italian Communist partisans as proxies.

The success rate of escape of former Nazi SS, including many of the most notorious war criminals, continued impressively. Most of these owing their freedom to the assistance of Bishop

Alois Hudal. Adolf Eichmann, the operational creator of the extermination camps to implement Henrich Himmler's Jewish genocide, the *Final Solution*, fled to Argentina in 1948. Josef Mengele, the macabre *Angel of Death* of Auschwitz-Birkenau concentration-extermination camp, fled to Argentina in 1949. Eduard Roschmann, former commander of the Riga, Latvia ghetto, fled to Argentina in 1948. Franz Stangl, former commandant of Sobibór and Treblinka concentration camps, fled first to Syria in 1948 then to Brazil in 1950. Gustav Wagner, former deputy commandant of Sobibór fled to Brazil in 1950 along with Stangl.

The Croatian priest and Fascist Ustaše officer Father Krunoslav Draganović did not achieve an equivalent record for helping as many of the most notorious major war criminals. However, he made up in volume of lessor wanted Nazi and Ustaše. His principle focus featured helping former brethren of the Croatian Ustaše, the ultranationalist Nazi-allied paramilitary force organized against Communist Yugoslavia during WWII.

Draganović's greatest achievement was engineering the escape into exile of Ante Pavelić, the Croatian general and military dictator who founded and headed the Ustaše in 1929. Pavelić bore responsibility for the murders of 500,000 Serbs, 30,000 Jews, and 40,000 Gypsies.

Following German surrender, Pavelić fled to Rome in the spring of 1946 disguised as a Catholic priest. The Vatican provided shelter in various Church properties in Rome and Naples. In 1948, Father Draganović helped him obtain a Red Cross passport as a Hungarian refugee and facilitating his flight to Argentina.

As a staunch Fascist and anti-Communist, Draganović not only arranged passage out of Europe for Croatian Ustaše, but their ideological brethren, German Nazis. This corrupt senior priest willingly arranged the escape of Klaus Barbie, the *Butcher of Lyon* to Argentina and then to Bolivia in 1950 at the request of U.S. Army Counterintelligence.

Fraser learned of Barbie's escape to South America from the same CIA source who informed him of the American CIC in Bavaria employing Barbie. Still serving out of the U.S. Embassy in Paris, Hugh Granger paid Fraser and Marchand an unexpected visit to their apartment in the autumn of 1950.

The news agitated Fraser and dismayed Marchand recognizing the depth of hatred her husband still held for Barbie.

Granger said, "Afraid I have some unsettling news. It's about Klaus Barbie. My sources in Army counterintelligence report he recently fled to Buenos Aries. Seems his discovery of employment by U.S. Army counterintelligence proved too great an embarrassment. Interestingly the origin of that leak was never discovered."

Granger smiled conspiratorially, "However, the government doubled down. Perhaps just a bunch of bungling clowns left behind to manage intelligence during the occupation, but to continue to hide this monster compounded the stupidity. The mess simply became too rotten to risk exposure by suddenly arresting Barbie then handing him over to the French."

Fraser said, "I never understood what intelligence value the CIC in Barbie. What use could he be in anti-Soviet counterintelligence?"

"Can't answer that either," Granger said. "But I can tell you unofficially, American counterintelligence operations in occupied Europe are in sorry shape. Actually non-existent. We have outsourced everything to a former *Wehrmacht* intelligence general, Reinhard Gehlen, former chief of FHO. The clever little bastard turned over all his files concerning running networks into the Soviet Union and Eastern Europe.

"Gehlen convinced Washington to hire him and much of his former staff to reactivate his network of agents. Christ, we have no means of even vetting the intelligence he provides.

"But I digress. My point being, perhaps these Neanderthals in the CIC were just scavenging about for any functionaries of the Third Reich that might offer anti-Soviet intelligence since the bastards occupy all of Eastern Germany.

"Knowing your history related to Barbie, here is the worse part, the American Army contracted with some Nazi-loving

Catholic priest to smuggle Barbie to South America with a new identity. The Army was aware of this priest running what they called a ratline. A rather bizarre set of circumstances but my sources are reliable."

With the conditional approval by Ben-Gurion to proceed with planning an attack on the *Komeradenwerk* in Madrid, Trakonitz needed to convince Marc Fraser of his help. Not only agreement to use remaining SS funds, but also the delicate matter imposed by Ben-Gurion of revealing to the Israeli cabinet how he came by the money.

If the operational team to be the Italian partisans he formerly recruited, then Fraser must also agree to be the figurehead originator of the mission to deflect suspicion away from Israel.

If Fraser refused all or any part of participation, Trakonitz had no alternative except abandon the Madrid venture. Clearly, this was not something for a telephone discussion. The day following the Ben-Gurion meeting, Trakonitz boarded a flight for Paris.

On the plane, Trakonitz reflected on events since he last saw Fraser. Occupied with the lead up to the Arab war then consumed with the desperate year of war, they communicated only occasionally by letter.

Their last conversation occurred over two years ago following the violent events in Italy. After describing the shootings of the SS in guarded language, he recalled Fraser saying, "Things did not go as planned, Pavel. You perhaps will read about in it the newspapers, however it is primarily an Italian issue. The premise made sense, however the execution was flawed. I am finished, my friend. Finished with pursuing my demons with the gun. Whatever comes next will be with the written word. Promised Fiona to return us to a normal life."

It was by no means certain Fraser would sign on to this after all this time. Best to arrive unannounced to avoid giving advance explanation for his visit.

Trakonitz buzzed the intercom from the lobby and responded to Marchand in Italian, "*Ciao, Fiona, c'est Pavel Trakonitz.*"

Arriving at their apartment door, both Fraser and Marchand greeted him hugs and kisses to both cheeks.

"Such a surprise," Marchand said. Fraser smiled. Knowing Trakonitz, this likely was not a social visit and said, "Please come in and sit down. Can I offer you a drink?"

"Perhaps later. Better I get to the purpose of my visit. It concerns the network of former SS. Specifically those we believe operating a sort of headquarters from Madrid. Heinrich Müller among the most prominent wanted war criminals among them."

The mention of Müller elicited responsive expressions in both Fraser and Marchand.

"I am now with the newly formed Israeli intelligence service, the Mossad. Assembled from the ranks of former Haganah, even the Irgun, and those served during WWII.

"The Jews of Israel have not abandoned the memory of the Holocaust. The obligation to seek justice seen as the means of signaling to the world, *never again*. More specifically, I am authorized to mount an operation against this Nazi *Komeradenwerk* that you first identified after their failed attack on you and Fiona here in Paris."

Fraser began shaking his head as he looked at the expression of concern on Fiona's face.

"Pavel, I told you after what happened in Italy two years ago that I was done with this sort of thing. Should have learned after my failed attempt to capture Barbie in Germany. Then the failures in Italy."

"Not failures, Marc. Justice delivered to three mass murderers," Trakonitz said.

"Your justice solution, Pavel. Three executions. I wanted to see them face public justice."

"A distinction with no difference."

"Probably. Nevertheless, society should impose the death sentence not individuals acting as avengers. The publicity itself adding impact. Regardless, both my ventures were poorly conceived."

His execution of Rudolf Lange haunted him. Unlike his killing of Cabrera or Leitner in 1943, Lange was not personal, only a symbol. An emotional response during a moment of rage.

This was not going the way Trakonitz planned. He was never good at this sort of thing. "I appreciate that, Marc. Yet I believe you and Fiona are still disturbed with the thousands guilty of committing the most heinous crimes in modern history going unpunished. Mankind must attempt to balance the ledger.

"Let me be specific. Israel cannot be directly involved in retributive operations in foreign countries. Israel's very existence remains precarious. Surprised the Prime Minister even considered my proposal. He therefore placed difficult restrictions before authorizing the operation. Even within Mossad, only your old acquaintance from Spain Felix Martel and Sandor Herczeg know this to be an Israeli sponsored mission."

"I am not about to participate in a raid on Madrid. I am not a soldier like you, Pavel. Furthermore, I may still be wanted by the Franco regime for espionage during the Spanish Civil War."

"Marc. I need only three things. Nothing involves you taking up a gun or traveling to Spain. Most importantly, the State of Israel fears a money trail. I offered that I knew of a possible funding source but declined to discuss specifics even with Ben-Gurion. However, that is not good enough. Ben-Gurion insists on the Cabinet knowing the origin of the money."

Fraser reflected for a moment before saying, "Very well, if that is what it takes. Tell him the money comes from SS secret Swiss bank accounts. Product of an American OSS intelligence operation. The Americans never acted on the information, so I took the initiative. Thought the money could better serve rescuing Jewish Holocaust survivors. As a Jew, I shall trust the Israeli Cabinet to keep that knowledge buried. No written record."

Trakonitz smiled broadly. "Agreed. The old man will appreciate the irony. Thank you. Is there enough money remaining to finance this?"

"How much is required?"

"That will depend on several factors."

"I believe there should be enough money. Who do you get to do this?"

"The operational resources must not know this is an Israeli operation."

Fraser laughed. "How do you intend to pull that off?"

"By using those former Italian partisans you assembled. Impressive what you and Fiona put together by yourself."

"I see. So you sell this as another independent Fraser operation."

Trakonitz nodded. "I assume these partisans might participate as mercenaries given enough money. That and logistical expenses represent the financial commitment. We could use your help in Rome to sell the plan to your partisans."

"Anything else?"

"The incident blamed on the Soviet NKVD. Martel will do his part to lay false evidence pointing to the Soviets with aid from clandestine Spanish Communists harboring resentment against Nazi military support for the Fascists in the civil war. You can help by adding fuel to published stories with backgrounds and crimes of the Madrid SS. Besides Müller, Martel has identified others using sources in Madrid much the same way as you did in Rome."

Fraser admittedly was interested. The recent news that Klaus Barbie had now escaped to South America with the help of American Army counterintelligence incited a provocation to continue to make trouble.

"What do you plan doing in Madrid?"

"Kill Heinrich Müller and as many other SS as possible. An assault with automatic weapons. Kill as many as possible then bring down everything with fertilizer bombs. Eliminate whatever role these Nazis play in supporting the ratlines. Send a message to those still evading capture. No safe havens. There are those coming after you."

Fraser replied, "Another one of your missions behind enemy lines, Pavel?"

"Something like that. I seemed destined for my wars never to end."

Clearly enticed to further strike at the remnants of the Nazi SS, Fraser turned to Fiona, "Am I still honoring my pledge to you if I help in this?"

She stood up and came over to Fraser touching his cheek. "As long as you do not directly participate by going to Spain. And provided I join this conspiracy and go with you to Rome for my own peace of mind."

Marchand realized the depth of her personal hatred for Heinrich Müller for sending those killers to Paris. The thought of what they were about to do to her and what she did forever a vivid memory. Only a fleeting sense of guilt for relishing the possibility of participating in this violent act of revenge.

"Who leads this mission?" Fraser asked.

"I do. My idea and I speak Italian."

"I thought you said Israel cannot risk involvement?"

"Quite so. I am just another Italian partisan with no intention of being captured or killed. If all goes according to plan, Ben-Gurion will not know until after. I will sell this as another rogue operation like in Rome in '48 by former American intelligence operative Marc Fraser. Perhaps implying you will head the mission. Would not be the first time I lied to a superior."

Fraser could not contain his smile while silently wishing he could directly participate.

Marchand said, "Since that is settled, I think we all need a drink before getting into the details of our roles.

# CHAPTER 29

MADRID, SPAIN | NOVEMBER 1950

---

Israeli Prime Minister David Ben-Gurion approved the mission to destroy the Nazi SS *Komeradenwerk* in Madrid. With a mixed response from the Israeli cabinet, Trakonitz attributed Ben-Gurion's authorization to proceed to Felix Martel's presentation of the plan. Martel conceived the mission, selling Trakonitz on the idea later. Something he began working on as a personal project after hearing of the attack years earlier on his old acquaintance the American Marc Fraser.

To Martel, it was another affront to his nationalist pride as a Spaniard. A democratic republic overthrown by a Fascist military revolt. A dictator supporting Nazi Germany throughout the war while enjoying the benefits of neutrality. While working within the Haganah for years, Martel continued to cultivate former contacts in Spain. His range of clandestine sources in the Spanish-speaking world proved invaluable now to Israeli intelligence.

With those sources extending to South America, Martel became one of the first to learn of former Nazis fleeing to Argentina. The dictatorship of a former army colonel, Juan Perón, actively encouraged German immigration even before the war. As in Francoist Spain, the Catholic Church held enormous power in Argentina, aligning itself with the most conservative political elements. Now, this unholy collaboration conspired to perpetuate Fascist ideology and Roman Catholic influence.

Mossad Director Reuven Shiloah added his approval to the raid. Although not from a military background, Shiloah possessed political imagination and a talent for analysis of international affairs. Well aware of Trakonitz's activities to smuggle Jewish refugees into Palestine, Trakonitz's explanation of the source of the funding hit a responsive chord. His comment to Ben-Gurion in support of the mission, *Mossad is the sharp end of the Jewish spear. We fight all enemies of Israel, including those not yet fully vanquished. I shall personally work with Trakonitz and Martel to lend support where possible while maintaining the internal cover story with Mossad.*

Trakonitz tackled the delicate explanation of the funding and the function served by the American Fraser. "I have consulted my friend Marc Fraser and his wife Fiona Marchand. They have agreed to participate in this mission.

"By way of background, I met Fiona Marchand in Italy during the war. Her work involved liaison between Italian partisans and U.S. intelligence. Both she and Marc Fraser worked for the American OSS out of Switzerland. Previously both participated in the French Resistance before fleeing France in 1943. Both have personal reasons for seeking retribution on the Nazi SS. Fraser's mother was also Jewish from the wealthy Rothschild European banking dynasty.

"Fraser masterminded a clever plan seizing control of certain SS Swiss bank accounts. Fraser reported the bank accounts to the OSS, but American intelligence did not act on the information. The reason given as continuing disputes with Switzerland concerning larger Nazi deposits in Swiss banks of looted national treasuries of occupied countries.

"Discovering the funds missing led Heinrich Müller to order three former SS officers to Paris to determine what happened in Switzerland. Fiona Marchand killed two of the assailants. The surviving assailant confessed to Fraser they operated under orders from former *Gestapo* chief Heinrich Müller. The French tried the former SS officer sentencing him to life imprisonment for war crimes committed while serving in Paris during the war. None of these details reached the newspapers.

"Even for the resourceful Fraser and Marchand, the Nazi enclave in Madrid was out of reach. After meeting with prominent Nazi hunter Simon Wiesenthal, they pursued a more active form of Nazi hunting. Tracking down Nazi war criminals like Wiesenthal with the expectation of governments to pursue prosecutions, seemed a frustrating endeavor for Fraser.

"The Allies ceased pursuit of war criminals after conclusion of the various war crimes trials before military tribunals. With thousands of Nazi fugitives, arrest of a significant number of Holocaust perpetrators seemed unlikely. Fraser therefore devised a more aggressive plan to capture at least a handful of war criminals while disrupting the Nazi ratlines.

"In a daring independent operation financed with the seized SS funds, Fraser and Marchand enlisted former Italian partisans as operational assets. With archival photos of wanted SS fugitives provided by Wiesenthal, they set up an elaborate surveillance operation on two suspected Catholic Church locations in Rome suspected of running escape routes for former Nazis.

"That was in 1948. The effort achieved minor success netting three significant SS war criminals. One was Rudolf Lange previously thought killed in Poznań in 1945. Lange was responsible for the murder of 35,000 Latvian Jews. The effort worthwhile for that alone.

"Fraser's importance to this Madrid mission is threefold. He becomes the fictional architect behind yet another independent attack on former Nazis by this rogue former journalist. Second, he agrees to fund the mission deflecting the money trail away from Israel. He and Marchand will also aid in recruiting the same Italian partisans as mercenaries under the pretext of this as another independent mission funded by an undisclosed Jewish-American benefactor."

Ben-Gurion interrupted knowing Trakonitz's reluctance to be specific on this issue, "You told me earlier that he also financed your refugee smuggling to Palestine. If this was an American intelligence operation, how did Fraser acquire control of the money?"

"Fraser refuses to be any more specific. However, he authorized me to say the money is unaccounted Nazi SS funds. The transactions giving him control protected under strict Swiss banking secrecy laws. The reason for the attempt on his life in Paris by the *Komeradenwerk.* "

Trakonitz concealed his knowledge of Fraser's scheme and Sandor Herczeg's participation by producing the necessary false documents.

Someone said, "He stole Nazi funds?"

Someone else said, "How do we know he is still not working as a front for U.S. intelligence."

Trakonitz said, "We do not know for sure, but no investigation by U.S. Intelligence ever resulted. Furthermore, I have personal knowledge of an event that suggests otherwise.

"Perhaps you recall the allegations by France of the United States harboring the wanted war criminal Klaus Barbie, the Butcher of Lyon. Tried in absentia, the Provisional French government at the time sentenced Barbie to death. The person making the public allegation of U.S. complicity in the incident was Marc Fraser.

"My guess is the American OSS confiscated the SS funds in a sophisticated intelligence operation involving Fraser. By some bureaucratic means, Fraser acquired access off the books using Swiss banking secrecy regulations to conceal the scheme. His use of those funds to finance smuggling of Jewish refugees and buying arms for Israel I believe proves his motives."

After an exhausting two hours, Ben-Gurion looked about the cabinet room, silent for several moments before pronouncing, "Proceed with this Madrid mission. Be mindful of the political sensitivities. Director Shiloah, please keep me informed."

From that day, preparations advanced rapidly. Everyone, except Mossad Director Shiloah, came to Rome to work out the tactical details before beginning the recruiting process. That process would not only involve the former Italian partisans used in the operation against the Catholic ratlines, but also several former Spanish expatriate republican army officers now living in France. These men still harbored a hatred for the Fascist Franco regime and the horrors of three years of the Spanish Civil War in the late 1930s.

Marchand rented rooms and a working suite at the Hotel Farnese.

That first morning together, Martel took charge of the briefing to describe the many details comprising the plan he and Trakonitz developed. Fraser and Marchand were there to understand the mission and help sell those Italians taking part in the Rome operations two years earlier.

A much tougher sell than before. Lorenz Giordano and the other partisan shot that night in Rome did not survive their wounds. Their deaths at the hands of Rudolf Lange's SS bodyguards as the capture went wrong. The reason Fraser became sufficiently enraged to put a bullet in Lange's head. This mission far more dangerous in a hostile foreign country.

"The plan now calls for a team of eleven plus Pavel and me," Martel said. "Six of these from the group of former Italian partisans you recruited two years ago. Two of those well known to Pavel from WWII. These six will be the assault force led directly by Pavel. The other four will be Spaniards. Former Republican army officers I know well now living in France. Fluency in Spanish necessary for certain logistical tasks. They will do the driving. The eleventh member is the bomb maker known to Pavel."

Trakonitz said, "He is a former soldier in the Jewish Brigade. Married an Italian following the war. Lives in Bologna. He is interested and can use the money."

Martel said, "Speaking of money, do you have access to sufficient funds here in Rome, Marc?"

"Been doing my own rough calculation. I do not know the entire plan, but I believe so. The largest expense is for this mercenary team. Even though they all have their personal motivations, they have families and this is risky. I suggest offering five thousand U.S. dollars to each. For maybe two weeks work, that should be financially motivating."

"Yes. Very good," Martel said. "How are payments for expenses handled?"

"Everything is already in place. For any direct payments to suppliers, just let me know specifics. I wire from a Paris bank. From the same accounts for shell companies created to fund Pavel's smuggling schemes. On paper, these service companies appear real, even filing French taxes. No money trail leading back to Israel.

"For cash, same thing except someone picks up the money at a designated bank. For large sums of cash such as for the partisans, we spread around to different Rome banks into whatever currency required. The funds are held in stable Swiss francs so exchange rates are irrelevant."

"Very impressive trade craft," Martel said.

Trakonitz took up the briefing. "Every team member is armed with false identification. Italian or Spanish passports according to language proficiency with appropriate Spanish entry visas. The passports are virtually indistinguishable from authentic government issue. Created by Sandor Herczeg from virgin official passport stock."

Fraser smiled recalling the talented forger used in the Krüger Swiss banking fraud. "Can you describe how you plan to take these people out with a bomb?"

"Two bombs actually. They become the secondary means. First, the assault team makes entry. Moving quickly through the building, we take out everyone we come across with automatic weapons. No more than ninety seconds allocated for the assault.

"We then exit quickly. The bombs already in the lorries carrying the assault force. Ready to detonate by timer. We allow enough time to get clear of the blast radius. The team then escapes in two waiting lorries used for surveillance. Escape routes previously planned driven by the Spaniards familiar with Madrid."

"How do you smuggle bombs into Spain?" Marchand asked.

"Unnecessary. We create the bombs from fertilizer. Ammonium nitrate specifically. Widely available from any agricultural supply distributor even in Spain. Farmers also use it routinely for clearing rocks and stumps. Felix and his Spanish sources in Madrid purchase the fertilizer and other materials in advance.

"Unbelievably easy to make. You simply mix with some sort of petroleum product like fuel oil, spent motor oil, or kerosene. The petrol increases the explosive force after igniting the mixture. In our case, the ignition source will be a small military grade explosive charge detonated by a blasting cap powered by a battery and rigged to a timer. All these components acquired from surplus war material. American origin to deflect away from Israel. The Soviets used many American-made armaments acquired through WWII Lend-Lease. Easily smuggled through Spanish customs as individual components."

Marchand asked, "What is the cover story for the Italians entering Spain?"

Martel answered, "I play the part of a Spanish contractor bringing in Italian artisans for a wealthy client's remodeling project. The Italians each carry a letter of employment from my fictitious firm to support their work visa status."

Trakonitz said, "The location is a large walled estate on the outskirts of Madrid. We want to catch as many of the bigger fish as possible. Müller becomes the critical objective. Once we know he is inside, I will determine if the target is rich enough with opportunities to signal the attack. Your two week window seems reasonable, Marc. We do not want to remain in Spain any longer than necessary. The team stationed ready to move within less than an hour. We leave immediately following the assault.

"The entrance is closed by a gate typically manned by only one guard. I drive the first lorry, stopping at the gate. I distract the man by speaking to him in German, possibly getting him to unlock the gate. Regardless, I shoot him with a silenced weapon. It the wrought iron gate remains locked, Moretti in the passenger seat scales the wall and unlocks the gate."

Martel resumed the narrative, "The Spaniards of the team will load and drive the trucks. Pavel's bomb maker rigs the explosives and sets the timer as the assault teams enter the buildings. The time clock is ticking from that point."

Fraser asked, "Have you identified primary targets other than Müller? I assume they all hold false identities. Same problem we had in Rome."

"We used the same approach as you did. Over six months of painstaking work. After ten years of Franco's rule, there is no shortage of those willing to work against the ruling Fascist regime. The effort produced a list of twenty-one former SS. Trained analysts matched the images to our extensive archival records. The most prominent of course being Heinrich Müller, known in Spain as Heinrich Möller.

"But there are others. Mostly lower or middle ranked former intelligence officers of the *Sicherheitsdienst des Reichsführers*-SS or *Gestapo* being of most interest. Otto Skorzeny has taken up residence in Madrid a few months ago. Known to be active in the *Komeradenwerk,* previously hiding in Bavaria after his escape from U.S. denazification detention. A group of former *Waffen-SS,* former paratroop commandos under Skorzeny provide a military contingent to the Nazi enclave, functioning much like an embassy."

Trakonitz interjected, "As Spain announces the dead with their false identities you will counter by publishing their actual identities, supported with their SS photographs and service backgrounds. As a journalist, you refuse to reveal your sources. Spain undoubtedly counters by arguing this is Israeli disinformation.

"Subsequently, you release additional information attributing the attack to the Soviet Union's NKVD further mudding the picture. We will provide you with certain planted evidence and Mossad acquired intelligence. You speculate this as a possible NKVD inspired attack using unidentified proxy European Communists. Stalin's continued overreaching ambitions in Europe. To former Nazis SS, the message is clear. This is likely an organized Jewish retaliation for the Holocaust. Ben-Gurion will settle for plausible deniability."

Before joining everyone in Rome, Felix Martel traveled to Marseille, France to finalize arrangements with his former Spanish army colleagues.

Arrangements went well in Rome. The Italian team included Flavio Moretti and Raphael Pariatore from Fraser's former capture team. The Polish Jew and former TTG demolition expert relished the idea of killing Nazis. Everyone respected this American and his French wife for continuing to go after Nazis. Fraser explained he was not going to Spain with them. This was more within Pavel Trakonitz's expertise as a veteran commando working behind enemy lines. The former Spanish intelligence colonel Felix Martel fought his own war against Fascism and knew Madrid.

Before departing, Marchand distributed new identity papers and rehearsed the overall cover story. Uncomfortable going unarmed, she assured them weapons would be provided once in Madrid. Too dangerous to cross the Spanish border armed. Once the bombs detonated, they would follow prescribed escape routes planned by Colonel Martel.

Lastly, Marchand paid them their mercenary fee in advance.

Located to the southwest of central Madrid just across the River Manzanares, the headquarters of the Madrid *Komeradenwerk* was a former Catholic monastery. Its location became a battleground in the Spanish Civil War. Between 1936 and 1939, Madrid suffered siege by rebel Fascist forces assisted by Italian troops and German aircraft. The River Manzanares provided a natural defensive position for the Republican government defenders. Caught in the frontline, the monastery suffered extensive damage.

Following the end of hostilities, the relocated monastic order sold the property and the surrounding agricultural acreage. In the spring of 1944, Otto Skorzeny purchased the damaged building compound using Nazi SS funds. Close to central Madrid yet still somewhat isolated. Heinrich Himmler was already looking ahead anticipating German defeat. The neutral and friendly Spanish Fascist state ruled by Generalissimo Francisco Franco provided an ideally suited exile location still in Europe. Rebuilding commenced immediately with funding continuing to the end of the war a year later.

Knowing of its existence, Heinrich Müller made his way to Madrid after escaping Berlin and took charge of finishing the project. The main building and former abbot's house by now rebuilt, Müller set about work on the larger building. The former Spartan dormitory cells and work areas of the monks converted to office and conference areas with sleeping quarters for a contingent of armed personnel and armory in the cellars. The abbot's house remodeled to serve as Müller's working residence.

Surveillance photographs showed an eight-foot high stone wall surrounding the entire compound with a wrought iron gate at the driveway entrance. Looking beyond the gate showed the driveway curving in front of the main building and extending in front of the former abbot's house. A fifty-foot high long-range communication radio tower stood on the grounds behind the main building.

Everyone boarded a train in Rome to travel to Marseille, France. Here they joined the four former Spanish army officers at the railway station. Two hours later, they all departed south crossing the border into Spain to Barcelona then changing trains for Madrid. Trakonitz and Martel used the time to rehearse everyone on key planning details.

"The weapons are in a secure location," Trakonitz said in Italian to the assault team. "Soviet PPD-40 submachine guns. Fires a 7.62×25mm Tokarev cartridge from a 71-round drum magazine. Plenty of firepower. Your Spanish colleagues are familiar with the weapon and will instruct you in its features once we reach Madrid. Everyone also issued a handgun."

The Soviet made PPD-40 submachine gun selected as the assault weapon for the raid was standard Red Army issue since 1935. A cache of these weapons existed in Madrid.

Stalin shipped significant numbers the PPD-40s among other war materials to the Spanish Republic government. They fought a brutal civil war against superior rebel Army forces commanded by General Franco aided by Nazi Germany and Fascist Italy providing significant military support. The Soviet Union was the only country to provide material support to the legitimate Spanish Republican government.

Following defeat of Spanish government forces in 1939, many of these weapons went into hiding for later use. The former Republican Army officers participating in this mission maintained contact with anti-Fascist Spanish dissidents. A dozen of these submachine guns now hidden in a secure location awaiting arrival of the assault force.

Using these weapons would provide tangible evidence pointing to the perpetrators as dissident Spanish Communist.

Trakonitz turned to the bomb maker Aleksy Wójcik, "Aleksy, the quantity of ammonium nitrate and fuel oil you require is also in secure storage. Plastique explosives, detonators, and timers previously smuggled into Madrid."

Martel passed around a stack of photo enlargements to the Spaniards. "These are photographs of known Nazi SS. All known to frequent the *Komeradenwerk* compound. On the back is an assigned number. To establish the precise time of the assault, we need to ensure the maximum number from this group of twenty-one Nazis is present. The principal target is the former head of the Nazi *Gestapo,* Heinrich Müller. Killing him alone makes the mission a success, yet we hope to cripple this vital link of the *Komeradenwerk* by killing as many influential SS as possible.

"To accomplish that, we maintain constant visual surveillance. You will maintain watch using field glasses. Even after dark, floodlights illuminate the entrance gate. You will radio by two-way radio the image number as you observe any one of these entering or leaving.

"The surveillance vehicles are delivery lorries same as the assault vehicles. They will serve as escape transportation. Once Pavel Trakonitz feels sufficient SS are present, he signals to execute the attack. The two lorries with the assault team will arrive within thirty minutes of the signal.

Trakonitz took over. "The assault team has ninety seconds to inflict damage once they enter the buildings. Wójcik activates the timers leaving another ninety seconds for the assault time to escape the blast perimeter once outside the compound walls before the bombs detonate."

Passing around a diagram of the compound, Trakonitz said, "After entering through the gate, the two lorries come to a stop at these precise locations up next to the buildings. Wójcik says the blast should bring down both buildings. The initial assault inside is to kill as many as possible forcing others to take up defensive positions. The explosions will then bring the structure down on those remaining."

Both Trakonitz and Martel briefed the group alternating in Italian and Spanish to cover everyone including Fraser and Marchand. Confident of the collective combat skills of everyone, they reinforced the need to study their false identifications. Mentally adopt the details in case questioned at the border. Make these new identities your own. Understand these false papers are indistinguishable from actual government issued documents. Stay relaxed and look relaxed.

Martel then explained the escape routes. The group would split for returning to France by train. Martel would lead one group to San Sebastián and from there cross the border to Biarritz, France. Trakonitz would lead the other group traveling to Barcelona then cross the border to Perpignan, France.

Moretti asked, "Will we still be armed at this point?"

Trakonitz answered, "Following the raid, keep your sidearm. However, before you cross the border into France, get rid of it."

For Fraser and Marchand, their part of the mission finished here. Funding for the mission logistics concluded. The partisans paid in advance. From the Paris bank accounts of fictitious companies and the Rome bank used to fund the operations against the ratlines, they added another layer of laundering. Armed with false Italian identification produced by the Mossad forger Herczeg, Marchand opened a bank account in Rome with a large cash deposit. The name on the account ethnically Russian. From here, they wired funds to Martel to a bank in Madrid also opened with false identification. There was still a slight risk if there was a concerted effort to follow the money from Rome to Madrid. However, the original source as Nazi SS funds by now underwent repeated transformation.

Departing north to return to Paris, proved an emotional farewell for Fraser and Marchand. Fraser's reunion with Felix Martel, the cousin of Loretta Elizalde tortured by Klaus Barbie. The strong bond they both shared with Pavel Trakonitz. The comradery with these former Italian partisans. The satisfaction that Jews were inflicting a measure of justice on Nazi SS plotting a place in the future. The personal satisfaction of participating in the execution of Heinrich Müller.

When the team arrived in Madrid, they settled into a leased agricultural warehouse. Just two miles from the target location, the facility was another causality of the civil war. Commandeered to act as an ordinance depot for the attacking Nationalist rebel forces laying siege to Madrid, the building saw a succession of tenants over succeeding years.

A section of the warehouse contained makeshift living quarters with toilet and cooking facilities. Parked inside were four delivery lorries with different commercial markings.

Upon arrival, Martel announced. "Today we settle in. My Spanish associates will purchase food, coffee, water, and other necessities. The bulk materials for the explosives are in that far corner of the warehouse purchased from an agricultural supply. Aleksy Wójcik will supervise the bomb preparation. By the following day, everything needs to be ready. Once the Nazis cooperate by congregating at the compound we must prepare to mount the assault within thirty minutes."

"The weapons, Felix?" Trakonitz said. Like the partisans, he too was uncomfortable without a gun.

"We pick them up tomorrow. The same people used for the months of surveillance to capture the photographs also have the weapons and detonation components for the bombs. These are people that managed to survive the purges following the civil war, yet are still willing to resist Fascism."

Having arrived on Sunday, by Friday everything was well underway. Four days of surveillance identified only six of the most wanted. Heinrich Müller was among them, rarely leaving the compound. At any time there was a handful of unidentified men coming and going. These unidentified individuals assumed to be Skorzeny-recruited *Waffen-SS* paratroopers. Skorzeny himself rumored to be in Madrid yet not spotted entering the compound.

Saturday afternoon, circumstances changed. As usual, Martel manned one of the lorries driven by one of the Spaniards. They alternated with the other lorry of a different color to break up the routine. Equipped with long-range field glasses, they could stand off at a discreet distance and still observe faces of those entering. They positioned the lorry to view the driver of any vehicle as they rolled down the window to speak to the gate guard on duty.

Obviously imperfect, however it gave them a sense of those inside. From previous surveillance photographs, most of these wanted SS officers drove themselves. Even after a few days surveillance, the watchers could associate certain individuals with license plates.

Late in the afternoon, a significant number of those identified by photograph entered over the period of one hour. Martel himself tallied eleven of the most wanted arriving. Possibly more if others were also in the cars unobserved. Müller already in residence. Possibly some sort of gathering.

Radioing Trakonitz, Martel said in Spanish, "*Doce.*" Indicating twelve on the list inside.

The radio crackled for several seconds before the response from Trakonitz, "*Nos movemos.*" The signal for the attack to commence.

At the warehouse, the team crammed into the two lorries behind the six drums of ammonium nitrate mixed with fuel oil in each vehicle. Before departing for the short drive to the target, each man carefully gathered their few personal possessions careful not to leave behind any incriminating items. They would not return to the warehouse. Once the mission was over, everyone would escape in the two surveillance lorries.

Martel watched as the first lorry driven by Trakonitz drove to the gate pulling up behind a car just entering. With his field glasses, he saw Trakonitz edging the lorry forward to keep the gate from closing. Then the gate guard collapsed, shot by Trakonitz.

Trakonitz accelerated, braking to a stop a few feet from the front steps of the former abbot's residence. He intended to personally kill Heinrich Müller. The *Gestapo* chief responsible for sending millions of Jews to their death.

The second lorry pulled to a stop at its assigned position close to the front entrance of the main building. The bomb maker Wójcik set the detonator timers in each lorry.

Armed with stopwatches hung from lanyards around their necks, each assault member pressed the button as they sprang from the rear doors of the lorries. The allocated ninety seconds started.

Two men arriving in the vehicle ahead of Trakonitz exited their car with bewildered expressions. They became the first casualties hit by bursts of automatic fire.

Once inside the main building, two partisans rushed up the staircase to the second level while two others moved into a large reception room on the ground floor. Tables of food and liquor. A target-rich opportunity. Fifteen seconds later their two colleagues returned from upstairs and finished the slaughter of everyone in sight.

Looking down a stairwell descending to a lower level, automatic gunfire coming from below drove them back. Checking the time remaining they poured fire into the stairwell for several seconds.

It was Flavio Moretti in command of this team that yelled, "*Tempo di muoversi*!"

In the former residence of the abbot, Trakonitz found Heinrich Müller standing behind a large desk holding a 9mm Luger pistol.

Instead of firing, Müller placed the pistol on his desk seeing the submachine gun in Trakonitz's hands.

In German he said, "Who are you?"

"I represent all the Jews you murdered. They sentenced you to death."

Trakonitz then unleased a sustained burst from his submachine gun.

Having picked up the assault team, the two escape lorries exited the compound gate, pulling to a stop a safe distance down the road. Ninety seconds later the first explosion caused the total collapse of the former abbot's residence while inflicting damage to the main building. By design, the second blast timed for ten seconds later caused two thirds of the main building to collapse burying much of the Nazi SS *Komeradenwerk* in Madrid.

# EPILOGUE

LYON, FRANCE | MAY 1987

---

Marc Fraser and Fiona Marchand returned to Paris in 1950. Both satisfied in their efforts to hunt Nazi war criminals. While Fraser would keep up journalistic attacks on Nazi war criminals and their benefactors, he now felt ready to resume a normal life writing novels.

The episode in Madrid made international headlines. The Franco government first blamed the attack on dissident Spanish Communists. Possibly backed by the Soviet Union. Once Fraser published evidence revealing the Nazi SS identities of wanted war criminals among the victims, Spain switched to blaming the attack on the State of Israel.

Within weeks, further disinformation efforts orchestrated by Felix Martel, produced endless stories in the international press speculating on the many alternative possibilities. Within months, the Madrid attack was no longer front-page news, pushed off with the escalating military conflict on the Korean Peninsula.

Given twenty years of adventures starting as an investigative reporter in Los Angeles, Fraser had plenty of material to call on for developing novels. Marchand resumed her career at the Louvre while travelling frequently as a much in demand restorer of oil paintings.

Ten years following the proxy assassination of Henrich Müller, the dark memories of the Holocaust still demanded a cry for retribution in the State of Israel. Now, more established as a nation, an emboldened State of Israel set loose the Mossad to kidnap Adolf Eichmann from Buenos Aires and smuggle him back to Israel to stand trial in Israel in 1960.

While Argentina was outraged, the audacious Israeli operation achieved a unique respect for the young nation. Given the new medium of television, the world remained riveted to the televised trial broadcast live. With the horrors of the Holocaust still a vivid memory, the Eichmann trial provided a more vivid portrayal of Nazi war crimes than the Nuremberg trials fifteen years earlier.

Sentenced to death and found guilty, Adolf Eichmann went to the gallows in 1962.

Throughout four decades following occasional newspaper pieces on Klaus Barbie, he remained a festering sore point to Marc Fraser. More troubling when identified residing in Bolivia under that government's protection for many years. In the early 1970s, French Nazi hunters Serge and Beate Klarsfeld began a crusade to bring Barbie to justice. Fraser followed their efforts closely, even sending money to help support Beate Klarsfeld's costly trips to South America.

With changing political winds, Bolivia eventually extradited Barbie to France in 1983. However, the decades-long journey of Nazi fugitive Klaus Barbie to escape his war crimes continued with protracted legal wrangling. France it seemed needed to pass a new law allowing Barbie to face trial for crimes against humanity and a waiver circumventing French statutes of limitations.

Finally indicted in 1984, the legal process dragged on with the defense team arguing the legal basis for France to try Barbie. Not until May 11, 1987 did the seventy-four year old Klaus Barbie face trial.

Due to the international notoriety of the case, the proceedings took place in a large converted court venue at the Rhone

Coor d'Assises in Lyon, France. A balcony surrounded a great central hall modified with temporary seating to accommodate 700 spectators. All trial participants including the defendant, the defense team, the prosecution, the magistrate, and other court functionaries sat in a raised tiered arrangement affording visibility to rows of seated spectators.

Reporters and selected others occupied reserved seats in the first row immediately in front of the raised proceedings section. Marc Fraser used his influence to secure a seat in the front row seated next to Serge and Beate Klarsfeld as those chiefly responsible for seeing Barbie face justice.

In the absolute silence of the courtroom, Klaus Barbie arrived from the wings of the building. To ascend the steps to the raised section he first walked escorted past the front row spectators.

As Barbie passed in front of Fraser, Barbie slowed his steps as Fraser drew his attention by tapping a finger to his forehead. At a distance of no more than five feet, Fraser could see a large web of noticeably white scars on the side of Barbie's forehead. Obviously from wounds inflicted when striking Barbie with his gun forty years ago in Memmingen, Germany.

As Fraser smiled a broad grin, a flicker of recognition crossed Barbie's eyes. Fraser nodded.

Found guilty two months later and sentenced to life imprisonment, Klaus Barbie, the *Butcher of Lyon,* died of cancer in a prison hospital in 1991.

www.ingramcontent.com/pod-product-compliance
Lightning Source LLC
Chambersburg PA
CBHW020634020726
47494CB00001B/183

* 9 7 8 1 9 5 1 9 8 5 2 1 9 *